P9-DVO-903

ONE YEAR AFTER

BOOKS BY WILLIAM R. FORSTCHEN
FROM TOM DOHERTY ASSOCIATES

We Look Like Men of War
One Second After
Pillar to the Sky
One Year After

William R. Forstchen

ONE YEAR AFTER

A TOM DOHERTY ASSOCIATES BOOK New York

ONE YEAR AFTER

Copyright © 2015 by William R. Forstchen

A Forge Book
Published by Tom Doherty Associates, LLC
175 Fifth Avenue
New York, NY 10010

www.tor-forge.com

Forge® is a registered trademark of Tom Doherty Associates, LLC.

The Library of Congress Cataloging-in-Publication Data is available upon request.

ISBN 978-0-7653-7670-1 (hardcover)
ISBN 978-1-4668-5189-4 (e-book)

Forge books may be purchased for educational, business, or promotional use. For information on bulk purchases, please contact the Macmillan Corporate and Premium Sales Department at 1-800-221-7945, extension 5442, or write to specialmarkets@macmillan.com.

First Edition: September 2015

Printed in the United States of America

0 9 8 7 6 5 4 3 2 1

For Congressman Roscoe Bartlett and Dr. Richard Pry, who first sounded the warning about EMP. And for the real "Franklin Clan," who have become a true blessing in my life.

PREFACE AND ACKNOWLEDGMENTS

When *One Second After* was released early in 2009, I never anticipated all that would follow. I had actually started thinking about a book regarding the threat of an EMP attack back in 2004, after a congressional committee, chaired by Congressman Roscoe Bartlett, released a report on EMP that should have served as a wake-up call to the nation; a report that the media, and therefore the general public, ignored. In a conversation with that re-markable, brilliant gentleman, he lamented that the core problem was that the issue of a catastrophic "first-strike attack," using an EMP against the continental United States by a nation such as Iran, North Korea, or a terrorist group backed by them, sounded like science fiction, and therefore it lacked a public constituency to demand a more robust foreign policy and defensive preparedness. Bartlett and others asked if I could write a "fact-based" novel about the threat to try to raise public awareness.

It took a year for the idea to even begin to jell. For the longest time my thinking ran along the classic (no offense intended) "Clancy-esque" model of a hero racing to stop the disaster. And then it was the students at my college and my daughter who created the inspiration. I am blessed to teach at Montreat College (yes, it is a real school) where, with a student body of five hundred, a professor forms close bonds with his students across four years. Graduation day, therefore, is a special moment, filled with both pride

and poignancy as one sees "their kids" moving on. It was yet another graduation day, yet another speaker droning on . . . I was looking at "my kids,"
politely listening to the speaker, but obviously eager to get on with things, and
then it struck me—what would happen to them if, at this moment, America was hit with an EMP strike? What would happen to my college, my
beloved small town of Black Mountain, to my daughter, to all of us? Two
hours later I was at the keyboard and began to write the story that became
One Second After.

It wasn't until 2009 that the book was published. (Rather amusing that a
number of major houses rejected it, to the delight of my publisher and editor who did pick it up, and see it turned into a *New York Times* bestseller.)
At the time of its release, I had no idea what was about to happen. I was
actually attending a conference about EMP out in Albuquerque with my
good friend Captain Bill Sanders, who wrote the technical afterword for
the book, when my agent called with the news that we had hit the bestseller list. I was flabbergasted, and there is no other word for it.

The full impact really didn't hit until several months later. I wasn't even
aware, at the time I was writing the book, that there was an emerging
movement of people who called themselves "preppers." A couple in a nearby
community had started a business, "Carolina Readiness Supply," and asked
if I'd come speak at a conference they were organizing. "How many do you
expect to be there?" I asked and they replied around a hundred or so. On
the day I arrived, that wonderful couple was standing in a jammed parking
lot to greet me, and I found myself facing an audience of more than five
hundred, some coming from as far as Atlanta and Charlotte. Something
was definitely happening!

And thus it has been in the years afterward. Some say that I was a driving force in the creation of the prepper movement, but I beg to differ.
Maybe my book helped to serve, but the movement was already "a-forming."
Tens of millions of Americans were again thinking as Americans, that
planning for self-reliance *before* a disaster hits is a smart move. For those
new to the concept of "prepping," I do have to forcefully say, ignore how
mainstream media too often portray such people in absurd television programs. Nearly without exception I have found preppers to be decent, honest
folks who think not only of themselves but also of their neighbors, com-

munity, and nation as well. If "the stuff" ever does "hit the fan," pray that your neighbors are preppers. And a major thank-you here for the thousands of preppers I have met. All I can say is thank you for your friendship.

As this book goes to print, it has been more than six years since *One Second After* was released. Much has changed but, frustratingly, much is still the same. I had hoped that by now there would have been government action at the national level to better secure our power grid, create plans both for defense and for public preparedness, and a more robust foreign policy that makes clear that the acquisition by rogue nations of a weapon that could generate an EMP will NEVER be tolerated. None of this has happened. The historian in me recalls the 1930s. We watched passively as the threats grew, which exploded into our nation's life on December 7, 1941. We are asleep again, while North Korea tests nuclear weapons and ballistic missiles, Iran is not far behind, and ISIS, a movement as brutal and psychotic as Nazism, emerges.

It had never been my intention to write a sequel to *One Second After,* but wherever I spoke that was always a question: What happens next? I resisted for five years; my publisher, Tom Doherty, and his senior editor Bob Gleason dropping major "hints" that they wanted more. During those years I did give them a book which I truly enjoyed writing, offering a positive vision of our future in space, and also a couple of books about the Civil War and the American Revolution with my good friend Newt Gingrich, and then a self-published book about the threat of ISIS. Finally, I could no longer say no and decided to pick up the narrative thread of what happens to John Matherson, his family, his village, and his college. Thus this book, and a third one to follow several months after this publication to round out the story.

This is supposed to be a preface and an acknowledgments page, and it is time I get into that. I feel like someone at an award's ceremony who is admonished to keep it to a minute or less, but has a list ten minutes long! So here goes:

Special thanks to Newt Gingrich, Roscoe Bartlett, and others who have, for decades, worked the political front of this issue. In an age of such bitter partisan infighting, how I wish both sides of the aisle, both houses of Congress, and the executive would realize that this is a national threat that if not addressed, will indeed result in a government in exile in some underground bunker far outside the ruins of D.C., struggling and perhaps fumbling to put the pieces back together again, like Humpty Dumpty's horsemen and soldiers.

As always, my special thanks to Tom Doherty, Bob Gleason, and the wonderful team at Tor/Forge. As a fledgling writer thirty years ago, when I first met Tom Doherty, I hoped that someday I could actually be part of "his team." We've done half a dozen books together, and there is no one else in this business I hold in higher regard. On the business side as well, eternal gratitude to my agent, Eleanor Wood; my film agent, Josh Morris; the ASCOT media publicity team and my near daily contact there with Monica Foster. A book is a team effort.

When I first showed a draft of the book to my college president, Dan Struble, he asked why I just didn't name things for real rather than give fictional names for my town and college. Thank you, Dan, for that suggestion. It gives a "real place" to the books that otherwise would be lacking. I am blessed to be living in Black Mountain, North Carolina, (yes, a real place!) and Montreat College. The permission to use the real names helped me with the writing and apparently has helped many a reader to have personal association with the story as well. Most of the names in the books are fictional, but some are real, and those "real" characters are drawn on how I see them as my friends. I hope they take delight rather than offense.

And finally, a very personal acknowledgment: A couple of years ago, I was speaking at a prepper conference and afterward signing books. Robin Shoemaker stepped up to the table, there was eye contact . . . and well . . . that once in a lifetime moment hit. I think the line in *The Godfather* is that we were hit by the "Sicilian Lightning Bolt." The best reward of my life for writing a book.

It's time to close this acknowledgments and get on with the tale. If you are like me, I tend to skip the acknowledgments stuff. It is usually a lot of names I don't recognize and definitely not the reason I purchased the book in the first place! But since my publisher is paying for the ink and paper, at least for old-fashioned printing rather than electronic, I do feel compelled to close with one final thought. The books are fiction, but the scenario could be real. It might very well be real. Our parents and grandparents of the

"Greatest Generation" allowed their leaders to close their eyes to the growing threats around the world saying "it will never touch us here," and a terrible price was paid. History has a hundred such examples. Do we read this as a novel or as a warning? If it is a warning, do we act or fall back upon "someone else will make sure this doesn't happen?" I pray that thirty years hence, these books are forgotten as dark tales of warning that never came true. If so, I will be happy and content for my daughter and grandchildren. I pray that I never one day hear, "Bill, you were right."

That, my friends, is undoubtedly up to you. The issue is in our hands to, as Abraham Lincoln once said, "nobly save, or meanly lose, the last best hope on earth."

William R. Forstchen
Black Mountain, North Carolina
September 2015

ONE YEAR AFTER

PROLOGUE

This is BBC News. It's 3:00 a.m., Greenwich War Time, and this is the news for today.

This day marks the second anniversary of the start of the war that saw the detonation of three EMP weapons over the continental United States, another off the coast of Japan, and a fifth weapon believed to have veered off course and detonated over Eastern Europe. The effects of this attack—never fully confirmed but believed to have been an act between Iranian-supported terrorists and North Korea—continue to reverberate around the world. It is estimated that upwards of 80 percent of all Americans, and more than half the population of Japan, Eastern Europe, and what had been western Russia and the Ukraine have died as a result. China has been seen as the new superpower in the wake of the attack, with significant Chinese forces, defined as humanitarian, now occupying the West Coast of the United States and Japan. Western Europe and our own United Kingdom, though spared the direct results of the attack, are still feeling the profound economic impact as the world attempts to reestablish economic and political balance. In south Asia, intense fighting continues in the wake of a limited nuclear exchange between Pakistan and India.

The second anniversary of what most now call "the Day" was commemorated today by the king, who attended a memorial service at Westminster Abbey. After the service, a renewed pledge was made by the prime minister to help our European neighbors with their rebuilding efforts and to extend continued aid to the United States.

More on that memorial service and the lasting impact of the Day, but first, this report from the provisional government of the United States capitol at Bluemont, Virginia. The administration's announcement two weeks ago of the mobilization of a million men and women for the Americans' Army of National Recovery, or ANR, is now in full swing with draft notices having been sent out in a move unprecedented since the Second World War. The majority of America's armed forces, which were based overseas on the day of the attack, have now been deployed to the western and southern borders to contain further expansion by foreign powers.

Therefore, the purpose of this Army of National Recovery, according to the administration, was reiterated today: to establish security in those regions within the United States still ruled by lawlessness, to restore domestic tranquility, to aid in reconstruction, and—when necessary—to augment the military presence along those borders claimed to be in dispute. Our panel of experts will discuss the implications of the creation of this new military force within the United States later in the hour.

And this message for our friends in Montreal: "The chair is against the door." I repeat, "The chair is against the door."

Now for other news from around the world . . .

CHAPTER ONE

"Daddy, I've been drafted."

John Matherson, who had endured so many shocks in life, sighed, wearily sat back in his office chair, and looked up at his daughter Elizabeth. Elizabeth's eyes revealed an aging far beyond her eighteen years, as did the eyes of nearly all of her generation. As a boy, John would gaze at the photo books about World War II; how hard it was to believe that the "old men" in the pictures really were just eighteen and nineteen . . . their eyes, however, revealed the inner torment of all that they had endured, features haunted and remote. They were no longer kids that should still be in high school or freshmen in college . . . they had aged a lifetime, often within a matter of days, and as one author described them, they were "forever aged far beyond their precious years of youth."

"Sit down, sweetheart." He sighed, motioning to the far side of his desk in the town hall of Black Mountain, North Carolina, of what he hoped was still the United States of America. His desk was piled high with all the paperwork he had to deal with as the town administrator, all of it handwritten or punched out on an old Underwood typewriter.

In the terrible months after the Day, he had finally taken on something of a dictatorial position under martial law. As some semblance of stability finally returned within the last year, he gladly surrendered those powers back to a town council. Regardless of the loss of electricity and a national infrastructure, one thing did appear to hang on—paperwork—and as town administrator, he was stuck with the job. He often looked longingly at the dead computer in the corner of his office, a relic of a bygone world that now simply gathered dust, just as the Underwood typewriter—half forgotten in a closet for years—had before their world was turned upside down.

His former hyperclean world of daily or twice-daily showers on hot summer days, starched white shirts with clean collars, and dress shoes instead of worn boots had been replaced by once-a-week baths in a kitchen basin on Saturday night with a once-weekly, slightly bloody shave using a straight razor scavenged from an antique store to prepare for church on Sunday. Clothes were washed by hand in the creek that trickled down behind his house, and the collars of all his shirts were beginning to fray and were permanently stained with grit and sweat.

John's brave new world had a grimy, battered edge to it. As a historian, he used to wonder what life 150 years earlier actually did smell like, look like, feel like. He was living it now, where a crowded room during a meeting on a warm spring evening had a distinctive musky, gamy smell to it, and folks who once wore jackets and ties or neatly pressed dresses now showed up in worn jeans and wrinkled, faded shirts. Sunday was the one day of the week when people did try to scrub up, though unless someone in the household was handy with an old-fashioned needle and thread, most wore suits and dresses several sizes too big. Their appearance made him think of the old daguerreotypes of a bygone era. It was rare to see someone overweight in those old photographs. Most had a lean, sinewy look, and their clothing, on close examination—except for the wealthy—a well-worn look.

His office in the town hall had that same worn feel to it. Gone were the scents of antiseptic scrubbing and buffing, brilliant fluorescent lights on day and night, fresh coffee from a machine that would take a dollar bill, air-conditioning in summer, and electric heat in winter. All of it gone ever since the Day.

Elizabeth still struggled to maintain some semblance of freshness with a semiclean college T-shirt and jeans and a red ribbon tied to her dark, nearly black ponytail. Her wiry frame was typical of everyone, her jeans belted tightly around her narrow waist. What little extra weight she had put on when carrying Ben a year ago was long gone

She put a crumpled piece of paper onto his desk and pushed it across to him. He opened it up and spread it out, quietly rubbing his jaw.

He, like everyone else, had heard rumors about an impending draft to be issued by a remote and seldom-heard-from national government that had evacuated Washington, D.C., and now functioned out of an old Cold War bunker system in northern Virginia. The vague rumors had become true with this single sheet of paper his only surviving daughter placed on his desk.

He looked up at her again. She was eighteen, had seen war and starvation, and was already a mother, the father of her child killed in the fight against the invading Posse that had attacked their community a year and a half earlier. In so many ways, she did look like those long-ago photographs of eighteen-year-old veterans of Normandy and Iwo Jima, aged far beyond their years. But this was his daughter, his only child. He could still see the face of the newborn, the eyes of her long-deceased mother, the eyes that would well up with tears when she came for comfort for a skinned knee, the sparkling eyes of a laughing twelve-year-old, the knowing gaze of a sixteen-year-old who knew that with a glance and a smile she could still con her "daddy." Like all parents who across the years had gazed into the eyes of their children, whom the government suddenly declared were old enough to fight and to die, his heart was filled with fear. They were taking *his* child away, most likely never to return.

He gazed at the paper while motioning again for her to sit down.

As she settled into the chair by the side of the desk she offered a gesture a bit uncharacteristic since she had grown up—reaching out to take his hand while he gazed down at the letter.

"Greetings, Fellow Citizen, and by order of the President of the United States of America . . ."

The president?

The president of the United States. He still thought at times of the one who was in office on the Day. No. Word was that the White House had received some forewarning of the attack, scrambled the president out of D.C. aboard Air Force One . . . but amazingly, the plane was not sufficiently "hardened," against a high-level EMP and went down somewhere over West Virginia. The president now? There was actually some debate; a junior senator out west claiming he was the legitimate successor, but most, especially survivors in the east, acknowledging a junior cabinet member headquartered in Bluemont, Virginia. The letter was the standard formula, reminiscent of draft letters of long-ago conflicts, ending with the forceful statement that she was to report to the office of the "federal administrator" in the Buncombe County Courthouse within three days for induction into the Army of National Recovery—or face the full penalty of the law.

He finished it and then quickly reread it. He was tired after having sat through a night rotation of watch duty, and he rubbed his eyes as he looked at Elizabeth, who sat across from him. No tears on her face, no hysteria, no reaction.

The federal administrator in Asheville. That must be this new official, Dale Fredericks, who had moved into Asheville a month or so earlier to replace the full battalion of regular army troops, which had quartered there over the previous winter but were then ordered to move out and head for Texas.

John found the regular army unit to be of tremendous help with attempting to reorganize the region, opening up some lines of communication with radio gear brought back from overseas deployment, their technicians even helped local ham radio operators to fix their equipment and establish some semblance of a network. They had been helpful as well with at least containing some of the raider groups known collectively as reivers, an old Scot/Irish term for outlaws.

As the army pulled out, some administrative replacements arrived via helicopter from Charleston, South Carolina. A printed notice had arrived for John from the postal courier from Asheville, announcing their arrival and that in the near future he would be contacted along with other community leaders for a meeting to discuss reorganizing the communities of western North Carolina. This was welcoming news given the continued trouble with border raiders from north of the Mount Mitchell range, who were calling themselves reivers, but after that notice, nothing else . . . until today.

And now, this first notice of reestablishing the entity that all spoke of with pride and nostalgia—the United States of America—had come as a draft notice from some distant entity to take his Elizabeth away. *I've lost one child,* he thought. *Dear God, not another.*

His thoughts drifted to Jennifer, Elizabeth's younger sister who had died when the so-taken-for-granted medical supply system of America had collapsed and insulin was no longer available. For want of a few vials of insulin, his youngest had died in his arms. That was part of his life he blocked off to keep his sanity. No parent should ever have to bury his child, but he had. He kept his gaze on Elizabeth even as he hid his thoughts about Jennifer, attempting to maintain a calm, even exterior.

He looked at her, trying to collect his thoughts. *I'm her father. This is my eighteen-year-old daughter who should still be a kid, not a young mother about to be drafted.* He shook his head and then forced a reassuring smile and tossed the document back across the table.

"Ridiculous. You're a mother of a fourteen-month-old baby. That's always been a draft deferment."

"Not anymore, Daddy. You didn't read it carefully," she replied, taking the letter from his hand and turning it over. In this age of paper shortages, the document was printed on both sides, front and back. He had actually forgotten to turn the single sheet of paper over to read the addendum.

"By executive order during this national emergency," she read in a flat, emotionless monotone, "all prior grounds of deferment have, as of this date, been waived, except for demonstration of severe physical disability. Those mobilized with dependent children must find suitable placement for their dependents. Failure to do so will result in punishment as outlined in Emergency Executive Order 303."

He reread the line and it chilled him. He remembered hearing about Order 303. It gave a government official the right to invoke capital punishment. He had executed people in the months after the Day, starting with the two drug thieves, with no executive orders other than the decision of the town to support such draconian measures during a time when the survival of the town was at stake. He had wrestled with those decisions then; he still did in his nightmares. As he looked up at his daughter, though, the irony did strike him that she was subject to such, as well.

She handed the page back to him.

"This came in with the morning mail from Asheville?" he asked.

"Yup, and I'm not the only one. Mabel at the post office said there were notices for 113 with the overnight post from Asheville."

"You sure of that—113?"

"Yes, Daddy." There was now a slight touch of a scared girl in her voice. "I ran up here to tell you. A crowd is already gathering at the post office, and they are definitely not happy."

He took that in, stood up, and went out the door to the next room where the town's telephone operator was on duty.

"Jim, would you patch me in to Mabel?" he asked, and then he returned to his office and picked up his old-style phone.

A retro 1930s telephone switchboard, taken from the local museum down on State Street, had been rigged up in the town hall. "Long distance," as it was once called, now meant a call to Asheville to the west and Old Fort to the east, though there was talk that Morganton, forty miles off, had managed to pull together enough copper wire to run a line to them. His phone jangled a ring familiar from his childhood, and he picked it up.

"United States Post Office. Mabel Parsons speaking."

He smiled. She held to the old rituals even though she was the only one who ever worked at the post office, which, beyond its old traditional service, had become something of the town center for news and gossip.

"John Matherson here. How you doing, Mabel? Your husband feeling better?"

"He stabilized out yesterday afternoon, John; thanks for pushing through that request for antibiotics. We really owe you one."

"Sure, Mabel. The kids at the college are starting to turn out a surplus in their chemistry lab, so no problem."

"So why are you calling, John? Certainly not to check on George's health."

He could sense the challenge in her voice. Mabel was not someone to mince words with.

"Okay, Mabel. My daughter Elizabeth just walked up here from your office with this draft notice thing. Said a whole bunch of them came in with the Asheville mail delivery. What the hell is going on?"

"I sorted through 113 of them, John. You know I'm not supposed to discuss other people's mail. Old post office pledge and all that. But, yup, I'm sticking them in the mailboxes right now. I think it's okay to tell you that it looks like half the notices are for kids still living up at the college; the rest are from town who are being called into this ANR thing."

"I'll be right down," John replied and hung up without waiting for a reply. Again he glanced toward his daughter. He was supposed to be the arbitrator and leader for the entire community, but at that moment, regardless of his overall responsibilities and long years of training and service in the military, the issue in his heart was about his daughter, his one remaining child, a mother herself. It was about his blood, his child, the way any parent would react.

He rubbed the stubble on his chin. It was Saturday morning. Tonight, his wife, Makala, would shave him with an old-fashioned straight razor, an art he had never mastered. Perhaps it was her years as a senior nurse in a cardiology unit that gave her confidence with a blade. Throw-away safety razors were indeed a thing of the past.

After a long night of watch duty, he felt grubby and unkempt, and beyond that, his jaw ached from the damned tooth that had started troubling him the month before. Makala had at last talked him into enduring a dreaded visit to the town dentist later and then a bath in the creek and a good shave afterward, followed by relaxation on his day off from duty. But all that had to wait as he looked at Elizabeth.

"Come on, kiddo, let's get going."

"Can I drive, Daddy?" Elizabeth asked as they left his office, holding out her hand and offering a smile, the sight of which warmed his heart. A touch of the old days of a teenage daughter conning a father with a smile as she requested the family car.

The 1958 Edsel, once the proud possession of his mother-in-law, had become the highly recognizable official car for John Matherson. It was increasingly a source of guilt, as well. Having moved to Montreat after his home was destroyed during the battle with the Posse, he now lived two and a half miles from the town office. At times, especially on beautiful spring and autumn days, he enjoyed the walk. After all, there was a time when for anything less than several miles, everyone walked until the advent of the auto. But more than once while he took his time walking to the town hall, taking an hour each way, something serious that needed his immediate attention had transpired. So after much official wrangling and arguing, the town council insisted he accept a ration of five gallons of gasoline a week, enough for seventy-five miles.

There was still a reserve of a couple thousand gallons in the underground tank for city vehicles, carefully doled out. As for gas taken from abandoned cars, it was increasingly useless, breaking down over time, though the town's Volkswagen man, Jim Bartlett, claimed he was developing a formula to make that fuel useable.

Having the Edsel strictly for business use was a luxury that still hit his guilt nerve, and whenever he did see someone walking in or out of town, he'd pull over to give a lift to assuage that guilt.

"We're walking, Elizabeth. It is exactly half a block from here to the post office." He set off with a long-legged stride befitting his six-foot-five frame, glad to breathe in the morning air after a long night's watch in the town hall. While heading out, he told Jim where he would be and asked him to tell Reverend Black, who was coming on duty, that the night had passed quietly for once.

There had been rumors that the Mount Mitchell border reivers were again prowling along the northern edge of his community. The Stepp families, who lived up along the edge of the towering mountains, were complaining constantly about missing chickens and hogs . . . though of course they were mum about their moonshining operations and surreptitious trading with those same reivers that at times degenerated into violence. At times, he didn't know if he should be blaming the Stepps rather than the outsiders. But at least this night had passed without incident or vendetta raids.

Leaving the parking lot of the town hall complex of administrative offices, fire department, and police station behind, John and Elizabeth crossed State Street, which had once been a main thoroughfare. The ice storm of the winter before had finally taken down the darkened traffic light. The bank across the street, long abandoned, had burned the year before, the once-prosperous building now an empty shell. The chamber of commerce and visitors' center for tourists on the other corner ironically was still intact, though the thousands of brochures advertising local attractions had of course been looted out for basic fundamental use. A roll of the original material that the brochures had replaced was worth far more than its weight in silver or the standard medium of exchange—ammunition. It was yet another one of those things hardly anyone thought to stockpile before things went down.

As soon as they crossed the street, he regretted the decision to come down here. About 150 years earlier, the village post office was the community gathering place, fitting a Norman Rockwellish image of the potbellied stove, the local village philosophers and rubes gathered within trading gossip and news, waiting for the morning mail and news from afar over a game of checkers.

Mabel had taken her job to heart; she had been assistant postmistress. For a year, she had little if anything to do, but once the army had for a short time set up headquarters in Asheville, a trickle of mail had indeed started to come in, increasing in flow until, thrice weekly, an actual courier had come from the "big city."

Delighted to be back to work, Mabel—with the help of her husband, George—had installed a woodstove in the foyer, set out a couple of checkerboards and a chess set, and did a thriving entrepreneurial business on the side with her fresh-baked corn bread that she brought in every morning, as well as herbal teas from various roots and sprouts. John decided to just turn a blind eye to the fact that her special medicinal corn bread for those who needed medication for pain management had been illegal in most states, except Colorado, prior to the Day.

And so the post office was again a community gathering place for the local rubes, philosophers, and more than a few community wags, especially on cold winter days and rainy spring days when there was little work to be done in the fields.

Before he was even across State Street, John was spotted by the ever-increasing crowd milling about the post office, most obviously in an angry mood, and—like any crowd in a democracy—they were looking for someone to vent their anger on, and John was the obvious target. He took a deep breath and pressed on.

Several tried to waylay him, and he turned on his most disarming smile.

"Hey, whatever it is, my daughter is caught up in it too. Let me talk to Mabel, and I'll be right back out," he announced while trying to slip his way through the crowd.

Even as he spoke, he saw Ernie of the infamous Franklin clan clattering up in his battered four-wheel-drive off-road vehicle. Word of the draft notices was spreading like wildfire, and he wished Mabel had called him the moment the morning mail delivery from Asheville had come in so he could've prepared a response. He spotted his old neighbor and friend Lee Robinson in the crowd and hurried over to him.

"Lee, if you could ask folks to just wait outside," he implored.

Lee's ancestors had settled the valley over two hundred years earlier, and four of them had fought in, as Lee said, "the War of Southern Independence." For John, Lee was the embodiment of this precious valley, representative of all that was best of its traditional, down-to-earth character, a man of moral strength and a cherished neighbor. His son Seth, who was a couple of years older than Elizabeth, had kept a watchful eye on her like an older brother and had passed along his approval of Ben, the boy Elizabeth had fallen for who became the father of her son, while Lee's youngest daughter had been Jennifer's best friend. Both he and Lee harbored the hope that perhaps someday the two would notice each other in a different way.

Lee nodded and John motioned for Elizabeth to stay with his friend as he went into the back of the post office.

Mabel held the place down on her own. There was no more door-to-door rural mail delivery service, of course; folks had to come into town to pick up the occasional letter or notice that came from the outside world. There had actually been something of a celebration at the office a month earlier when a letter had arrived all the way from Indiana. It was a mystery how it had even gotten through, addressed to Abe and Myra Cohen from their daughter, a student up at Purdue. She had survived the Day, married, and Abe and Myra were now grandparents of twins.

On the Day, so many families had been cut off from children attending distant colleges, husbands and wives on business trips, elderly parents off on vacation. Only a handful had made it back in the days and weeks afterward. To have been down in Raleigh or Atlanta on the afternoon of the attack had placed so many beyond the pale, never to be heard from again. So on any day when word spread that a delivery had come in from Asheville, the post office filled up with those still holding hope of news from the distant outside world.

Beyond being the postmistress, Mabel had learned to be a professional counselor, as well as a shoulder to cry on when the mail slot was again empty. Word from distant loved ones, news of the outside world, a place to gather and share local news and gossip—this was Mabel's domain; she offered a place to share moments of happiness, to console in sorrow, to offer encouragement, and to hope that at least some of the old traditions still worked . . . and she cherished it all. But not today.

Before he could even get one word in, Mabel authoritatively held up her hand. "Yes, John, I know—perhaps it was a mistake letting those letters out before tipping you off. Maybe I should have called you first before sorting and sticking the letters in mailboxes. It wasn't until your daughter opened it here that I even knew what it was, but by then, it was too late; word was out."

John sighed, looking at the hundreds of small postal boxes from Mabel's side of the world inside the mail sorting room, morning sunlight filtering through the tiny glass windows, illuminating the darkness within. The blue-tinted envelopes were in more than a hundred slots.

"Pull them out," John said. "I need time to deal with this."

Mabel shook her head firmly, a withering glance telling him he had overstepped when it came to her august employer, the USPS.

"John, you might run this town even after you've resigned from that martial law routine, and in general, folks agree with nearly everything you've done. But not in here." She braced herself up to all of her five-foot-two-inch frame and looked up at him towering over her. "I used to be an official employee of the United States Postal Service, and by heaven, I was proud of that. Remember that book some years back and the wretched movie made afterwards about how the postal service reunites America after a disaster like the one we had for real? That stupid movie was something of a cult favorite with us postal workers . . . Folks used to joke about us and our job—'going postal' and stuff like that. But we did make things run, and damn it, John, don't get between me and my work now, or you'll have the United States Postal Service to answer to!"

She nearly shouted the last words.

"Okay, Mabel, I'm backing up."

"And remember this for good measure: I am required by the law that used to exist to ensure the proper posting of mail without censorship, and please don't try to stop me."

John gazed at her, ready for a frustrated retort when she pushed that final point in, but she defused the moment by exhaling nosily and then offering the flicker of a friendly smile.

"Sorry, John. Now that I know what is in those envelopes I'm as upset as anyone. One of them is addressed to my son-in-law. Just like you, there are times I hate the job I have to do, but I do it anyhow, the same as you."

John made the gesture of stepping forward again, leaning over to offer a friendly kiss to her forehead and she gave him a hug, the situation defused.

Even as he stood there, he saw one of the glass doors opening. It was Ernie Franklin, elbowing his way past Lee Robinson, and sure enough, seconds later, there was an explosion of expletives from the foyer.

"Now I got to deal with it," John finally replied, wearily shaking his head, looking back down at Mabel.

She sighed, reached out, and took his hand. "Hey, I'm just the messenger, as they used to say, so don't shoot me." She hesitated, now a bit embarrassed, because in his former career, which was essentially that of dictator, he had indeed shot more than one person. "Sorry," she fumbled, red faced.

He smiled. "I know what you mean, and no insult taken, Mabel. It used to be a popular metaphor for the bringer of bad news—and this morning, it is bad news."

"My God, John. I owe you everything for what you helped to do with George, pushing the town to release some antibiotics for that last bout of pneumonia. But I'm sorry—if things are to one day work out, I have to do my job, the same as you do." She hesitated, gulped, and stepped back slightly. "I can't stop you from pulling those envelopes out of the mailboxes, but if you do, you will have lost my respect, John."

How could he respond to that challenge? And now more and more of the mailboxes were being pulled open. Ernie was continuing his expletive-laden tirade and whipping up a potential explosion, right in the lobby of the post office.

"Well, it's already out there, Mabel," he replied, pointing to the boxes.

She stepped back closer and again squeezed his hand. "You're the leader in this town, John. You'll manage somehow; you always do."

"Yeah, sure," he said, shaking his head. He looked at the mailboxes and at the friends and neighbors gathering on the other side. "Damn it, Mabel," he said, forcing a friendly smile. "At least next time, give me a call first so I can either figure out what to do first, or . . ." His voice trailed off, and he didn't add, *Or find a place to hide.*

How often, from the very first days, had he wished he could do just that as he opened the door and stepped back out into the foyer.

Ernie Franklin was, of course, immediately in his face. Though in his midseventies, he radiated a definite "don't ever mess with me" aura. Head of what all called "the Franklin clan," who lived on the far side of Ridgecrest. Some had defined them as survivalists even before the Day. Ernie and his wife had, prior to the war, been tech heads—programmers starting way back in the 1960s. He had proudly let everyone know that he and his wife Linda had written some of the software for Apollo and the shuttle programs. Foreseeing the future, which finally did happen, he had bought up a hundred acres of mountain and built his fortresslike retirement home at the edge of town. It was well stocked with food that obviously was still supplying his "clan," which now included a couple of sons, their families, a daughter, and a reclusive author who had come into their lives before the Day. They had survived on their own since the first day, never requesting rations or help from the town. On the day of the cataclysmic battle with the marauding Posse, the enemy's flanking attack had swept along the edge of Ernie's property but then shied back when confronted by an explosion of automatic weapons fire. Indirectly, his clan's efforts had contributed to the town's victory by forcing the enemy to funnel in along a narrow hiking path rather than using an old logging road, that would have flanked his own position along the Ridgecrest Heights and the Baptist conference center. As a result the main battle had been fought along Interstate 40, but whenever possible, Ernie let everyone know on a regular basis that whether part of the organized fighting force or not, his clan had played a crucial role in the battle and deserved recognition.

And now he was ready to unleash on John, and he did so in no uncertain and most definitely scatological language. John long ago learned to let him vent until he finally took a deep breath.

Finally, Ernie relented, breathing hard, and John held his hand up.

The foyer of the post office was packed, and given the level of sanitation all now lived with, it was a bit rank. He had always been sensitive to smells, something his boot camp drill sergeant picked up on and had made sure John's job was to scrub out the barrack's bathroom after the first round of use in the morning, with John usually vomiting up his breakfast while he worked. After two years, the natural scents of his irregularly washed neighbors had become something of a background norm, but it still troubled him at times.

"How about we all step outside?" John offered. "Let's sit down, take a deep breath, and talk about this. Could you help me with that, Ernie?"

Caught a bit off guard by John's standard maneuver to ask someone to help him, especially in a moment of crisis, the response was almost always the same. Ernie muttered an agreement and motioned to the door as if he were in charge—and the crowd followed him out.

As they stepped outside, John saw Ed, the police chief, who had most likely been summoned by Jim at the switchboard and had come down from the town office to keep an eye on things. John made eye contact and gave him a subtle hand gesture to just relax and walk away as if nothing was amiss. In this new world of theirs, everyone walked about armed. John always kept a light Ruger concealed in his pocket; most of the neighbors present had a rifle or shotgun casually slung over the shoulder or cradled under an arm. But Ed was the town's armed authority, and he did not want to convey the slightest concern that he might need armed support to this ever-growing and angry crowd.

More than a hundred were now gathered, many clutching the draft notices for themselves or their children and kin, and John made it a point to let people see that he had one in his hand. Folks began to sit down along the curb, leaning against the odd assortment of old vehicles folks had retrofitted to function again after the EMP burst had blown out the electronics. Several of the cars had huge canvas bags strapped to the roof to store the gas from the charcoal burners that Mabel's husband had figured out could actually power a car . . . just barely but enough at least to drive around town and out to the fields that were now their farmlands.

He cleared his throat and motioned for a moment of silence. That had become traditional with town meetings, formal and informal. If Reverend Black were there, there would have been a prayer, nonsectarian, an appeal for guidance and calm, but without his presence, there would just be silence for a moment.

John finally cleared his throat again and spoke. "I have no answers for you."

"Well, that is one helluva start!" Ernie interjected sarcastically.

John looked over at him and held his hand out in a calming gesture. "Just let me say my piece, and then we'll all have a chance," John offered, and he saw that he had the support of the rest of the group.

Ernie reluctantly nodded and went to sit in the driver's seat of his Polaris.

"My daughter Elizabeth got the same letter the rest of you got to report in three days for mobilization into this Army of National Recovery that we've been hearing about. We kind of knew that this draft would sooner or later be at our doorsteps—and today, it is. I'm asking that we hold our tempers for now. I'll go into Asheville, talk to this new federal administrator that came in last month, Dale Fredericks, and see what he has to say, since chances are it came out of his office. I'll call him right now and let him know I'm coming."

He looked up at the sky and then back at the crowd. "Weather looks good for today." His next move was definitely a calculated one on his part—some would say even cynical manipulation, others one of the basic principles of leadership. "Some of the boys at the college actually managed to get a wild boar night before last after trying to lure it in for weeks. They're butchering it even now, and our friend Pete of barbecue fame is helping them. Rather than salt it down or smoke it, let's just indulge ourselves this evening. I'll ask Pete if he can get a roasting pit going right now in the town square. Ernie, maybe you and some others could help. How about we have a community meeting—say, at six—and I'll have more information then and a bit of a meal, as well? It won't be Pete's finest pulled pork, but it should still be pretty good. And no ration cards for this. It's time to celebrate after spring planting and all the good weather we've been blessed with."

"Cook something like that takes days," Ernie interjected. A glance from John, though, to at least give him a break on this point had its effect. "Yeah, okay, John. We'll help Pete try to make the pig somewhat edible and ready for the meeting tonight when I'm sure you'll return with some damn good answers," Ernie replied.

There were outright cries of delight from those who were still trying to just barely get by on the public rations. A meal of real meat, no matter how tough, was always a lure and a promise.

"But before you go, John, I have something to say first," Ernie announced, but John held up his hand.

"As I said before, Ernie, I know nothing more than the rest of you. I want to get that call in now and get on the road. Is that all right with all of you?"

John dreaded such informal sidewalk meetings. Everyone felt they had to have their say, and it would drag on for hours. His nature was such that he wanted to get the real information and get it now, sort it out, and then deliver the hard message as quickly as possible. He wondered if this mobilization of his community's fittest and healthiest young men and women had more behind it than just simply a call-up for national service, such as what happened in the Second World War. He could see already from those who were waving the blue envelopes that the community's most able-bodied, who were the backbone of their town's defenses and hardest workers in the fields, were the first to be called.

CHAPTER TWO

"You sure you don't mind driving?" John asked.

Makala Turner Matherson smiled and shook her head, a smile that always captivated him. She was petite, of slender build even before the starving times, and still had striking blond hair—and unlike most women now, she had kept it long. They had met literally on the Day. She lived in Charlotte and had been heading to Mission Hospital in Asheville to attend a conference for nurses specializing in cardiovascular surgery when her car stalled out, like nearly every other car on the roads that day . . . fortunately for her, and for him, she became stuck at the Black Mountain exit. He had spoken briefly to her that first evening, as she stood by the side of the road. Even then, it was her eyes that had first captivated him. That first instant of eye contact—her unique eye color, sometimes near golden, other times more brownish green—had caught the evening light and actually seemed to sparkle. He had not let it register then; on that evening he was an anxious father looking for one of his daughters along with trying to figure out what had happened.

A day later they crossed paths again and in the weeks that followed she gradually became part of his life, literally saving his life when he was hit with a staph infection, and then stepped far deeper into his family, and his heart, as she helped to nurse his youngest daughter, Jennifer, as her life slipped away due to diabetes. Prior to the the Day, he never believed anyone could replace his first wife, Mary, who had been taken by cancer years earlier, but during the initial months of crisis, and then the long winter afterward, he came to realize that not only did he depend upon her as a friend and ally, but that they had fallen in love as well. He could no longer imagine life without her . . . her emotional strength, her empathy, and a strong moral compass that he completely trusted and relied upon.

Since they were heading to Asheville, she decided to dress a bit more formally, wearing a light-blue knee-length skirt and gray blouse. Hardly anyone wore white anymore. What little bleach remained was for water purification and manufacturing a couple of different medications. Hearing of the mission he was setting out on, she had even disappeared into the woods a bit downstream from their house for a very chilly dip to clean up, and thus she exuded a fresh, scrubbed, nearly cheery glow that he always found so appealing.

When heading out of town, he preferred that she did the driving; it freed both of his hands if a weapon was needed.

"Just wish I was driving my old Bimmer rather than this beast," she announced. "My God, to have that BMW and something like the parkway with a good radar detector . . . now *that* was driving! It was one of the reasons I loved it up here and wanted to move here out of Charlotte after the divorce. So now I am here, and no Bimmer—just your beat-up Edsel, John Matherson."

She reached out to take his left hand. His other hand rested on the Glock holstered on his right hip.

If not for the nature of the trip and always the slight sense of danger when heading outside the confines of Black Mountain, he actually was enjoying this ride on the open road.

It was a delight to be on an absolutely empty Interstate 40. The tires of the old Edsel were starting to bald—new tires for such a car were of course impossible to find—so for safety, they kept it at a stately thirty-five miles per hour.

The road had always been a favorite of his. A long, sloping climb a couple of miles west of the entry ramp at Exit 64 revealed a magnificent view of the Mount Mitchell range to his right, the highest mountains east of the

Rockies at over 6,600 feet. At this time of year, the lower slopes were a lush green, but the peaks even in mid-May could still be dusted with snow, which was indeed the case this morning. The lower range of mountains to the left of the highway, rising up only four thousand feet, was awash with the spring coloration of pale brilliant green.

The interstate was beginning to show the effects of two years without maintenance other than work crews pushing the hundreds of abandoned cars aside. The first year, the grass had not been cut, and now in the second year, spring saplings were beginning to sprout along the shoulders.

Houses out along the fringe of town had long been abandoned, with folks moving into vacated homes in town for security. Many of the abandoned homes had broken windows, vines creeping up along the outside walls, overgrown walkways, and abandoned cars with flattened tires beginning to rust in driveways. In one sense, it could be a depressing sight, but in another way, John saw it as nature reclaiming the lushness of this land, working to erase some of the monuments of man.

The flat, rich farmland flanked the road; nearly all of it was under cultivation. Precious gas was rationed out for the tractors, and that had been a deeply troubling concern for John and the town council. Gasoline might hold out for another two years or so, if rationed wisely and treated to maintain its volatility, but then what? He still harbored fantasies of trying to build steam-powered tractors, machines he had always been fascinated with as a historian.

Several such tractors had actually been located in the barns of remote farms, rusted solid and forgotten. It was hoped that parts from the machines might be cobbled together by the time of autumn harvest into one tractor that could actually run on wood rather than gasoline. Again, his wish was that the community had more old-fashioned machinists and tool and die makers who could build such things from scratch.

They drove past several well-guarded pastures along the highway, where the few precious horses that had not been killed for food in the first year were kept. He caught sight of a newborn colt frolicking about, and he smiled at the sight. It was not just the beauty of new life; it might be their main source of energy for farming in a few more years if the technological infrastructure of their world—at least to an early- to mid-twentieth-century level—was not restored.

The scent of an apple orchard wafted through the car, and he breathed deeply. The last of the petals of spring were still falling and swirling about on the late-morning breeze.

It had been a beautiful land when he had arrived there over a decade earlier, and it still was. In spite of human folly, the land was breathtakingly beautiful, whether cloaked in the glory of spring or covered with the mantle of winter snows. He had to keep reminding himself to look past the crisis, the terror and fear, that today was a good day to be alive up in the mountains of western North Carolina.

Ahead was the barrier his community had set up just beyond the Exit 59 turnoff. The sight of it refocused him on the reason for a noonday drive along an empty interstate highway.

He had called the new federal administrator in Asheville, Dale Fredericks, as he had promised Ernie and the gathering in front of the post office, and when told that the administrator was busy but could see him later in the week, John had offered a few choice words to the unidentified assistant and said he would arrive at noon and hung up. The game of bureaucrats, a game he knew well from his time serving in the Pentagon, had attuned him to how power was played—and to wait hat in hand for a callback was an admission of subservience. Beyond that, he had promised the community he would have some answers by evening, and to tell everyone to wait would definitely not play well at all.

John looked to the backseat of the Edsel. Ed, Black Mountain's chief of police, was riding on the left side with a sawed-off twelve gauge, and one of his students from the college, Grace Freeman, was on the right side with a well-tended, carefully maintained M4. Her intelligent, attractive look belied the fact that she came from a family that had worked in the security business and that she had grown up around firearms, knew how to use them, and had a good grasp of tactics and the ability to think under stress. She had thus risen to senior student in command of the company of troops fielded by the college.

Once clear of the security barrier, the fifteen-mile drive to Asheville would be a journey into no-man's-land, and the old Edsel could be a tempting snatch and grab for some, even now. A month earlier, the Quentin family had embarked on their twice-monthly bartering run to Asheville; it was rumored that they had some hidden fields of corn up on the far side of Route 9 and were running moonshine. They had never come back. Speculation was that a band of the border reivers—though others said it was a gang out of Asheville—had snatched the lot of them. Jim Quentin's bullet-ridden body was found in a ditch by the highway three days later, the searchers drawn to where he lay by the buzzards wheeling overhead.

Makala slowed and waved to their security team guarding the highway barrier, nearly coming to a complete stop so John could shout that they were heading into Asheville and would be back by late afternoon. That was standard procedure: let the border guards know your expected return time, and if you did not show up, a search operation would be mounted. They were waved through, and the gate closed.

Ed perked up once beyond the Swannanoa gate, his gaze scanning the side of the road, and John eased his Glock 21 out of its holster and cradled it in his lap. He kept the lightweight Ruger for when he walked about town, but beyond town, he wanted a .45 loaded and ready. The road ahead was cleared, though scores of abandoned cars still littered the shoulder of the highway, nearly all of them looted of their tires, gas tanks pumped out, oil drained from engine blocks, and some of his own crews now scavenging the wiring from alternators. Medieval Romans tore up finished stones from the roadways, aqueducts, coliseums, and monuments of their ancient ancestors; modern Americans looted abandoned cars.

Makala sighed and nodded toward a dust-coated BMW, identical to the one she had abandoned by Exit 65 and was now a burned-out wreck from the battle with the Posse. Every time they drove past it, her commentary was nearly the same. "Maybe someday we can get that one towed back home." She sighed wistfully. "Rewire it, find some treads, some premium gas, and go for a drive again."

He chuckled, glad for the diversion.

"How about cranking up some Emerson, Lake & Palmer on the sound system while we drive?"

She laughed. "I keep forgetting, dear husband, you're from another generation. That is old folks' music. Give me some Meat Loaf."

Ed sighed, muttering a rude comment under his breath at that; he was strictly country music. Grace, eyes still glued watchfully to the side of the road, asked what in the world they were talking about, having heard of none of the performers.

"Never did get to take you out to a nice dinner at the Grove Park," John replied wistfully. "Their Friday-night buffet of seafood—all the snow crab legs you could eat."

"Champagne, *real* champagne. I'll dress up in a skirt and four-inch heels so I can see you eye to eye."

More groans erupted from the sixty-five-year-old police chief and the twenty-one-year-old student who was deadly at six hundred yards with a scoped, bolt-action rifle.

He let his hand slip out of Makala's grasp as they drove on. If anything happened, she'd have to maneuver quickly with both hands on the wheel. Makala slowed for a moment, pointing out someone on the overpass for the old parkway, and then speeding up, John watching carefully for any threatening move. The location was a good one for an ambush since the road narrowed as it went through a defile, with a blind corner just beyond where a barrier line could be hastily erected. The person on the bridge wisely held up both hands as a peaceful gesture that at least he had no weapon, and then he actually waved. It seemed friendly, but it could also be a signal to an ambush waiting around the bend.

Ed and Grace were tense in the backseat. John chambered a round into his Glock and now had a reserve clip out and on the car seat beside him. Makala was ready with both hands on the wheel. They cleared the bridge and continued on to the turnoff into Asheville where the road widened. All four gave inward sighs of relief as they slowed for the entry barrier to Asheville set up at the intersection of Interstates 40 and 240. They showed identification at the city barrier line and then were waved through. John recognized one of the men guarding the approach: it was the friendly cop he had met long ago on his first visit to Asheville after the Day. There was even an exchange of pleasantries, and then Makala drove on, exiting at Charlotte Street and finally arriving in front of the old courthouse complex.

The complex was made up of three buildings—the county office, a rather ugly and imposing fifteen-story structure; a smaller city office to the south side of the complex, which was an elegant building of art deco design; and a fortresslike, foreboding county prison downslope and behind the two buildings.

John felt an instinctive chill even as they parked and got out. When the army occupied this place, the sight of young men and women in traditional U.S. Army uniforms had been a comforting sight for him. That had once been his world. The uniforms were different now.

On the steps of the county office were two guards wearing flak jackets, and one of them stepped forward, an M4 carbine half raised. "Identification. And no weapons allowed in the building."

John had cleared the chambered round out of his Glock and holstered his weapon before getting out of the car. The sharp command uttered by the guard made him hesitate. Carrying in the open had become very much the norm in the two years after the Day, and the tone of the guard set him off. Ed and Grace were falling in behind him, their weapons slung casually over their shoulders.

Makala stepped forward in front of John.

"Here's my ID." She held up her old North Carolina driver's license. "John, why don't you put your pistol back in the car? Ed and Grace, how about waiting for us there?"

She handled it smoothly, as she always did, and rather than react as tempted, John carefully pulled his pistol out, handed it over to Ed, and reached for his own wallet.

"Ma'am, this ID has lapsed and is therefore not valid."

John actually started to chuckle at the absurdity of the guard's comment. "Should we go down to the North Carolina DMV and get a new one right now? We definitely don't want her to get a ticket for driving."

He meant it as a joke, but the officious guard did not take it that way. It was the type of response that had always set John off.

"I'd prefer to see some current federal identification, such as your ration card."

"Didn't think to bring it," she replied smoothly, stepping a bit closer to cut John off from a far angrier response. She then gave an innocent smile. "I'm sorry, I wasn't aware that was now required."

"I'm John Matherson of Black Mountain, here to see Dale Fredericks,"

John announced coldly, coming up to his wife's side. "And this is my old military ID as a colonel in the United States Army. I assume that will vouch for me." He shifted into his well-trained command voice.

"Whom do you wish to see?"

John bristled up. "I just told you—Dale Fredericks. I wasn't aware that I had to be announced."

"You mean the director of Carolina District Eleven," the guard replied.

"I wasn't aware I had to address him by his formal title."

"Sir, I'm following my orders, and henceforth, proper titles are to be used."

John glanced down at the guard's sleeve. "All right, Sergeant, then I am Colonel John Matherson of the United States Army Reserve. You will address me as *sir* and inform whomever it is that put you out here that I am here to see Dale Fredericks."

"Wait here." There was a hesitation on the guard's part. "Sir," he finally added in.

He jogged back into the building, the other guard just standing silent, blocking their way and not making eye contact with either of them.

A moment later, his interrogator was at the doorway and gestured for them to climb the steps and come in. John slowed as he approached and flashed an angry glance at the guard. "Sergeant, I'll let it pass this time, but in the future, you not only address me as *sir*, you salute my rank when I inform you who I am and show proper identification, and you do not wave me about as a traffic cop. You could have walked back down the few steps to tell me to come in, which I would have done anyhow. Do I make myself clear?"

The guard was silent.

"Do I make myself clear, Sergeant?" John snapped.

There was a muttered "Yes, sir," and John opened the door on his own and held it for Makala to go in first.

"That last bit wasn't necessary, John," she whispered.

"Hell yes it was," he replied, following her into the courthouse, and as he stepped within, he came to a sudden stop.

The interior was lit . . . *with electric lights*. The county courthouse had an open foyer that rose several stories, the upper floors facing the foyer cordoned off with ornate iron balcony railings that had a heavy, oppressive look, almost like the bars of a cell. Though no critic of architecture, John always felt that the 1920s-era building had a bit of a Stalinist-era feel to it when compared to the far more attractive county offices next to it. The half dozen fluorescent lights illuminating the foyer fluttered slightly as if the electrical current was not constant.

Of course, it was not the first time he had seen electric lighting since the Day. Mission Hospital had brought a generator online, which, when powered up, provided electricity for two operating rooms and an adjoining ICU established on the first floor next to the emergency room. A number of private and even some older industrial generators had survived the attack, but it was now, after two years, a question of fuel to run them. The vast majority of families that had tried to think ahead long before the Day and had put in backup power had been thinking in terms of days or weeks at most. The ones with ten to twenty gallons of gas on hand had run out within the first week. A couple of families in Black Mountain, such as the Franklins, had kept mum about their thousand-gallon propane tanks, but even those went dry after the bitterness of the previous winter.

The army had left a couple of generators behind, and it was now obvious where one of them was in use, and the sight of it set John on edge given how much fuel was being used just to provide lighting. For a moment, he stood there wondering if he was feeling the cooling touch of air-conditioning, as well.

"John Matherson of Black Mountain?"

John felt a bit embarrassed; he had actually been standing there as if he were a gape-mouthed tourist, gazing up at the electric lights. He caught sight of the man he assumed was Dale Fredericks coming out of his office, located on the ground floor of the courthouse. There was a friendly enough smile as the man approached, hand extended, which John took, and there was a firm enough handshake. Dale stood half a foot shorter than John, light, sandy hair worn a bit long and combed across his forehead to cover the fact that his hairline was receding. He was wearing a blue jacket, standard light-blue shirt, and red tie, the way most professionals dressed before everything had gone down. John didn't know if the man's clothes were setting him off or if they were actually a touch of reassurance that somehow, in some ways, things were coming back to normal. It made John awkwardly aware of his own well-worn dress shirt, collar frayed and permanently darkened from sweat, his jeans and hiking boots both a bit the worse for wear, as well.

Dale's face was round, again a strange sight in a way for the survivors of what they now called the starving times, which had left a permanent mark on all who had survived it. Perhaps the only positive thing that could be said of those days was that the American slide into near universal obesity had finally come to a stop. Something else caught John's attention. The man was freshly showered and shaved, a fact that made John feel suddenly out of place.

Dale's pale gray eyes darted to Makala. His smile broadened slightly, and he offered his hand, which Makala took firmly, introducing herself.

"I assume this is Mrs. Matherson. My assistant told me you were coming."

"It's Makala Turner Matherson," she replied, her smile as broad as his. "Director of public health and safety for our community. And I assume you are Dale Fredericks."

There was a slight flicker of a frown from Dale, and then he regained instant composure over his faux pas. "Oh, sorry; I did not properly introduce myself. Yes, I am Dale Fredericks."

She gave a sidelong glance to John as if nudging him. Though he felt comfortable with all of the aspects of his jobs as a colonel, a college professor, and the one who took on the role of near dictator operating under martial law during the darkest days of the crisis, there were nuances of the games of diplomacy at which he knew Makala was superior, and he caught it now as if she were saying, *Don't let the fact that the guy is clean and well dressed put us off.*

"If my administrative assistant had clearly understood who was calling, she most certainly would have scheduled you in. Please accept my apologies for the confusion. Let's go into my office and see what I can do for you."

He led the way, graciously helping Makala to take a seat and offering water, which both Makala and John accepted. To John's utter disbelief, the water was freezing cold.

"Oh, that?" Dale replied with a chuckle. "Indeed a luxury, I realize. We have an old-fashioned water cooler. I know it's a bit of an excess, but on some of these hot days, it means a lot for staff morale."

"Did I feel air-conditioning when we came in?" Makala asked innocently. "It really did feel wonderful."

"We turn it on for a few minutes each day," Dale said.

"Oh, how wonderful," Makala whispered, and then she set her glass down after only one sip.

There was a moment of nervous silence, and Dale cleared his throat, pale eyes fixed on John. "I think I can guess why you came here today, but why don't you open the discussion? But I have to warn you, I'm really tied up today, so we'll have to keep it fairly short for now."

John pulled Elizabeth's draft notice out of his pocket and put it on the table. Before he could speak, Dale leaned over, took it, and held it up.

"Your daughter?" he asked.

"For starters, yes."

Dale smiled disarmingly. "Well, in that case, I know I can work an arrangement for you. We'll figure out some sort of deferment."

John now actually did sit up straighter, and Makala gently reached over and put a light restraining hand on his arm.

"I didn't come here to just plead for my daughter, sir."

Dale's features clouded for a second, and his gaze dropped. "Oh, I'm sorry. Forgive me, sir," Dale replied hastily. "You see, these notices started going out a couple of weeks back. Mail to your town was a bit delayed, so it only went out there with this morning's delivery from our post office. It's why I'm in semi-hiding at the moment," he said with a rueful chuckle. "I've got parents, wives, husbands, kids all pleading for deferments. I actually had a mother try to bribe me yesterday with a pie that had a silver dollar stuck in it. So please excuse me if I misspoke. I know an honorable man such as you would not come here just to ask for special treatment for a member of his family."

John nodded, even feeling a touch of understanding. Across the last two years, he had presided over many a hard decision, the most dreadful of them executions, first starting with the two young men who had stolen medications from the nursing home. He never regretted or second-thought the decisions once made, affirming to himself that in taking one life, he had spared others anguish and deterred a descent into anarchy. Nevertheless, the appeals of loved ones and having to firmly say no could be grueling.

And attempts at bribes ranged from what could just be called a friendly neighborly gesture of some rations or a bottle of bootleg moonshine appearing on his doorstep with a friendly note attached to outright criminal threats.

"Thus the reaction of the guards outside the building when we first came in," Makala ventured.

"Ah yes, regrettable but necessary," Dale replied. "Otherwise, that foyer out there would be swamped. Apologies if it seemed rude."

"I understand, but I would suggest that your man out there gets a little training in proper procedure and some basic manners."

"I'll have a talk with him, John," Dale said with an apologetic smile, brushing an errant lock of hair back from his forehead. "So how can I help you?"

"I'm here on behalf of many of the citizens of Black Mountain, Montreat, and Swannanoa," John said. "It is not just about my daughter."

"I see," Dale replied, leaning back in his swivel chair, bringing his fingertips together and resting his chin on them. "Many of the citizens, you say?"

"I didn't speak to everyone who got the notices this morning, but I daresay yes, it will be the majority. Our first question: just what is this all about? We hear nothing from the federal government for a year. After the worst of the crisis is over, an army battalion shows up, but then they are pulled out—and now these notices of draft into this new organization, this ANR. I have an understanding of the need to create a centralized force to restore this nation, but on the other side of the coin, these notices were a shock that hit without warning. I'll also add that nearly all of those being drafted are citizens crucial to my community, not just for protection but also for food production and our first steps at rebuilding. It comes as a tough blow."

Dale stood up and sighed. He walked about behind his desk for a moment and then pointed to an old map of the United States on the wall behind his desk. "The federal government is reconstituting at last," Dale announced, and he nodded toward the map. The gesture seemed a bit hamhanded to John, a professor for many years, but he could sense that Dale was nervous and building a case, so he did not show anything other than a forced expression of interest.

"The situation overseas, though unstable, is at least for the moment relatively calm. Our overseas nuclear assets survived intact, and, as you undoubtedly know, a swift and terrible retribution was rained down on North Korea and Iran. After that, secondary wars did break out, such as the conflict raging now between India and Pakistan, which we are standing clear of. There are numerous low-intensity wars raging around the globe. The only thing ensuring our security is the certain knowledge that our nuclear boomers are still out there under the seas ready with swift retaliation if there is another launch against the United States."

"Wish we had made that message clearer before the Day," Makala said softly, her voice filled with bitterness.

"We all do," Dale replied.

John said nothing. Was it really Iran and Korea, or were others involved? Those were questions for which no one had a clear answer. If it had been Russia that provided technical support for the attack, they were suffering now as well because an EMP burst, which—believed by some to have been off course—had detonated over Eastern Europe rather than what many assumed was the target of Western Europe. Moscow and Saint Petersburg had ceased to exist in the months afterward, the same as every major city in America.

"But here," Dale continued, "we are struggling to regain our national borders. The rhetoric with the so-called Chinese aid and fraternity mission is clearly transitioning into a permanent occupation force. The president has decided that we must mobilize for this national emergency, and thus the letters arrived here in Asheville shortly after my own arrival. John, I wish I had been able to establish better community relations with everyone after arriving here before these draft notices hit. All our regular military assets and the army that existed prior to the attack that have returned to the continental United States are being shifted to our southern and western borders. The new Army of National Recovery is therefore needed to help reestablish order and government control in the rest of the country. I heard how you organized the fight against a group called the Posse and soundly defeated them. John, there are still scores of Posse-like groups wandering the countryside, some of them in our own backyard, such as these so-called reiver groups harassing law-abiding communities like yours.

"I tell you . . ." He sighed, sitting back down in his chair, taking a long drink of cold water, and then setting the glass down. "This was not what I thought my job would be when I first got here. I thought it would be to help network communities together, stitch back the fabric of our society, getting us working again as a single team as we did in the old days, and our flag would again represent a real working nation and not just a memory. It was a shock to me when orders came down to mobilize several thousand out of my district for national service and that my first job was to be the bearer of these tidings."

He nodded toward the draft notice resting on the desk between them, his features remorseful.

"Whoever thought this up—the selection of personnel—I assume it is not you?" John asked.

"Oh, definitely not. Most definitely not."

"Well, whoever did is clueless about the situation here. We barely hung on by the skin of our teeth when the Posse hit us a year and a half ago. I assume you are aware of that situation?"

"I know about the fight you put up and your leadership. A masterful victory."

"It was a bloody slaughter for both sides. If that is the definition of victory, I pray I do not have another like it. The young men and women receiving draft notices are the backbone of our own internal defense force. We've had a dozen incidents since with raiders, gangs of thieves, and now these reivers just on the other side of Mount Mitchell. Strip out the backbone of my command and we are defenseless."

"Your command?" Dale asked softly.

John hesitated and then nodded. "Yes, I am commander of the local self-defense force."

"Isn't it perhaps time that we began to shift that a bit, to work together more as a team, bring back state and federal authority? That is the intent of the Army of National Recovery—a federally organized force to bring stability back to America nationwide. When fully in place, local communities will no longer have to fend for themselves. I would think that would actually be welcome news for you, John."

John was silent with that. Of course that was an ideal. But how could they make it a working, functional ideal?

"When I can see and feel clearly that such is the case and that our local security is firmly in place, maybe then I'd feel more comfortable with so many of my community's personnel being pulled out for duty elsewhere."

"The times are no longer Fort Apache on the frontier or medieval barons holed up in their castles," Dale replied. "It is time to bring back a broader authority and stability."

"But stripping out the core of the strength of my community now? I'd like to see something else in place first."

"In fact, you're about to see that, John. I have assets reporting in this weekend that I think you'll find to be rather impressive and definitely reassuring. I wish they had come in first before the draft notices went out. Their presence would have alleviated your concerns about defense of your community in the future."

"Like what?"

"I've been promised some air support, for starters."

"Air?"

"Not for public consumption, so keep that under your hat for now. For some folks here, I'd prefer it to be a surprise, if you know what I mean."

"Air support from where? Nearly everything stateside was fried by the EMP."

"Again, not allowed to discuss that. Let's just say some overseas equipment is finally making its way back here. The government decided some of it can be spared as needed by local administrative areas. I put in a strong request. So even as your personnel head off for training, I'll have some darn good backup in place for your community and this entire region. Is that fair enough?"

"We'll see, but there is a second question just as burning. Just where in the hell are these kids going to serve with this ANR?"

"Ours not to reason why," Dale said softly.

"'Theirs but to do and die'?" Makala interjected.

Dale looked at her a bit taken aback, and John realized that Dale did not know the line from the ironic poem.

"Tennyson describing the disaster of the Charge of the Light Brigade in a long-ago war," Makala said. "That is not a fate for any of the young men and women of our town."

"I spoke too flippantly; forgive me," Dale replied. "John—" He hesitated and then nodded to Makala. "And you too, ma'am—I have no idea as to where your daughter will be assigned. This is a national mobilization, a million strong. We need to constitute an army within our own continent. Most of our military based here in the States when all this started was as decimated as the civilian population. We have, at best, a few hundred thousand under arms within our borders. We have to secure our borders, hopefully just by a show of will."

"Why not just federalize the National Guard?" John asked.

"Good question, John. That was seriously discussed, but it was quickly realized it would be all but impossible. The high casualty rate within the United States decimated Guard members the same as everyone else. Databases have been lost, and there isn't a single state government that is running efficiently enough to coordinate bringing Guard units into national service. It was realized we needed to start from scratch again—and thus the Army of National Recovery. This force, once created, will not even have to fight other than containing lawlessness in some regions. Once our borders are resecured, the military can return to its mission of stabilizing places still in chaos. When that happens, the ANR stands down, and all your sons and daughters will be back home by Christmas."

"I seem to recall that kind of promise at the start of nearly every war," Makala replied coolly. "'They'll be home by Christmas.' That is most reassuring."

There appeared to be a glint of anger in Dale's eyes, even though he held his smile without flinching. "I'll tell you what," he said, standing up, clearly indicating the meeting was drawing to a close. "I can at least do this, but for heaven's sake, don't let anyone outside your community know this. The notices said to report here in three days. Let's just say that was a misprint, and it is thirty days hence. That will give me time to file your concerns back to Bluemont and give you a chance to see that I am a man of my word when it comes to the fact that I promise we'll have a region-wide defense force in place to cover for communities such as yours so that you no longer need your small, independent commands—and I'll see if I can better clarify terms of service. Is that fair for right now?"

John hesitated but then finally nodded in agreement. He looked over to Makala, who smiled, nodded as well, and actually said, "Thank you, sir."

"Good, then that's settled. Now you must excuse me; I am swamped, which I think you can understand. Get back to your people, calm things down, and we'll be in touch and see what can be done, let's say in a week or so. Does that work for you?"

John stood and nodded.

"And please don't construe this the wrong way. Your daughter's age?"

"Eighteen, and she is the mother of a fourteen-month-old boy whose father was killed in the fighting with the Posse." He hesitated, ashamed to mention it as if seeking sympathy, but it spilled from him. "Her younger sister died of diabetes last year, as well. She is all we have left."

Dale looked at Makala with soulful eyes. "I am sorry about the loss of your daughter, ma'am. I know deferments for draftees with dependent children have been dropped, but—and again, please don't take this the wrong way—I think you have good grounds for an appeal that I can move forward. Especially if she is serving as your assistant or in some capacity vital to the area's security beyond that of just simply carrying arms."

"Elizabeth is my adopted daughter," Makala replied. "And at the moment, she serves in the local militia, helps with the community farm acreage, and takes care of her son and her grandmother, like so many of the other kids in our community." She stared straight at him, and his eyes dropped.

"We've all lost someone," he said.

"And you?"

He hesitated. "Strange, but maybe lucky. I had no one special when the Day hit. I was part of the personnel evacuated out of Washington. I had two sisters; we were never close, really. I married some years ago and then divorced and lost track of where my ex was even before the war hit us. And so I just buried myself in work."

"Such as?" Makala pressed.

There was a look in his eyes, but it passed like a shadow. "Working for the federal government, of course, to try to bring order out of chaos. I was ordered to report up to Bluemont to help with the work of reorganization and then was assigned to the field—meaning here—two months ago. Now, if you'll excuse me, I really am late for my next meeting. I'll take care of the thirty-day extension on the draft in your community and will be in touch. I know you'll clearly see that our district has become safe for law-abiding citizens within a matter of days."

John looked at him quizzically, but long experience told him that this man was not going to say anything more. He had at least gotten a temporary reprieve for his entire community. Whatever Fredericks's actions were going to be, he'd have to let him play them out.

Dale stepped out from behind his desk, opened the door to his office, and motioned for Makala, who nodded her thanks as she exited with John following her. Dale shook John's hand in the hallway and then returned to his office while they headed for the exit and out into the early afternoon heat. John spared a sharp glance for the sergeant who had troubled him earlier, but the man's gaze was fixed straight ahead as if John didn't exist. John and Makala walked slowly to where Ed and Grace were leaning against the hood of the Edsel.

"What do you think?" Makala whispered.

"Well, I didn't expect the extension. I'm highly skeptical that a central government can secure our communities. We understand the nuances and threats better than they ever can. If they had shown up with a million extra rations as a reserve for the winter ahead, some farming equipment, electrical generators, additional communications gear, some tech people to help us get things up and running, or a darn-good, fully stocked field medical unit that can move from community to community, now those would be blessings I'd be overjoyed to see. That's the kind of help I was hoping for, not this pulling out of those we need the most not just for defense but also for rebuilding."

"All of those would be great," Makala replied. "I don't like the idea of them being plucked from our midst, and six weeks from now, they're thrown into some godforsaken no-man's-land fighting Posse groups in New York or the nightmare in Chicago."

He sighed as they headed to the car where Ed and Grace stood, weapons slung, both of them relieved to see John and Makala out of the building and heading their way.

"If everything he said is true, it is essentially a lawful order of the emergency government. But to go against it?" Makala said.

He shook his head ruefully. "I was a military man once, Makala. I swore an oath to defend the Constitution, and as long as that point held, I followed orders, even when I didn't like them. I feel caught in the middle with this thing. This is about Elizabeth but also about damn near every other family I feel responsible for."

"Let's go home and try to calm things down first. He certainly didn't volunteer to come with us. And once we get back, you have that postponed appointment with your friendly dentist, Doc Weiderman."

The mere mention of it reminded him of the damned toothache. The crisis of the moment had diverted him from the pain, but mention of it was a forceful reminder.

She gave him that reassuring nurse smile that usually meant what was coming would not be pleasant. He sighed and nodded.

"What do you think?" he asked.

"About your tooth or Dale?" she asked.

"Dale."

She took his hand and squeezed it. "I think he's full of shit."

CHAPTER THREE

"Come on in, John; no more dodging now."

Richard Weiderman was an old friend from long before the Day—the family dentist who had taken care of his kids and had even belonged to the town's Civil War Roundtable group. Richard took delight in giving talks on what medicine and dentistry were like back then, and that knowledge had put him into an important position after the Day. Gone were pneumatic-driven, high-speed dental drills and suction tubes, and the mere sight of a Novocain needle always creeped John out.

When John came in for checkups, he used to nervously joke with Richard about a favorite comedy musical that featured an insane dentist who winds up getting fed to a man-eating plant. Everyone had some sort of dark joke about dentists, but on the other hand, all were darn grateful for their existence and took it as an ordinary part of their lives even if it was a few unpleasant hours a year in the chair.

No longer. Richard's supply of Novocain and other anesthesia had immediately gone into the town's emergency supply. He had become more than "just a dentist" during the battle with the Posse, helping to patch up facial wounds and repair shattered jaws and agonizing wounds to the mouth. In the year and a half after those dreadful days, he had resumed his practice, using what had been a hobby knowledge of dental history to put himself back into business. In the basement storage room of a long-deceased dentist, he found a foot-powered treadle drill and a variety of dental tools not used in a hundred years. From a hidden reserve in a jewelry store, he snatched up thin sheets of hammered-out gold for fillings. He had moved his office from a posh location in an upscale development at the edge of town into an abandoned jewelry store on Cherry Street, where reluctant patients came for treatment. There was even a hand-lettered sign over the entryway, painted in ornate, nineteenth-century script, complete with the image of a tooth, proclaiming, "Pain-free extraction!"

That at least was no longer just an advertising line. The chemistry teacher at the college had put together a team at Makala's behest, and they had actually managed to start the production of ether. It had, after all, first been manufactured in the early nineteenth century with supplies and equipment any modern college or even high school chemistry classroom lab could duplicate.

When first discovered in the early nineteenth century and for nearly forty years afterward, ether and nitrous oxide were not used for medical purposes, but instead for what could be called "stoner parties." The "ether man" traveled from town to town with bottles of ether and tightly woven bags containing the nitrous oxide to be dispensed at two bits a whiff—a favorite form of entertainment. It was finally a dentist in Georgia in the early 1840s who had connected the dots that ether was far more than just entertainment. The Civil War historian in John was always grateful for that realization when he contemplated the agony of the hundreds of thousands of wounded who, if the war had been fought but twenty years earlier, would have gone under the saw and knife wide awake. Ether and chloroform were readily available then, and they were even sent through the lines as a humanitarian gesture if an enemy's hospital was running short. The tragedy after the Day was that the art of making anesthesia locally had to be re-learned, and thus many of the wounded after the war with the Posse had indeed suffered. After that experience, Makala made it a top priority for the college lab to resume manufacturing the precious gas and fumes, along with silver-based antibiotics.

As Richard motioned for John to take a seat in the chair, he looked around the office and felt that it indeed had a Civil War–era look to it.

A woodstove in the corner was burning, in spite of the heat of the day, to sterilize instruments in a boiling pot. X-ray readers and a computer screen providing soothing images to divert a patient in the chair were replaced with some old-fashioned charts of the mouth and teeth—gruesome but illustrative when Richard had to point out where a problem was.

John tried to settle back into the chair, Richard gossiping with him for a few minutes about the draft; his oldest daughter was one of those called up. And then the moment came.

"Come on, John, open up; let's take a look." Then the dreaded "Ah, I think this is the one." He tapped the sore tooth with the end of a probe, nearly sending John out of the chair.

Richard sat back, nodding thoughtfully. "In the old days, I'd send you to a specialist for a root canal; I don't even need an x-ray to tell you this one is bad. I can have it out in two minutes, John."

John looked at him wide eyed. "I'll skip it for now, Rich," he replied hoarsely. "Maybe in a couple of days after things settle down. I got a couple of meetings to attend to later today."

"Come on, John, I even got ether now. Have you under, tooth out, and you're on your way an hour from now."

John shook his head. "I gotta be clear headed—too much going on at the moment."

"I think you're begging off, John," Richard replied with a knowing smile.

"Yeah, well, maybe I am."

"Open your mouth again."

"Why?"

"I thought I saw something else. Promise I won't touch the sore tooth, but John, you and I know that kind of thing actually used to kill people two hundred years ago. It's an upper molar—gets infected, gets into your sinuses, and then you got real agony that could eventually kill you. Come on; let's get it taken care of."

John kept his mouth closed and shook his head, willing himself to think that it really didn't hurt all that bad and could wait.

"Well, at least let me take a quick look-see at something else. Promise I'll leave that bad boy alone."

John reluctantly complied. Richard leaned in, tapping John's lower-left canine, and John winced a bit.

"Yeah, thought so," Richard announced while still peering into John's mouth. "Start of a cavity that could go nasty there."

All John could do was mutter a strangled "Damn it."

"I can take care of that nice and quick," Richard continued, sitting back up and rubbing his hands on his apron. Gone were the days of latex gloves and masks, the few in the town's supply reserved for major surgeries only. "Drill that sucker out in five minutes and pack a filling into it."

John looked at him wide eyed.

"Compromise with ya, John. Let me fill that before it goes bad, and you get off free until tomorrow with the bad one. Otherwise, I go to Makala, and she lays some mandatory treatment order on you as the public health official."

John glared angrily at Richard for pulling that trump card and finally nodded a reluctant agreement.

Richard smiled, and whistling, he went over to the boiling pot, tossed in the instrument he had been using to probe John, and pulled out several others with tongs. John tried to look the other way as Richard pushed the foot-powered drill up alongside the chair and clamped a drill bit in.

It was yet another reason why, before the Day, John would shake his head when folks waxed too enthusiastically about the alleged beauty of living in the nineteenth century. They never thought about medicine and sanitation, let alone dentistry.

Richard pulled out a rubberized bag from under a counter. It looked like an oversized balloon with a nozzle on the end.

"I'll open the tap on this," Richard said with a grin. "You take a good deep breath in. Nitrous will chill you out for a few minutes."

Richard stuck the nozzle into John's mouth and then opened the valve.

"Go for it," Richard said, and he did have a bit of a maniacal grin as John breathed in deeply.

Within seconds, it hit, and John actually did feel mellowed out, even giddy, as Richard closed the valve, put the bag down, swung the old-fashioned drill around in front of John, and started to pedal furiously.

There was a low humming as the oiled cables spun in their sprockets, the drill bit spinning. Richard moved quickly, prying John's mouth open and pushing the drill bit down on to the cavity.

John felt like his entire head was vibrating, the sound of the drill bit flashing him back to early childhood, a dreaded dentist who had yet to go high tech and used an old-fashioned cable-driven drill, but at least that one was electrically powered.

For the first minute or so, it really didn't bother him; in fact, he was tempted to crack a joke. There was pain within seconds, but for a blessed moment, he really didn't care. It was strange how nitrous allowed one to feel pain but not care about it.

And then it hit. The gulp of nitrous was wearing off, the treadle-powered drill was setting up an awful racket, he felt like his mouth was vibrating apart, and the pain was building.

He started to gasp, waving his arm for Richard to stop.

"Hang in there, John, just another minute—almost got it all."

Gone was the electrical-powered suction tube. John's mouth was filling up with saliva and drilled-out bits of tooth, and it smelled like something was burning. He began to gag, waving frantically for Richard to back off.

Richard pulled the drill out and held up an old-fashioned spittoon, John gagging, spitting, and cursing.

"Think I got it all," Richard stated.

"*Think* you got it all?" John cried.

"Well, you were putting on such a show there."

"You're damn right. I swear you're a sadist, Richard."

Richard grinned. "I'll pack it with a filling, and we're done."

There was no argument; John couldn't very well walk out with a hole in his tooth on top of the other one that was throbbing away.

Richard opened a drawer in the old-fashioned, white-enamel-topped table behind him, drew out a tissue-thin sheet of gold, clipped off a small piece, gingerly rolled it up, and then worked it with a miniature-sized jeweler's hammer, turning it over and over. He finally picked it up with a pair of tweezers and dropped it into a petri dish filled with moonshine that served as an antiseptic wash.

"Now rinse good. Make sure the stuff gets into that tooth, and it's okay to swallow."

Richard handed him a mason jar of clear white lightning, and John did as ordered, nearly yelping with pain as the high-test moonshine swirled around his aching tooth as well as the one that Richard had drilled. He so wanted to swallow, but thoughts of the town meeting to come caused him to spit it out into the bucket, though Richard was not above a quick swig for himself before getting back to work, fishing the gold filling out of its anti-septic wash. After another agonizing minute, he had it firmly worked into the drilled-out hole.

"There. All done," Richard announced proudly. "Don't chew on that for a few days. If it starts to get infected, get in here, and I definitely expect you back in here in another day so I can get that rotting tooth out of you before it really goes bad. We can't fool around with those things the way we used to. Remember old man Parker died last month from a tooth infection."

John could only nod. Now both sides of his mouth hurt.

"How much do I owe you?" he muttered, standing up.

"Let's see, one drilling, one filling with gold foil . . . make that a buck in silver; that covers the cost of the gold more than anything else. We'll say a buck in silver or twenty rounds of ammo—prefer .22."

John fished into his pocket and pulled out a well-worn Barber quarter and two Mercury dimes. Over the previous year, silver money, hoarded by more than a few before the Day, had started to slip back into circulation as money that was accepted by nearly all.

"All I got on me. Can I pay you the rest tomorrow?"

"Yup, but that tooth pull, that'll be an extra fifty cents," Richard said with a smile. "Only twenty-five cents if you want to skip the ether."

"Yeah, right." John sighed. "I'll be back tomorrow and pay you the rest then, along with the extra two bits for ether when you pull the tooth out. Okay?"

Richard smiled and nodded. "You'd definitely better be back in, John. It's no joking matter, and you know that better than most. Stupid to die because of a lousy tooth after all you've been through."

John all but fled the office and then turned to walk up Cherry Street, pausing to look in nostalgically at the used bookstore, a favorite haunt before the Day. The owner had died in the battle with the Posse. It had been turned into a borrowing library by his friend's widow—bring a book in to trade for one taken out—and it thus continued to flourish, but he missed his old friend, the games of chess over coffee, a world where he did not face the situation waiting just around the corner. A sign hung on the door: "Closed for the town meeting. Chess tournament later tonight."

Nearly half a thousand had shown up in the town square for the hastily called gathering to find out the news about John's visit to the new federal administrator. The pig roast lent a slightly festive air to the occasion; it wasn't every day—or even week or month—when an open meal was offered to the town without requirement of ration cards, and more than a few showed for the roasted pork and then wandered off if their families were not directly affected by the draft.

Phil, a favorite in the town where everyone still spoke nostalgically of his legendary barbecue restaurant, had presided over the roasting. He complained that he should have been given a week or so to properly prepare the wild boar, but John had left word with him to do his best and have it ready by six for the sake of all, which he faithfully did. The fire pit had been burning all day, Phil butchering off hunks of meat from the wild boar and just roasting them over the fire, muttering throughout the hot day that if given the time, he could have made the six-hundred-pound boar into a real feast. The meat was tough but at least edible, and any meat, especially in midspring, was welcome after the long, lean days of winter.

There was nearly half a pound of meat for everyone present, and that had settled things a bit. Eventually, though, the meeting degenerated into angry questions, fueled primarily by Ernie Franklin and his extended family of kin and followers. John had no answers to give Ernie other than the fact that the draft had been pushed back to thirty days, that Fredericks had promised that assets were coming in to ensure public safety, and that the federal government was finally started to reach out to their region. It was a bit difficult to speak clearly; his mouth still throbbing from the ordeal with Richard, so it was a relief to announce he had another meeting to get to. He turned things over to Reverend Black and with a sigh of relief piled into the old Edsel with his family for the three-mile drive up to the college campus and Lake Susan to an event John had been looking forward to for a long time.

Paul and Becka Hawkins had arranged for the secret meeting up at Lake Susan long before the crisis over the draft had hit. Paul was one of the IT guys for Montreat College, and Becka was an assistant librarian. Both were students who had stayed on after graduation, found jobs at the college, and then eventually married. After the Day, the library, the place where they hung out together as students, had become their permanent home when they set up an apartment in the basement. Friends familiar with the old *Twilight Zone* series joked that the couple reminded them of a famous episode starring Burgess Meredith in which a bookworm finds paradise in a library after a nuclear war.

Their shared passion was poking around old books and magazines, looking for anything that might be helpful to the community, such as articles in *Mother Earth News* on how to identify which mushrooms were safe to eat. Six months before, they had finally hit the mother lode of treasures.

The reason it had taken so long to find this particular treasure trove was twofold. Years earlier, the library had gone over to electronic cataloging. The old card-filing system, once so familiar in all libraries, had finally been carted to a back room and not updated since the turn of the century. Anything that had come in since had simply been entered into the campus database— now long lost, of course.

One of the great weaknesses of the now lost digital age was its total dependence on electronic databases rather than old-fashioned backups with ink on paper. A poignant pastime for some was to gaze at a dust-covered iPhone, trying to remember something called phone numbers of friends and even that of children and parents. Older folks could still rattle off a number and address from a quarter century earlier, but from the day before all systems went down? Where were the addresses, even photographic images of life in the decade before the Day now? It was symbolic of just how much had been wiped out of their lives, most likely never to return. Thus in the library—as in so many millions of other locations, from federal government offices down to iPhones and iPads—nearly all data from the decade prior to the attack had been lost.

The second factor behind the long delay of discovering the hidden treasure was that, every spring, locals emptying out attics and garages would haul thousands of moldering books and magazines into the library for the annual Fourth of July book sale and fund-raiser. Of course, the sale had never happened after the war started, and the hundreds of boxes of donations were all but forgotten in the basement. It took the Paul and Becka prowling around the damp, moldy basement for yet more curios and things interesting to read to find the treasure: a complete set of the *Journal of the AIEE*—the American Institute of Electrical Engineers—dating all the way back to 1884.

Nearly anyone else in the world would have consigned the moldy, sneeze-inducing magazines to the kindling pile, but fortunately, not those two. Months earlier, they had burst into John's office—unlike most in the town, they still called him "Doc" out of memory of his days as their history professor—and tossed a dusty, brittle magazine on his desk without preamble or explanation.

"Doc, this is a gold mine!" Paul cried. "They even got the first edition here from 1884! And check this out—articles actually written by Tesla, Nikola Tesla himself!"

It had been a quiet, snowy day when they arrived, and he had indeed been in a mellow mood after a romantic night with Makala in front of the fireplace and no new crisis to deal with, so he was initially in an indulgent frame of mind. Hardly a day passed without someone presenting a hare-brained idea to solve the town's problems with everything from cold fusion machines to perpetual motion. When Mabel's husband, George, first walked in with plans for how to run a car off charcoal fumes, he thought the man crazy, but a year later, half a dozen such vehicles were chugging around the community.

As a professor, John had always turned to Paul when it came to the inevitable computer glitches in his classroom, and Becka could always track down some obscure journal via interlibrary loan for an article he was writing, so of course he would listen to them. Within minutes after they dumped the journal on his desk, he was as excited as they were. They brought in a box of the journals and spent a delightful afternoon poring over them. Beyond being the onetime head of this town, he was a historian, and the journals were a remarkable glimpse into a most remarkable time in global history where the world was coming out of the darkness and into the future brilliance of electrical power . . . and in so doing would set itself up for the greatest disaster in human history since the great plagues of the fourteenth century.

The monthly journals dated all the way back to the first days of the electrical industry. The infamous "current wars"—the conflict between Edison on one side supporting the use of direct current and Tesla and Westinghouse on the other pushing for alternating current—had been fought out for years on the pages of the magazine. Historically, that was interesting enough, but far more important were the details of the genesis of the modern electrical current grid from generating station to transformers to household appliances with detailed plans and patents set out for everything.

It was a time of excitement and new inventions nearly every month. It was also a time of bitter infighting, turf wars, patent arguments, claim jumping on who invented what first, character assassinations, and outright thievery and sabotage.

Becka's librarian skills came to the fore as she laboriously indexed and cross indexed the material they had uncovered. That was an essential step since the magazines had been printed on cheap, wood-pulp-based paper, and many were as brittle as glass, about to disintegrate if handled more than a few times. The secrets of the past could literally disintegrate in a reader's hands, and she therefore became their guardian, ensuring the magazines were not pawed over in a frivolous manner. What she was protecting covered the development of the entire industry, from just a few years after the first commercial incandescent lightbulbs and power plants went online up until the 1960s when the AIEE had merged with another organization to include advanced electronics—unknowingly beginning to lay the groundwork for disaster with an increasingly delicate infrastructure.

The library had already proven its worth innumerable times over since the Day. There had been a rush to uncover half-forgotten issues of *Mother Earth News* and the *Foxfire* series of books for some retro learning about food gathering and preparation. The college had set up seminars for students and the general public to teach canning, mushroom gathering, hunting, trapping, and folk medicine. But this? It was like some lost tablets had been found by archaeologists that would explain a forgotten language, a language that could unlock one of the great secrets of the universe—how to restore electrical power. More than a few, especially the ham radio operators and a few other hobbyists, understood how it all had once worked, but to see the actual diagrams and patents once written and filed by Tesla and company was undreamed of.

John had called an emergency meeting of the town council that same evening, unable to contain his excitement, and within the hour, the proposal by Paul had been passed with a full allocation of whatever resources were necessary—if and when they could be found—and even a boost in precious rations from the town reserve for those doing the heavy, dirty work for the project.

The proposal: to retrofit the dam at Lake Susan down below the college and turn it into a hydroelectric generating system. The few old-timers still alive in Montreat—John's mother-in-law, Jen, being one of them—could recall how there actually had been a hydroelectric power plant a couple of miles above Lake Susan that first provided electricity to Montreat until the big power companies had moved in and taken things over in the 1930s, abandoning the smaller mills and letting them fall into ruins. Jen, as a small girl, used to hike up to the abandoned site and prowl around the wreckage.

The day after the decision was made, Paul led an expedition up there to scavenge through the bits of wreckage in hopes of finding abandoned equipment. Some useable pipe, a few rusted gears, and some disintegrating switchboards were dug out, but not much else—other than a rattlesnake, which was quickly dispatched. No matter how hungry he was, John could not stomach the thought as several students quickly skinned the still-twitching snake and made a meal of it.

The list of necessary supplies put forth by Paul seemed insurmountable at first glance. So many of the items listed in the journals from the 1880s were readily at hand in that long-ago world. But to find them now? In the world of the 1880s, Tesla and Westinghouse could cook up their ideas about this revolutionary thing called AC current and then turn to an army of men with technical skills—wire makers, steel molders, and lathe operators on down to the sandhogs digging tunnels. The details of how they ventured to harness the power of Niagara Falls for the great megaproject of that time were outlined in the journals in the breathless detail that the Victorians loved to read about. They made it seem easy in comparison to turning tiny Lake Susan into a new source of energy.

It presented the classic paradox of attempting to recover a lost technology when the entire infrastructure had been shattered. Tesla, Westinghouse, and Edison created one of the most significant technological advances in history, the ability to create energy at one location and move it to another to perform myriad tasks as yet undreamed of in the 1880s. They created a system that would lead to radio, television, medical technologies that nearly doubled the average life span from that of the year 1900, and limitless energy at the flick of a switch—everything that the world of the twenty-first century assumed was part of ordinary life until the Day.

As they conceptualized those first ideas regarding the still barely understood thing called electricity, they could turn over their drawings to master tool and die makers, precision lathe operators, smelters running blast furnaces, wire makers, and even blueprint drawers. There was a nineteenth-century infrastructure already in place to make the great wonders of the nineteenth century, not just the generating of electricity but the means to get it out there and keep it running 24-7-365.

As a historian, when he was first looking at the plans that Paul and Becka drew up for the town's approval, John felt overwhelming despair. Nearly everything they envisioned for their project had to be made from scratch, reshaped from the salvaged refuse of a collapsed national infrastructure, and it would all have to be manufactured locally. As he examined Tesla's patent application for the essential converters—the precision-made tools that converted the electrical current blasting out of a generator turned by water-power into 60-hertz alternating current—it seemed nearly impossible to replicate. So to for the transformers, another of Tesla's near genie-like creations, that could step voltage up for transmission and then step it back down again for final distribution into homes and factories.

Paul shrugged off John's concerns with a smile. "I helped with rigging up Internet to this campus and kept it running; this is no big deal in comparison."

The challenge presented to Paul and Becka by their discovery was ultimately to start the rebuilding of a modern community from scratch.

The Day had taught all that electricity was the fundamental bedrock of their entire civilization, so ubiquitous that no one really fully grasped how crucial it was until it was gone. John's former students, if successful, would begin the long journey back. If they said it was possible, he and the rest of the community could do nothing less than support them, and all had given the go-ahead even as it strained the community resources, taking dozens of workers out of food production—the bare essentials of survival—with the hope that the investment would indeed start the long journey back from the darkness. As John voted to approve their plan and requests for resources, he quoted the old Joni Mitchell song with the refrain "You don't know what you've got 'til it's gone."

So the plan had moved forward. Anderson Auditorium, a beautiful old structure that was actually a twelve-sided, three-story-high building—a popular architectural style for conference centers back in the 1920s—was cleared out and converted into a huge workshop. The interior of a day care center next to Flat Creek, which emptied out of Lake Susan, was gutted out to be converted into the town's new power station. Out along the front of the dam, part of that structure was torn down, the lake was drained, and even during the coldest days of winter and early spring, piping was laid in and the dam face rebuilt.

Lake Susan was a relic of a time when people actually built dams and created lakes for strictly scenic reasons. No one until Paul and Becka came along looked upon the sparkling water falling over the dam's spillway as representing quite a few megawatts of energy.

When Paul and Becka, now sporting official titles as electrical engineers, presented their wish list of necessary material, John had told them to move forward, but he did wonder if it was all turning into a pipe dream.

The generator would have to be woven by hand with a dozen miles of copper wire. Most of the freestanding, old-fashioned copper wires in the community had literally melted off the poles when hit by the EMP or had been looted afterward for other such uses as the barely functional telephone system. The turbine of welded steel had to be perfectly balanced; if not, within minutes, it would burn out its bearings and either seize up or fly apart. New transformers had to be made, miles of wire needed to be re-strung to run the power from the dam clear down to Black Mountain, and all the other intricacies of actually building a power grid from scratch had to be accomplished.

Regarding the copper wire, Paul had uncovered yet another treasure trove that was under their noses: the old electrical substation at the base of the hill where John used to live. It had been heavily damaged by the EMP and further damaged in the battle with the Posse, which had been stopped in the area around the station. Paul began to tear the old transformers apart and pull out the copper wiring within them. Most of it was fused into a solid mass from the electrical overload of the EMP. The answer—and Paul, in his enthusiasm, made it sound simple—was just melt it down and draw new wire out of the molten mass.

It had taken weeks of experimenting, of remastering a common tech-nology of the nineteenth century. One student was severely burned, but they had finally figured it out, and the interior of Anderson Auditorium was now a thunderous, smoke-filled workshop of wood-fired kilns, a foundry, wire works, and lathes powered by a somewhat gasping old VW engine provided by the town's auto mechanic, Jim Bartlett. Teams were sent out to pull generators and alternators from abandoned cars for their wiring and batteries for the acid and lead inside.

The fact that a meeting and a demonstration had been planned for the evening after the meeting with Fredericks actually came as a welcome diver-sion after dealing with the crisis of the day, and it was a good excuse for John to keep the open community meeting from turning into an hours-long, dragged-out debate.

A small crowd, the team of students and elderly workers who had once labored in the heavy industries of a long-ago industrialized America, was gathered outside the old children's day care center, rechristened "Montreat Power Station #1," and actually applauded with enthusiastic delight as John and his family pulled up in the old Edsel.

In a way, it was simply a publicity show and test run; the real turbine and generator were still several weeks away from final placement. What Paul and Becka had set up for the evening's demonstration was a one-sixth-scale test model housed off to one side of the main floor where the main generator was still under construction.

The pipe from the dam face snaked downslope to the powerhouse, thus adding a dozen more feet of elevation drop from the dam face and thus more energy.

It was obvious that Paul, Becka, and their workforce had been waiting excitedly for his arrival. Elizabeth, her worries of the moment forgotten, bounded out of the car with young and very sleepy Ben in her arms. Makala gently helped John's aged mother-in-law, Jen, ever the elegant lady even at eighty, as she braced herself and slowly walked down to where the crowd waited, exchanging greetings with old friends and neighbors. Makala fell in behind her, John by her side, both ready to leap forward and grab the fragile woman if she should start to totter. The previous two years had aged her ten, and no one needed to be told that in this terrible new age after the Day, a fall resulting in a broken hip was a lingering and most painful death sentence.

"So how are the wizards of electricity?" John asked cheerfully as he approached the waiting crowd in the gathering gloom.

There were warm smiles and handshakes all around. John suggested that the two who first cooked up the idea offer a brief explanation of what they had accomplished. Paul was eager to go into a tech-laden lecture, but after a few minutes, Becka simply leaned up, kissed him on the cheek, and lovingly put a hand over his mouth.

"He'll go on all night like that," she said with a laugh. "He even does it in his sleep. Doc, we got a good head of water coming through the pipe; all we need to do is open the valve that feeds into our model turbine. Would you do us the honors?"

John shook his head and smiled. "You guys built it. You turn it on."

They hesitated, and he sensed they were nervous. They had actually resisted testing this out until now, so no one was sure all those old diagrams and their months of hard labor actually would amount to something. They were fearful a premature test run might blow apart all they had labored for so far. The two looked at each other and the several dozen who had worked with them throughout the winter and into the spring. The crowd laughed and urged them on. Together, they stepped into the power-house, and a joke was shouted that now was not the time to make out in the dark but to get to work.

"I'm not sure how long she'll run, so here goes!" Paul shouted through the open doorway, and together he and Becka first opened a valve that diverted water from the overflow pipe, shifting it to run against the turbine blades of their test model. All could hear a vibrating rumble as the turbine began to turn faster and faster, coming up to speed, as Paul watched an old-fashioned gauge monitoring the RPMs. He said something to Becka, the two barely visible inside the gloomy exterior of the control room. Together, they took hold of a switch that John thought looked like something straight out of a Frankenstein movie and forced it down to connect the generator and bring it to life.

A gasp erupted from the small crowd. Light! Electric light!

Electric lighting, not seen in their valley for over two years, shined forth from a community power station. Old hundred-watt bulbs inside the power station instantly flashing into brilliant darkness-shattering life. A string of bulbs along the roofline of the building began to glow as Paul and Becka threw a second switch, and even a salvaged string of Christmas bulbs draped along the eaves of the small power station, the same lights that had once decorated the campus tree every winter, sparkled in their multicolored hues.

"Ben, look at the lights, the lights!" Elizabeth shouted as she hugged her squirming toddler, who was now awake and pointing at the multicolored Christmas lights, squealing with laughter.

John pulled Makala in closer, hugging her. He looked over at his grandson's shining face, and tears came to his eyes. The child, for the first time, was seeing what half a dozen generations before him had experienced from their first seconds of life and knew throughout their lives. And now those around him were laughing and cheering. And then, as an added thrill to it all, music! An old-fashioned boom box Becka had mounted on a windowsill came to life, blaring out an old song—"Blinded by the Light." Within seconds, all were dancing to the music, laughing and cheering like wild children, some of the elderly in the crowd showing the college kids how to form up for a line dance.

Then the music seemed to go slightly out of beat, slowing down and then speeding up, reminding John of when he was a kid and he and his friends would put 45 RPM records on and crank the player up to 78 RPM and think it wildly funny. The hundred-watt bulbs glowed with hot intensity. One winked off, and another actually burst, and before Paul could throw the switch off, the Christmas lights shorted out.

The music and dancing stopped, and the scent of ozone filled the air. Becka raced back inside the power station to switch the water back to the outflow pipe. A grinding sound came from the turbine housing as its blades clattered to a stop. The crowd outside stood silent, not sure how to react.

John quickly stepped forward, breaking the tension, clapping his hands. "Bravo, you guys! Magnificent!"

The two engineers peeked out nervously from the power station building, ready with excuses and explanations about this being a test run, that the real turbine would be far more finely tuned and that they still had to get more precise with Tesla's alternating generator system, but they were drowned out by the enthusiastic applause and hugs from their coworkers, the uproar growing even louder when Becka let slip that she could not be picked up and tossed around because she was expecting. The promise of any new life in their so tragically depleted community was greeted with laughter, cheers, and more than a few ribald jokes about what had been going on in the library basement other than research.

John and Makala worked their way through the crowd, and the act took on something of a ritual as John warmly grasped Paul's hand, congratulating him first on the good news with Becka and then for their miraculous achievement with the power plant.

Makala warmly embraced Becka. "First thing in the morning, I want you to stop by so we can talk over your diet, and Paul, let this lady rest for a while. If need be, the power plant can wait; your baby is far more important to us."

Far too many pregnancies had been lost in the first year after the Day, and more than a few mothers actually died due to malnourishment. The entire community now gave top priority to expectant mothers. For John, there was a flash memory of the sacrifice he had decided on for Elizabeth, the death of their beloved golden retriever, Ginger, a decision he had made without hesitation and which still filled him with tears.

John sensed it was time to leave the electricity wizards to their cele-bration; it had already been an exhausting day after a sleepless night. Re-turning home, he slipped off to be by himself while the rest of the family went to bed.

A half hour later, he sensed a presence behind him and turned to see Makala standing in the moonlight. He didn't say anything other than to slip over on the bench by Jennifer's grave so that she could join him.

Makala offered him a glass of blackberry wine, the last of half a dozen bottles that had been a Christmas gift from one of his old students. Makala took a sip from her glass and remained silent.

"You know, there are times I still crave a damn good cigarette." He sighed, finally opening up. "And this is one of them."

"One of the few benefits of what happened, it made you kick that loath-some habit," Makala offered, leaning in against his shoulder.

He struggled not to let her know that he had been crying, but he could not hide it. It still hit him at times when he came out at night to sit by his daughter's grave for a few minutes for silent thought and a prayer before going to bed.

"I should be at least somewhat over it all." He nodded to the grave. Nightmares still haunted him, her last words coming back to him, whisper-ing that she wanted to be buried in the yard so she could remain close to him and for him to take good care of her beloved stuffed animal Rabs, whom he now held whenever he visited with her.

He finally sat back, coughing, embarrassed, wiping his face with a soiled handkerchief, Makala kissing him on the cheek again.

He nodded an embarrassed thanks even though she had witnessed mo-ments like this scores of times, but he was glad to feel her close by his side. "And now they want to take Elizabeth away from me," he gasped, strug-gling for control. "If she goes off, she'll never come back."

Makala remained silent as she always did at such moments to give him room to finally let his feelings out, a luxury he could not indulge in when in front of others who expected his stoic leadership.

"There are times I am so sick to death of the role I have to play," he said. "The rock-solid leader, the one that everyone else comes to for strength. I can't bear the thought of her going, but I have to stand by silent and let her go if that is the way this plays out. To do otherwise is pure hypocrisy. I have to tell her to go if others are forced to go." He sighed, looking off. "When we went in on the attack against Iraq, I wanted to be on the front line, not stuck a couple of miles back in a well-armored command vehicle. When several of my men were killed, I had to take it in calmly, reassure the other troopers, tell them to push on, even though I wanted to scream with frustration and pain, since I knew those kids well. When we came back to the States, I went to see their families; one was married with two kids. The whole rest of the country was celebrating what they thought was an easy win, but it still cost hundreds of lives. What could I tell those who had lost a son or husband? They died in a good cause? They were heroes?

"The three in my unit who died? Their Humvee took a rocket-propelled grenade, and there was no heroism about it. One second, they were alive—the next second, dead. And they left behind families that will never really heal no matter what the platitudes and honors."

He looked up, gazing at the moon. "And so now I will be the parent that stands by and waits, with my gut instincts telling me she'll not come back. Part of me wants to race back to Fredericks tomorrow and take the deal I know he'd give me to exempt Elizabeth. Then what? Frankly, it's not how the town will react that bothers me, though I know I'd be a pariah. You and Jen would understand, but I think the respect of both of you would be gone if I did."

He fell silent, and she did not reply.

He continued, "It's that I know Elizabeth will tell me to go to hell and enlist anyhow, because she believes it is her duty, even though it means being torn away from her child." His gaze returned to Jennifer's grave. "Damn this world. Damn what we allowed it to become."

"We had nothing to do with what happened," Makala began, but he cut her off with a glare.

"We did have a lot to do with it. We had all grown so fat, so complacent, and we always let someone else worry about such things, even though we knew that those we allowed to be in charge were far too often incompetent—or worse, self-serving and blind in their arrogance."

There was no reprimand in his words, only a deep sadness. "I feel like a balled-up knot, becoming the archetype of the way it is in all wars, of old men pointing to the front lines and telling the young to go out and die. But this time, it is now my daughter, her friends, the ones who fought and saved this town a year ago."

He sighed again, absently petting the well-worn fabric of Jennifer's stuffed animal.

"When Dale made that first offer, of course I refused; it was so damn insulting. But now, after hours of thinking about it, it does tear at me even as I know I have to resist it."

"I don't trust that son of a bitch as far as I can spit," Makala snapped back in reply. "He tried to bribe you right up front with offering a deferment to Elizabeth and not the others. He knew what he was doing."

A bit taken aback, John said nothing, just looking at her for a moment.

"What do you think of him?" she finally asked. "You're the ex-military type, not me."

"My first reaction today was not good. I mean, the guards out front . . . you could see it in his eyes; he's a thug. That type has always been a plague since pharaoh first organized an army. They get in a uniform, and God save anyone who crosses them. A good unit commander weeds that type out quick or at least keeps them on a really short leash. So that was a bad first impression. But I'm not going to judge Fredericks solely on that. He explained why he made what you call a bribe. He just thought I was there only for Elizabeth. The guy most likely is swamped with hundreds of families, each asking for special treatment. At least my war in the Gulf and the ones after it were fought by an all-volunteer force. No one likes a draft, but there is some logic to it here and now if we are to resecure our borders and start rebuilding the entire United States as it once was."

He wearily shook his head. "So now I am hoisted up on the spike of my own ethics and convictions."

"Look at it cynically and him far more cynically, John. You want to believe that the motivation of this leader is good, along with those behind him all the way up to those in Bluemont."

John was silent for a long time.

He gazed at Jennifer's grave, moonlight casting a shadow from the ceramic golden retriever placed at the head of the grave in memory of Ginger, whom Jennifer had loved with all her heart and whom John had actually killed the day after Jennifer died in order to feed Elizabeth, struggling with her pregnancy. That memory nearly choked him up again.

It was all too much. He stood up, stepping back into the sunroom to place Rabs on his perch where he kept watch over Jennifer. Makala followed him.

"I just don't know," John whispered. He looked appealingly at Makala. "Give me a couple of days to sort this one out. See what Fredericks comes back with. Okay?"

His tone indicated he was worn down with the conversation and needed some what he called "introvert time," to just think things through. She kissed him on the cheek, whispered a good night, and left his side.

He returned to the sitting room and sat down at the old rolltop desk that had once belonged to his father-in-law. Mounted to one side was a true luxury.

One of the ham operators had shown up at his doorstep several weeks earlier with a small multiband shortwave from the 1960s dug out of an abandoned antique store. He also gave John a solar-powered battery charger, and though the batteries were wearing down after hundreds of recharges, they did allow him to tune in for a half hour or so before having to charge them back up again. He settled down by the radio and clicked it on, the old-fashioned analog dial glowing and fine-tuned into a familiar voice . . . the BBC. The timing was good—late in the evening here, three in the morning over there. There was the familiar, comforting chime of Big Ben marking three and the always-so-well-modulated voice of the news broadcaster.

It is 3:00 a.m., Greenwich War Time, and this is the news of the hour.

Heavy fighting was reported today in Chicago, Illinois; Indianapolis, Indiana; and Fort Wayne, Indiana. The American government in Bluemont announced an offensive against a gang controlling that region, deploying troops from the newly formed Army of National Recovery, or ANR. The government spokesperson stated that the offensive is a clear first step to eliminate lawlessness and restore national unity. There is an unconfirmed report, transmitted by a former BBC correspondent in Ottawa, that American federal forces have taken heavy casualties not only in this action but in others in Cleveland and other cities bordering Canada along the Great Lakes.

The federal government also announced that it will bring whatever forces, and I quote, "up to strategic level if need be into this fight to bring about unification," end quote. There was no specific answer as to what is implied by this statement when asked about the definition of "strategic level."

A message now for our friends in Quebec: "The chair is against the door." I repeat, "The chair is against the door."

Here in England, the government announced that, contrary to earlier promises, the rationing of petrol must continue for the foreseeable future. The prime minister stated . . .

Strategic forces? He shook his head. Surely that did not mean what he feared. "Damn it." He sighed, putting his head down on the desk and closing his eyes.

CHAPTER FOUR

John was still in his office, having dozed off at his desk, when the piercing jangle of the old rotary phone snapped him awake.

The windows facing Jennifer's grave were open, and between the insistent ringing of the phone, he thought he heard something else . . . gunfire.

He looked at the luminescent face of his old-style windup wristwatch; it was just after three o'clock, local time. He felt absolutely drained with exhaustion as he picked up the phone.

"John, it's Richard Black down at the town hall. We just got a report phoned in from our watch station up by the North Fork Reservoir. A firefight."

John stifled a yawn, trying to focus. "Okay. I'm coming down to the office. Call Maury Hurt; ask him to roll out his Jeep and wake up the reaction team."

The team, a squad of eight from the town's military company, pulled weeklong rotation shifts and were bunked in the firehouse next to the town hall. Exchanges of gunfire and skirmishes along the northern border of the community were nothing new. It was most likely the border reivers raiding for food or a continuation of their ongoing feud with the Stepp families, who lived at the base of the Mount Mitchell range. The raids were more annoyance rather than a real threat, though several had died on both sides over the last year. And there was always the threat, as well, that some far deadlier gang had moved into the region. Rumors that survivors of the Posse lingered, that they were coalescing again and bent on vengeance against Black Mountain.

Regardless of who had started the flare-up tonight, like a marshal of the Old West, he felt obligated to see about it.

He pulled on trousers and a flannel shirt, an early morning chill still in the air. Makala helped him don a Kevlar vest, a present from the army before they had left Asheville. He holstered his .45 and headed for the door.

"Most likely another damned feud." John sighed. "But it could be some other group setting us up. Until I find out who exactly is shooting at whom and why, we got to assume the worst—that some splinter group of reivers are hitting us. So if they do get into this cove, you know what to do."

She was already holding the twelve gauge as if to reassure him that his home would be safe, and she kissed him lightly. "Be careful."

He smiled. "Soul of caution." It had become his standard reply. Then he was out the door. The Edsel reluctantly turned over after thirty seconds of grinding and John's muttered curses.

He roared out of the driveway, through the gateway into Montreat, where the one guard was obviously awake and offered a half wave, half salute, and two minutes later, he was at the town hall. The reaction squad was already loaded up into a heavy, four-wheel-drive pickup truck. His old friend Maury Hurt rolled up in his WWII Jeep just as John pulled in.

Reverend Black was at the door of the town hall.

"Anything new?" John shouted.

"Just that one call from the watch post reporting an intrusion. Firing has stopped, though some sort of building is burning above the north bank of the reservoir."

He hoped that whatever the ruckus was, it was over. It could be nothing other than some drunks shooting at each other, or it could be an infiltration, the team at the outpost dead and raiders pouring into the valley of the North Fork. He had received more than one chewing out from old vets, the town council, and others that, at such moments, his job was to stay in the town hall and let others do the job. He had been forced to do that in Iraq and swore he would never do it again. If his people were going to put their asses on the line, he would be there with them.

He settled into the Jeep beside Maury and pointed to the road. The two-vehicle task force set out, rolling west along State Street. The once-thriving shops, the town hardware store, and the wine and chocolate shop all had long ago shuttered up, windows boarded up or broken. No traffic lights blinking, just an empty road, the stalled vehicles from the Day long ago hauled off for salvage. Dropping down the slope on the west side of town, everything was dark. It was still a few hours till dawn, the air chilled but rich with the scent of spring, the wind flowing around the Jeep slapping him awake.

Maury turned off onto old Highway 70 past John's favorite hot dog stand, looted and burned out long ago, then past the state veterans' cemetery, where it had been decided that those who had died in defense of the town were to be buried rather than the golf course. Instinctively, he raised his hand to his hat brim in salute, Maury, a veteran of the air force, doing the same.

It was a chilly journey in the open Jeep, a vehicle Maury had purchased years before and had lovingly restored. Even now, riding in it made John think of the movie *Patton*, except unlike that eccentric leader, John did not stand up and take on the affectations of a siren throughout the ride.

They reached what had been a minimum-security detention center with its ugly and now useless barrier fence and turned onto the winding road up to the North Fork Reservoir, the main water supply for the entire city of Asheville.

"Something's burning," Maury announced. John didn't need to be told, the red glare of it reflecting off the surface of the lake.

They reached the dam face of the reservoir where he had a watch station in place. The two students assigned there came out of the concealed bunker, reporting that they had heard voices echoing across the lake, followed by a couple of minutes of sustained gunfire and then something going up in flames.

If voices alone could echo across the lake, then most certainly their arrival in a Jeep and four-wheel-drive truck could certainly be heard, as well.

He stood silent for several minutes, gazing across the quarter-mile-wide lake. It looked like a shack of some kind was indeed burning on the far shore. Back before the Day, this had been the reservoir for the city of Asheville, and any kind of building within the watershed was strictly forbidden. Chances were it was some kind of still or squatter's shack burning over there.

Was it worth the risk to check it out, or should they wait until dawn?

The Stepps, who had settled this valley over two hundred years earlier, had hung on rather well compared to many after the Day. Over the last year, they had produced enough of a surplus to start breeding hogs, chickens, and drop off the town rationing, and they traded well and fairly with the community. The raid might be aimed at their food. One branch of the family, however, lived more on the fringe, and it was they who usually were either trading with or wrangling with the reivers. He guessed this was some kind of payback attack. Illegal still or not, something was going on, and he had to find out what it was.

Darkness played to his advantage if it was raiders; he knew this territory, and they most likely did not. If it was just the Stepps doing something stupid, he had to deal with that, as well . . . and hoped that was all it was.

He motioned for his reaction team to gather round. He looked at their young faces in the waning moonlight. They were tense but ready to go in.

"I'll take point. I want you deployed back fifty yards behind me in a skirmish line."

"Sir, that's our job to be point, not yours." It was Grace, typical of her to speak up.

"Not this time," John offered. "If it's just the Stepps, they know me; they might not know you and fire first and ask questions later."

He stood up, indicating there would be no more debate, stepped out from behind the bunker, and started along the access road that followed the west shore of the lake. He heard someone behind him, turned back, and saw that it was Maury, his World War II–era M1 carbine raised.

"What the hell are you doing?" John asked.

"Just taking a walk with you, that's all," Maury replied.

"Okay, but let's not go off half-cocked. If it's the reivers, they usually hightail out rather than face a fight with a full squad of our troops. If it's someone else . . ." His voice trailed off.

They moved silently along the bank of the river. All was silent except for the crackling of the fire, the lake reflecting the light and that of the moon.

He began to think of the notoriously bad line from old movies—"It's quiet; *too* quiet"—just before all hell broke loose.

A gut instinct suddenly kicked in; something didn't feel right. Long ago, instructors in advanced infantry training had drilled into him that in combat, listen to gut instincts; chances were that something your conscious thinking had not even registered—the faint crack of a broken branch, a barely detected scent on the air, just a feeling that something wasn't right— was screaming at you to react.

"Hey! Whoever's coming, we need help up here!" The cry for help close by. It sounded like old Wilson Stepp.

"Wilson Stepp, is that you?" John shouted.

There was no reply.

"Wilson, it's John Matherson. What the hell is going on?"

A momentary pause, and then Wilson's voice, sounding strained. "Hurt, John. I need help."

"We'll go up and check it out, sir."

Turning, he saw Grace creeping up behind him, crouched low. He motioned for her to freeze in place, deciding that she was going to get one hell of a chewing out once this was over for breaking orders.

Only a couple of years older than Elizabeth, Grace had made the campus her home after the Day. Her family lived in Jacksonville. It was ironic that he had actually discussed with her parents what would happen if ever there was a serious crisis, her folks telling John to make sure she stayed put at the school, where they knew she would be safe. It was almost as if they had some insider word that something bad was coming. As he looked at her, he thought of the risks she had already taken and wanted to now take again—and how he would ever be able to face her parents if one day they did show up on the campus. How he would feel if Elizabeth went off and one day he confronted her commanding officer.

That made his decision as to what to do next all so clear.

If someday they finally show up for their daughter, do I tell them she died because I sent her into a trap?

"Stay put," he whispered.

He suddenly felt an overwhelming urge for a cigarette. He could make out Maury's features, his friend tight lipped, eyes wide.

"It smells bad, John," Maury whispered.

"No shit," was all he could say. He was suddenly afraid, but he could not let that take control of his judgment now.

"Hey, for God's sake, someone help me!" The cry sounded weak, strained. From behind him, he could hear voices. It was some of the Stepp family coming up the road, armed.

Either the raiders are gone, or this could turn into a bloodbath, John realized. They were not the type of people to stop if they thought one of their kin was hurt.

"Grace, go back. Tell those folks to stay back, and the same for the rest of you."

"Sir?"

"Just do it," John hissed. "Maury, keep them back. I'm going up."

"Are you flipping crazy, John?" Maury snapped. "You go back, and I'll go forward and check it out. Your job is back there, not getting your ass blown off by some damn drunk reiver. And if that is old man Stepp hurt up there, it's most likely because he fell down drunk."

"So I send your ass to get blown off, is that it?" John replied, and he forced a smile. "Chances are there aren't even any reivers—just these damn fools got drunk and started shooting at their own shadows."

He stood up.

Maury was right, and he knew it. But given all that had happened against the Posse and just hours earlier with Fredericks, he realized he was sick to death of sending others forward. At the moment, it was so much easier to just do it himself.

"I'll let you know when it's cleared," he announced, and then he went forward, crouching low in the ditch, his .45 out.

He pressed up alongside the road another fifty yards. He saw someone lying in the road, half sitting up, clutching his side. It was old man Wilson Stepp.

He drew closer, Wilson half turning to look in his direction. He suddenly realized his own field training was definitely rusty. The lake, illuminated by the burning shed and moonlight, was behind him, thus clearly showing his silhouette if anyone was on the other side of the road.

"Hey, John—get down," Wilson gasped.

At that same instant, he saw it—a bright-red spot of light sparkling on his chest.

"Oh shit." The words barely slipped out of him.

"Okay, Matherson, just hold your hands up, and walk up this road real easy like."

"Sorry, John," Wilson gasped. "You stupid ass, shouting out your name like that. They're just behind me."

His response was instinct, lowering his pistol to shoot at the laser sight that he could see glinting from a concealed position upslope from the road.

Less than a second later, the impact of the shot hitting his chest knocked the wind out of him, and he went down on his knees. He heard running, more shots. He started to turn—it looked like Maury was going down just behind him—then a stunning blow to the back of his head and a falling away into darkness.

Dawn.

The sound of an engine, a jolt of pain, a feeling that he was falling, even as he looked up at the canopy of trees overhead. A bounce that made him gasp from the pain, the back of his head, his chest.

He tried to move, but his hands and feet were bound. *What in the hell?*

He tried to sit up. A harsh voice close to his ear, breath stinking. "I'd stay right where you are if I was you. Otherwise, you get another tap to the head."

He was silent for a moment, each jostling bounce triggering a wave of pain. He felt light-headed, disoriented—a concussion, most likely. He half opened one eye, caught a glimpse of a rough-hewn-looking character, bearded, in camo fatigues, cradling a short-barrel M4 with laser sights, sitting in the bed of the truck.

The sun was up, golden light filtering through the forest canopy softened with morning mist. They were on a downhill grade that kept going and going. Something told him that they must be on the far side of the Mount Mitchell range, heading down the long slope of over six thousand feet of altitude to the inhabited valleys on the far side of the mountain. The driver shifted out of gear for a moment; John heard at least one other vehicle, some laughter—and a strange sound then . . . squealing. It sounded like pigs.

Damn it, he thought. *I get tangled up in this for some damn pigs and moonshine. What a reason to get taken by whoever this is.*

He looked up at his captor. "Where am I?"

"You'll find out soon enough."

Silence for a moment, his head throbbing. "Thirsty. Could I have something to drink?"

His captor chuckled, waited a few minutes, looking off as if to convey who exactly was in charge, and then he reached into a pocket, pulled out a bottle, and uncorked it, offering it over.

"Hands tied," John said, and his captor grinned.

"Yup, well, have a touch of this." He held the bottle to John's lips. It was shine, pure shine, but John took a gulp anyhow, coughing and gasping, and a moment later, he vomited it back up, his captor cursing him and then laughing even as he passed out again.

"All right, drag the son of a bitch out."

John came back to consciousness as someone pulled him by his feet toward the tailgate of the truck. He opened his eyes, and there was a moment of barely suppressed panic at the sight of a hunting knife, wondering if he was about to have his throat cut. Someone cut the bonds around his ankles and roughly pulled him upright, ordering him to turn around. His hands were freed, a slice of skin from his wrist going with the rope.

He flashed back to his nightmare experience of POW training as a green second lieutenant during a time when outright physical abuse was an accepted part of the program. Even though all knew they were in Fort Bragg, North Carolina, more than a few cracked under the torment. He limped out of that training with a sprained ankle, one eye swollen shut, and a cracked rib when he had attempted an escape, which all were expected to try. He had run afoul of a Green Beret "guard," whom he had at least had the pleasure of kicking in the groin, which triggered the "guards" into giving him some payback.

Try never to show pain, don't show fear—it had been drilled into him then. He hated to admit it now, but he definitely felt pain, and it was hard not to show fear.

They were in a forest clearing, definitely miles north of Mount Mitchell, its peak and ridgeline clearly visible in the early morning light. Somewhere up in the Burnsville area, he guessed.

Reiver country.

"Bring him over here."

He was shoved hard, nearly falling over, struggling to maintain his footing and some semblance of dignity. They were at a mountain crossroad, of all things a local fire station, engine still within, a burned-out gas station next door and a few run-down houses and single-wide trailers, run-down long before the Day. Whoever called for him was sitting in an overstuffed lounge chair inside the open fire station. Several men, all dressed in camo gear, were gathered around the chair, whispering, glancing back at John.

In spite of his dazed condition, his thoughts flashed to a movie about some dumb-ass canoeists going out for a weekend in the mountains of Georgia, a movie that scared the crap out of every Northern boy. When he moved from New Jersey to attend college at Duke, his Southern friends often teased him with suggestions they go canoeing and see if they could find some locals for him to meet.

A couple of the men inside the fire station definitely looked like extras from the film, especially the one that he assumed had shot him, his few remaining teeth blackened as he gazed sardonically at John. The only thing missing to make the moment terrifyingly complete was a mentally disabled kid playing a banjo. It fit every worst stereotype ever held about folks living in the mountains of southern Appalachia.

"So this is the great John Matherson?"

Things were out of focus, his head aching from the blow that had knocked him out. His damned tooth was throbbing, and another wave of nausea was hitting. This was certainly turning into one hell of a rotten day.

Shoved again from behind, John staggered into the gloom of the fire station, the shadowy figure in the lounge chair chuckling at his obvious discomfort and then ordering someone to fetch a chair for their guest.

Knees trembling, John half collapsed into the chair and leaned forward, gasping for air, each breath a torment thanks to what he assumed must be a cracked rib or two from the bullet impact.

"Get a medic. George might've cracked this poor man's skull."

"Lucky if that was all I cracked," a voice replied. "I popped him square in the chest before tapping him on the back of his head. If it weren't for that fancy Kevlar vest of his, you'd be talking to a corpse now."

"Nice vest, Matherson. You'd be dead now if you didn't have it on," the voice interjected. "Someone help him out of it. We can use it ourselves."

John did not object as the flak vest was pulled off, suppressing a gasp as the one taking it off none too gently pointed out the impact point, bruised black and blue.

"Vest is mine now; I claim it," his captor announced. "I'm the one that shot him, then took him prisoner."

"We settle that later. All captured supplies go into the common store."

"The hell you say!" the man with the blackened teeth exclaimed.

There was a moment of silent confrontation between George and the apparent group leader sitting in the lounge chair. With a curse, George finally tossed the vest aside and walked out.

Relieved of the Kevlar, John sat back in the padded chair, stretching his shoulders, breathing deeply, trying to judge for himself how badly he was hurt. Every breath hurt, but better that than an exit wound the size of his fist with his heart going with it.

"So where is this bastard?"

It was a woman's voice, older. He looked back out the doorway at a gray-haired, slightly bent woman in faded jeans and a flannel shirt carrying an old-style medical bag.

She approached John, took out a flashlight, and shined it into his eyes so that he winced, telling him to follow the light, rough, callused hands fingering his head. It hurt like hell as she did so, the light causing him to lose focus for a moment.

She taped his chest, feeling along his sternum so that he winced when she pressed in hard. Sticking a dirty finger into his mouth and then pulling it out and examining it for a moment, she finally wiped the finger on her flannel shirt.

"Don't see any blood in your spit. You cough any blood up?" she asked.

He said nothing, slowly shaking his head.

"Good. Just a cracked rib, no lung punctured by it. You puke at all?"

"Yes, a bit earlier."

"Concussion, not too bad—that and a cracked rib or two. That's all."

Without further comment, she picked up her medical bag, opened it, pulled out an oversized bottle of aspirin, shook out two, and handed them to John.

"Take these and call me in the morning," was all she said, and she walked out.

"That's one helluva medic." John sighed, and his host laughed.

"Maggie is the best. She pulled two bullets out of me last fall with nothing more than a quick shot of white lightning before digging in."

Focus was coming back, and John looked over at his host. The man, like so many now, had that ageless look—on the surface maybe in his mid-thirties but infinitely older inside. His skin was weather beaten, leathery. He was dressed a bit more neatly than the group of several dozen hanging about the fire station—jeans, a combat blouse with the eagle of the famed 101st Airborne draped around his narrow shoulders, left sleeve empty and pinned up at the shoulder, left eye covered with a patch, and jawline twisted and gnarled like the bark of an old oak.

"Name's Forrest Burnett, once a first sergeant with the 101st." He pointed at the empty sleeve with his right hand. "Lost that in some shit hole of a valley in Afghanistan about ten years back." He smiled, pointing up to the eye patch and twisted scars of his face.

"Actually lost the arm first to an IED. Rest of my squad dead. When the bastards came up to check us, oh good Lord, how I wasted them all, but lost the eye and my good looks before I killed the last of them." He laughed softly. "Not like your war . . . it's Colonel, isn't it?"

"Something like that," John said cautiously.

Burnett looked to those gathered around. "We got us a special guest here," Burnett announced loudly so all around him could hear. "A real live colonel. Oh, I know his record. Book-learning-type colonel. Even in the Pentagon, not like one of us grunts they sent out in that last war. Now a hero in these mountains for how he turned back that pagan Posse group."

"Shit, fifty of us," one of the group interjected, "would have kicked their stinking asses clear back to Greensboro."

There was a laughing chorus of agreements.

The leader shot an angry glance back at the man who spoke up. "Keep your damn mouth shut!" he snarled, and the one he spoke to dropped his head and backed up.

John said nothing, for after all, what could he say? In a way, Burnett was right. He had received many an advantage ever since college and his decision to go into the military with the immediate rank of second lieutenant. From the accent, John knew Burnett to be a local, most likely a volunteer out of patriotic fervor or poverty after 9/11, sent back from Afghanistan twisted up in body and mind.

"Got the Silver Star for that, wasting those bastards, and then years of bullshit afterwards. How was your retirement, Colonel?"

John said nothing. Burnett was taking him into the game of who had it worse, and in that case, John would most certainly lose. John would always be the first to admit that, especially in the years just prior to the Day. Retired colonels did get far more perks. A one-armed sergeant with a twisted face and missing an eye might get a lot of sympathy at least and compassion—especially after the crap that had been heaped on the veterans of Vietnam—but in the long run?

"Look, Sergeant. You want to shoot me or hang me, then just do it and get it over with. So let's cut the crap. It's your call," John snapped back, knowing that Burnett had every right to be bitter, and making an appeal for mercy would fall on deaf ears.

Most fell silent, though a few, led by George standing outside the firehouse, offered to help him with his suggestion of a firing squad.

Burnett gazed at him intently, and finally a smile creased his face. "Damn you, Matherson. At least you got some sand in your craw. George, find him a cot; let him sleep off his headache."

The man who had been his captor sighed, stepped out from the group watching the encounter, and roughly pulled John to his feet.

"Lucky son of a bitch," George announced to all.

"Just see to him," Burnett said, "and cuff his ankle to the bed. Bet he got

ONE YEAR AFTER 87

one of those bullshit escape-and-evasion courses, and now thinks he can pull a Rambo and split on us."

John looked at Burnett.

"I escaped from mine," Burnett asked. "How'd you do?"

"Got the crap kicked out of me," John answered honestly.

"Figured."

"Just one question."

"Sure, Colonel Matherson."

"The rest of my unit with me . . . what happened?"

"Think we killed one, the guy following you."

John took that in, not trying to show any emotion. *Was Maury wearing a Kevlar vest?*

"Friend of yours?" Burnett asked.

"Yeah."

"And if we killed him?"

"You know what I'll do if I get out of this."

Burnett nodded.

"Your Stepp friends started it. Traded us some bad moonshine a month back. Had lead in it. Damn near killed George over there. So we were paying a return visit to burn out their still and pick up a bit of food, and it went bad. Didn't expect you as a prize, though, Matherson."

"The Stepp family?"

"We don't kill civilians unless we got to," Burnett snapped.

John turned to look at George. "If you killed my friend and I get out of this, it's personal for me, and you're a dead man," he said slowly, forcefully.

The punch to the jaw put John out cold for several more hours.

"**You** are one stupid bastard, you know that, Colonel?"

John forced his eyes open. He had actually been awake for at least a half hour or more but had mimicked sleep, trying to gather his thoughts and figure out what to do next. His defiance might have earned him a touch of respect, but the aching jaw from the uppercut was numbing, and he wondered if a couple of teeth had been knocked loose. Unfortunately, the blow hit on the other side of his mouth, so the toothache was still with him.

Opening his eyes wide, he found he could at least focus somewhat. It was Burnett, chair pulled up by the side of John's cot, and he was holding a steaming mug. The scent all but overwhelmed John; it was real coffee.

He sat up, stifling a groan, and took the cup. He wondered if this was now "good cop" time with Burnett offering a treat that no one in Black Mountain had seen in nearly two years. But he accepted it anyhow, half gulping it down, though it was scalding hot, regretting it a few minutes later when the coffee hit his empty stomach.

"Here, eat this; it will settle your guts." Burnett held out a slice of fresh-baked bread slathered with—of all things—real butter. It was slightly sour but still heavenly, which John took and wolfed down, trying not to sigh with delight. *God in heaven,* he thought. *Real coffee, bread, and butter, and we all took it for granted our entire lives.*

"What in the hell am I going to do with you?" Burnett opened without any preamble. "The way I see it, I got three choices. One, we shoot you or hang you as a warning to any who try to mess with us. You really have quite a name around here, and killing you would be, as the natives of the region once said, a real coup. Two, we make you a slave. You know what most of the tribes and white folks did two hundred and fifty years ago when they had a captive they wanted to keep?"

"Cut their Achilles tendons so they couldn't run—and if still a problem, castrate them."

"Yeah, something like that."

"And the third?" John ventured. "Let me go or trade me back."

"Good thinking, but still not certain on any of the three," Burnett replied. "No sense asking you what you think. Pride will prevent you from appealing to the third choice; fear definitely the second one; defiance might make you ask for the first—and at the moment, I think a majority of folks with me would lean towards that. George was the one who put that round into your chest, and believe me, he was shooting to kill you. He'd have finished you if not for that nurse who took care of you. I heard Maggie kicked his gun up and told him to bring you in."

"So why don't you just finish the job publicly? Will win a lot of prestige points with some."

Burnett took back the empty coffee mug and plate, setting them on the floor. "Response that I kind of assumed from you, Colonel. You ain't the whining type. Whether that is really you or just a game you're playing, it does work to a certain extent. Though the big drawback to shooting or hanging you is it will set off the biggest feud these mountains have seen since the Civil War. Your people won't rest until a lot of dead have been piled up. So, Colonel, that's an argument in your favor."

"Can we cut the *colonel*-and-*sergeant* routine?" John said, and at that moment, he thought of his lost friend Washington, the security guard at the college who had taken a frightened group of kids and whipped them into a potent military force able to defeat the Posse, dying in that fight. Washington had never dropped the *colonel*-and-*sergeant* routine, and it had always rankled John and would for the rest of his life. It haunted him, because between himself and his lost friend, he felt Washington was indeed the better man.

"All right, Mr. Matherson—or is it *Doc* or *Professor*?"

"Cut the shit. Just John. Hell, I walked into your ambush. So what do I call you?"

Burnett leaned back and laughed. "There's a crazy coot up over the mountains in Tennessee who insists he be called Your Holiness. Down in Haywood County, an ex-preacher is saying he is Christ reborn in this time of troubles. I bet there are a thousand nutcases with a thousand names."

He smiled, and John could not help but smile as well in reply. The coffee and food had settled down in his stomach, and he was beginning to feel somewhat better. He also sensed that if Burnett was talking like this, the prospect of an unpleasant ending had diminished.

"I actually rather liked the stories I read about that Mongol guy, Genghis, after seeing a movie about him and a weird high school teacher who went over to where the guy lived and kept talking about riding with the Mongols and drinking fermented horse milk. But if I named myself after him, people would think I was into *Star Trek* movies. Thought as well about using Napoleon, but everyone who ever called themselves Napoleon is definitely a nut job."

"So Forrest then?" John asked.

"Yeah, for the moment, that's okay with me, but out there, it's *sir*, if you get my drift."

"Okay."

"I assume you want the third alternative—that I let you go or trade you for something."

"Who wouldn't? I want to live the same as you."

"So then, damn you, why do you and others like you keep hunting us?" There was a flash of anger from Burnett as he spoke.

John looked at him quizzically, shook his head, and then regretted the action since the dizziness set back in. "What the hell do you mean?"

"You sent a punitive expedition over Mount Mitchell last fall before the snow set in—killed three of my people in an ambush."

"Now wait a minute," John replied, his temper rising up. "You and yours have been harassing us all along the north slope of the mountains ever since the shit hit the fan two years ago. Folks killed, food stolen. What am I supposed to do? Just sit back and let you rob us?"

"Half the time, it was most likely someone else doing that. We picked off a couple of dozen of that Posse gang that fled up this way after you kicked their asses. Whoever is killing each other, do you know how barren it is up here? Over on your side of the mountains, you got good crop and grazing lands. After everything went to hell, you had barriers up on the road, and unless someone was a damn doctor or you took a liking to them—like that hot nurse I heard you married—it was move along and get the hell out of town."

He had nothing to say for a moment to that. It was mostly true. Makala, though, an "outsider," had at least been in the town when the EMP hit. But the way Burnett spoke of her as "that hot nurse" ticked him off.

"Insult me, but don't insult my wife," John snapped. "She was in the town that day it happened—a nurse from a cardiology unit—and she saved a helluva lot of lives afterwards, me being one of them. So back off on that, Forrest."

Burnett nodded. "Okay. My apologies."

That was something about the culture of this region that John always admired coming from New Jersey. Contrary to stereotypes, there were aspects of Southern culture that nearly all observed. One was respect for women, something that too many called sexist but John saw as just basic, decent politeness. Burnett had crossed a line regarding another man's wife and had immediately pulled back. It raised his opinion of him a few notches.

"It was survival, Forrest. If we took in everyone who came up through the pass after everything went to hell—and yes, over the mountains too—we'd have been feeding ten times as many, and everyone would have died within two months. I got forced into the position. I didn't like it, but I had to make decisions that were tough, and if I didn't, no one would have lived. And I'll bet you would have done the same and most likely did and are still making those decisions."

"Yeah, well, the same with us here."

"Didn't give you the right to raid us as you do."

"That granny woman who looked at your head used to be a nurse at Memorial Mission in Asheville," Burnett replied as if shifting the subject to safer ground. "I got people up here with me, the same as you, before everything went sour. Mostly working folks born in these mountains, un-like the rich bastards that started to flood into Asheville, too many of them trust-fund brats playing at being hippies and jacking the price of a few acres of land through the roof because they liked the view. Then they turn around and wanted taxes raised for their pet projects and pushed us out. Oh, we were good enough to do the hard labor when things were good, but the day after the power died, it was get the hell out and stay out.

"George, who damn near killed you . . . his family has lived up here for near on to two hundred years. A damn good carpenter. Most of his family starved to death by the first winter, then one of your trigger-happy shooters killed his older brother in that ambush last fall. You're lucky he didn't blow your head off."

"Maybe he wants to castrate me in front of everybody," John retorted angrily.

"Don't joke. You ain't far from the truth. He sees it as payback."

John fell silent.

"Point is, we are trying to survive, same as you. We might look like a ragged lot, no fancy civility like you got down in Black Mountain and that college where I heard you were a professor before all of this. Difference was that a lot of those up here were of tougher stuff and refused to conveniently die off. Up here, folks still had a handle on a lot of the old ways. Oh, we were quaint for the tourists from Atlanta driving through along the parkway or coming up here once a year to buy Christmas trees. That was actually our biggest cash crop back then, other than weed. Ever think how many folks are buying Christmas trees now or making a living on farmland that was played out generations ago?"

John did not reply, sensing the wisdom to not interrupt.

"So how do we survive, when every town like yours sealed itself off? Too many folks for too little good land, and within several months, the forests hunted out so completely I ain't had a taste of venison in over a year, and someone bringing in a greasy possum was a reason to celebrate."

John did not say anything or reveal that after the cup of coffee and the long hours of being either tied or handcuffed to the bed, he was about to explode.

Burnett, sensing his distress, pulled out a key, unclipped the cuff around John's ankle, and motioned to the door, which John gratefully headed for.

"John."

He looked back.

Burnett was casually holding his .45. "Nice gun, John. Hate to shoot you with it if you try to run. It would spoil George's day, me killing you rather than him getting to."

Even if the temptation to run had been there, as John staggered off to the edge of the tree line, he knew it would be hopeless. Whoever these reivers were, there were certainly a hell of a lot of them around, and they knew the ground far better than he could ever hope to figure out. The clearing around the mountain crossroads was an encampment, a hodgepodge of old RVs and pickup trucks with canopies rigged over the rear bed. Some fires were burning—over one of them, a pig was speared and being turned over the fire, most likely one of Stepps' spring sucklings. There were nearly as many children as adults, a ragged lot most of them, just like the children in Black Mountain the winter after the Day, hanging about whenever someone had managed to snag some game. The scent of it wafted out into the street.

Finished with his task, John slowly walked back to the hut they had put him in. Burnett nodded, uncocking the semiautomatic and holstering it, the holster John had been wearing just hours before.

"You ever shoot a man before everything went bad?" Burnett asked as John sat back down.

"I never fired a shot at someone with intent to kill until I had to execute that kid who stole drugs from the nursing home. I think it best not to ask what you went through in Afghanistan."

"Something like that," Burnett replied calmly.

"Look, let's cut the crap with this working-class sergeant from the mountains versus a colonel who you think had a silver spoon up his butt. I didn't grow up in the mountains, but I sure as hell grew up in a tough place in New Jersey, so I know the game. If you hate my guts for that, so be it. All of us are in a world of shit now, so what is it you want from me if you decide not to kill me? Or is this just some head game for your entertainment before you string me up or blow my brains out?"

Burnett nodded and stood up after several minutes of silence.

"My wife, well, she left me the year after I came back from the war minus an arm, an eye, and half my mind. Had a son—heard they're dead, along with the bastard she hooked up with . . . killed or executed." He hesitated. "They were living down in Charlotte. I heard long afterwards they fell in with that Posse."

John lowered his head. "Merciful God," he whispered.

"Maybe you or one of yours was the ones that shot her. I don't give a good damn about the bum she hooked up with—I hope someone did kill him, slowly. But still, she was once my wife, and my boy was with her. You shoot any kids with that group, John Matherson? He'd have been twelve."

John looked up at Burnett. "No, we didn't shoot any kids that day. If any were still traveling with them, they were left behind before the fight and scattered afterwards. If she was with them, Forrest, you know what I had to do. They were literally cannibals, and that was beyond the pale of any civilized society, or at least the civilization we're trying to rebuild."

Burnett was silent just looking down at him as if weighing the life-or-death decision.

"What would you have done?" John finally snapped back. "If you had taken any prisoners from that group of cannibal barbarians, what would you have done?"

"Are you pleading with me, Matherson?"

"Hell no," he snapped back. "Whatever you're going to do will most likely happen no matter what I say."

"You shoot my people for snatching a few pigs."

"And again, in this mad world, you're doing the same—killing mine. Maybe one of my closest friends is dead because of what happened a few hours ago. And if he is, you know all bets with me are off if you let me go."

Burnett started for the door and then looked back. "A helluva shitty world we've been handed, Matherson. Makes Afghanistan look like paradise. It's what America is sinking into now, Colonel. Think about it. America, the new Afghanistan."

"Was that what we fought for over there?" John asked. "Is that what we're fighting to prevent now?"

Burnett smiled, and for a moment, there was that frightful two-thousand-yard stare. "You'll have my decision regarding what to do with you at sundown," he snapped as he slammed the door shut and locked it.

CHAPTER FIVE

"There's the flag of truce," Burnett whispered. "Now remember, the slightest wrong move, and everyone is wasted."

Things were still slightly blurry, the lingering aftereffects of the concussion.

"My people honor their word. I'm more worried about yours."

They were sitting in an old Polaris four-wheel-drive off-road vehicle that had been upgraded with an attempt at some armor across the front to protect the engine. John and Burnett sat in the backseat, a couple of the reivers—heavily armed men—up front. A half dozen other vehicles of Burnett's had stopped a quarter mile back above the north shore of the reservoir and with professional skill spread out on foot to either flank. John did worry now that maybe the entire thing was a setup, an ambush to wipe out some of his best before putting a bullet in his head.

It was good at least to be back out in the open after three days locked up in the fetid cabin. He got twice-daily visits from Maggie, who advised him to just stay in bed and let the concussion heal, and the food had actually been rather good—indulgent, even, given that it was pork stolen from the Stepp family, and rather than saving or rationing it, the group had been gorging themselves on it as if there were no concern for tomorrow. Only problem was chewing it, between the sore jaw on one side from getting slugged and the bad tooth on the other side. Maggie actually took a look at it and offered to "pop that little ole thing out," but he adamantly refused.

Burnett had dropped in a few times, conversations short and a bit taunting that the group was still debating his fate—implying that execution was still an option—but John knew that was just a sham to see how he'd react. Why waste precious food on a doomed prisoner?

Then this morning, they had blindfolded him and led him out of the hut he was quartered in. He could hear the crowd gathered around to watch some jeering, and for a moment, his heart sank. Without comment from Burnett, he was shoved into the backseat of the Polaris, and the expedition left the encampment.

He said nothing, but there was definitely a wave of relief. Execution would have been a public affair. They were most certainly not just driving off into the woods for a private shooting. He could sense they were going back up over the Mount Mitchell range. It was a tedious, hammering, head-splitting climb of a couple of hours and then an equally jolting drive back down what must have been a fire road through the forest until coming to a stop, and Burnett unfastened the blindfold.

"So you're letting me go."

"Trading you." Burnett chuckled. "Your weight in salt. We got plenty of ammo and food, but salt is getting hard to find."

John took that in, not really feeling humiliated. A long time ago, trading prisoners for salt had been a practiced norm. Weight in silver also? For Burnett's group, salt was more valuable than silver. Salt meant preserved food. Silver was to those living in a barter world just metal—though Doc Wagner was experimenting with grinding pure silver into a formula for antibiotics—but salt could preserve hundreds of pounds of meat and was a dire necessity of diet, especially in the heat of summer.

There was a long stretch of straightaway ahead paralleling the left shore of the reservoir—the same place where he had been ambushed—and in the distance, John could see his people deploying out.

"The negotiated agreement was twenty on each side as escorts, salt to be left in the road. But I suspect your people got a lot more hidden to the flanks."

"Same with yours," John said, looking back at the assortment of vehicles. He could sense the tension. Though confined in the squalid cabin during his stay with the reivers, he could easily hear the conversations and arguments, George indeed arguing it would bring prestige to them if they strung John up and then sent his body back as a warning.

"So why didn't you kill me?" John asked.

"I have a hankering for salt," Burnett replied, "and this is the easiest way to get it."

"It's more than that," John replied, and he actually forced a smile. "The real reason."

Burnett sat back, asking the two escorts who were sitting up front—one of them George—to get out and go up the other road and signal when everything was clear. They were not happy with the assignment but followed his orders.

"Let's talk," Burnett announced, and then he did something remarkable for John. He pulled out a pack of cigarettes—merciful God, they were actually Dunhills—opened the pack, lit one up, and offered it to John, who was nearly trembling at the sight of them. He finally shook his head.

"I heard you were quite the smoker," Burnett said.

"You seem to know a lot about me."

"I had a few people in with you for a while."

John gazed longingly at the cigarettes but then remembered the day he quit. *Once an addict, always an addict,* he thought. *And if I have one now, I'll be begging for more, giving this man the advantage.*

He shook his head in refusal, though he did breathe in deeply as the smoke curled around him.

Burnett shrugged at his refusal and stuffed the pack into his battle jacket tunic.

"This is about more than me being traded for salt," John said.

"Yup. Ball is in your court, Matherson. So start talking. I can still change my mind and blow your brains out here in front of those people of yours, toss your body out, and boogie back over the mountain."

"You want a war? Because that will trigger it."

"My camp is mobile; you saw that. I can be twenty miles away before nightfall. You and yours are stuck in one place, and we'll just keep pecking away at you. I have all the advantages of mobile offense over static defense, and you know it. And you don't have the manpower to send an army up over my mountains; we know far better than your people. We'll run you ragged, wear you down, and just keep picking you off."

"So you are telling me you hold all the cards."

Burnett smiled. "Most of them. If you throw in with this new government in Asheville, you just might have more, but word is half your strength is getting drafted off, making you even more vulnerable."

"So back to the original question," John said. "Why the trade? It's about more than salt."

Burnett shrugged. "You tell me."

"You want a truce?" John replied.

"A trade in our favor, I'd prefer to call it."

"I don't give away favors without a quid pro quo," John snapped. "And besides, I said it the first day and will say it again now just so everything is perfectly clear. If I find out my friend Maury was killed by your people—especially that psycho of yours, George—it becomes personal for me, mayor of the town or not. You'll have a personal vendetta on your hands."

"Ballsy talk for someone I could still shoot now," Burnett said, and he actually smiled and then nodded. "Your friend is okay. My negotiator checked on that."

"Wish you had told me earlier, spared me some anxiety."

"Psychological advantage, Matherson."

"Yeah, thanks." There was an inward sigh of relief with that news.

"You are beginning to sound like a professor, John, with this quid pro quo stuff, but I know what you mean . . . what's in it for you and yours?"

"Exactly."

"Other than your life, of course."

John nodded.

"I want a secure southern flank," Burnett said, nodding back to the high range of Mount Mitchell.

"You already have that. My folks don't venture over it. The area is pretty well hunted over for food, anyhow. So you have no worries, if that is your big concern."

"Not from you, Matherson. From the feds setting up in Asheville. We kept clear of them when the army was there, though they did send a few expeditions up Interstate 26 to Johnson City and back. That was a joke; we could have shredded them but didn't want to pick the fight, and they really didn't want to go off chasing us. But this new group moving in . . . there's been news reports, even on the shortwave, of this million-man army they're forming up. I figure those poor bastards will be off to Texas and California, but they are also talking about taking out groups like us. We get jumped out in the open by one Apache helicopter while on the move and a couple hundred of my people get killed."

"Apache helicopter?"

Burnett took a deep drag on his cigarette, tossed the still smoldering butt, fished another one out, and lit it with an old Zippo bearing the insignia of the 101st Airborne—a deft act for a man with one arm.

"Yeah, you've been out of the loop for a few days. My spotters saw four choppers—two of them Apaches—come in and land at the old shopping mall parking lot. They've got a defensive perimeter up there—a regular base, it seems. Did you know about this?"

"News for me too," John replied, honestly surprised by the information. "When I met with Fredericks, he said they were getting some assets in. I had no idea it'd be Apaches."

"Still in desert paint," Burnett said. "They must have shipped them back from the Middle East. Anyhow, I got enough worries without dealing with that, as well. You put in a word to just leave us alone, and I'll count that as part of this quid pro quo thing of yours."

John shook his head. "I doubt if I'll have any influence, but I'll see what I can find out. But I'm making no promises, Forrest."

"You weren't in Afghanistan. I was, and I'm paranoid about someone having air superiority over us, since it was the only real advantage we had against the Taliban. I let you go, you negotiate on my behalf with that person down in Asheville to leave us alone, and other than some pig and chicken raiding, we'll leave them alone." He paused. "And you too."

"I won't be your proxy," John said. "You have one helluva murderous record."

"Pot calling the kettle black, Matherson. How many did you kill in the Old Fort pass? How many did you personally execute, starting with those two drug-addled punks?"

"Different situation," John said softly.

"They're still dead, and my ex and my son may be two of them. And over the last three days, I thought more than once I should just even the score and be done with you."

John took a deep breath. "So again, why didn't you?"

"Because I'm stuck in the same boat you are at times. You officer types maybe read Machiavelli; you'd be surprised how many of us waiting it out in barracks read some of the same shit. Machiavelli said a prince had to transcend traditional morality for the greater good of those he led."

John looked at him, unable to contain his surprise.

Burnett cleared his throat. "I might be a good ole boy, John, but that doesn't mean I don't read. You know the old line about soldiering being long months of boredom interspersed with occasional moments of pure terror. A lot of time to read. I even thought about making the army a career until this happened." He pointed to his empty sleeve and torn face.

John felt genuine admiration for the man. He was a consummate actor in many ways, but then again, most good leaders were, knowing how to play their audience. Now, with just the two of them, he realized Burnett could easily slip into an academic discussion on the literature of war.

There was an awkward moment of silence between the two, finally broken with Burnett leaning over the side of the Polaris to spit and mutter an obscenity. "Look, John, for now, you agree not to come over the mountain, and we'll try to do the same."

"Try?"

"You saw my group. I can only order them so far."

"You know if any of my people get hurt, we'll come after those who did it."

"To the top of the mountains, no farther."

"That's a bit one sided, Forrest."

"That or nothing. I'll at least try to restrain things a bit along this front. Over toward Tennessee, there's a lot of easier pickings there anyhow for right now—better crop and grazing lands than what you got."

John hesitated. He knew he wasn't going to get any further than where they were. Of course, he most certainly did not want to get shot now, so close to freedom, an act that would trigger a deadly firefight between the two sides, but he did not want to just sell out.

"I'll agree to this. You try to hold your people back, and I'd suggest that you break camp and move north. Do so, and you got no concerns from us."

"Fully intended to anyhow once back in case you decided to try to screw me over and launch an attack tonight, but I warn you, none of you will get over the mountain. We know it better than you do and will be watching."

John nodded. "Understood, but I'd suggest moving anyhow for now. Gives me a bit of leverage. You can look down our throats at any time from up at Craggy Pass."

That fact had always made John uncomfortable. From the top of Craggy Pass along the old Blue Ridge Parkway, anyone posted there with a good spotter scope could look straight down into Black Mountain.

Within a few more days, he was going to have airpower, as well, a classified project that apparently Burnett did not know about. The wreckage of the old L-3, piloted by his friend Don Barber, who had been killed in the fight for the pass, had been ever so slowly reconstructed. There were enough pilots still alive in the community itching to get back up, and with the plane, he could again monitor things out in every direction for seventy-five miles or more, including the reivers' territory and their perch atop Craggy Pass.

"I can recall from drives up along Craggy years ago that you can see the town hall."

"One of the reasons we like having a watch station up there," Burnett replied. "And if you are asking me to give it up, the answer is no."

He knew Burnett was not going to concede giving up a vantage point like Craggy and other points along the old Blue Ridge Parkway that allowed him to watch any movement in a fifty-mile radius. Perhaps it could be turned to an advantage and help avoid future problems.

"Let's do this," John offered. "If I feel there's a problem between us, I'll run up a signal on the big flagpole at the old car dealership. Three American flags, one atop the other."

"And?"

"I'm trying to set something up between us to avoid future hassles. I'll use that as a signal that I want to talk. You fly some sort of flag in return up at Craggy when ready to meet, and we meet here. If you feel we need to talk, send a messenger down to my watch post at the end of the reservoir here.

We both work to keep our people back from each other. You keep that nut-case George away, and I'll make sure the Stepps aren't running amok."

"Why talk?"

"We're doing it now, aren't we? It's better than continuing to kill each other."

"Yeah, okay."

"Forrest, differences are going to come up. We're trying to step back from what eventually was going to be a full-scale blowout. We both have people who'd want that. So we set up a means of talking at times to smooth things over. Better than continuing to kill each other, isn't it?"

Burnett took it in and finally nodded.

"Okay, John, deal. Now get the hell out of here. I think your people and mine are getting itchy, and I don't want any mistakes."

John got out of the Polaris feeling a bit light-headed, but then he steadied himself.

"I wouldn't mind getting my vest and .45 back. The gun belonged to my dad, who carried it in Nam."

"Kiss my ass," Burnett replied with a wry smile. "Spoils of war."

John shrugged and started to turn.

"Matherson."

He looked back, and Burnett was extending his hand. At first, John thought he wanted to shake, and he reached out. Burnett put a cigarette into his hand and laughed.

"You'll trade big time for these if I get you hooked again. I got cartons of 'em." Laughing, he called for the driver to get back in and start to back up.

"You are one lucky son of a bitch, Matherson." It wasn't Burnett; it was George casually pointing a rifle in his direction. "I should have put my second round right into your face."

John knew better than to reply. He just started the long walk of several hundred yards along the lakeshore, and as he drew closer to his own side, there was an immense sigh of relief. He could see Maury in the passenger seat of the lead Jeep, left arm in a sling. There was no reason now for a vendetta. Burnett must have known his friend was alive all along.

He slowed and started to turn to look back and actually offer a salute, a symbolic gesture in front of both sides that issues above and beyond his mere release in exchange for some bags of salt had just transpired.

It was a sudden move that saved his life. At the same instant, he felt the frightful crack of a bullet snapping past his face just a few inches away. He dived for the gravel pavement.

More shots.

Burnett was standing in the back of his vehicle, .45 drawn, and for a split second, John thought the man had betrayed him, after all.

Then he saw the pistol recoil again, but it was aimed downward at George, sprawled out on the pavement, George's body twitching as Burnett put a full clip into the man.

John sprang to his feet, waving to those who were waiting for him. "Don't shoot! Don't shoot! I'm all right!"

For a terrifying few seconds, he thought the situation was about to spin out of control. Someone from his side actually did empty out half a dozen rounds, causing Burnett to duck, a sickening thought that the man was hit and a full-scale war had just started. Burnett, though, was suddenly back on his feet, facing backward, shouting the same as John did for his side to hold fire.

Before anything more erupted, John forced himself to jog down the road, waving his arms, shouting for his people to hold their fire. He caught a glimpse of movement in the woods to either flank, his own reaction team. *Back in my territory,* he thought. It was strange, this realization, as if he were a medieval baron captured by a rival, negotiated over with an uneasy peace coming out of the encounter.

He reached the Jeep, head swimming, gasping for breath. Ed was driving the Jeep. Maury was in the backseat, his left arm in a sling but with the M1 carbine raised in his right hand.

"Get the hell out of here!" John shouted as Ed pulled him in, threw the Jeep into reverse, and floored it back down the road until they were finally around the bend.

A score of vehicles were parked up along the road, concealed from view. His troops, actually a hundred or more, were carefully filtering back and beginning to mount up. He stepped out, wanting to shake their hands, but then arms were around him. It was Makala and Elizabeth, both of them sobbing with relief.

"I'm okay, just a little banged up," he said, wincing as the two women held him tightly, not yet aware of his cracked rib.

"We thought you were dead until yesterday when that negotiation team appeared!" Makala cried. "Even now, we feared it was a trap to lure us in."

"I think we can still flank the bastard," Ed said, holding up one of the two precious mobile shortwaves owned by the town. "I got our second company up above the quarry ready to swing in behind them."

"And knowing those people, they're waiting for just that. No, what happened back there just now was a mistake, and their leader handled it. Now let's just get the hell out of here and go home."

He looked down at his hand. The cigarette was still intact, and he smiled, hesitated, thinking of his lost daughter and the promise he made to her to quit smoking. He crumbled it up and tossed it to the ground.

He stood up, looking around and watching as the reaction teams came back in. Thankfully, no more shots echoed. He got back out of the Jeep, making it a point to go up to as many as possible and thank them, many of his students—some in tears—coming up to salute him and more than a few flinging their arms around him, so grateful that he was alive, after all.

He spotted Grace, went up to her, and actually started to point a finger at her to chew her out for her disobedience in following him. He saw the tears of joy and loving concern in her eyes and relented.

"So glad you're alive, sir," she gasped, and then she turned around to shout for her team to mount up as ordered.

He waited until the last of his students, his troops, were safely into the vehicles and heading back to town before getting back in the Jeep.

"What the hell happened, John?" Maury asked. "I saw you go down, thought you were dead, and then they dropped me. By the time we got up to where you were, you were gone."

"Anyone else hurt?"

"Wilson Stepp shot in the leg, but you must have seen him lying there. He said they were minding their own business and got ambushed."

"You believe that?" John asked.

Maury shook his head. "But we do have a problem. Pat Stepp is dead. We found him in the morning, or what was left of him, inside that shack."

"Damn all this," John said. He thought he had an agreement, but it was one the Stepps would never observe. Feuds that lasted for generations, such as memories of the Shelton Laurel Massacre over in Madison County during the Civil War, still caused tensions between the descendants of those on opposing sides 150 years later. Truce or not with one of the border reiver gangs, the Stepps would continue to wage their own war, and nothing he could say would stop it.

He sighed. "I got a bit of a concussion and a cracked rib. How about we go home? I'll fill everyone in on what happened. It actually turns out the whole affair could be to our advantage, though we'll have to figure out how to deal with the fact that old Pat got killed."

"Not tomorrow morning," Ed said.

"Why?"

"Yesterday afternoon, Fredericks has ordered 'select leaders of the community,' as he put it, to come to Asheville."

"Did he know I was captured?"

"Of course. It was news across the entire valley."

John took it in. It was getting hard to think. "I'm going home for now," he replied, and he looked at Makala, who was gazing intently at him and pressed in close to his right side in the backseat of the Jeep, Elizabeth on his left.

"Damn right. A week of rest and bed for a concussion, at the least." It wasn't a suggestion; it was an order.

"And this meeting?"

"The hell with him," she said. "He figured you were dead, John, and was summoning the rest of us for an audience. Don't respond at all, and let's see what he does in reply."

John looked at her and smiled. "You ever read Machiavelli?" he asked.

CHAPTER SIX

The day promised to be a hot one even in the cove of Montreat. He had slept peacefully through the night and now rested on the sofa bed out on the sunporch. Someone had actually stopped by with two freshly laid eggs for John, and Makala had fried them up for breakfast. There was no coffee, of course, to help kick-start him awake, and he had to chew even the eggs carefully because of his tooth. Makala had vetoed having it pulled while he recovered from the concussion.

Sunlight streamed in through the south-facing windows, the world outside the open windows quiet, peaceful, the silence disturbed by the sharp ringing of the phone. Makala answered, spoke briefly, and hung up.

"You were masterful." He pitched his voice higher in a vain attempt to sound like his wife. "'I'm so sorry, Mr. Fredericks. Yes, thank you, John is fine, but he's suffered a severe concussion. He's confined to bed rest for at least the next three days and not able to travel.'"

She smiled.

"Well, it's the truth. I'd prefer a week, and that granny nurse you told me about was right; you got a cracked rib next to your sternum." Her features became serious. "Another hard blow there, the rib breaks free and gets driven right into your heart or lungs, so no driving around in that damn Jeep until it starts to knit."

"Yes, ma'am."

She kissed him on the forehead.

"Anyhow, what did Fredericks say?"

"He tried to force the issue of you going to Asheville, but he backed off."
She shrugged. "You heard the rest. He's coming here in an hour."

"There must be some fire under his butt from further up if he's doing that.
I guess I should get dressed and go to the office."

"You idiot, that defeats what I just said about you not being able to move.
I'll prop you up and get a clean shirt on you and a shave. You really do look
like hell."

"At least I had real coffee while being held."

"What?"

"I'd darn near kill for a cup now."

"Cruel even to mention it," she replied, and there was a real touch of
longing in her voice.

Propped up on the sofa in the sunroom, John caught a glimpse of Fredericks's Humvee pulling into his driveway. The driver looked like the character he had tangled with in front of the courthouse earlier in the week.

In spite of the heat, Dale still wore the blue blazer as if it were a uniform
but, perhaps in a gesture of informality, had foregone the necktie, which, ever
since the Day, was something rarely seen. Makala was out to meet him with
a courteous smile, directing him around the back walkway to the sunroom.
Elizabeth, with Ben in her arms, had agreed with the suggestion that she
take the toddler for a walk to avoid any maudlin encounter and for Jen to just
stand clear, even though the woman was eager to "give that bastard a piece of
my mind"—said, of course, with proper Southern ladylike charm.

John made a slight gesture to get up, but Dale, smiling, extended a hand.

"Don't bother; you're the one that's wounded. Just relax, John."

Makala, role-playing a proper hostess, returned a few minutes later with
a tray and two cups of fresh mint tea, and then she left the room, closing the
door behind her.

"How you doing, John? When I heard what happened, I was preparing
to send an operation up over the mountain to see if we could pull you out."

That would have been one helluva mess, John thought without replying at first, sipping the soothing brew. Not coffee, with which Burnett had spoiled him for several days, but still good.

"So what happened?" Dale asked, leaning forward attentively. Then he hesitated. "If you feel okay to talk. Your wife said you were pretty banged up."

"Not too bad, actually. They didn't kill me on the spot, and once the trade for salt was arranged, I knew I'd get out of it alive."

He didn't mention that he had also been shot and if not for the Kevlar vest, he most certainly would have been dead.

"Trading you for salt. Damn barbaric. Perhaps we should talk about working together on this. It's about time these—what do you call them? Reivers? I just call them damn bandits—got taken out."

John sipped at his tea and nodded. Perhaps it was the way Makala had first reacted to Dale, but his instinct was to just sit back and play the concussed and very fatigued ex-prisoner for a while.

"Do you have the personnel to launch that kind of operation?" John finally asked. "Once off Interstate 26, you get into some pretty wild country now. There are reiver groups holed up in every county from Tennessee clear on up to Virginia and most likely beyond."

Dale smiled. "More assets are coming in every day. Bluemont is really pulling out all the stops to bring places like this back in line. From what I've learned about you, John, you're a man worth saving."

"Appreciate that, Dale. But it didn't prove necessary, after all."

There was a long pause, Dale absently stirring his untouched tea with a spoon and then looking back at John. "I think I got some good news for you regarding that draft call."

With that, John did sit up slightly.

"I kicked your concerns straight up the ladder to Bluemont. We have a good radio hookup now. Even got through to the new secretary of National Unification."

"The what?"

"Secretary of National Unification."

"Never heard of it till just now."

"Well, word does travel a bit slow yet. The president decided that the task of reestablishing functioning government in the lower forty-eight states required a separate branch of government."

"What about the Department of Defense? Its mission since the day the Constitution went into effect was to protect and defend this nation."

"But that does get a bit dicey when it is matters of internal security, John. As a military man, you know that. We're fighting a situation here on two fronts. Foreign incursions under the guise of humanitarian aid, but we all know they came here maybe to help at the start but are now here to stay. That is obviously a task for our traditional military. The lawlessness inside our country, though, that used to be the job of the various states themselves. It was decided we needed a new kind of national force to address that while Department of Defense handled the border situations."

"So who is this secretary of National Unification?"

"Secretary Jensen. Used to be a senator from the Midwest. Good, solid man—I know him personally. He's the one who pushed for this new national mobilization."

"I see. And the men and women mobilized, will they be sworn into our army or into some new force?"

"Standard oath to defend the Constitution and acknowledge the president as commander in chief, but they will answer in chain of command through Jensen to the president," he replied casually. "We're trying to work at the local levels to find out who did service in the traditional military and call them back in to train and lead these new troops. It is one of the reasons I felt it essential to see you as soon as possible, and thank God you are alive."

"Why?" John asked cautiously.

"I spoke personally to Jensen about you. What you accomplished. John, though you're over fifty, we feel your country needs you. You've done your job here in Black Mountain; in fact, it could serve as a model for a thousand other towns that all but collapsed. They want to promote you to the rank of major general—in fact, even arrange transport by air up to Bluemont and put you to work up there."

"My God," John whispered. *Major general?* He had turned down a one-star promotion because of Mary and cancer, moving here so many years ago. The path in life not taken, which he never for a moment regretted. But major general?

"John, you accomplished a miracle here, and everyone knows it. Think of what you could do for your country working at the federal level at Blue-mont, helping to pull things back together."

"But what about here?" John asked.

"I have a second piece of news for you, General Matherson," Dale said, smiling broadly, interrupting John's musings.

"Don't call me that yet," John replied, his tone a bit icy. "A soldier is not addressed by a rank until it becomes formal, sir."

Dale fumbled a bit and muttered an apology.

"So what's the news?" John asked, trying to sound relaxed again.

"I got deferments from the draft for most of your people from this town, so you don't have to worry about security here."

"What?"

"Deferments for the draft from your community. It took some talking, but Secretary Jensen relented—said we can cut the number by half with you coming aboard. I explained that with your leaving, additional personnel needed to be left behind for security purposes." He paused. "At least for now."

"For now? What do you mean?"

"I daresay by the time there would be any additional call-ups, you and the team up in Bluemont will have set things straight. But anyhow, the draft allotment for Black Mountain, Montreat, and Swannanoa has been cut from 113 to 56. We'll need to discuss who you have here who are vets with combat experience. If they are not on the draft list but volunteer, they'll most likely step in as NCOs and officers. That will cut the number drafted, as well. We got a promise as well that the unit from here will most likely go with you to Bluemont to help provide security there. Light duty and not some of the tougher assignments like the rebellions in Pittsburgh, Cleveland, and Chicago."

"Who will pick the fifty-six?" John asked.

"You, of course," Dale replied, smiling broadly. "You know the community, the hardship cases, the ones that can be called up without too much stress on their families."

"So I become the judge, the head of the draft board, is that it?"

"I think you are the best man qualified. I read that was how it was done back during the Second World War and Vietnam. Local draft boards. If you feel strongly about particular cases, you can assign someone else to go.

When we drew up the draft list, we had to rely on a list of those who signed up for ration cards when the army was here last year. I worried that the list was incomplete and believe you can work it out in a fair manner."

So that is how they got the names, John thought. There had been some limited allotments of rations, MREs from the army battalion based in Asheville, but those who took them had to fill out ration cards.

"John, I know you are a man of integrity and fair play. I assume you'll pick your daughter for the draft as an example for the rest of the community. Do so and she can then serve as your adjutant up in Bluemont. I heard how you trained the unit here and the way they fought in the action against the Posse and provided security for the community ever since. I think with experienced young men and women like that, the basic training can be skipped, and they just go into a unit that would serve directly under you."

"It sounds good, Dale, and I appreciate your effort on my behalf. Please don't think I'm not grateful, but honestly, at the moment, I feel like a size-ten head stuffed into a size-five hat. I need a little time to think this over."

"Sure, John, sure. Sleep on it. Why don't you and your lovely wife come up my way for dinner when you're feeling better, and we can talk about it more then?"

John nodded, not replying.

Dale stood up as if to leave, saying he'd show himself out. He reached for the back door and then stopped. "Say. I heard some of your old students got a new electrical generator system running and are looking at starting to wire up the town. Is that right?"

"How did you hear that?"

"Word of such wonders travels fast. Mind if I go up to take a look at what they're doing? If those kids are all that some are reporting, I got far bigger projects waiting for them in Asheville."

"I'm sure they'll be glad to show you around their workshop and power plant."

"Thanks, John. Now get some rest."

As the screen door slammed shut, the Humvee outside roared to life.

There was a gentle tapping on the door. It cracked open, and Makala peeked in.

"Enter?" she asked with a smile, and he nodded. "You look exhausted,

John. We'll talk about whatever happened later, but for now, dear patient, you need to get some sleep."

She slipped out of the darkened room, but sleep would not come. There was far too much to think about now.

CHAPTER SEVEN

"So that's the offer," John said to the hundreds gathered in the town square, finishing up a recounting of his discussion with Dale two days earlier.

The members of the town council had come to sit down with John the day after Fredericks's visit. No one was really sure how to read their new district administrator. He seemed friendly enough, but all were bothered by the fact that, after finishing his visit with John, he had spent a fair part of the day "poking around," as Ed put it. He had indeed been up to the dam to talk to Paul and Becka, then to the campus to watch as the students still living there were running through a practice drill of clearing a house, using the Mac-Gregor dorm with several "aggressors" hiding inside. The fact that Dale had seen only that troubled John; he was concerned it would leave the wrong impression that the college had become nothing more than a military barrack.

Fredericks had then made a show of going about town in his Humvee, rarely talking to anyone. John knew the reaction to Fredericks was actually rather normal. Across the previous two years, he and the community had learned how to function on their own. What Ed and the others saw as "poking around" was a normal part of an inspection tour upon taking a new command. Most would look askew at new guys until they had proven themselves. Though John had his own questions—and Makala had outright disdain—he was willing to concede a testing-out time.

"The few that cornered him long enough to ask about the draft," Ed continued, "were given a stock reply, John, that the two of you were working out an arrangement that 'everyone will be happy with.'"

So the word was out. After the visit by the town council, it was decided to call for a town-square meeting to be held in the town park if the weather was good. Makala had objected to the physical strain of him addressing what might be several hundred or more who might get a bit ugly, but he felt it had to be done before he went back to Asheville. The town still had a functional bullhorn, and she insisted that everyone understood why he was sitting down rather than his usual method of delivery, which was on his feet, walking about and into the crowd.

The crowd was far bigger than he had expected, five hundred or more. A mixed array of vehicles were parked along State and Main—motorcycles and mopeds, precomputerized cars from the '50s and '60s, tractors, vehicles that ran on recycled cooking oil, an old flatbed tractor trailer from up in Swannanoa that hauled fifty or more people in, even half a dozen cars with the strange-looking canvas balloons on their roofs storing gas from charcoal burners strapped to tailgates or pickup truck flatbeds. How those worked John still couldn't figure out, but apparently they had been something of a fixture on the streets of Japan in the final months of the Second World War.

They opened with what was now the firm tradition of Reverend Black offering a prayer, followed by the news. The public announcement was made of Pat Stepp's death; at John's behest, Reverend Black did not state the cause of death, and then he quickly moved on to the happy news of three births in the community. Then the group sang the national anthem and pledged to the flag.

The first question from the crowd actually asked for a brief account of what had transpired with the reivers. With a couple dozen of the Stepp family present, he thought it best not to have two controversies blow in one night, so he simply said he was taken prisoner, traded for salt—for which, since it came from the town supplies, he would personally find a way to compensate the community—expressed remorse for the loss the Stepps had endured, and said that, henceforth, the guard along that border would be doubled. He felt it best to talk to the Stepps afterward, in private, to ask how they felt about a truce rather than seeing them go out on a vendetta raid.

And then he recounted the discussion with Dale, struggling a bit to remember precisely the nature of the exchange, asking for forgiveness if he had forgotten anything but that he was still rather battered up when Dale had arrived. Taking a deep breath, he opened the meeting for questions, asking that folks step up in front of all and speak loudly so all could hear, and that if anyone wished to comment, to keep it to the agreed-upon limit of two minutes; otherwise, they would be at it half the night.

The community had reverted in many ways to the old New England tradition of open town meetings, except in cases of actual trials for crimes, which were again handled as they had been before the Day. Norm Schiach, the town's well-respected lawyer, acted as judge. There was no town jail other than a holding tank in the police station for the drunk and disorderly. Theft of food was still considered to be just about the most heinous of offenses, and several times, the punishment of banishment from the community had been the sentence. The starving times were still such a close memory that all saw such an act as close to murder.

John finished his description of the conversation with Dale Fredericks and then dropped the bomb—that he had been offered a position with the federal government and that if he accepted, the draft for their community would be cut in half. That caused a stir, and it was several minutes before the meeting came somewhat back to order. He sighed inwardly.

Ernie Franklin was already on his feet, and half a dozen followed him, ready to pull the parliamentarian game that as Ernie's time was up, the next person behind him would just announce, "I yield my time to speak to Ernie," who could then continue to press whatever it was he was peeved about.

It was going to be a long night, and regardless of how his head still throbbed, John would have to play his role.

"So let me get this straight," Ernie said without preamble or need for introduction. "You volunteer to go in with the fancy rank of major general and half of those who got draft notices are let off the hook. Is that it, John?"

"Yes. If I volunteer, the draft quota is cut in half."

"So which half goes if you accept?"

"I didn't say I'd volunteer," John replied. "I just said that was the offer."

"Well, are you going to volunteer, John? I mean, what the hell . . . you get to be a major general. Rations must be damn good with those pencil pushers who created this mess in the first place and then ran to their bunkers up in Virginia, most likely even get some sort of pay, as well."

"Like I said, Ernie, I haven't decided yet."

"Why not volunteer? You get to be a major general, the draft for our town is cut in half, and the other half gets a safe assignment with you. It strikes me as a darn good deal, John, for you and for us."

There was a loud muttering of agreement from the crowd.

"I have to look at all the factors, Ernie, and ultimately, it's a personal decision."

"Personal? This is about more than a hundred families here. I don't see that as a personal decision just for you to make."

Maury Hurt, arm still in a sling, came to his feet. "Who the hell are you, Ernie, to tell him what to do? Frankly, I think the offer stinks, putting John in a position of damned if he does and damned if he doesn't. The way it was offered, putting John on the spot like this, tells me something isn't kosher with this deal. I think we should have a vote that regardless of John's decision, either we go along with the full draft or say no to the whole damn thing."

"Easy for you to say, Hurt," Ernie retorted. "Your kids aren't being called up."

That triggered an explosion of arguments and accusations. Reverend Black and Ed stood up by John's side, shouting for order.

Ed finally seized the bullhorn, yelling that if folks didn't shut the hell up, the meeting was over and he'd clear the town square by force if need be. The crowd finally settled down, and Ed handed the bullhorn back to John.

"I'm not comfortable with this offer of cutting the draft in half. Fredericks threw in the caveat that the cut was 'for now.'"

"Then get the statement in writing," Ernie interjected. "John, it's about whose ox is getting gored today, at this moment. I've lost one grandson in this already in the fight against the Posse; I'm not about to see others getting shipped off, and your decision can be a difference for all of us."

"Time's up, Ernie," Reverend Black announced calmly, holding up his watch. "Next question or comment."

"I yield my time to Mr. Franklin," the man behind Ernie announced.

John sighed inwardly but forced a nod of agreement.

"So what is it, John?" Ernie pressed.

"I'll decide after tomorrow."

"Why not now? That means fifty-six families can breathe easier to-night."

"Hey, Ernie, why don't you back the hell off?" It was Lee Robinson, John's old neighbor before both their homes were gutted out in the battle with the Posse. "My boy's been called up, but I'll be damned if I'll pressure John to volunteer on the fifty-fifty chance just to save his hide from this. John's done more than enough already."

There were mutterings of agreement from the crowd, even though Lee had spoken out of turn.

"Why don't we see a show of hands here from those who got draft notices if they're willing to volunteer to go," Lee pressed in.

Reverend Black picked up on it. "Good suggestion, Lee. How many who received draft notices are willing to volunteer to go?"

John could not help but look over at Elizabeth, who was standing next to Makala, Ben in her arms, nuzzled in against his mother and nearly asleep. She raised her right hand.

He felt a deep swelling of pride but also anguish. It was the torment all loving parents feel when they see their child making a difficult and perhaps dangerous decision as an adult when, in memory, they still see the small innocent child of years long gone.

It seemed as if every person in the crowd looked to her, the daughter of John Matherson. Hand after hand now went up, some swiftly, others reluctantly. One of Ernie's grandsons raised his hand, even though he had not received a draft notice.

More than half were willing to volunteer, and John felt a lump in his throat. The idealism of youth. Nearly every last one of them had fought in the battle against the Posse. Every one of them had seen death in all the vicious multitude of forms that only a battlefield can deliver, all of them had lost friends and loved ones that day. One of the hands raised was a hollow-eyed young man in his early twenties, and John remembered how he had to be restrained from committing suicide on that day when he found his girlfriend dead, lying in the gutter by the side of the highway where the final minutes of the battle had been fought out. The boy had never recovered, just going through the motions of living, and he most likely welcomed this chance to perhaps honorably end it all at last.

"This is hardly fair," John said softly, megaphone off so that only those sitting closest to him could hear. He raised his head and motioned for the volunteers to put their hands down, shaking his head. "Ernie, could I have a few minutes?" he asked, and to his surprise, Ernie relented. John was not sure if his opponent of the moment had been taken off guard by the response, including that of one of his grandsons.

"Don't do this now," John said, keeping the megaphone off but coming to his feet so that all could see and hear him. "I don't want to sound like the professor type, but remember, I used to study and teach about stuff like this. We, we here, have made some hard decisions together, and at times, you had to trust me to make them on my own or that the council back in city hall had to make, clear back to that day when those two damned souls, the drug thieves, had to be shot.

"Lee made a fair call with asking who would actually volunteer, but that becomes a group pressure thing, and history has shown us that nine times out of ten, it can be manipulated or go astray. A few score hands go up, and the rest feel guilty, some afraid they'll be called cowards, others because it is what their friends are doing. And at times, it is dead wrong when a group, whipped up by emotion, is called to make a decision that should be made in private and after deep reflection."

"How do you feel about this draft?" Ernie replied.

"Personally or in my position in this town?"

"Cut the horseshit. Just how do you really feel about it?"

"I'm a soldier. You never really take the uniform off for as long as you live. We still call ourselves Americans. Some people might think it hokey, but we still sing the national anthem and salute the flag here. So in light of that, if this is a legitimate order from a legitimate government, then I will say that for the sake of national unity, we obey it."

The crowd now erupted into various factions, some shouting approval, others crying out that they had received damn near nothing from the federal government for two years other than a few rations, and now half of their surviving defenders were being ordered to God knows where. And some shouted that there was no longer a government at all and those in Bluemont could go to hell for getting them into this mess to start with.

The meeting was rapidly breaking down, angry shouting when one of the young women who had raised her hand to volunteer turned on a friend who had refused, called her a traitor and a coward; a fistfight erupted, half a dozen then wading in to break it up.

John felt it a good excuse to try to close things off. He bent over to pick up the bullhorn, feeling light-headed when he stood back up, and clicked it several times to get attention. "A suggestion for all of us," he announced, and the crowd, which had been focused on the brawl, turned back toward him.

"Ed, could you do me a favor and haul those two hotheads off to the drunk tank until morning and they've calmed down?"

There was a time during the first year that none would have dared a brawl at the town meetings, a major reason being that the starving time was so intense that few had the energy. It was also because the draconian response then needed, especially when it came to days when public rations were issued and guards at the favorite pizza restaurant—which had been converted into the bakery for two slices of bread per citizen, heavily laced with sawdust—were ordered by him to shoot to kill if a riot over food broke out.

"Let's call it a night," John offered. "We can stay here for hours and argue ourselves blue in the face, and it won't change anything for the moment."

"I second John Matherson's motion," Reverend Black announced quickly, "and suggest we call it a night. Dawn comes early now, and there's a lot of work for all of us to see to tomorrow."

John smiled inwardly at that. For nearly everyone, it was no longer an annoying alarm clock set to a particular hour. In winter, one slept in late and went to bed early; in summer, especially now at spring planting time, it really was up before dawn with twelve or more hours of heavy, backbreaking labor ahead for the majority.

John exchanged glances with Ernie. "Okay with you, Ernie?" John asked.

Ernie could see the hands going up in agreement to end the meeting for now and reluctantly nodded, outmaneuvered in the public forum. "After the meeting with this Fredericks, we'd like a report, John, and to hear your decision about yourself."

"Agreed."

"And we'd like as well to learn a helluva lot more about just who these people in Bluemont are with their orders."

"It's the government, our government!" someone shouted back.

"Maybe yours," Ernie retorted, "but they got to prove a lot more to me than some bullshit orders stuffed into a mailbox before I'll stand back and watch kids here being sent off to God knows where, whether they want to or not."

Things were about to go out of control again, but Reverend Black masterfully stepped forward, taking the bullhorn from John. He raised his hand, delivered a quick benediction and the Lord's Prayer—their traditional closing—and the group began to break up.

John slowly walked to the Edsel, grateful that the meeting had ended early. His head was throbbing.

"John."

"Ernie, can't it wait?" He sighed. He looked over his shoulder as Ernie came up to his side.

"Just one thought to put in that swollen head of yours."

John was about to react at what he felt was one insult too many for the night, but Ernie smiled.

"I'm talking about the damn concussion, John."

"Oh, yeah. So what is it? I'm really beat."

"Ask yourself this. Just who in the hell are these people? We didn't elect them. Even when we did elect them, a lot of 'em were the dumbest, most grasping bastards on God's good earth, and if they had done their jobs right in the first place, we wouldn't be in this mess."

"No one ever said representative government was going to be a cakewalk."

"Exactly. More than a few were not all that upset when the whole thing went down."

"Such as you?"

"I didn't say that, damn it. But at least my family and I saw the future and were ready for it. The rest of you trusted them, and now four out of five are dead as a result. Worse than the plague or any war in history."

"Your point, Ernie? And yeah, my head really is swollen."

"Find out what you can about who is actually running things in Bluemont, Virginia, and what exactly this million-man mobilization is really about."

John nodded.

"I'll drop by for a visit after you get some more answers."

John put up his hand. "Ernie, don't pressure me. I'll go to the town council first; then, if necessary, we hold another meeting like this one."

Ernie stared at him for a moment and then nodded.

"And Ernie, I'm changing the rules."

"What rules?"

"Two minutes per person, and that's it. You got more to say than that, write it down and hand it to someone else. It's a meeting, not a monopoly."

"You're the one doing most of the talking. What about you?"

"I got stuck as leader when everything went to shit. I didn't see you come rushing out to do it."

There was an angry glare for a moment and then the crease of a smile. "You do have guts, Matherson." He then reached into his pocket and pulled out a cigar and offered it.

"Oh, for God's sake, don't offer me one of those now. I'll be your damn slave if I ever go back to smoking."

"Precisely the reason I'm offering them," he replied with a smile.

John reluctantly shook his head.

"Well, you know where you can get one if you need it, General."

"It's John, just John, so lay off it. Okay?"

"Good luck tomorrow, John."

Ernie actually offered his hand and walked off. John was ever so grateful when Makala slipped into the driver's seat, Elizabeth getting into the back, cradling Ben, who was fast asleep in her arms.

"Elizabeth, once home, when you get the little guy settled in, can we talk."

"You're ticked off that I volunteered."

"Let's sit out on the porch and talk there."

She was silent the rest of the way back, not waiting for him as they parked in the driveway and she went into the house.

"You know why she did it, don't you?" Makala asked.

"Yeah, being my daughter and all that. But damn it, she has a baby to think of."

The two walked out to the porch and settled down. It was quiet, and peaceful night sounds drifted in . . . spring peepers and the hooting of an owl. Habit was to pick up Rabs, but he did not—not for this conversation.

Elizabeth came out and sat down casually in the overstuffed chair across from the sofa. Illuminated by the moonlight, she triggered an inhalation of breath from John, who at that instant suffered from the duality that all loving fathers must deal with. She had grown into a beautiful young woman. Everyone in their community, if seen by someone from before the Day, would think them borderline malnourished. All now had a lean, sinewy look common in the somber faces of ancestors eternally looking out from old daguerreotypes of the Civil War. Nearly every woman now kept her hair short, with any length drawn back in a short ponytail. Some still dressed in something formal—that, with skillful sewing, had been tucked in several sizes—for church or synagogue. As the food supply was finally beginning to stabilize out, they were drawing back from the edge of starvation, but it was still a far cry from the world they had lost.

Elizabeth, after the long months of worry during her pregnancy and the first months after Ben was born, had actually filled out a bit, and so he did see the beautiful young woman and mother. But like all fathers, he also saw the four-year-old who still would call him Daddy, want "smoochies," ask to play tea party with her stuffed animals, and squeal with delight when he pushed her too hard on the playground swing and she'd cry that she was going to fly away.

"I know what you're going to say, Dad," she announced.

"Oh, really?"

Makala, who was holding his hand, squeezed it, a clear message to shut up and let the girl speak first.

"Okay, then enlighten me."

Again a squeeze, this time of reproach for his tone. He was getting angrier by the second just looking at her. She had a one-year-old baby. What about him? Her dead sister was buried out in the yard just feet away. If she went off with this damned army—and he had a gut sense that would be it—she would never come back, the way so many never came back from too many wars, leaving with the naïve promise that all would be okay and not to worry.

"When the question was asked who would volunteer, I had to put my hand up, Dad."

"Why?"

"To support you, that's why. How do you think it would look if your daughter didn't put her hand up? Everyone would say you were pulling in favoritism, and you wouldn't have stood a chance at the meeting tonight."

That caught him a bit off guard, and he lowered his head, filled with a sudden pride.

"Thank you, angel. But you know it puts you on the spot now."

"I know that."

"And that was it?"

She hesitated. "No, there were other things."

He looked back up at her. "Such as?"

"I want to go."

Now he did lean forward with that one. "In God's name, why?"

"*You* did."

"What do you mean I did?"

"Back when you graduated from college. You volunteered, and if not for Mom getting sick, you would have made general. If you went, why shouldn't I? You always said the military, medicine, teaching, and the church were the noblest of professions. And you chose the military first."

"But it was different then, sweetie. We weren't at war."

"And you and your buddies most likely talked damn near every day about proving yourselves if and when there was one."

"You know my service record, Elizabeth. I was under fire for less than a hundred hours, miles back from the front line, never fired a shot in anger."

"And inside, you chastised yourself for that. You can't deny it, Dad."

"It's all different now, Elizabeth. You'll be fighting for a government we don't know, that we did not vote into power, fighting in a war we're not even sure about. It'll take years, maybe a generation, before we can really say things are back to normal—if ever they will be again."

"And what the hell have I done for it?" she asked.

"You have a baby to think of."

"Don't you think I considered that? So, yeah, my complete contribution to all this is I got pregnant, and then my baby's father goes out and gets himself killed. Just great—my total contribution to civilization."

"Ben is the future," John offered.

"I know that." She started to choke up. "But nevertheless, you know I love him with all my heart, but I feel I have to go. Go and do something the way his father did."

John wanted to snap, *Sure, Ben's dad was a hero—killed in a bloody butchery of a fight, and in retrospect, if given any choice, the kid would have wanted to live.* And now, Elizabeth—like eighteen-year-olds throughout history—was imbued with an idealism to do her part and not questioning the deeper reasons of why.

"*Dulce et decorum est pro patria mori.*" John sighed.

"What does that mean?" Elizabeth asked.

John just shook his head and saw the curse that all fathers who have seen war know far too well. It was one thing for them to go, but it was something else entirely when they came for your children. He realized he was playing the guilt line on her while sitting only feet away from Jennifer's grave. It wasn't fair to her; what he was saying was now about him, and he felt a wave of shame for playing that card, but at the moment, he could not help it.

Sighing, he said, "I can't stop you. I just ask that you give me a few days to figure things out."

"Just please don't try to pressure me, Dad," she replied forcefully. "If that's it, I'm going to sleep. Little Ben wore me ragged today, and I'm part of the work team for picking ramps tomorrow."

She got up, kissing Makala and then John on the cheek. She hesitated for a second and then leaned in and hugged him so fiercely that he winced.

"Hey, the rib still hurts too."

She hit him with the smile that could always disarm him and left the room.

"I never had children, John." Makala sighed. "I wish I had one like her."

"You do. She sees you as her mother now."

"You know what I mean," Makala whispered and then cleared her throat. "She got you with that opening argument. She's right, and you know it."

He could only nod his head in agreement.

"Let's go to bed, John. You need to be fresh, for tomorrow morning's excitement and then the meeting with Fredericks tomorrow night."

She got up and left the room, leaving him to his nightly ritual of picking up Rabs and going out by Jennifer's grave to say good night.

"You have one helluva sister, Jennifer, but then you always knew that," he whispered. "But dear God, I can't bear losing her too."

CHAPTER EIGHT

John got out of his Edsel, the sun just breaking the horizon beyond the Swannanoa Gap, the air perfectly calm and clear, and he could not help but grin and whistle an old-fashioned wolf whistle at the beauty that was in front of him.

It was Don Barber's old Aeronca L-3B World War II recon bird, fully restored. The plane had served as the crucial all-seeing eyes of their community in the months after the Day. With no electronics in it whatsoever, to start it, one had to pump an old-fashioned primer, with a brave soul out front grabbing hold of the propeller and throwing it to bring the engine to life. The plane had played a crucial role in first monitoring the approach of the Posse, providing recon on their attack deployment and flanking moves up Swannanoa Gap. Against strict orders, Don had tried to provide close air support during the battle by dropping pipe bombs, and he was shot down. Don was killed, and the canvas-fabric plane burned, one entire wing gone. And he had assumed, as had everyone else, that it was a write-off.

Rare indeed was the private plane that had survived the Day and the chaos afterward, but there were still more than a few old pilots alive who, like any pilot, felt only half alive if he didn't get his hands on a plane on a regular basis. Billy Tyndall was such a pilot, and Maury Hurt, the owner of the WWII-era Jeep—though not a pilot—was a master mechanic with equipment from that war. They were joined by Danny Mullen, an airplane mechanic from the Vietnam era who had serviced B-52s, who said if you work on one plane, you just get a feel for any type of plane. They had hauled the wreckage back to an abandoned warehouse by the Ingrams' market. They scrounged up tools, canvas, and even spruce spars from the garage of old man Quinten, who had been working on a homebuilt plane but had died from heart failure in the first weeks after the start of things.

Now, two years and a couple of thousand man-hours later, she was ready for her checkout flight. The paint job was army green, taken from Maury's workshop, with the original touch of white and black stripes from aircraft that had flown on D-day. They towed the plane up to the interstate as their landing strip, the test postponed for several days until finally dawn revealed clear skies and no wind.

It had become a source of concern for John that word might leak beyond Black Mountain that they were rebuilding a plane, and he made sure, as best as he could, that all were sworn to secrecy as to what was going on in "hangar one." It was something Dale had not picked up on during his visit, and John was pleased that the hangar crowd had kept their mouths shut.

The alleged secret project was now public when they towed the plane out of its hangar. Word rapidly spread that the big day was at hand, and several hundred spectators had come down to watch and definitely pray.

The team who labored so hard for this moment now stood in a tight circle, quietly arguing about the next step. Danny, Maury, and a couple of others who had flown were saying that Billy should just stick to what was called "crow hopping," getting a few feet off the ground and then gliding back to a landing.

"It's the way the FAA used to insist upon it being done," someone said.

Billy sighed. "There ain't no FAA anymore."

There was a time when one mentioned the FAA and most pilots started to mutter under their breath, but at that moment, there were no certified inspectors to check the work, no professional pilots to take on the risky job of the first test flight. This was yet another throwback to a long, long time ago when those who wanted to reach the clouds built a plane in their barns from some basic designs in an old magazine, rolled it out, said a prayer, and took off.

"Look, either it flies or it doesn't. And there's only one way to find out."

The circle around him fell silent. Danny finally extended his hand and patted Billy on the shoulder.

"Okay, but if you kill yourself, I'm going to be really pissed that you wrecked the plane again."

John knew better than to go over and stick his head into it. His own military experience had taught him a way for a colonel to get a royal chewing out from a sergeant was to interrupt a pilot and ground crew during a preflight check.

Billy's wife was obviously not happy in the slightest with the entire routine, running up to hug him fiercely before he finally broke loose and climbed into the narrow cockpit. She looked back at John, the gaze conveying that if something went wrong, she would hold him personally responsible.

Danny went forward, calling to Billy to check that the magnetos were off, and then he turned the prop a dozen rotations to work oil into the pistons and called for three shots of primer.

Danny now ran down the brief checklist yet again, Billy checking that ailerons, rudder, and elevators were clear and the primer closed. "Mags hot! Contact! Clear prop!"

Danny threw the propeller downward with his right hand, stepping back to one side and away as he did so, and the engine started to fire up on the very first try. There was backfiring, and black smoke blew out with the exhaust, and it nearly stalled. Billy eased in the throttle. There was more backfiring, and then it settled down to a steady low roar. A cheer erupted from all, John thrilling to the sound of it. Yet another connector back to the world before the Day, coming back into their lives.

Danny was around to the side of the door on the starboard side of the plane. He pulled it half open and talked with Billy, the engine running up, checking oil pressure and temperature, and switching mags on and off amid the occasional backfire. Dan finally stepped back, latching the door shut. He leaned down low and pulled out the wheel chocks.

Billy looked over at the crowd with a boyish grin of delight. He had taken to sporting a handlebar mustache and goatee, looking like an aviator of the First World War. He raised his hand and saluted. Dan, John, and Maury, all vets, formally returned the salute.

Billy revved the engine up, and there was more backfiring and dark smoke exhaust, the aircraft trembling as if eager to be away. Billy looked over at Dan and held up two fingers and then one.

"Twenty-one hundred RPM," Maury announced. "Would like a hundred more, but what the hell. He's got miles of runway ahead of him."

Billy released the brakes, and the plane seemed to leap forward as if alive and eager to get back to where she truly belonged, as if the follies of foolish humanity had kept too many planes grounded for far too long.

Dan was absolutely rigid. "He's at twenty . . . twenty-five . . ." There were a couple more backfires, Dan wincing with each, now cursing steadily.

The tail of the plane was up, and the plane swerved a few feet off the centerline of the highway.

"Dance on those pedals, damn it," Danny snarled.

And then, ever so gracefully, she was up, leveling off a half a dozen feet above the highway, gaining speed now that she was free of the ground. The crowd cheered and swarmed around Danny and Maury, slapping them on the back, Danny yelling for everyone to get back, still intent on following Billy, who was easing the stick back, beginning to climb, still flying straight and level until nearly out of sight.

Danny suddenly gasped as Billy pulled the stick back even more and pushed the plane into a turning bank of at least thirty degrees or more.

"Damn him!" Danny shouted. "Take it easy!"

Billy continued the turn, banking around, disappearing behind the trees for a moment where the highway curved to the north on the far side of town. There was a moment of silence and then another rousing cheer as he reappeared a hundred or more feet up, flying level and straight back toward them. He came straight on, and then a couple hundred yards out, he nosed over as if going into a dive, leveled off ten feet above the crowd gathered on the highway, and roared over them, everyone now cheering wildly.

"Stupid son of a bitch. There was a time when he'd lose his license for that dumb trick!" Dan cried, but no one was paying attention; even John was caught up in the moment. Billy continued to climb, and then, in a moment that drew nervous comments from some, he pulled the nose up higher and higher, engine still running full out.

"Stall check, damn it, not this time, Billy," Dan whispered. The plane appeared to hang motionless for several seconds, nose pitched high at over forty-five degrees, and then it suddenly dropped, one wing dipping a bit. It leveled out, the throttle cut back to idle.

"Keep this damn road cleared!" Danny shouted. "He's coming in to land. Clear the road!"

Danny muttered suggestions that only he could hear as the plane drifted down, gliding past where John, Maury, and Danny stood, still up by half a dozen feet.

"A bit too high, too high," Danny groaned. "Let her settle, let it settle—don't flare yet."

Still several feet off the ground, the plane appeared to just fall, bouncing hard, tires squealing in protest. The plane bounced back up several feet.

"Don't fight it!" Danny shouted. "Just let her settle!"

The plane leveled off, the nose a bit high again, easing down a hundred yards farther on. With two small puffs of white smoke from the tires and a slight swerve to port side, it straightened out and then rolled to a stop.

Billy hit hard rudder, turning the plane around, taxiing back the several hundred yards to where the crowd waited expectantly and then shut the engine down. He had the door open and was grinning like a kid, the way so many pilots grinned after a flight and a safe landing.

"Damn you!" Maury and Dan shouted at the same time, launching into separate tirades about taking off in the first place, pulling such a sharp bank, going for a power-on stall, and the bounced landing. Billy just stood there smiling, taking it in.

"She flies, and she's a beauty," was all he said before finally lapsing into a review. He suggested that the replacement wing was most likely causing the plane to yaw to the left, the fabric under the starboard wing was fluttering, and he couldn't get the engine up above 2,200 RPM even when flying straight and level, but he did apologize for the sloppy landing—it had been well over two years since he had last flown.

"We have an air force," John said with a smile, looking over at Reverend Black. "Guess I should get back home and get ready to find out what the hell is really going on in Asheville."

"The meal was excellent, thank you," Makala said politely, sliding her chair back slightly and putting her napkin on the table.

John had been filled with barely contained excitement for most of the day because of the successful test flight, trying not to think too much about the meeting with Fredericks. He had taken a cold bath, plunging into the creek to clean up. Jen, still the matriarch of the house, had laid out his one good set of slacks and blue dress shirt, but he refused to wear a blazer. It might work for Fredericks but not for him. Makala had carefully shaved him, noting with disapproval that his cheek appeared to be swelling from the bad tooth. She reminded him that with the effects of the concussion clearing up, it was time for a visit to the dentist.

For John, this ritual of dressing up almost felt like they were going out on a date rather than a meeting that would most likely decide their futures. Following their routine of her driving while he kept careful watch—this time with a twelve gauge laid across his lap—they made their way to Asheville. He insisted the two of them take this trip alone; having his guards waiting outside just struck him as wrong.

Dale nodded his thanks for her compliment regarding dinner. "Amazing this long-term survival food that was being sold before the Day," Dale said. "I thank heavens FEMA thought to buy up a billion rations before things went bad—beef stroganoff that tastes almost as good as I remember it once being and strawberries that you just add water to and chill."

"What we would have given for just a couple thousand of these after the Day," Makala said quietly, looking over at John.

John looked to Dale, wondering if he was picking up on his wife's barely veiled rebuke.

"So where did these come from?" she asked.

"I managed to get two hundred thousand rations on order. They're shipping them in now."

"Oh? From where?" Makala asked.

Dale smiled. "I really wish I could tell you that, Makala, but it is still one of those classified things for now." Dale stood up from the table, which was set up in a private side room to the courthouse dining hall, and he motioned for the door. "Let's head over to my office where we can relax and talk a little business."

"I think I'll take a walk around town while you two have your meeting," Makala announced.

"Mind if I have one of my security people tag along?" Dale offered. "Asheville is secure, but after dark, we still do have a problem now and again. And with you dressed as nicely as you are and obviously a bit better fed than most, it might be a concern."

A bit better fed. John caught that one and wondered if it was a veiled insult. More than a few who had supposedly been running Asheville until the army arrived had obviously been more than "a bit better fed." Most had disappeared when the army commander started to inquire into exactly how the city was managed after the Day, fleeing to God knows where in several well-stocked vehicles. Rumor was they had run afoul of a reivers community in the highlands along the South Carolina border, and no one expressed regret as to whatever their fate had been.

"I can take care of myself," Makala replied as she reached into her purse and drew out a hammerless .38 revolver.

Dale looked at the gun, a bit surprised, and then he sighed. "I hate to remind you, but in the future, weapons really should be checked at the door when you come in the building. We're trying to reestablish some rules, Mrs. Matherson."

"Oh, but of course. Sorry. I just plain forgot." Without further comment, she was out the door and heading for the exit.

John just smiled.

"She's an interesting woman, John. Bet there is a tough side to her beneath all that charm."

"There's a tough side to any of us who survived out here," John replied, still smiling.

There was silence as they headed to Dale's office, the foyer dimly illuminated by a single fluorescent bulb overhead. Once into the office, Dale closed the door and threw the light switch, the fluorescent lights overhead winking on, a gesture that startled John a bit. For months after the Day, nearly everyone at times, when walking into a dark room, fumbled for the light switch and then stood there confused for a few seconds before reaching for a precious match to light a kerosene lamp—if they still had any fuel left—or just settling down into the darkness. The casual reality of just flicking a light switch was startling.

"We do run a little power at night to keep our communications gear on-line, and the fluorescent bulbs only burn a couple of dozen watts. It's a luxury you are not used to, I know."

What happened next really put John off balance. Dale sat down at his desk, reached to a cupboard behind him, and pulled out a real bottle of prewar scotch. Without asking, he took out two tumblers, pouring a couple of ounces into each and handed one to John.

"To the restored United States of America," Dale said solemnly, raising his glass, and John could not help but follow. Memory of old traditions of the officers' mess on formal occasions hit John, with toasts to the republic, the president, and whoever might be an honored guest.

John sipped the scotch and let out a sigh of pleasure. He had not tasted real twelve-year-old scotch since before the Day. Dale settled back in his chair, loosened his tie, and put his feet up on the desk. "Well, I guess folks down here call this next step 'time to talk turkey.' "

"Where you from originally, Dale?"

"Massachusetts. Why?"

"I can't recall a single soul here every saying 'talk turkey' when it was time to get down to business."

Dale nodded, still smiling. "Thanks for telling me. I know I am seen as an outsider sent in by some distant entity. More than a few around here are grumbling that a local should have been appointed to run this administrative district. But I think you'll agree with the report sent up by the army commander that was here before me that more than a few in this county office were not up to the job, and others were downright corrupt, taking care of themselves first and the hell with you folks stuck out in the boondocks."

"You mean folks like me in places like Black Mountain, Waynesville, Brevard, and Canton? I could name fifty other towns, if you wish."

"Well, yes, places like yours."

"In that, I'll agree. You undoubtedly read the reports. I turned in a few myself to the army. The crew that took over running this city had more than enough food for themselves while the rest of us were on our own. They tried to confiscate what we did have, and when the crap really hit the fan with the murdering gangs, they cut us off, sealed up the highway leading into the city, and just looked out for themselves without offering any help. So, yes, I can understand why some thought it was best to bring in new blood."

"Good, I'm glad you see it that way. Thank you." He extended his hand, which John took, and then he offered a refill of his glass, which John refused. Whether it was going to be talking turkey or down to real business, two ounces was enough, and the glass was not yet drained.

"John, I've been sent here by the federal government to reestablish overall stability to the entire region. My district encompasses all of western North Carolina, down to Interstate 77."

"So that includes Charlotte, as well?"

"Eventually, but Charlotte right now is still a no-man's-land. The few still living there are considered lawless, and once our strength is secured here, we'll eventually head down that way to bring things back under control."

"Who is *we*?"

"That's a long way off. Right now, I got my hands full just with those border reivers you dealt with last week. John, I'll be frank. Your town is a model of how to survive and then rebuild, and I'm not blowing smoke at you with that compliment. That's why the administration up in Bluemont sat up and took notice when I sent in a report with the recommendation you go back into federal service as a major general, and they jumped on it. Your country, *our* country, needs damn near every skill possible to rebuild. You have those administrative skills, and I'm anxious to hear your decision." He paused and continued to smile. "I heard there was a bit of an upset meeting yesterday regarding the draft notices."

"How did you hear that?"

"People talk, and right now, the call for help from our country with the creation of the Army of National Recovery is the buzz conversation around here."

Dale offered a drink again, which John refused, holding his glass up to show there was still some left. Dale poured another few ounces for himself and put the bottle back in the cabinet.

"I really haven't seen a bottle like that since the Day," John said. "The liquor store was looted clean within forty-eight hours, and those that had some kept mighty quiet about it after that. So where did that come from?" he asked casually.

"Oh, I traded for it just before coming here with the pilot who brought me and the rest of the administrative team up from the coast."

"So the folks on the coast have such things again?"

"A lot more than here. England, as you know, wasn't hit by the EMP. So some trade is back up, and thank you, dear Lord, quite a few cases of real scotch did come into Charleston several months back."

"What else do they have down there?"

"Part of Charleston has power again, feeding off the carrier anchored at Patriots Point. John, you step foot on that carrier and you swear nothing ever went wrong. Computers still run onboard the ship, hot showers, real food, and not just emergency rations . . ." His voice trailed off as if sensing the frustration John was feeling.

"How about hospitals? And what about insulin?" John asked. "They ever run out of that?"

Dale hesitated for a moment, not sure of the meaning, and then he nodded, his features solemn. "Sorry, John, I did read about that in your profile report. And no, things were just as hellish down there during the first months after the attack, even more so with the summer heat than up your way until the navy arrived in force."

"My profile report?"

"Sure. It's been two years since the war started, but some things are slowly coming back online. They had some backup database systems in Bluemont; remember, it was always one of the fallback positions in the event of a major attack hitting the lower forty-eight and taking out Washington, D.C. When I put your name in, they said your dossier from your service in the Pentagon was still intact, and they mentioned that you had a daughter with diabetes. Damn all, John, if only you had been evacuated up to Bluemont when this hit rather than being down here, it might have turned out different."

"Don't go anywhere near there, Dale," John replied. Whenever the death of Jennifer came anywhere near a conversation, he always felt something about to break inside. "We weren't, she wasn't, we had no insulin, and she died—and that was it." He glared at Dale icily.

Dale lowered his head. "Sorry I mentioned it."

John sat silent for several minutes. It was his weakest spot, and Dale had just touched it. Of course, he had thought of all the alternatives—one of the worse of them that, on the day things had hit, before everyone else began to catch on, he should have just stormed into the pharmacy and cleaned out their supply rather than accept the six bottles the pharmacist had offered him the day after. But then again, would he really have done that? He knew that regardless of his anguish, that was a moral boundary. Condemning others to death to save his own was not something he could ultimately live with.

"Perhaps we should talk about this commission your people want to give me and how it will affect the draft in my town," John said, shifting the subject back to the main point of this visit.

Dale, who apparently regretted his misstep with his reference to Jennifer, looked back up, his pensive gaze gone. "Sorry if I hit a bad nerve, John. Just my clumsiness at times."

"No harm done," John replied. There was a moment of awkward silence, which John finally broke. "I think I asked where you were on the day the war started."

"I was out in the field that day on an inspection tour for a government agency, fortunately near Bluemont."

"What agency?"

"The White House," Dale said without elaborating.

"Oh?" Again there was an awkward moment, as if both were stumbling to keep the conversation going, Dale obviously not yet feeling ready to push John further regarding the offer of a return to government service.

"So is it true that Air Force One was not sufficiently hardened and went down?" John finally asked, breaking the silence.

"Something like that."

"Too bad."

Dale stared at him intently for a moment, John returning the gaze unflinchingly. His tone had not conveyed horror at such news; it was a response of complete detachment. Where once the entire nation dwelled on the latest actions of the celebrity of the moment—and the president was definitely in that classification—now there was a distancing by all. Each had endured horrors unimagined before the electricity went down, and there was little room for empathy for what occurred outside of their sight and hearing.

When half, three-quarters, or more of your community dies, a death rate unprecedented in all of Western history since the great plague of the fourteenth century, survivors focused on their survival and that of their families, blocking out what was no longer part of their world.

"And the president now," John finally offered. "You feel she's qualified?"

"Constitutional line of succession. Secretary of Health and Human Services was the highest-ranking survivor, but you already know that. The vice president was the secretary of Homeland Security."

"This is a presidential election year. What's going to happen?"

"That's a tough one, John. We first need a census. Do we stick with the Constitution as written and reestablish the Electoral College or just go with a national vote?"

"Electoral College," John replied instantly. "The Constitution must stand untouched. That is a rock-solid bottom line for this country and for me personally. I will not serve a government that abrogates the Constitution. Yes, we had to move to martial law, but I pray those times are passing, regardless of the crisis that continues in many regions. If we tear out the bedrock of the Constitution, we will find ourselves on shifting sands that will eventually swallow all of us up into the darkness."

"Easy to say, John, but think of the complexities—and then think of why you are being asked to come back to serve. May I just rattle off a few points?"

"Go ahead."

"A year after the attack, we ran an analysis up in Bluemont and cataloged some classifications for the various states."

"Classifications?"

"Rating each state from a level one—meaning fully stabilized based on a number of different criteria—down to a level five, which means currently occupied either by a hostile nation or a nation claiming it is neutral and alleging it is here to help—to complete anarchy into lawlessness, of which Florida is still the worst case."

"And the results?"

"Not one state has reached what we define as a level one, with functioning local and state governments in conformity with federal law, as well."

"Conformity to federal law?" He was a bit cautious now.

"Come on, John. You do recall the Thirteenth Amendment, right? Do you know there are places where slavery is back, one of them in what used to be Charlotte?"

John sighed, not really surprised, and then he sadly nodded.

"Twelve states are level five. We got a few zones at level one, but not an entire state yet as it existed prior to the attack. I'm proud to say a hundred-mile radius around Bluemont is level one, touching into four states—West Virginia, Maryland, Virginia, and Pennsylvania. The rail corridor of the B&O for a couple of hundred miles is actually up and running. They pulled out half a dozen old steam locomotives from museums and got them running since we're smack in the middle of the coal region."

What about all the anticoal rhetoric of several years back? John thought, but he decided not to throw that into the conversation.

"Anyhow, back to your original point about elections this year. I think you can see it's impossible if we are going to do so within the proscriptions of the Constitution. We need a census—and out of that, a redrawing of congressional districts, most likely a significant reduction in total members of the House given the blow to our population. It has not always been 435, as you know. Some are saying we only need a hundred or so, the same as the Senate."

"I got no thoughts on that right now," John replied.

"And what about senators from level-five states? The vast majority of senators and members of the House were in D.C. on the Day with Congress in session. Not many made it to Bluemont."

"Have either houses even met since the war started?"

"The thought of even reaching a quorum to make the meeting legal is of course absurd. There's been advisory meetings with the president by surviving members of both houses who are now living in Bluemont, but that's it for right now until we can hold legitimate elections."

"What you are telling me is that elections have been postponed indefinitely?"

"Hopefully by next year we'll be ready again," Dale replied quickly. "John, it's obvious by your questions you are passionate about the Constitution."

"We all should be; it's the only thing we have to hang on to if this country's ever going to recover."

"That is a major reason we need the Army of National Recovery and men with your convictions serving in it. We have to restore internal order, John. Once that is achieved, we can focus on containing the obvious expansionism of China. If need be, a redeployment to the West Coast by some of the ANR units will show China we mean business; they back off, and with the West Coast secured, Mexico will pull back, as well. Mission accomplished. We then move to a full restoration of our government under the Constitution."

John nodded thoughtfully with that. *This man fumbled more than one point over the last week, but he certainly must have studied my file well,* John thought. While in the army, John had written more than one paper about the constitutional constraints regarding the use of military force, and though a strong pro-Union supporter when it came to the Civil War, he was more than a bit bemused at times with how Lincoln skirted the limits of his office to preserve the country as a single entity.

Lincoln made the tough decisions necessary to save the Union, and John believed that if Lincoln had lived, he would have relinquished his powers that transcended constitutional limits and restored proper balance in the months after the Confederacy collapsed. He was, ultimately, an honorable man.

Was this president, who did hold her office as defined by the Constitution, of the same character and moral fiber as Lincoln? If not, what might the ANR devolve into?

At this moment, he realized, perhaps the only way to find out for sure was to take the commission, go to Bluemont, and find out directly. *I can always resign if not satisfied,* he reasoned.

"If I enlist, your offer to cut the draft in half for my community stands firm?"

"Absolutely, John!" Dale cried. "Yes, absolutely, yes! Some of them can go with you to Bluemont—your daughter, of course, and even your wife and grandson, if you wish. Provisions like that are made for someone with your rank."

"Oh, really?"

"Come on, John. I remember reading somewhere that Grant's wife accompanied him into the field, sent there to help ease the migraines he suffered from. Lincoln had his son placed on Grant's staff near the end of the war rather than see him go into a combat unit. Lee pulled his youngest son out of combat and had him moved to a staff position. Generals and admirals often did and still do such things."

"And yet I recall that one of Teddy Roosevelt's sons went down in flames over France in 1918," John replied. "And though I don't think much of some of the things FDR did, his son was up on the front lines and was in the thick of it on Midway Island when everyone figured the Japanese were going to overrun the island, and he'd have been killed or taken prisoner. So it does go both ways."

Even as he spoke, John realized this man certainly had studied him to have so quickly pulled up examples of Lincoln, Grant, and Lee to assuage any guilt he might feel about favoritism.

"How soon can you report?" Dale asked, stepping around this debate with a historian.

"I'll go in with the rest," John said, "which, based on your offer of the other day, gives me about three and a half weeks to settle things."

"We're establishing some air transport this weekend, John. Think of it! Planes, transports coming in from an airbase near Bluemont and another air link down to Charleston. A lot of our assets that were positioned overseas are finally going into service back here in the States. We'll most likely be able to fly you up there rather than risk road transport for you and yours."

"Okay, that sounds fine."

"And we now have air assets as I told you about when we first met. The government allocated two Apache helicopters and two Black Hawks, to be permanently based in Asheville."

"I heard about that," John replied, not revealing that it was Forrest Burnett who had told him of the arrival of the choppers. "Apaches. I think they'd be needed more in Texas, for starters."

"Each district is getting at least a couple of aircraft for local security."

He wasn't sure how to react and did not reply.

"By the way," Dale said, still smiling, "I heard about your own air force."

"You seem to hear a lot," John replied.

Dale shrugged. "It's my job." There was something about the way he said it, but John let it pass. "It's a nice asset, John. I'd really like to have access to it at times."

"You'll have to take that up with the town council. I'm stepping back from those types of decisions."

"Oh, of course, but please do mention it to them at the next meeting."

"I'll do that."

Dale stood up, smiled, and extended his hand. "Can I make an official announcement of your decision to serve?"

"For the moment, Dale, let's just hold on that. I still have to clear it with my family and the town council. So can you ride with that for several days?"

"Of course, John—or should I say General Matherson?"

John did not reply to Dale pinning the title of rank on him before he had officially signed. He sensed the purpose of their meeting was at an end and stood up.

They shook hands. John turned to leave, looked down at the glass with the ounce of scotch still in it, and with "talking turkey" done, he gladly downed the second ounce.

"You can take the bottle along if you want, John."

John smiled and shook his head. "Wouldn't think of it. Some people see that and they'll think it's a bribe."

"Okay then. Let's plan on meeting the middle of next week for an update. Before I forget, I was really impressed with the work your people have been doing with the phone and electrical systems. Could you ask those overseeing the work if they'd mind if they'd come see me and perhaps lend some advice for operations here in Asheville?"

"Will do."

He was out the door and surprised to see Makala sitting in the dim light of the lobby, head bowed, nearly asleep.

"Come on, sweetheart, wake up."

She stood up with a start, smiled, and leaned up to kiss him. "What in the hell have you been drinking?" she asked sharply.

"A scotch."

"He actually had scotch, real scotch?"

He merely nodded. She was silent as they went for the main exit.

"Do you need to pick up your pistol on the way out?" John whispered.

"As if I'd actually obey that one? You are kidding, aren't you?"

They went to the car, parked outside in the darkness, not commenting to the uniformed guards, who did not acknowledge their passing.

"You still have a concussion and have been drinking, so I'll drive," Makala announced, opening the door for him over his objections.

They drove in silence, John scanning intently, shotgun on his lap and pistol by his side, not relaxing until they reached the roadblock into their own territory near Exit 59. Once cleared, he finally relaxed.

"So what happened?" Makala asked.

"I took the job. I felt I had to."

Not another word was exchanged during the long ride home. And for several hours after they slipped into the house, with Elizabeth, Ben, and Jen fast asleep, John sat alone in the garden by Jennifer's grave. When he finally went to bed, Makala was asleep, as well.

CHAPTER NINE

This is BBC News. It is 3:00 a.m., Greenwich War Time.

In a surprise move that is triggering comment around the world, the United States administration in Bluemont, Virginia, just announced less than an hour ago that it will release an undisclosed number of tactical nuclear weapons, commonly known as neutron bombs, for use against, and I quote, "indigenous groups in rebellion against the authority of the federal government within the continental United States." The government official went on to explain that such weapons are in no way intended as a threat or, and I again quote, "a counterforce threat against other nations currently engaged in aiding our civilian population or occupying territory within the United States," end quote. The announcement stated that if used, such weapons will only be employed east of the Continental Divide and north of the Red River, thereby sending a clear signal to the governments of China and Mexico that such weapons are not intended as a threat against their forces on American soil.

It was also reported today by Radio Free Canada that the American federal forces known as the ANR were dealt a serious setback in Chicago with the reported annihilation of a full battalion of troops, with several hundred taken prisoner by one of the groups in rebellion in that city occupying the downtown area. There is no word yet as to their fate.

Later in this program, we'll have a panel of experts joining us to discuss the nature of these weapons and the political ramifications of this announcement. Colonel Peter Ramsey, professor of strategic warfare studies at Sandhurst, was reached by this reporter for clarification as to the nature and use of so-called neutron bombs. He explained that they are low-yield nuclear weapons developed during the 1970s for tactical battlefield use and are by no means to be confused with the type of weapons used two years ago to trigger electromagnetic pulses. A neutron bomb is designed, at the instant of detonation, to release a highly lethal dose of radiation out to a very limited distance but with a very low blast area, damaging buildings only within several hundred yards of the point of detonation. The high radiation yield, however, can kill out to a mile or more, often within minutes. It is a weapon designed to kill but not physically destroy urban areas, and the federal government is threatening to use them in light of its frustration in suppressing rebellions in nearly every major city.

This now for our friends in Budapest and Prague: "The languid sobs of the violin wound my heart deeply." I repeat, "The languid sobs of the violin wound my heart deeply."

As John parked in front of the town hall, he dwelled on the fact that he had an appointment to see Doc Weiderman and finally get the tooth out—that and the word phoned in by Ernie Franklin, who claimed to have heard a BBC report regarding something about the feds announcing they were going to release tactical nukes for use inside the continental United States. There had been plenty of rumors over the last two years about further use of nukes, and indeed, in the days after the attack, North Korea and Iran had been blanketed in retaliation, while India and Pakistan finally escalated over the edge, and most of their major cities were gone, as well. But here, against ourselves? Insanity. It had to be a rumor.

Before he even managed to get out of his car, Ed was out of the office, running to meet him. "John, we've been trying to find you for the last twenty minutes. Where the hell have you been?"

"Do I have to report in every time I stop to go to the bathroom and walk around for a few minutes before coming in?" He didn't add that he had stalled for a few minutes just inside the Montreat gate, nerving himself for the dental visit.

"Don't you hear it?" Ed shouted.

"Hear what?"

"That!" Ed pointed up toward the Mount Mitchell range.

Damn it, not another raid. John cocked his head but heard nothing. "Perhaps I'm not over the concussion yet, but I don't hear a damn thing."

Ed stood silent, turning to face the mountain, and John saw a crowd gathered where street traders had set up their booths down on State Street for the twice-weekly market, looking up toward their beloved peak, several pointing excitedly.

"There it is again!" Ed cried, but John heard nothing. "An Apache— and it's shooting the crap out of something!"

"What?"

"Started about a half hour ago. I think they're hitting the reivers up along Craggy Pass."

John gazed at the mountain for a moment and finally caught a glimpse of a helicopter soaring up sharply over the pass and then turning to dive back down the far slope, disappearing from sight.

"Call Billy Tyndall now," John snapped. "I want the plane ready to go immediately."

"John?"

"Ed, just please do it; I'll explain later. And once that's done, I want you to go down to the big flagpole at the car dealership. Find three American flags and run them up the pole, one above the other."

"What?"

He repeated the order, falling back into the older routine of making decisions quickly, passing the order, and expecting it to be done without debate.

"Ed, just please do it."

He drove the half mile down to the hangar, which was open, fortunately with Billy already running through a preflight check.

John jumped out of his car. "Can you take me up now? I mean right now?"

"Sure, John, but what's the rush?"

"Get me up over Mount Mitchell. I want to see what the hell is going on over there."

Billy looked out the hangar door, his eyes going a bit wide. "It's a bit gusty out there. Turbulence over the mountain can get wicked for a small plane like this."

"You telling me it's unsafe?"

Billy hesitated. "How serious is this, John?"

"Could be damn serious."

"Okay, we'll go, but grab a barf bag out of the back well before we go up, because you're going to need it."

Billy called for Danny to help throw the prop as the two climbed in. Billy ran down the short checklist, shouting for Danny that mags were hot and to clear prop, and seconds later, they were taxiing across the Ingrams' parking lot, down a short stretch of Main Street, which was kept well clear for passage of the plane, and then up the exit ramp. Billy stopped for moment to check mags again and to be sure that John was strapped in with seat belt tight, and then he throttled up. John could hear him muttering curses over the headset as they rolled far past where he had lifted off on their first test flight.

"How much do you weigh, John?" Billy shouted. "I should've asked that before we took off."

"One eighty-five."

"Ah shit. Okay, just hang on."

They rolled another five hundred feet before the ground started to drop away, climbing slowly, and once above the trees flanking the interstate, Billy gently banked the plane to almost due north.

"You're my first passenger in this plane, John. I'd prefer somebody lighter for that."

"You want to back out of this?"

He knew it was the wrong way to ask the question; it came out as a challenge to play chicken rather than an offer to follow Billy's best judgment. *Dumb thing for a commander to do at such a moment,* John thought, but as he looked over Billy's shoulder, he caught another glimpse of a helicopter, this one a Black Hawk sweeping low above the old Blue Ridge Parkway, flaring and settling to land.

The plane bounced as they passed Allen Mountain to their right, the turbulence catching John by surprise. As an officer in the army, he had spent hundreds of hours in choppers, but this was actually his first flight in a small aircraft like this since childhood, and he was beginning to regret his rash decision to take a personal look. But he was committed now.

"Look, Billy, if you think the turbulence is outside what this old bird can handle, turn back at your discretion."

"Yes, sir." There was a bit of a chuckle. "But don't say I didn't warn you. We'll have to circle a few times; with you in the backseat, climb rate is only several hundred feet a minute, and it's nearly five thousand feet straight up."

Fifteen minutes later, by the time Billy had completed the second full turn, circling over the North Fork Reservoir, John was firmly clutching the barf bag and wiping the sweat from his brow. He knew he was about to let go, but at least the air at six thousand feet was actually chilly this morning, which helped a bit. Coming out of the long, sweeping turn, Billy announced they were just above the level of Craggy Gap but that he'd like to get another five hundred feet altitude before venturing closer. The turbulence was indeed bad, and John could sense Billy tensing up with each sideways, up-and-down jolt from unseen winds that rattled the plane, at one point lifting John out of his seat and then slamming him back down a second later.

"Well, we're certainly shaking out the G stress-load testing for real," Billy gasped after one hammer-like shock. "Just did it with sandbags piled up on the wings when on the ground before. Guess we'll find out for real if that replacement wing will fold up."

"Thanks for sharing that," John gasped, as he sealed up the barf bag he had just used.

They were running a mile or so south of the gap, and John could clearly see black-clad troops on the ground along the parkway, the helicopter that had carried them lifting off and heading back toward Asheville.

There were people on the ground other than the ones in black uniforms, half a dozen at least, and as they flew closer, John could see they were down, not moving, and then the realization hit. They were dead.

"Damn it," John whispered.

"What? Reivers? So what?" Billy responded in the casual tone of someone who had seen bodies and fighting before. For that matter, all of them down to four years old had seen bodies lying prone and motionless like that, twisted up into impossible contortions with blood pooling out beneath them. The troops on the ground, a team of eight from the looks of it, gazed up at them, one of them raising a weapon to his shoulder and pointing it in their direction.

"Don't shoot, damn you," Billy said, and a second later, he nearly stood the plane on its starboard wing, in an evasive turn, zigzagging back and forth.

Someone was by the side of the man who had raised the gun, motioning at the plane. The weapon was half lowered but still poised toward them.

"Go over the gap, down there!" John shouted, pointing to the north-side slope of Mount Mitchell where, half a dozen miles away, the two Apache helicopters were circling in a long oval pattern, lifting up at one end in a near-vertical turn, coming about, and then sweeping back down.

"They're shooting the crap out of something down there," Billy announced and pointed, but John did not need to be told. He could see the trail of gun smoke streaming aft of the helicopter. He had seen it often in their mad rush into Iraq during Desert Storm, driving past the twisted, torn wreckage of a convoy of Iraqi vehicles, bodies within cut to shreds by the deadly twenty-millimeter rounds of the chin turret and side-mounted miniguns.

Down at the base of the slope of Mount Mitchell, there was a secondary explosion, a vehicle igniting, an old RV that appeared to lift off the ground, a fireball erupting, most likely its propane tank blowing.

They were still several miles out, and John now guessed that this was in fact the same encampment site he had been dragged into as a prisoner. So contrary to what Burnett had said, they had not pulled up stakes. Moving a camp like that would drink up a lot of gas, and Burnett had rightly guessed that John had dampened down the calls for a vengeance raid.

"If only we had those Apaches when facing the Posse, it wouldn't even have been a fight!" Billy exclaimed. "Seems like a waste of good ammo on a bunch of junk vehicles."

A couple dozen fires were burning in the clearing below. The second helicopter began its strafing run, no longer aiming at the vehicles but instead at a stretch of woods several hundred yards east of the clearing, and a few seconds later, John could see a couple dozen people sprinting out of the woods, breaking cover, running across a road.

"Jesus Christ, those are kids!" Billy cried. "Look at them."

The attacking helicopter yawed slightly, its rounds stitching the road, bodies tumbling, bursting, going down into twisted heaps.

"John, what in God's name are they doing?"

"Killing people," John said coldly.

Its run completed, the helicopter banked up and away to the north.

"Ah shit, we got company!" Billy cried.

John turned to look straight ahead and barely had time to cry out as the first helicopter, which they had lost track of while watching the attack, was now coming straight at them, at eye level. There was that frightful split second, which John had faced several times before in his life, when he figured that all was finished and he was about to die.

Billy slammed the L-3 hard to starboard, and the helicopter shot past them.

"That son of a bitch was playing chicken, and I blinked, damn it!"

"Here comes the other one!" John shouted. And indeed, the second one was closing in, gun turret swiveled toward them. A quick burst of tracers shot across in front of them fifty yards ahead.

"Damn him!"

"He's warning us off, otherwise we'd be dead now!" John shouted.

"Hell with this. I'm turning back. First time I ever get shot at in the air, and it's by my own side, damn it!"

"Billy, you got one of those signal-to-ground streamers in the back well?"

"Yeah. Why?"

John turned, having to unbuckle his seat belt in order to lean into the storage well, and he pulled out a six-foot-long, bright-orange streamer, tearing off the rubber band so that it would unravel. He fumbled in his pocket. *Damn it, no pen!* "You got a marker pen back here?"

"In the side pocket well, with the maps. A grease pen."

"Fine. Now I want you to turn about and fly straight over where those vehicles are burning; edge it in alongside the woods. It'll be tight from the way that smoke is blowing. I don't want this going into the woods or the fires."

"What in the hell are you doing, John? That son of a bitch just fired at us."

"He knows who we are. He was trying to warn us off. He won't shoot us down."

And as if in answer, there was a popping sound, the aft overhead plastic window behind John cracking with a neat bullet hole through it.

"What the hell?" Billy cried.

"Ground fire, that's all. Just keep weaving!"

"Oh shit, great!"

The first helicopter was back, slowing as it came up along their portside wing. John could clearly see the gunner looking at him, turret swiveling to point straight at them.

John held his hand up and actually waved. The gunner just gazed at him, looked forward, another warning burst in front of them. John grabbed the head of the streamer, braced it on his knee, and quickly jotted a note on the streamer. *Forrest, it wasn't us. John M.*

It had struck him that the survivors below, who had without doubt been watching every move of his community for months from atop Craggy Gap, had most likely seen the first flight of the L-3. There was a chance the reivers might link his town's ability to fly with this attack. If he had stayed well clear of it all just now, chances were their rage would be focused on Asheville. But flying over like this, he had to make it clear that though the town's plane had been seen in the middle of this attack, they had nothing to do with it. Otherwise, they might catch the blame for it with a murderous vendetta rather than just a food-gathering raid—that is, if any down below had survived this onslaught.

John held on to the end of the streamer and tossed the weighted head out the side window. Another shot fired from below hit the wing just a few feet from his face. He let the end of the now extended message streamer go and saw it flutter down to land by the edge of the woods.

"Okay, Billy, get us the hell out of here!"

John suppressed a yelp of fear as Billy stood the plane on its starboard wing and pivoted sharply, dropping the nose and then leveling out and skimming low over the trees, turning back toward Craggy Gap. One of the helicopters was again beside them, the pilot looking toward them, pointing at them, then to the southwest, back toward Asheville.

John shook his head in reply, pointing due south. There was a tense moment, the gunner looking at them again, chin turret swiveled. John kept pointing south. The helicopter sped up a bit and then swung in front of them, Billy cursing loudly, swerving to the west as they were hit by the turbulence it kicked up. For several minutes, it was a game of cat and mouse, the helicopter repeatedly trying to force them to follow its lead.

"Okay, Billy, act like we're going along!" John shouted. "We're too low yet to climb over the mountain anyhow."

"Thank God you finally got some sense, John," Billy replied as he turned on a heading toward Asheville, pointing straight ahead to the watching gunner, who nodded a reply and repeated the gesture that they were to follow him back. The two helicopters backed off slightly to a hundred yards out, the three aircraft beginning to climb to clear Bull Gap, which was half the altitude of Mount Mitchell and an easy enough ascent for the L-3. The turbulence picked up severely as they cleared over the south side of the mountain and began to descend into the Swannanoa Valley. John could see home eight miles or so to the east, Asheville looming up straight ahead.

As they reached the eastern end of town, one of the choppers edged back alongside the L-3, the pilot pointing toward the parking lot of the long-abandoned and burned-out mall. Their operational base was apparently set up there; both of the Black Hawks were on the ground there. Parked nearby were half a dozen trucks and an equal number of Humvees. A couple of military fuel bladders, each capable of holding a thousand gallons, were deployed out, the Black Hawks apparently being loaded up again.

One of the helicopters edged in closer, the pilot motioning down to the parking lot. Billy vehemently shook his head. "That guy's an idiot if he thinks I'll put this girl in there. I might be able to land, but there's not enough room to take off again."

Billy pointed to I-240, motioning again and again, circling the road at five hundred feet until the helicopter pilot finally relented and nodded in agreement.

"Billy, you know what to do. If we land there, this plane, all your hard work, belongs to them forever after. Act like you're setting up to land. How good are you at tree hopping?"

"Used to love it, but then again, no one was shooting at me for real."

"Your call. You're the pilot in command."

"Well, damn glad you finally realize that, John. Make sure you're buckled in tight and hang on. You still feel like puking?"

John chuckled. "Been there, done that. Then I was so terrified back there I forgot about puking again."

"Just don't mess the plane up now."

Billy turned the plane where Interstate 40 merged with 240 and started to drop as if setting up to land. Just as he passed the abandoned Walmart to his right, he shouted for John to hang on. He slammed up to full throttle, pushed the nose forward, and dived, skimming over the store's parking lot and going under a power line, a move that left John speechless.

"Always wanted to do that—no FAA now to take away my license!" Billy laughed.

It was eight air miles back to Black Mountain, but it turned into nearly fifteen as they played cat and mouse with one of the Apaches that took off in pursuit after them. The helicopter was just as maneuverable as they were with the added advantage that it could come to a complete stop and hover if necessary. It was up to Billy to outnerve that Apache's pilot, and John wondered if the pilot of the helicopter pursuing them was just being an annoying bastard or if maybe he was actually having a bit of fun with this game of who could outfly whom.

By the time they reached Swannanoa proper, John knew that it was turning into something more than just a game. The Apache pilot was getting increasingly aggressive, with Billy pushing the edge of sane piloting in response. He started to line up to go underneath a highway overpass, John finally asserting himself and shouting for Billy to break it off.

Skimming only half a dozen feet above Interstate 40 for the last few miles, the helicopter circled wide and came across their front, the pilot half saluting them, but Billy returned the gesture with finger extended as he instantly pulled full back on the joystick and clawed for altitude, the plane shaking violently from the rotor downwash that would have slammed them into the pavement if he had not reacted.

"I think that bastard was trying to crash us at the end!" Billy shouted.

John did not reply. With the tension of the last hour at an end, he finally relaxed enough to reopen the barf bag and let go for a second time. There was a crosswind as they came in to touch down, Billy tensing up as much as when dodging the helicopters, landing with portside wing down low and rudder in the opposite direction, the plane coming down a bit hard and then rolling out. A couple of cars were parked on the westbound side of the highway, one of them Ed's much-battered patrol car, the other Maury's Jeep.

They rolled to a stop while still on the highway, Billy popping the door, staggering out, and walking around the plane to look at the bullet hole in the wing and the one through the cab farther aft, which had shattered the overhead window. Then, like John, he just leaned over and vomited. "Damned if I ever fly you again, John," he gasped.

Leaping the highway crash barriers, Ed, Danny, and Maury approached the two, all three shouting questions as Ed grabbed hold of John, who was definitely shaking from the experience. He well understood now a conversation shared long ago with a general who had been a veteran, first wave in on Omaha Beach, and from there led his battalion all the way to the Elbe in 1945. He had once asked his elderly friend what was the most frightening moment of the war, and the general laughed, saying he was trained for Omaha and too busy on the beach that day trying to bring order out of chaos to be scared, but the time he had gone up with his recon pilot, the experience had scared him half to death. Though frightened by the game of chicken with the helicopter pilots, John was now furious, as well.

Ed was still holding him by the arm. After all the noise, shouting, and confusion, it was hard to sort out what the police chief was saying, and then he caught it. "Fredericks wants to see you now, John."

John nodded. "You're damn straight he does, and I want to see him now!"

Twenty minutes later, they pulled into the parking area in front of the courthouse, John having quickly briefed Ed on what he had seen and what happened afterward.

They got out of the car and headed for the courthouse entrance. The same sergeant who had hassled John on an earlier visit was out front and came toward him as if waiting to strike. John slowed and glared at him coldly. "Son, either you get the hell out of my way or you're going to quickly find out if that gun of yours is for show or not."

The guard hesitated, and John stepped around him.

"Bullshit trooper," John snapped as they continued on. "No guts when facing someone really pissed off."

"Keep it calm, John," Ed whispered.

"Not after what I just saw," John snapped.

They stepped into the cool darkness of the courthouse. The fluorescent lights were off this morning. Another security guard blocked their way as they came into the foyer.

"Your weapons," he snapped as a preemptive order.

"Yeah, right," John growled, reaching into his pocket, pulling out a pocket Ruger semiautomatic, and slapping it on to the table. "Careful, son. It's actually loaded."

The guard glared at him but said nothing then turned to Ed.

"Like hell," Ed announced loudly, his voice echoing in the foyer. "I am chief of police of my town, and for fifteen years, I've walked in and out of here and never surrendered a weapon unless going into a courtroom. So like hell, son."

He started to step around the table, and the guard stepped back, unclipping the safety strap of his holster.

"Listen, boy, you are an amateur," Ed snarled. "If I wanted you dead, you'd already be before the devil or Saint Peter. So just leave your gun in that holster."

"Sir, step back three feet, turn around, and keep your hands over your head."

"Go ahead and try it." Ed was actually grinning. "I was sick of your type before the war, and I'm doubly sick of you now."

"Sir, I will shoot to disable you."

"Oh, really? Go ahead, damn you!"

John began to step between the two.

"Charlie, back off." It was Dale, storming out of his office with two security guards in tow.

The guard looked away from Ed, and John's friend laughed. "You village idiot. Wrong move, Charlie. Bang-bang, you're dead." Ed was holding up his empty hand, forefinger pointed at the guard, thumb moving like a gun hammer.

One of Dale's guards did have his gun out and drawn in reaction to Ed's gesture, and for a frightful instant, John thought Ed was a dead man.

Dale actually came to a stop, letting the guards move in front of him.

"Everybody just freeze!" John shouted, and his command voice was firmly in place, echoing in the cavernous foyer.

All looked to John, except Ed, whose hand was not on his holster but only inches away with the safety strap unbuttoned.

"Now everyone work with me, and let's calm down. Mr. Fredericks, please ask your personnel to relax. Ed, can I have your permission to remove your weapon myself and put it on the table?"

"Go to hell, John."

"Ed, please, let's defuse this calmly. Okay, my friend?"

Ed continued to stare intently at the guard who had drawn a weapon but finally nodded in agreement. John stepped up to his friend, deliberately letting the jumpy guard at the front desk and the ones now blocking off Dale from harm see him draw Ed's weapon out with thumb and forefinger and place it on the table next to his Ruger.

There seemed to be a collective sigh of relief, and Dale stepped around his two guards. "John, can I see you in my office?"

John and Ed fell in behind Dale, Ed looking back over his shoulder menacingly at the two security guards who followed them all the way into Dale's office. The guards stood unmoving until Dale finally gave a nod of dismissal.

"Don't let the door hit your ass on the way out," Ed quipped as the two exited.

"Damn it," Dale snapped as soon as the door was closed. "I got enough trouble around here today without you two pulling that scene out there."

"*Us* pulling it?" Ed replied hotly. "I've been chief of police for fifteen years. Rules were I kept my sidearm in the building. Hell, there was even an incident in here some years back where folks were damn glad I was armed. Only time I was to disarm was when I went into a courtroom to testify. I'll be damned if some black-uniformed rent-a-cop orders me to disarm and is so damn stupid I could have blown his ass away in response."

"And you two would have been dead," Dale retorted icily. "Those two you just insulted are trained security specialists, and they know their business."

"Your personal bodyguards, Mr. Fredericks?" Ed cried.

Dale was silent.

"Well, if they're so damn professionally trained, they forgot something." Ed reached down and lifted up his right pant leg to reveal a Ruger like the one John had strapped to his ankle. "Some frigging security, Dale."

Dale gazed at him coldly.

"So do I keep it, or do you call your goons?"

"I suggest you leave this meeting now," Dale replied, and there was a flicker of a smile, but John could see the coldness behind the mask.

"And if I say no?"

"I'll have you escorted out. The rules here are now firm. No firearms carried into this building."

"Then call your goons, and let's see what happens."

"Oh, for God's sake, Ed," John interjected. "Let's all cool it down here. We didn't come here to argue about the policy of carrying in this building. Ed, there are bigger fish to fry at the moment."

"You telling me to leave, John? Is that an order? Because I'll be damned if I part with my ankle shooter now."

John put a reassuring hand on the shoulder of this man who had stood by his side through two long, terrible years. "Ed, for the sake of the moment, as a favor, please go along with it."

"That was our problem before the Day. Just go along with it. It was always 'just go along with things' as we kept stepping backwards, and look where it landed us." As he spoke, his gaze was fixed firmly on Dale.

Dale did not move, but John could see his eyes going wide, features paling. "I will call my security team in ten seconds," Dale replied.

"Oh, now the threat to bring in the gestapo."

"The what? How dare you!"

"Ed, please cool off," John whispered, trying to sound reassuring. "Please help me with this."

There was eye contact, and Ed finally nodded and without a word turned and walked out of the office, slamming the door hard.

"He's a hothead, John."

"He's saved my life more than once. He helped keep our town together, and frankly, he had every right to be pissed off just now."

Dale opened the cabinet and motioned to the bottle of scotch. "I think we could both use a drink after this."

John shook his head in refusal.

"John, this country is still at war, and some rules have to change. For the security of this building, no weapons except by designated personnel is now firmly one of them."

"Rules changed. Like killing innocent civilians?"

"Sit down, John. You've had a hard day."

"You're damn straight it's been a hard day after what I saw a few hours ago and what your hotshot pilots pulled on me after that."

"I heard you were up in that plane. Why in God's name did you go up and stick yourself into the middle of that fight?"

"Because it bordered territory I feel responsible for. That's why."

"A bit of advice. There are times when a man in our position has to learn to delegate. And second, as a military man, you should have immediately grasped it was a military operation under way, and to go sticking yourself smack in the middle of it was foolhardy, and you know it."

"A military operation authorized by you?" John asked coldly.

"John, regarding you. Thank God my pilots are well trained. One of them radioed in about your plane, and I ordered him to hold his fire. Otherwise, they were about to dump you out of the sky, thinking you were one of the gangs we were taking care of today."

"Gangs?" John exhaled noisily. "Have you debriefed your pilots yet? Have you looked at the gun camera footage?"

"No to the first question, other than a brief radio report, and as for the second, we don't have gun camera footage anymore."

"Why?"

"Because the equipment doesn't exist. We're cobbling aircraft back together once they are shipped back here to the States, and as quickly as we get them flying, they're dispatched out. Gun cameras are just about the last damn thing we worry about as long as the machine flies."

"Well, I wish to God you rethought that one."

"Why?"

"Because when I wandered on to the scene, it wasn't that those hotshots were tearing up some vehicles belonging to gangs and murderous thugs— they were strafing the woods where noncombatants, women, children, and old people were hiding." He paused, forcing himself to calm down, to shift out of an emotional response, to fall back on to the long years of training to be dispassionate, in control of himself. He took a deep breath. "I witnessed the last firing run. The pilot lit up a stretch of woods, and a couple dozen people, many of them obviously women and children, broke cover in panic. They were gunned down without mercy."

"How many?"

"A couple dozen, at least. Nearly all were hit."

Dale took that in, again putting fingertips together in the shape of an inverted V, chin resting on the tips, looking pensive. "Hmm. They didn't report that."

"What were their mission orders? But before that, why the attack in the first place?"

"You didn't hear?"

"Hear what?"

"A supply convoy running from here up to Johnson City was hit just north of Mars Hill. Two of my people dead, half a dozen wounded, one ve- hicle destroyed. That was yesterday afternoon."

"Mars Hill—that's in Madison County. Word is that the border reivers up there are an entirely different group."

"How do you know that?"

At that moment, he felt it best not to elaborate too much. "Dale, I've been dealing with these issues for two years. You've been here how long? A month?"

Dale did not reply.

"May I suggest you get a better feel for who is what before you start send- ing out strike missions. There's a nut job over in Madison and down into Haywood County who claims he talks directly to God and gets his march- ing orders from him, and that includes killing. They were the ones who most likely hit your convoy. Even with that in mind, is an attack on your convoy justification for slaughtering dozens of civilians in reply? How can you be sure you even were hitting the group that attacked your people on the highway?"

"Damn sure." Dale's tone was getting sharp, disturbed that his judgment had been challenged. "I had a drone up to check it out before we went in."

"You've got drones?"

"Of course we do. Did a survey several hours after the attack on the highway—spotted a couple of vehicles heading from the direction of Mars Hill straight back to the encampment I ordered to be attacked today. It was and is intended to be a message to all in the region that, henceforth, official federal operations and convoys are not to be harassed. It is a necessary message to everyone if we are to restore order in my district."

"But no confirmed identification that it was definitely them?"

"John, are you trying to defend these people?"

"No, Dale," he replied quietly, making direct eye contact. "But what I can confirm is that I saw your people gun down innocent civilians."

"If they are running with the reivers, they are not innocent civilians. If innocent, they'd have come out of the backcountry long ago, registered for rations, lived in safe areas as designated by the government. The army unit that was here before me put out that appeal, and I've done the same thing. Therefore, after they hit my convoy, I saw that as justified reason to send the strongest possible message that things have changed around here."

"Dale, your people were shooting up civilians. They are people who were living up there before the war, and those that are left see it as their land still. And the fact that this drone of yours—which apparently has video equipment while your helicopters do not—spots two vehicles is slim evidence to me. These people are far too savvy to pull a hit on a convoy and then be spotted two hours later."

"I made the decision and stand by it." He paused. "Though I should have given you a call to get your view since you seem to know these reivers a lot better than you let on."

"You implying something?"

"Well, it is curious that you get taken prisoner by them, and four days later, you come walking out of the woods as if nothing had happened."

"What are you implying, Dale?" John repeated, this time more forcefully.

"Just that it was strange. You should have filed a report with me about what happened while you were their prisoner. It seems a lot more transpired than you let on in our last conversation. Otherwise, you would not be defending them now." He paused. "Did you strike any deals with them?"

"I didn't receive any memo from you that henceforth I was to report all activities to you."

"I am the representative of the government here. If you had been more forthright with me, maybe what happened today could have been avoided."

John glared at him without responding to this classic maneuver to transfer responsibility and guilt if something went sour.

"Yeah, the reivers over the mountain from me are a tough bunch, but they're mostly into raiding for food, gas, and whatever they think they need. Yes, they've killed, and we've killed some of them, but outright murdering for a pig, a bushel of wheat, a few gallons of gas . . . that's not their style or mine. Taking on an armed convoy sounds more like the reivers farther west following one of those nut jobs than the ones north of me who I have found are mostly folks just trying to survive, the same as you and me." He paused for a moment. "In spite of our differences, I still see them as Americans."

"And I see them as what you locals here call reivers. They got a hundred different names for them around the country, but they all come down to the same type, and one of my jobs is to either bring them back under legal control and compliance with the law or else."

"Or else what, Dale? And while we're on that, what is this rumor about the release of neutron bombs for use within the continental United States?"

"The situation in some urban areas is beyond retrieval. But come on— to actually use them? We both know the game of threat, and that's all I can tell you." Dale sighed and extended his hands in a gesture of frustration. "But back to here and now. I'd rather try persuasion than what I had to do this morning."

"Twenty-millimeter miniguns are a rather permanent and uncompromising way of persuasion."

"Damn it, John." Now his voice was cold. "Have you been anywhere outside of your small town since the Day?"

John gazed at Dale, a bit startled after all their previous conversations—which, though grating at times, reminded him of a typical smiling mid-level bureaucrat in the prewar world. "Go on."

"I sure as hell have—or at least seen reports you never laid eyes on. Every major city in America is down, most of them abandoned wastelands, those left controlled by ruthless mobs like those you call reivers. More than fifty thousand of them control Chicago and have declared a dictatorship under some whack job who calls himself 'the Great.' The prisoners he takes? The lucky ones get thrown off the top of the old Sears Tower. The rest he crucifies along the shores of Lake Michigan. If those at Bluemont do decide to pop a neutron bomb, I hope he's the first to get it. Reports of human sacrifices with some cult running Saint Louis—another good candidate for a nuke. You want to see the reports, John, of what's left of our country?"

John shook his head sadly. "No, I was 'just here,' as you put it. But it was my town that stopped the Posse, and I saw more than enough of the depravity of men when turned desperate."

"That is what I am fighting to prevent here," Dale replied sharply.

"So perhaps using nukes in the cities and machine-gunning kids and women here is part of the reconstruction program now?"

"John, it was a combat situation, and you, veteran of Iraq, should understand that. They reported taking heavy ground fire and had only seconds to react. Air to ground, mistakes happen, including fratricide at times. You know that."

"Train your people better," John finally said coldly. "I could see they were kids, women, old folks—so could your pilots."

"Precisely why we need people like you, John, to see to things like that."

"And because you wanted to talk with me, you ordered your pilots to harass the crap out of my pilot and damn near kill us when we finally tried to land."

"John, I felt it essential to talk to you at once regarding the whole affair. My pilot got a little carried away, that's all."

"And once we landed in Asheville, you'd confiscate our plane?"

"Of course not," Dale replied smoothly as he reached back behind his desk for the bottle of scotch and offered John a drink.

"I'll pass for now. My stomach is still a bit queasy from that ride."

Dale poured himself another shot and put the bottle back into the cabinet. "I'll look into it and get back to you. These kids that fly can get wired up, and we both know that. Most likely, he figured your man could handle that final pass after the chase he had been led on, nothing more."

"Tell him to stand well clear next time."

"Or what will you do?"

"It's already been a long day, Dale. I didn't expect the ride I went on this morning. I think it's time I went home."

"Sure, John." Dale extended his hand. "No hard feelings."

"For what happened to me, no. But what happened to those civilians, yes—damn hard feelings. I'd like it thoroughly investigated. And believe me, Dale, this is from long experience here. Whether they did raid that convoy or not is no longer the issue. They will seek payback, and you just triggered a war along your northern border."

"Well, if they come at you, call me at once."

John just nodded.

"And, General, when can I announce your acceptance of a commission and get plans rolling for you to head up to Bluemont?" He asked the question as if the conversation of the previous twenty minutes had never taken place. "Arranging a transport flight just doesn't happen overnight."

"Let's talk about that some other time," John replied.

"Why not now?"

He fixed Dale with a hard stare. "Because frankly, I just don't feel like discussing it at the moment after what I saw this morning."

Without waiting for a reply, John headed out the door, stopped at the desk to pick up his Ruger, and found Ed sitting in his patrol car, still fuming mad.

"Ed, I don't want to hear a word, not a word for right now. Let's just get the hell out of here."

CHAPTER TEN

He sat in the town hall for most of the day, refusing to discuss anything of what happened in Asheville or during their earlier flight. Billy, however, had eagerly shared what he had seen, and the entire town knew. Reactions were mixed. Some were furious over the harassment of their flight, but many shrugged off the fate that had come down on the reivers.

John requested a town council meeting for noon, and behind closed doors, he reviewed what happened both in the air over the reivers' camp and in his subsequent meeting with Dale.

"I have a confession to make now," he finally announced. "While being held by the reivers, I struck an informal truce. No killing raids. Neither of us can fully control everyone when it comes to stealing some pigs and chickens and running stills up in the mountains, but their leader—his name is Forrest Burnett, ex-military, wounded vet who fought in Afghanistan—struck me as an honorable man. We shook hands to just back things off between us."

"I know Forrest," Ed interjected. "Lived up in Burnsville. A good kid. One of my cousins married into the Burnett family, so I had some dealings with them. Heard he volunteered for the army right after 9/11. Got shot up real bad in Iraq, or maybe it was . . . Afghanistan . . . anyhow, one of those places. Came back a bit messed up. I mean, his wounds—an arm and an eye—would mess up anyone, actually. Folks said it was that posttrauma thing. Couple of brushes with the law after he got back, but cops up there understood where he was coming from and tried to keep it light on him. So he's running the reivers?"

"It's what he claims," John said.

"A question, John," Reverend Black interjected. "When you got back, why didn't you just tell us?"

"My mistake. I realize now I should have been up front. Given that the Stepp family lost several in skirmishes with them, I knew that saying I had negotiated something of a truce wouldn't fly well with folks living over in the North Fork. Some might have seen it as me trading off for my own freedom. I was planning to go up there personally, talk to the families one-on-one, and smooth things over before going public. Things just got ahead of me."

"Hell, John," Maury interjected, "when you're a prisoner like that, anything is pretty well fair game as a promise to get you out as long as you don't compromise the military code. We know that."

"Forrest had promised that they were going to decamp and head north, which obviously he did not do. As we know, the Stepps did launch a vengeance raid over the weekend and walked straight into an ambush, and the reivers let them off with one man slightly wounded. Even the Stepps admitted the whole crew could have been wiped out but were let off. Maybe I screwed up by not going up there sooner. I'm sorry." John shrugged and looked out the window, no one speaking for a moment.

"So you figured on letting things settle down with these reivers," Reverend Black interjected to break the embarrassed tension, "and then go public, is that it? We stay on our side of the mountain, they stay on their side?"

John looked back over his shoulder and breathed a sigh of relief with the nods of agreement. More than once in the previous two years, he had held information back at times until he felt the timing was right. This had been a tough one, though. The reivers were viewed as outlaws in the old, literal sense of the word—that they were outside the law and thus fair game.

Ed, who had until this morning been the most passionate about confronting the reivers or any other raiders without remorse or mercy, had now changed his tune completely upon learning that a kin through marriage, a vet, was running the outfit. He spoke for several minutes of old friends he knew on the north side of the mountain—that they were decent, hardworking folks and perhaps the last year had been a tragic misunderstanding that could have been solved by talk rather than raid and counterraid.

"So what are you suggesting we do?" Reverend Black asked, looking to John and then Ed.

"I'm waiting for that right now," John replied. "I set up a signal with Forrest if either of us needed to parley. That was the three American flags I asked Ed to raise this morning down at the old auto dealership, and I'm waiting for a response. I hope to God he is okay and he does respond and not believe that we had anything to do with that attack. If he's dead and one of his hotheads takes over, and there were more than a few of them, we are in for a bad summer of raids. Even if he is alive and decides to fight rather than talk, it is going to be a bitter summer along the mountain slope. We're going to have to mobilize up a fair portion of our trained personnel for full-time border guard duty who should be working in the fields and rebuilding things instead. But the position I know they observed us from, Craggy Gap, there is now a squad of troops from Asheville up there now. So I don't know if he got the signal or not—or the one I dropped from the plane."

"Why did they deploy troops up there?" Maury asked.

He had not really thought about that up to this moment. Did Fredericks known more than he'd let on about what had happened between John and Burnett and for the time being was cutting communications between the two? Was there a plot within a plot on this one?

"I have no idea," John replied. "Perhaps they saw some of the reivers posted up there and went for it." He looked around at the group, which remained silent for several minutes.

Finally, it was Maury who spoke up. "Let's just keep it in here for now. There are a lot of conflicting issues to think about with this. Folks are still not settled on the draft, John, though most assume you are taking the commission to help out at least half the families, and there is a lot of grat-itude for that. Regarding the reivers, everyone knows about what hap-pened, and everyone is assuming a vengeance raid is coming. What is your suggestion?"

"For right now, we put all our reaction squads on full standby and move one up to near the reservoir to help keep an eye on the Stepps and their property. Other two squads here. Rest of our formations at the college, here in town, and in Swannanoa on notice for immediate mobilization. If I was Burnett, saw our plane, saw the troops up now at Craggy, I'd assume that we had shafted them over and it's time for payback. I just pray that he sees our signal and asks for a parley first." He looked around the room, and there were nods of agreement. "Okay, let's get moving on this. I'm heading down to the old Ford agency. You can call me at the hangar, which is just a few yards away."

He went out to the Edsel, Makala insisting that she drive, and once the doors were closed, the tension that had been between them since the dinner meeting with Fredericks let go. John sat silently as she roundly cursed Fredericks, John's decision to accept a commission, his foolishness for going into a combat area in a plane not yet fully tested out, and finally back to the point that it seemed like he was going through with the commission. There were less-than-veiled implications that she thought that the concus-sion really had addled his thinking.

They were parked by the flagpole for a good half hour before she was finished with the chewing out. He had learned that at such moments, si-lence was best until she was finished.

He didn't get time to reply, as Billy came running down from the hangar shouting there was a call from the town hall. John actually felt relief that he was getting out of the Edsel, and then he followed Billy up to the hangar and came back less than a minute later.

"Makala, would you mind driving me up to the reservoir?"

"What?"

"There's two men there, sent by the reivers. Forrest Burnett survived the attack and wants to meet."

"And you are crazy enough to go personally up to meet him?"

He leaned across the seat and kissed her on the cheek, a gesture that she did not respond to. "Am I supposed to send someone else in my place?"

She gave him a sidelong glance and then continued to stare straight ahead even as she started the car. "They damn near busted your skull, you still have a concussion, and you almost got shot by them this morning and nearly shot again by those stupid pilots. How in the hell do you think I'm supposed to react, John Matherson?"

He forced a smile. "Just saying you love me would be sufficient for now. We can argue about the rest later."

"You can be a manipulative bastard at times," she snapped. With tires squealing, she turned on to State Street, heading west, and a moment later, her hand slipped into his.

John stopped at the border watch station, which was positioned at the face of the reservoir dam. The two young guards gestured up the path.

"They came out about thirty minutes ago from right there. One had a white flag; the other handed me this, sir."

The young man, just a few years earlier a freshman in one of John's history classes, handed him the message streamer he had tossed out of the plane. Just below his scribbled message was a one-line reply: "Meet today, now. Otherwise, all bets are off. Forrest."

"Anything else?"

"They backed off. I tell you, sir, I feel like I'm in a crosshairs if I stick my head back up, and so are you."

John was glad he had convinced Makala to wait back with the car and had told the reaction forces to stay there, as well.

"You did good, son." John took the streamer, waved it above the top of the sandbagged watch station, and then just stood up.

"Sir? They can drop you. I swear they've got us scoped in."

John tried to smile, stepped out the back of the bunker, remaining up-right, and started to walk up along the west shore of the lake along the old maintenance road. Barely out of sight of the bunker, he heard a rustling, and two young men—lean, tough looking, one cradling an M4, the other a deer rifle with a high-powered scope—came out from hiding and wordlessly pointed for him to continue up the road. They walked thus for a half a mile or so, passing the north shore of the lake, the road turning, getting steeper.

"If you guys are proposing I walk all the way back to your territory, I hate to say it, but it's not going to work. My head is killing me, and I just don't have the wind I once had."

They didn't speak, just gesturing for him to continue on.

Have I just made myself a prisoner again? he wondered. For that matter, the two could have been a couple of survivors who had gone rogue and decided to kill for vengeance, and he had just walked into their trap. Burnett had most likely been killed in the raid, anyhow. If so, he truly felt a fool. Makala was right; of late, he was taking too many risks, and he wondered why he had lost an earlier sense of instinctive caution.

And then he reached a bend in the trail and stopped dead.

It was a caravan of half a dozen four-wheel-drive vehicles, all of them painted in camo pattern. How they had managed to negotiate the long-neglected fire road was beyond him. As he approached the lead vehicle, he saw Forrest sitting in the front seat, face ghostly white.

"Forrest?"

"Yeah, Matherson. I don't have time to bullshit around. I need a favor, a big favor."

"What is it?"

"Take a look in the beds of these trucks."

John nodded and realized he didn't need to look; he could hear them—children crying, the moaning of people in pain, the all-so-familiar sounds of this world they lived in.

John looked into the bed of the truck that Burnett was in. Half a dozen kids were crammed into it, all of them wrapped with bloody bandages. Several were sobbing, looking up at him with wide, terrified eyes. A boy of about twelve or so, yet another victim of war, just gazed at John. He was cradling a toddler, and the way the little girl hung limp in his arms, John could see that the child was dead. Blood was dripping off the open tailgate of the truck.

John did not even bother to go look at the other trucks. He pulled open the passenger door.

"Move over, Forrest."

"Yeah, but give me a second. I got one in the gut this time, damn it."

John grabbed hold of him and saw the bloody bandage—thank God on his left side; at least his liver was intact—and helped him ease over. He looked at the driver, who was gazing at him coldly.

"Drive, damn it!"

"Where?"

"Into town, you idiot. The hospital. Now drive!"

The road was rough, rubble strewn, in places nearly washed out, the truck swaying and rattling, and John winced with each bounce, the kids in the back crying in anguish. They finally reached the level stretch of the maintenance road and began to speed up, and then the thoughts struck him. "Slow down here. Let me get out!"

"Why?" Burnett gasped.

"You want to get shot again? I got a reaction squad down there. We weren't sure of things. I'll signal for you when you can start up again."

"You playing me straight, Matherson?"

"May I burn in the hell if I'm not," he snapped, jumping out of the vehicle and running down the road until he knew he was within sight of the observation bunker. He raised his arms, waving them. "We got vehicles coming in. It's okay!"

He looked back to the lead truck and motioned it to come on. Nearly out of breath, his cracked rib sending a wave of pain coursing through him with every breath and every step, he ran ahead of the vehicle, leading the way. He saw several of his reaction troops stepping out from concealment, weapons raised, and he motioned for them to lower their rifles.

Reaching the bunker, he jumped in and grabbed the phone, cursing under his breath, waiting for Elayne to pick up at the switchboard.

"This is Matherson!" he shouted. "We got a lot of wounded coming in. They're okay—friendlies. I want the alarm sounded. Get medical personnel over to our main hospital, and open it up. Move it. A lot of these wounded are kids. Get on it!"

He hung up and ran back to the lead truck. His lead reaction team had slung their rifles. A couple of them were crying as they looked into the flatbed.

"Damn it!" John shouted. "You're all trained in first aid. Stop crying, get into the vehicles, start helping these people. A couple of you stand up where you can be clearly seen as we drive into town, so everyone knows it's okay."

They started up again, John back in the lead truck alongside Forrest, heading down the road, past the entryway to a long-abandoned vacation development. He saw the Edsel ahead in the middle of the road. *What a difference a week makes,* John though grimly. Last time, he had come limping back, head nearly busted open, and now he was leading this pathetic caravan of wounded from the very group he had just tangled with, and had tangled with before throughout the last year.

John leaned out of the window, waving frantically as a signal to Makala standing in the middle of the road. The four trucks carrying the backup reaction squads, which someone had apparently thought to mobilize out when he had gone off on a walk into the woods with two armed men, were behind her. He told the driver to stop fifty yards short, and he got out. Gasping for air, he walked this time rather than run, which might just set off one of his troops who might get trigger-happy, his running misinterpreted as a signal that he was trying to escape.

"Makala, I need you here now!" he cried.

She came running up to him. "Jesus, what is it, John?"

He pointed to the first truck and now emotion took hold. "They're casualties from the air strike this morning. I've called ahead; the hospital is getting ready now to take them in. Just go look, look at what was done to them!" There was a bit of a hysterical edge to his voice. After so much death the last two years, he had wanted to believe that they were coming out of it. But now there was more and yet more, and the shocked boy holding the dead girl was just too much.

Makala went past him, up to the side of the truck, and looked in. Her hand went to her mouth. She stood in numbed silence for several seconds and then looked back to John. "Any of you with the reaction force who I trained as medics, up here now. Move it! Move it!" She climbed into the back of the flatbed.

John went up to the side and looked in at Forrest, who was obviously struggling to hang on to consciousness. "Thank God you came to us, Forrest. Hang in there, trooper. We're getting your people into a hospital now. Just hang in there."

Forrest looked up at him with a slight nod and reached out with his one hand, which was covered in blood. John squeezed it and turned to run to his car, shouting for the drivers of the trucks to clear the road and fall in at the rear of the convoy.

John swung the cumbersome old Edsel around and hit the gas, flooring it down the winding road straight onto Route 70, a good four-lane road that made the last few miles relatively pain-free for the sufferers who had somehow survived a grueling, torturous ride of over thirty miles on gravel- and rock-strewn fire lanes to swing around the Asheville troops deployed at Craggy Gap.

Hitting the main road, he slowed long enough for the six trucks that belonged to the reivers to gain the main road behind him, and then he floored it again, black exhaust bellowing out of his cracked muffler. Racing into Black Mountain, where the road began to narrow down as he passed the abandoned pharmacy, he laid on his horn. He could hear the old-fashioned siren that had been installed at the town hall wailing. People residing in the center of town were pouring out, running toward their mobilization points, which meant all doctors and nurses, either those licensed before the Day or trained as such afterward, were dashing to their assigned positions. Few knew yet what was actually going on, and at the sight of the old familiar Edsel, many turned and looked, shouting questions to John as he roared past them, narrowly avoiding T-boning an old pickup that came racing up out of Cherry Street, heading for the fire station. John cursed madly at the fool, actually thinking for a few seconds as the truck swerved to get out of his way that he would find the driver later and personally kick his butt, and then caught a glimpse of the driver—it was Reverend Black. John continued to honk and pointed for him to follow.

The hospital—which, a year and a half earlier, had handled over a thousand casualties after the battle with the Posse—was in the once-thriving furniture store across the street from the town square. After the last of the casualties of that battle had been moved out, Makala took charge of scrubbing the building down, stockpiling some supplies and then sealing it up if ever there were another mass disaster, epidemic, or battle. John skidded to a stop in front of the hospital, pointing for the truck behind him to stop in the street.

Makala leaped out of the back bed of the truck before it even came to a stop, and John could see she was crying. She was normally so professional as a nurse—now acting as a doctor—and trained to deal with such things, but the months of relative calm had taken the hard edge off her, as well.

"Merciful God, John, most of them are just kids."

He could not reply, and then in another second, as if a switch had been thrown within her heart, she became the professional again.

"Triage right here!" Makala shouted. "Someone get the triage bag inside. Bring it to me, and get a table out here. Move it!"

Several of the recently trained combat medics with the reaction teams were out of the vehicles, racing to follow her orders. She looked back at the line of trucks, her voice carrying as noisy engines were shut off.

"Everyone listen to me!" she shouted. "No one move for a moment, please! Those of you who drove your wounded in, we're going to offload your people as quick as possible, but wait for my personnel to do so. We don't want to make any injuries worse than they already are."

John felt as if he was slipping into shock, even as his wife took charge. *Injuries worse than they already are?* These people had endured a hellish exodus of thirty miles or more. It wasn't like each had been carefully strapped to a backboard seconds after getting shot and airlifted to a rear-line hospital.

Doc Wagner pulled up on his motorcycle and jumped off, running to his assigned position in the main clearing room inside the hospital. At the same time, he saw his dentist come running up the street from his office, carrying a precious jar of ether in one hand and a medical bag in the other, sprinting into the hospital to join Wagner.

Makala looked at the crowd of onlookers who were gathering in the park across the street but—as had been drilled again and again—were keeping clear. In the parking lot outside the town hall and fire station, troops were falling into place, having responded to the siren but not sure yet if this was a call for military action or not.

John caught the eye of Grace Freeman, the second in command of the campus company, as she came running down the slope from the town hall, seeking orders. He shouted for her to order all medics down to the hospital and for half the troops to deploy along the road and form a cordon to hold onlookers back, with Ed helping to take charge of that detail.

Makala was already calling for volunteers as stretcher teams, and several dozen citizens responded to her cry, being directed into the hospital and coming out a moment later carrying litters.

"Listen, people!" Makala shouted. "I want a medic to check each casualty before you try to get them on the stretcher. Any suspected back injuries, I want fully trained medical assistants to handle moving them onto a backboard rather than a stretcher. Now move it!"

John went up to the first vehicle and leaned in. "Come on, Forrest, let's get you inside."

Forrest smiled weakly. "Hey, Colonel, or whatever the hell you are now. Good officers go last, remember?"

John swallowed hard and took his hand again, noticing how the bandage was soaking wet with blood that was obviously still leaking out of his wound. He debated for a few seconds whether to just override Burnett and call that they had a priority two and move him now. He looked over his shoulder and saw that Makala and her assistant were at work, the first stretcher case coming up. As she had done at the battle with the Posse and had not done since, she was back into the most dreadful of roles—deciding who would receive immediate treatment, who would have to wait because their wounds were not life threatening, and who would be set aside to die because the time spent to try to save them could save half a dozen others instead or because they were simply too far gone for any help in this world other than a prayer from Reverend Black.

The triage bag held several old-fashioned tubes of lipstick. Makala pulled one out and opened it up. The first stretcher case was a girl of eight or so, stoically silent but clutching a blood-soaked bandage just below the knee, right leg leaning out at a drunken angle with a shard of bone visible.

She wrote the number two on the child's forehead, immediate priority to ensure no arterial bleeding. With what they had available for orthopedic reconstruction, chances were the child would have to endure an amputation later on.

Next one up was a girl in her twenties, broken arm dangling but with very little blood. Makala offered a few words of solace. The young woman grimaced and nodded, and Makala wrote the number one on her forehead. She would have to wait perhaps hours before someone would actually treat her, but she was in no danger of bleeding out or dying of shock.

On another stretcher was a young boy, naked, curled up nearly fetal and crying like an injured kitten as Makala gently tried to pry his hands free from his wound, calling on a couple of the nurses who had just come running in to help her. She gazed silently for a few seconds and then kissed the boy on the forehead, telling him that they would soon make him well, and then John saw her write the number three on his forehead. He was beyond help. What meager supply of painkillers and anesthesia they had on hand would have to go for the number twos facing surgery. She stood back up, wiping tears from her face and motioning for the next case, again a number one.

Then came the boy that John had seen in the back of the pickup truck, the toddler hanging limp in his arms. All those around them and those gathered across the street fell silent at the sight of him as he stoically walked up to Makala, and all could hear his appeal.

"Lady, it's my little sister. She's all I got. Rest of my kin are dead. Please make her better."

Makala knelt down by his side and made a gesture of looking at the toddler, taking off the scarf she had been wearing, opening it up and starting to cover the terrifying, gaping wound in the little girl's side. She had bled out long ago and had died, her features a ghastly gray.

"Can I hold her for a second and check her?" Makala whispered.

"Yes, ma'am."

Makala took the body, cradled it, and then went through the motions of acting like she was checking her as she wrapped her scarf around the child's torso to cover the wound. "I think she's a real special case. What's your name, son?"

"Vincent McNeill, ma'am."

"Vincent, let me take your sister to the doctor as a special case so he can help her now. Is that okay?"

He looked at her wide eyed. "Really? Will she be okay? She got real still as we were driving over the mountains."

"We'll treat her special, and you are a very brave young man. Now follow my friend inside, and the doctor will help you with your arm." Makala looked at her assistant. "Two, and *S* for shock. Put him to the front of the line. We still have a few valiums. Get one in him."

The young woman, another of John's old students, fought back tears as she tried to lead the boy inside, but he suddenly turned to look back. Makala was drawing her scarf up to cover the little girl's pain-distorted features in a desperate attempt to conceal the ravages inflicted on the little body of his sister.

"No!" Vincent screamed, and then he collapsed, sobbing.

"Get him inside now!" Makala cried.

Several from the crowd broke through the barrier line to rush over and help pick him up. Makala stood silent, clutching the child, breaking down sobbing and then looking at all who were staring at her.

"Is this child our enemy?" she screamed. "God forgive us. Dear God!" She sobbed as hugged the dead child.

John let go of Burnett's hand and ran over to her. Reverend Black was by her side, and after a brief struggle, the minister relieved Makala of the burden she was holding, John kneeling down to embrace her as she sobbed uncontrollably, pulling her in tightly into a soothing embrace.

Black, holding the child, looked about at the gathering. "I beg each of you to pray. Pray for these people, and pray that this type of madness ends." He slowly walked into the hospital carrying the dead child. John held Makala tightly.

"Oh, God, John, I thought of our Jennifer. That boy had the same look in his eyes that you did when she died. Why did they do this to these people?"

He looked up. The stretcher cases were lining up, waiting, wounded crying, while across the street, many were openly crying, as well, many on their knees in prayer. It was as if a vast wave of empathy had enveloped the town, and the pain of those viewed just hours earlier as foes had become their pain and source of anguish, as well.

"Makala, you have to get back to it," he whispered soothingly, rocking her back and forth as if comforting a child. "You are trained for this. I'm not."

She drew in a deep breath. "Help me get back to my feet, John," she whispered. She stood up, took a deep, shuddering breath, nodded, and then pushed him away. The assistant who had helped the boy into the hospital was back out, sobbing.

"Focus, Gina. You got to focus on the moment," Makala implored her. "Now help me."

John stepped back as Makala picked up the lipstick tube she had dropped and walked up to the next stretcher, leaning over. "Two. Try to get blood type." The next one was walking wounded, an elderly man, his skull cracked so wide open that John could actually see his brains. Makala wrote a three on his forehead and motioned for someone to guide him inside. The next case was a near-skeletal man in his twenties, gut shot and unconscious, obviously a three. The next case was another two; someone had roughly stitched up the carotid artery, but it was leaking blood and appeared ready to burst. The next one . . . then the next one . . . and the next one.

John stood by the truck, Burnett's hand in his. Burnett's voice was weak, telling him what had happened, denying they had anything to do with the raid on the convey. A couple of his people coming back from a trading mission with the cultlike reivers over in Madison County had witnessed it from afar and then ran for their base.

"Why didn't you move as you told me you would?" John asked.

Burnett laughed weakly. "You know how much gas it takes to move half a hundred vehicles and four hundred people fifty miles? Looks like a scene from one of those damn disaster movies. I was bluffing you, John, to see what you'd do. Then we heard those helicopters coming in, and I knew the shit was in the fan."

John could only nod.

"Thought you were in on it at first when I saw that plane. Yeah, we seen you fly it for the first time last weekend. Craggy Gap used to be a damn good perch to spy on you folks. So, yeah, I thought you were in on it. Your plane take a shot or two?"

"A couple. One damn near blew my head off, hit just behind me."

Burnett chuckled weakly. "One-armed but still good with a carbine."

"That was you?"

"Damn straight. But glad now I missed. Glad you dropped that note. Took a chance on believing you. Saw the way those Apaches bird-dogged you, as well."

He slipped off for a moment, John squeezing Burnett's hand with his right and reaching out with his left to check his pulse. It was weak and fluttery; he was definitely slipping deeper into shock. Throughout all this, the driver was silent, and John suddenly realized that he was wounded as well and had just quietly passed out.

Christ, these people are tough, John thought. Ragged and malnourished, they had struggled to survive. Black Mountain had managed to pull together in fair part because tactically it was a superb location, with only one pass in and one out, surrounded by mountains. But these people had somehow managed to survive while actually living in the mountains, narrow valleys, and hollows in the same way their ancestors had etched out a living 150 years earlier.

"Medic over here!" John shouted.

Burnett stirred. "Officers last, Matherson."

"To hell with that!"

A stretcher crew came up to John, and he pulled the door open and went around to the other side and opened the driver door and then recoiled. The driver's left side under his armpit was drenched red, blood actually trickling out from the open door and splashing on to John's boots. The young man had silently bled to death while waiting his turn in the old tradition of women and children first, and John wanted to scream with frustrated rage. How he managed to drive with that kind of injury was beyond comprehension. A stretcher team came up, and John shook his head.

"This one's dead." He sighed.

He went around to where Burnett was being eased out of the pickup truck and onto the stretcher, protesting weakly for the rest of the kids and women to be tended to ahead of him.

Makala came over to his side, looked down at him, drew a pair of scissors out of her pocket, and cut the bandage off, revealing a jagged hole in his left side just below his ribs. She sighed and raised the lipstick tube.

"He's a two," John snapped, and she hesitated. "It's Forrest Burnett, and he's a two."

Forrest, eyes going out of focus, looked up at him. "Officers last," he whispered.

"Yeah, Forrest, you're the last case, now relax." He turned his gaze back to Makala. "A two, and do it now."

She nodded. "You ex-military?" she asked, leaning down and shouting the question.

He stirred and smiled.

"What's your blood type?"

He looked confused.

"Trooper, what's your blood type?" John shouted.

"A positive." Then he slipped out of consciousness.

"Get him into surgery now!" Makala shouted. "Prep him. I'll go into him if need be if no one is working on him once I'm done out here."

John looked at her and nodded his thanks.

"Spleen's most likely blown apart," she whispered. "He's lost a lot of blood, John. We should just let him go."

"Would you have three years ago? Before everything fell apart?"

She did not reply. Outwardly, she was doing her job, but he could see she was in shock and struggling to barely maintain control.

John turned to face the silent crowd, many of whom were still praying. "People, listen up. We need blood donors now. Most of you know your types. O positives over here. A, B, and AB form separate lines off to the right. Tell the medic what type you are, and that will be marked on your forehead. We need blood now!"

Half a hundred onlookers stepped forward, and again, a lump was in John's throat. It took him back to the terrible days after the Posse fight, when those near death from malnourishment volunteered blood as a final gesture before dying.

Makala cleared the last casualty, an elderly woman who simply smiled at the lie that three meant they'd see to her soon.

"You're a good soul, nurse," the old woman whispered, "but I know I'm seeing my Maker today."

John looked at her and sighed. It was Nurse Maggie, who had checked his concussion. He went up to take her hand, and she smiled wanly.

"So it's you. Thank you for what you're doing for us," she said.

He could not reply.

"John?"

"Yes, ma'am."

"The trucks have to go back. There's fifty or more wounded waiting back at our camp. We sent the women, children, and badly hurt ahead first."

"I'll see to it."

"Don't trouble about me," she whispered, and then the stretcher-bearers took her off to that place that all knew and whispered about with dread— the dying room.

He looked at Makala, who came up and leaned against his shoulder as he put his arm around her.

"Fifty-three packed into those trucks. Nearly half were threes, after that trip. If I could have gotten to them in that first golden hour, we could have most likely saved all but three or four of them." A shuddering sob ran through her. "Oh, God, I could have saved that little girl if I had gotten to her quick enough."

He started to break, as well. And his Jennifer could have been saved if only they had some more vials of insulin. He knew hundreds were watching, and again he was forced to act his role, drawing in a deep breath. "We got to get to work," he whispered to her, and she nodded.

"Sorry we argued, John."

He kissed her on the forehead. "My fault, and I love you."

She looked up and smiled. "Same here," she managed to whisper, and then she drew in a deep breath and backed away from his embrace. "I got to scrub up." She again sounded all business. "You really want that Forrest character saved, don't you?"

"Hell yes I do."

"Why? He damn near had you killed."

"Because I respect him, that's why. He did what he had to do, same as I did. And besides, if for nothing else, he gave an arm and half his sight for this country long ago."

She kissed him lightly on the cheek. "I want to save him too. I'll try my best."

He started to step back.

"John, you have to call Memorial Mission. They have enough anesthesia and antibiotics and painkillers on hand now, and we need all of it. We got enough hoarded up to help with the primary surgeries, but to ease the suffering of the rest, there just isn't enough to go around. We're giving aspirins out as a primary painkiller, at least to those who aren't bleeding heavily. We have those batches of antibiotics made up from silver, but I'd prefer some stronger stuff, especially for the gut shots."

"I know; I was going to make the call. But you know what that means. Release of medications requires authorization, and Asheville then knows we're taking care of the wounded."

"Yes, and tell that son of a bitch to come down here and take a good look at his handiwork."

She kissed him again on the cheek and then went into the hospital. John looked at those of his community, many of them in line to donate blood.

"I need volunteers. Drivers for these trucks. There's more wounded back in their camp, and we got to get them in here. Two medics to go with each truck. I'll drive one of them."

Ed came up to his side, shaking his head. "John, you're staying here."

"The hell you say."

"John, be a leader again. You put your ass on the line once too often for any of us to sit back now. The shit will most likely hit the fan with Asheville when they find out what we are doing. Besides, I hunted the woods since I was a kid and know every fire lane and back trail. I'll lead them back."

To his surprise, a couple of the Stepps came forward to stand with Ed.

"Sons of bitches," one of them growled. "Someone tangles with someone we have fun squabbling with, it isn't right with us. Okay to shoot at each other man to man, but kids and women like this? We know the trails better than anyone. We'll get their wounded out."

Before he could argue any further, Ed and the Stepps were getting into the trucks, and volunteer medics were piling into the backs, calling for additional supplies of bandages, clean bottled water, and gear.

John stood silent, filled with pride, and watched them head out.

CHAPTER ELEVEN

"John, they're coming."

It was Maury, who was up at the Swannanoa roadblock just west of Exit 59.

"What do they have?"

"He's in a Humvee, a deuce and a half with a lot of heavy weapons on board following, and that's it."

"Okay."

"John. He's got a helluva lot of backup just over the hill. I got a watcher down at Exit 55 who just reported in. A dozen trucks, half a dozen Humvees with Kevlar armor curtains, and get this, they got a Bradley."

"A what?"

"You heard me straight. A Bradley, a big honking armored personnel carrier. My watcher says a kid came in on a moped by back roads reporting that all four helicopters are prepped, warmed up, and ready to lift off. He's loaded for bear, John."

"But just the Humvee and one truck for now?"

"That's a rog, John."

John could not help but smile. Fredericks was at least showing some nerve.

"Okay. No hassles. Let them through."

"You sure, John?"

"Time to talk, Maury. It's just time to talk and pray it stays that way."

"It's your call."

John put the phone down and smiled at the town council gathered in his office. "We wait here," John said. "But please, let me do the talking. Okay?"

He looked straight at Makala, who had not had a wink of sleep since the morning before. She had a lab coat on, and it was splattered with blood. He gently tried to suggest that she change but was met with silence and knew not to press the issue. Reverend Black was hollow eyed, obviously in shock. More wounded had come in just before dawn, brought back by Ed and his volunteers, most of them lightly injured, the trucks having been sent back, using town gas, to pick them up, parents of children who had been brought in with the first load making the trek, and Black had to perform the grim task of telling a number of them that their child was dead. The trucks also had four dead on board, and only five vehicles had returned. Slipping across the parkway at night, the last vehicle was ambushed, apparently by troops from Asheville, and it burst into flames, one of the Stepps dying in the ambush.

The way Reverend Black looked at John when he asked that all hold back from the conversation was chilling. Black had been a pillar of strength for the community ever since the Day. He had never fired a shot in anger, but he had presided over hundreds of funerals, he and his wonderful wife, Portia, taking the nursing and then physician assistant courses. They had bravely stood in with every emergency, included the dreaded epidemics that had swept the country in the year after the collapse, and were the moral strength of the community. The two of them were all so crucial to John and his family in the weeks after Jennifer died, stopping by every day to pray with him and offer comfort. And now John could see that long-suppressed anger was about to boil over.

He heard the vehicles pull up into the parking lot and now looked at Black. "Please, my friends, this might be our last chance to talk this thing out and prevent more killing, so let's stay calm," John whispered as he stood up to look out the window.

Dale, wearing his usual blue blazer, shirt, and tie, was getting out, and a dozen troops, heavily armed, were piling out of the back of the truck. John had wisely ordered his troops to form a cordon on the far side of State

Street, directly in front of the hospital, so the parking lot was empty of any armed response and the potential of an immediate confrontation. There was enough rage on his side that he feared a Lexington Green incident of someone intentionally or accidentally triggering a firefight.

The troops with Dale looked around cautiously, a sergeant, yet again the same one John had taken such an intense dislike for, was leading them. Dale said something to him, and the group spread out a few feet and formed a cordon around the two vehicles. Dale waited for a moment, as if expecting a welcoming committee or some sort of formal greeting, and it began to drag out.

"Oh, damn it, this is ridiculous." John sighed but did not move. Then finally, in frustration, he rapped loudly on the window. Dale looked over to him, and John just pointed to the front door, motioning for him to come in.

Dale, features flushed, waited another minute and then finally came into the building. Elayne, remaining at her switchboard, stuck her head out the door of her work cubical. "You want John? He's in his office down that way," she announced icily as Dale came through the door, and then she returned to work, doing exactly as John had ordered—acting as if nothing out of the ordinary was transpiring with Dale's visit.

John had left the door cracked open, and Dale pushed it open, coming in. "John, just what the hell—" He fell silent at the sight of the rest of the town committee silently gazing at him. "I'd prefer we talked alone."

"What you have to say to me you can say to them, as well. They're the town council and have a voice in all decisions here."

"This is private between us."

"It became very public yesterday."

"I insist we talk alone, and I'll have time later for the rest of you."

"It doesn't work that way here, Dale." There was a moment of silence, and then John smiled. "And besides, if I take that commission, it will be these folks here who will be running this town after I'm gone. And if Ernie Franklin is on the town committee after I've left, you'll really have your hands full."

Dale took that in as several of those gathered actually chuckled, the tension easing for just a brief moment with mention of Ernie, who had insisted upon sitting in on this meeting whether he was on the town council or not.

"We have to talk about that commission now, too, John. A lot has happened since yesterday morning. And I think that topic is still private between you and me."

"Yes, a helluva lot has happened, Dale. So either we talk here in front of the leaders of this community or not."

Dale stood his ground and then slowly reached into the breast pocket of his blazer, drew out an envelope, and handed it to John. "Open it." He spoke the two words as a command.

John took the envelope and then deliberately placed it on the desk, his eyes not leaving Dale. "From you, Bluemont, or whom?" he asked.

"I suggest you read it, Mr. Matherson. Then we can discuss the contents."

John made a very deliberate display of waiting another minute before finally picking the envelope back up and opening it. He scanned the note and tossed it on the table. Reverend Black picked it up.

"That is a legal document for your eyes only, John, not a community gathering."

"It is an arrest warrant for capital crimes," Black announced, holding the document up. "A list of names, twenty or more, with Forrest Burnett at the top."

John looked back at Dale. "You've got to be kidding, Dale. Capital crimes? Under what authorization?"

"Federal law. They raided interstate, which, even by prewar standards, brought in the federal government. They have been a threat to national security since the start of the war, and they have killed federal officers, two of them last night. That's grounds enough."

"I'll grant the first point, perhaps, but you damn well better be able to prove it was them."

"When you were their guest, they talked about raiding into Tennessee, and that is interstate."

Just how in the hell did he know the content of any conversation while he was being held prisoner? Had Fredericks infiltrated spies in all along and knew everything that had transpired?

"My response. Last night, a column of wounded refugees was ambushed. A truck with wounded aboard, several of them children driven by a member of my community on a mission mercy, was ambushed. Your people fired first; those in the trucks had a right to defend themselves from unknown assailants."

"Not by the report I got," Dale snapped back sharply. "They ambushed my personnel and attacked first."

"What kind of trial will these people get?" Black interjected.

Dale smiled. "Same one you folks gave to the Posse, the drug thieves, and others."

"That was martial law," John retorted. "We're moving away from that."

"I have not," Fredericks replied. "The federal government is acting in proper accordance in a time of national emergency. I represent that government and demand that those listed be turned over immediately. If not willing to comply, you know what that means."

"Whose law?" Black shouted, standing up. "You call machine-gunning kids an act of law?"

"Tragic collateral damage," Dale said.

"Go down to the hospital, damn you, and take a look at your collateral damage!" Black cried, and for an instant, John feared the minister was about to rush Dale. In all their years of friendship, he had never heard Black use a foul word or see him so publicly lose his temper. The man stood there trembling with rage, Makala standing up to come by his side, whispering for him to sit down.

"I *am* going down to the hospital," Dale said, features still fixed in a smile. "I know you have Burnett and most likely others on that list. I'm putting them under arrest and taking them back to Asheville."

"No, you are not," Makala said, emphasizing each word sharply, coldly. "They are under my care, and I will not release them, and I say that as director of public health and safety for this community."

"And this community is under my authority, Mrs. Matherson." Dale pointed at the document Black had tossed on the table. "You have been properly served with notification. I thank you in advance for your cooperation, and now I have to do my duty as the federal official in charge of this administrative district." Without waiting for a response, he turned on his heels and walked out of the room without a backward glance.

His departure left all of them stunned, eyes shifting to John. "Stay here," he snapped. "Reverend, call Maury at the checkpoint at Exit 59. Tell him to report if their helicopters start to lift off, and if so, send someone out to tell me. The rest of you please stay here."

His voice carried a sharp authority, and Black got up as John sprinted for the door, Makala and Ed moving to restrain him. John hated the fact that he was trailing behind Dale, who was already out the door and shouting orders for his squad to fall in with him. It was the wrong display in public for this moment, but he had to stop him now, or in another minute, there would be a fight . . . and killing.

John came up to his side and actually grabbed him by the shoulder, the gesture causing one of Dale's security team to raise a weapon.

"Step away from the director!" the man shouted. "Do it now!"

"So is that your title with them?" John asked sharply, glaring back at the black-clad trooper, that same damn sergeant.

Dale, startled with how John had grabbed him, tried to shrug John's grip off his shoulder, but John did not let go.

"What's it going to be, Dale?" he whispered softly. "Either I'm dead in five seconds and the rest of you are dead in ten seconds, or you and I talk this out."

John let his glance shift to the roof of the fire station to their right, which adjoined the town hall. A dozen of his best reaction team were up there, weapons half-raised but not yet aimed.

"You drop me and, orders or not, they'll slaughter all of you. Now I am going to take my hand off your shoulder, the two of us will smile as if there's been a foolish misunderstanding. We walk down to the park, sit down, and have a friendly little chat. It's your call, Dale."

And for the first time, John could see hatred in the man's eyes. After weeks of cat and mouse, of the smooth trained government bureaucrat, the darker gaze of the political maneuverer and climber had flashed out for a brief instant.

"Sure, John," he whispered. "Now get your hand off my shoulder, you son of a bitch."

John smiled and let his hand drop.

Dale looked at his troopers, and the threat clearly registered that for the survival of all, a little face saving had to be played out. "Just a brief misunderstanding. Everything is fine now," he said with a smile.

John returned his gaze to the roof of the fire station.

"Grace, let's not overreact. I want you and your troops to sit down and relax."

He chuckled inwardly as the sergeant heading Dale's security team looked up and for the first time actually noticed that a dozen trained killers, who two years earlier had been typical college students, were staring down at them with weapons raised.

"Your sergeant really is incompetent," John whispered. "He has a shoe-size IQ, and he'd never have made it when I commanded troops, other than perpetual KP and toilet cleaning."

John pointed toward the garden-like town square a few dozen yards away and started for it, Dale waiting an instant and then walking briskly, not wishing to lose any more face, coming up to John's side and keeping pace with him. John motioned to a wooden bench and sat down without waiting for Dale.

"I can signal for someone to bring us something cool to drink, if you need it after that," John said with a smile. "No booze, though, only water. But if you need some of what the locals call white lightning, I'm certain we can find a mason jar."

The sight of the troops up on the roof when Dale had foolishly believed he had the upper hand in the middle of what indeed was John's town had obviously shaken him. It showed John as well that this man had absolutely zero field experience. If it had been his intent to kill Dale, the entire unit would have been wiped out in a few seconds, as easily as swatting down a fly. His men might look tough in their black uniforms, but if they were indicative of what the so-called Army of National Recovery was made of, it was indeed a pathetic indicator. Up against a group like the Posse, they literally would have been dead meat for their dinner table.

Dale, obviously a bit shaken, unbuttoned his collar button and loosened his tie but then shook his head. "You didn't fall for a drink when negotiating with me; you think I'd fall for the same?"

"Just a friendly gesture in these parts," John said with a smile.

"You know I can't leave without Burnett and the others on the arrest list in tow."

"And you know I will not release them—actually, I should say in all honesty that the director of public health and safety, whose care those men are in, will not release them."

"Oh yes, your wife. So she follows every order of yours without question, I see. Or is it the other way around?"

John actually did laugh for real. "If only you knew." But his gesture did not break the tension.

"I have the arrest orders. They are terrorists, and you know it. You are harboring them, and in the eyes of the law, you know what that means."

"Terrorists, Dale? I recall before the war when it became politically incorrect to use that term when it came to *real* terrorists and ironically then applied to those who were not—and look at what it finally got us."

He gestured to the streetlight overhead, the burned-out bank at the corner, the world of silence, a nation with the electric switch thrown off.

Dale was silent.

"So is this the next step, Dale? Everyone who somehow survived the Day but is not in compliance with the central government will be branded a terrorist?"

"You had no problem executing over a hundred of the Posse. I heard their skeletons still litter what used to be a truck stop."

"You know damn well that was far different. They didn't even classify as human anymore. They were a satanic, cannibalistic horde gone amok, and it was kill them or be killed. And nearly all such have been wiped out since. Burnett and his people terrorists? Well, those screaming kids dying from gut shots that we took care of yesterday sure didn't look like terrorists to me. They looked like people to me who once were fellow citizens, not like the scum I was forced to kill."

"You and the border reivers have been at war with each other for over a year now, and one of my jobs is to clean them out. I thought you'd be glad to see me get rid of them for you."

"Merciful God," John snapped. "Was that the reason why? Kill them to impress me? My God, don't tell me that now."

Dale again said nothing.

"Or was it to intimidate all of us? You have the gunships, we don't, so it's time to obey?"

"It was an act of war, Matherson. We have to weld this country back together again if we are to survive. The Chinese are on our land, same with Mexico. What's left of Russia, with a nuclear arsenal aimed and the hammer clicked, is watching every move, and it better not be one of weakness. The only thing keeping them from finishing the job is our nuke subs sitting off their coast in the Arctic and Pacific. We have to show strength within, that we are willing to do whatever is necessary to pull this country back together, or else."

"Or else what, Dale?"

"The president herself said in the briefing to those of us being dispatched to reorganize the various administrative districts that we had an open hand to suppress any type of rebellion. We have a year to get the job done, or someone else will do it for us, and believe me, there are many who would be far more draconian than me."

John did not reply. The classic administrator told to do the job "or someone else will," and it was thus a lockstep to follow orders.

"The reivers, they were at war with you and then with me. So I fought war as I was told to do, the same as you did with the Posse."

"War? Yes, we've killed some of them, and they've killed some of my people, but they were not like the Posse, and I've come to realize that if anything, they were far more like us than some. Maybe if we had figured out how to talk a year ago, a lot of mistakes could have been avoided."

"And you'd have had maybe a thousand more to worry about feeding."

John nodded. "Maybe, but what's your answer? Kill them all, including the kids, and not have to worry about feeding them at all?"

"Either they come into observance of the law or there is no alternative any longer."

"I can't accept that."

"I *have* to accept that. Did you hear the news about what happened in Chicago? What about that?"

"Whoever was the dumb ass who sent half-trained kids in to fight there is an idiot, Dale. Just who in the hell is running this ANR, anyhow? For God's sake, it's an understanding going back to the Romans that it takes up to three years to train troops for that kind of fighting, and the schmuck running that action I bet wasn't with the kids who were killed or captured and then executed."

"That schmuck, as you call him, will be your commander," Dale retorted.

"If I enlist now."

Dale took that in and fell silent for a moment. "And if it is an order that you enlist immediately rather than a request as I first put it, John? Will you obey?"

"Is that a threat?"

"Not intended to be at all, John," Dale said smoothly. "But it is evolving out as reality now, and the reality at the moment is that I have an arrest warrant for Burnett and nineteen others for capital crimes, and I intend to see it carried out."

"And if I say that I will not comply, I am a terrorist, then, as well?"

Dale did not answer.

"So any order from on high, regardless of its moral worth, must be obeyed. Is that what America has really become? Did we let it slip away an inch at a time before we were attacked, and now we are finally driving straight off the cliff once and for all? When I was in the army and stationed in Germany just before Desert Storm, I met more than one man or woman who was called 'a good German.' When we did talk about the difficulty of the times they grew up in, they would admit that in the beginning their leaders did not seem all that bad. Oh yes, the Jewish issue was troubling, but no one figured it would really go anywhere serious. Besides, Hitler and crowd did promise social order, create jobs for all, and restore national pride and unity. '*Ein Volk, ein Reich, ein Führer.*' Is that what we are now, Dale?"

"What does that mean?"

"Look it up when you get back to your office, Dale, and then look in the mirror."

"I'm not liking the tone of this," Dale finally retorted.

John smiled. "Dale, you do realize I am holding all the cards at this moment? I cannot allow you to move Burnett. Makala dug a jagged piece of shrapnel out of his gut that shattered his spleen. How he even made it over the mountain is beyond me. That is one tough son of a bitch. He needed four units of blood. If he lapses into sepsis, he'll die anyhow. Makala is an okay surgeon now, but before the war, there'd of been a whole team working on that man. It'll be weeks before she releases him."

"Is it that you *cannot* release him or *will* not?"

"I don't see a difference at the moment."

"I do, John—a *big* difference. You tell me he can't be moved at the moment for 'humanitarian reasons,' and you give us both a face-saving out for the moment, and I'll go along with that. Nevertheless, the man is guilty; his case has already been reviewed. And I'll tell you right now, he'll be hung in front of the courthouse for his crimes along with the others on that list. But if you want to play a game for a week or so until he can be safely moved, I'll grant that to get us both out of this confrontation."

"Oh, I see. Summarily executed. Is that what we are, Dale?"

"You did it too, John!" Dale shouted, standing up so that the guards who had been waiting nervously up by the truck gazed at them intently. "The Posse, you give them a trial? So who in the hell are you to tell me what I can and cannot do now? I have an authorization signed by the secretary of National Reunification and countersigned by the president, and my job is to bring this district back in line to a level-one status. Burnett and his kind are finished. So either you join my team, John, or you know what I'll have to do."

John remained seated but was no longer playacting a friendly smile. "Fine, then, you've made yourself clear. But, Dale, you need a little bit more training on extracting your ass from a potentially fatal misstep. You are no longer in the halls of the White House or wherever you served, whomever you were assigned to. This is not some public relations job where you bullshit a stupid press corps and when the questioning gets too tough, you say time is up. You got twelve armed personnel fifty feet away, and though I think most of them are ridiculous, I don't want them hurt. But believe me, there's at least a hundred or more who are armed watching every move you and your troopers make, and they are ready to react. I want this to end peacefully, Dale, and you'd better want the same. First lesson of command, Dale: your troops come first, but if you are required to spend their lives, you'd better have a damn good reason for it and be the first one to go, as well. You willing to die today and have all your people killed in a vain attempt to get Burnett?"

"Why are you defending him like this, damn it? He'd have killed you without blinking twice a few weeks ago, and chances are, you'd have done the same if you'd had him in your sights when he was leading a raid into your territory."

"There used to be an old code of warfare, Dale. Hard to believe, a code, actual rules for warfare. Not the bullshit rules of engagement that tangled us so insanely in the Middle East and cost the lives of many a good kid we sent out. I mean the rules as they existed back fifty, seventy years ago."

"And is the history professor going to educate me?"

"You are damn straight I am, Dale, and in your exalted position, you should know them."

He sighed, shook his head, and motioned for Dale to sit back down, but Dale remained standing.

"An enemy on the field of action, it is kill or be killed, and that was Burnett and me just several weeks past. But then the next rule comes in, and in a more civilized age, most nations actually signed treaties that they would obey this. A wounded soldier no longer in action was out of the fight. He was not to be fired on. If captured, he was to receive the same medical treatment as one of your own. Some thought it was a paradox—try to kill him, then patch him up. But some saw it as at least trying to be civilized in the madness of war, to lessen its horrors, and I for one believed in it. I remember seeing a video on the computer, shortly before the Day, of one of our medics being hit by a sniper, wounded but still able to do his job. Minutes later, a couple of our troops dragged in the sniper who had hit the medic, and you know what he did?"

"Oh, let me guess," Dale retorted sarcastically. "He patched him up."

John nodded, and he felt a lump in his throat at the memory of that, of the pride he felt in the training of the medic and of all the troops he once served with. Had the last two years brutalized everyone to the point that the chopper pilots simply now fired on anything that moved? The thought was deeply disturbing.

"Burnett is my prisoner, and I gave him my word that he and those he brought in with him would be properly treated. He came to me for help after what you did to him. My community took him and those with him into our care without any conditions. To try to move him will kill him, most likely even before you can hang him. So the answer is not only can I not let him go, I refuse to let him go. I'll talk with you later about the charges against him and the others. Even if the charges are true, the gunning down of civilians who had nothing to do with the attack . . . in my world, we used to call that a war crime, Dale."

There was no response.

"Do I make myself clear, Mr. Fredericks? I see it as a war crime, I will report it as such, and if there is to be any trial someday of Forrest Burnett, a wounded veteran, formerly of the 101st Airborne, it will take place here in this jurisdiction and not Asheville, where I believe he will not receive a fair hearing."

"So you are going against my authority, then."

"I can't decide what you think."

"I thought I could trust you and work with you, Matherson. You had a chance for a job on a national level and could have made a difference there."

John did not reply.

"And if I come back with an order for you to report to Bluemont?"

"Dale, is that for your convenience, to get me out of the way as a troublesome thorn, to get shunted off into some paperwork cubbyhole? Has it even been the real thing since the first day you offered it?"

"You calling me a liar?"

"No, Dale, just asking a question any man has a right to ask."

There was no response.

"Dale, in about one minute, we end this one of two ways. You and your tin soldiers try to storm the hospital—and I promise you, you and they will not make it, though if there is shooting to be done, you will have to fire the first shot—or we make a show of it for the hundreds who are watching us that you and your men cannot even see, make a big show of shaking hands, and you get back in that Humvee and go back to Asheville. You do that, and I'll look deeper into the charges against Burnett's group and keep you informed of what I find as a face-saving compromise for you."

Dale looked back at the roof of the fire station where the rest of John's unit had squatted back down behind concealment, though Grace remained standing, M4 casually cradled in her arms.

John did feel a flash of sadness at the sight of her thus. She was a kid; this should be her senior year. In fact, graduation should have been taking place just about now. Instead, she was a hardened professional, veteran of the fight with the Posse and a dozen other smaller actions afterward. She had even dropped one of Burnett's group last winter when they were raiding for food, and she showed zero remorse about the girl she had killed who was nearly the same age as she. Yet again, such moments made John think of Thomas Hardy's poem "The Man He Killed." "I made the mistake of trusting you, John, when I came here."

"No you didn't, Dale. You thought you could bull your way through when anyone with real combat experience would never have walked into my kill zone."

"I'll remember that if there is a next time," Dale said while actually smiling, and his tone sent a chill through John.

Dale stood back up and actually put on the skilled bureaucrat's show of smiling and extending his hand, though when he clasped John's, there was no warmth in his handshake. "I expect you in my office in three days to report for duty," Dale said, again with that officious smile.

"What?" Now John was off guard for the moment.

"Forgot to add that in." Dale reached into the other pocket in his blazer.

"I'd advise you to do that real slowly," John whispered. "Some watching might think it's not just a piece a paper, and maybe, just maybe, you actually know how to carry a gun rather than a pen and paper."

Now there was a look of hatred, and John smiled.

Dale drew out a second envelope, held it up for a few seconds so anyone watching could see it clearly, and then made a formal gesture of handing it to John.

John did not comply by opening it. "What is it?"

"Your formal orders to report for federal duty in three days, John Matherson. It is no longer voluntary. You have been drafted, as well, for the good of the country. A transport is coming down from Bluemont for you. You have the choice of taking your wife with you or not, though I advise that you do, since the terms of the draft are for, and I quote, 'the duration of the national crisis as defined by the Secretary of the Office of National Reunification and the President of the United States,' so it could be for years. The second notice in that envelope is for the mobilization of fifty-six draftees, to be selected by you as your first official act as a major general in the service of the Army of National Recovery. Said draftees to report at the same time you do. I'm still willing to forego the other fifty-seven for the moment, so you can still play the hero one last time. I therefore expect you and your people in front of the courthouse at nine in the morning, three days hence. If not, you know the consequences." Dale smiled. "Show up, and I don't report this incident today. Don't show up, and you know the consequences. Ball's in your court now, John," he said, and without waiting for a reply, he headed back to the Humvee, actually waving in a friendly fashion to Grace and the troops on the roof of the fire station and then motioned for his own troops to get back in the truck.

The vehicles turned about, pulled out onto Montreat Road, and headed back to the interstate. John could sense a collective sigh of relief from the crowds that had gathered along the sidewalks in the center of town.

Clutching the envelope, he slowly walked back to the town hall, trying to act nonplussed, though that last maneuver by Dale had indeed put the ball back into his court.

Once inside the building, the town council swarmed about him, some slapping him on the back and bombarding him with questions, but Makala could sense something was still amiss.

John looked at Don King, president of the college. "I'll need Gaither Chapel this evening, Don. Let the kids up there know that all those who received draft notices are to report for the meeting. Let's make it for six while we still have plenty of light. Richard, could you go tell Elayne to call around town and let everyone who has a draft notice to please come to the chapel?"

Makala did not say a word. She knew him well enough that there were times it was best just not to ask.

CHAPTER TWELVE

John walked into Gaither Chapel of Montreat College, a place of so many beloved memories. Some of the weekly chapel services were a bit tedious at times; others were so moving they left him in tears, especially when Reverend Black—or his old friend Reverend Abel, who had died in the battle against the Posse—preached a service that could reach college kids and his intellectual soul, as well. There had been many a concert, recital, and guest lecture in it, and in the weeks after graduation each year, there was a flurry of weddings for students who had fallen in love, sometimes in the very classes he taught, in this cherished building. When the chestnut blight had hit the mountains in the 1930s, dying trees had been harvested off, the rich textured wood shaped into this building, right down to the pews. A group of chestnut enthusiasts would tour it every year, and as a historian, he enjoyed participating in their visit and hearing of their yearly pilgrimage to visit hallowed buildings like this one.

A month or so after the Day, it was the place where he had felt the first real stirrings of interest in Makala beyond that of gratitude for a nurse who had saved his life when he was hit with a deadly staph infection from—of all things—a cut finger. Elizabeth, holding Ben, was behind them. Grandma Jen walked slowly by Elizabeth's side; even then, she felt it necessary to walk with pride—erect, ramrod straight—and leave the cane in the car, though she would pay for it afterward with a painful backache. The chapel was packed with nearly all of the 113 who had received notices, as well as their families. John noticed Kevin Malady, the former head librarian who, due to his massive build and long black hair that was straight cut just above his shoulders, had the nickname Conan the Librarian. Kevin could, in happier times, even do a decent imitation of the famed actor—yet another icon of the prewar society that had disappeared, no one knowing of his fate.

John was startled when Kevin stood up, smiled, faced the gathering, and shouted, "Commanding officer present! Battalion attention!"

Those who had served in the Posse conflict and in the defense force afterward leaped to their feet. It troubled him that the display was taking place in the campus chapel, a place of prayer, meditation, and peace. He looked to Reverend Black for guidance in this, but even he was standing and smiling at John as he came down the aisle, motioning for him to take the podium. John stopped and asked him to first lead the gathering in a prayer, and after it was spoken, John stepped to the podium.

"Two traditions we have that we must never forget because it is one of the core values we believe in."

John turned toward the American flag, raised his hand, and started to recite the Pledge of Allegiance, and all joined in, some barely whispering the words in this time of confusion, others saying them forcefully. He had a terrible voice for singing, but Grace picked up the first words of the national anthem, and all joined in, John struggling to get through it since it hit him at such an emotional level. It always amazed him how some could be cynical about the song or would mock the fact that his community had embraced it with renewed vigor ever since the Day. For several months after 9/11, people heard it wherever they went, and then a cynicism seemed to take hold with some who mocked it and said it should be changed because it was too warlike or just expressed hatred of the country in general and turned their backs on any patriotic display. At least here, even in this current crisis, such had not taken hold.

The song finished, and John turned to face the gathering, scanning his audience for a moment, the upturned faces of kids who had sat in his history classes two years earlier, flashes of memory of so many who, in a different world, would have been standing here now or already graduated and getting on with their lives, buried instead up at veterans' cemetery.

For this meeting, so many members of the community had made the trek up to the college campus that it was standing room only, and at least a hundred or more stood outside in the parking lot, windows opened for a cooling evening breeze and so that they could hear what he was about to report.

John felt a bit nervous as he waited for the finish of the national anthem. Though he was a trained officer and felt he had been a rather good professor who knew all the tricks of public speaking and keeping an audience with him, what he was about to present to his neighbors and friends would be a bitter pill to swallow. It was not a rally cry to war, such as the one he gave when word arrived that the Posse was heading their way. This was far different, with so many shades of gray and not just simple black and white.

He looked to Makala and his family, who had taken seats in the front row, someone having saved them as a gesture of respect. He cleared his throat.

"My friends, I bring difficult news, and it is a time to make difficult decisions. I'm going to ask this of you. I'll say my piece, but after that, I am leaving so that you can freely debate things more without me present. I ask that our friend Reverend Black moderate after I leave."

He forced a smile and looked at Ernie Franklin and his contingent of family and kin, who filled a couple of pews. "And this time, a two-minute rule, Ernie, and no one can transfer their time to anyone else."

Ernie glared at him, but the gentle laughter that rippled through the room and even a scattering of applause with this decision finally caused Ernie to smile, stand up, wave an acknowledgment, and sit back down, shouting, "I've already passed note cards to others!"

John nodded and felt he had opened on a bit of a light touch to help folks settle down, and it was now time to dig in to the issues at hand.

"As all of you undoubtedly know, the head federal administrator based in Asheville, Dale Fredericks, was here this morning with an arrest warrant for members of the so-called border reivers, four of whom, including their leader, Forrest Burnett, are being tended to in our hospital. The warrant stated that they were guilty of capital crimes and under the current federal rules of martial law would almost undoubtedly face execution by hanging."

There was a murmuring in the audience, most reacting negatively but more than a few whispering that it was what the thieves deserved.

"I refused to comply, and feel I must explain my reasoning, though I know there will be repercussions for all of us. You all know I was a colonel in the United States Army prior to coming here. By the code of military justice, if enemy combatants surrender in the field, they are to be treated justly, and it is forbidden to inflict summary execution."

"Which is exactly what we should have done to those scum held at Gitmo!" someone shouted from where the Franklins were sitting, and more than a few nodded in agreement.

"We are not here to debate Gitmo," John replied, "but what happens in our own community, today. But let me add a second point. Burnett and those who came in yesterday were not captured. They were not attacked by us or taken by us in an engagement. I personally witnessed what happened, as did Billy Tyndall, who is sitting there in the back of this chapel, if you doubt my word. I felt it was a vicious, excessive use of force against a civilian encampment of people who were once our neighbors on the far side of the Mount Mitchell range—which, in the months after the Day, by necessity, we decided to seal ourselves off from since there was not enough food available even for ourselves.

"Yesterday, I witnessed fleeing children, women, and elderly being gunned down, and it sickened me. Those of you here who are veterans of our previous wars know that American troops, on the ground and in the air, went to extremes whenever possible—sometimes at grave and even fatal risks to themselves—to behave with honor and to spare innocent lives, even when it was for the families of enemies we fought.

"Later that same day, after witnessing the attack, I was summoned to a watch station by the reservoir and there met a convoy of vehicles, that many of you saw, bearing the wounded and dying of that attack. Forrest Burnett made the honorable gesture of surrender with an appeal for help, particularly for their children."

He paused for a moment in a flash memory of the young lad in deep shock, holding his dead sister. Makala told him earlier the boy had died during the night. His own wound was not truly fatal, but at times, shock went so deep that the will to live truly was gone. She wept as she told him and then stoically added that perhaps it was merciful that he had gone on with his sister, since their mother had died birthing his sister and his father had been killed in a clash with the reivers over in Madison County.

"He would have been a psychological case the rest of his life," she said, her voice suddenly distant and cold, hiding behind a professional demeanor. "Maybe it was for the best."

That now haunted him, as well, as so many deaths haunted him, starting with his own flesh and blood, Jennifer.

"If I did wrong," he continued, "by accepting their appeal for help and putting him and all those others under our protection, tell me now, and I will step aside."

It was Ernie whose voice carried through the chapel. "Okay, John, it was the moral thing to do. Yeah, you were right for a change."

After that endorsement, one of the few times Ernie had agreed with him publicly, any voices of protest, if there were any, remained silent.

"Thanks for that, Ernie," John replied.

"Don't expect it to become routine," Ernie replied. Again there was an easing of tension in the room.

John looked down at his notes. He felt what he was about to say next was so important that he needed something in writing to help guide him.

"Therefore, under the code I was trained to follow, I would not release those who came to us for protection to the federal authority who stated to me that the decision had already been made that those on the arrest warrant had been tried and would be executed."

No one spoke in reply, and there were finally nods of agreement with what John said. He looked about the room. "If anyone feels there is a need for a vote on this, speak up."

Folks looked one to the other, but no one stood, a few voices sounding out finally that nearly all were in agreement and to move on with things. That endorsement filled his heart with a deep satisfaction. In spite of all the horrors, his friends and neighbors had not lost their basic values of morality and fair play, some of the core beliefs that defined them as Americans.

"Thank you for accepting my decision," he finally continued. "Now to the difficult issue we face this evening and why I specifically asked that all who received draft notices should attend this meeting."

Now there was indeed a deadly silence in the chapel.

John reached into the back pocket of his jeans, pulled out a folded envelope, and drew out the papers Dale had handed to him in the park.

"This"—he held the papers up—"is a formal notice to all 113 who received draft notices early last week that they are to report in three days' time to the federal building in Asheville, where they shall be inducted into the ANR, the Army of National Recovery, and from there sent on to whatever training facilities and units as deemed necessary. Those who do not pass the primary physical shall nevertheless be retained for federal service as seen fit by the local administrator of our district. Those who refuse to comply with this notice shall be held in contempt of federal authority and face the full penalty as stated in Executive Order Number 1224A." He paused. "This means you shall be subject to arrest for desertion and face a military tribunal for treason, which can be a capital offense as defined in the Constitution of the United States."

And now the room was indeed astir, and Ernie was on his feet. "What the hell, John! And forgive me, Reverend Black, for blasphemy in a house of worship, but this is bullshit. We were told we had a month and that if you volunteered for service, the number to be inducted was cut in half to fifty-six. Just what in the hell are you telling us?"

John held both hands out in a calming gesture, but it took several minutes for the gathering to settle down.

"Ernie, you are right that if I volunteered, the draft for our community would be cut in half. I will not debate here and now the motivations behind that offer made by the federal administrator, Dale Fredericks, though for me, it was suspect from the moment it was offered. A draft quota is a draft quota. My identity is of course tied to this town—to you, my friends. Together, we forged our way through a terrible time. But on the other side, fifty-seven fewer being drafted here meant without doubt that the numbers would be made up somewhere else. We still think in terms of just our community struggling to survive, but that burden would go somewhere, someplace like Weaverville, Hendersonville, Fletcher, where we used to go for a night out or even had friends and relatives. The old saying that it is about whose ox is getting gored stayed with me. We cut our draft, someone else picks it up.

"I will add that at the same time it was offered, I was informed that my daughter would not face field service with a combat unit and could accompany me to Bluemont. That offer was later increased to incorporate the majority of those in this community who were mobilized as well to be sent to Bluemont, where they would be under my direct command as a support unit and most likely exempt from combat service."

"So if you take it," someone from the back cried, "half our kids and kin are exempt, and from what happened at the town meeting last week, there's more than enough volunteers to fill the quota! John, I think the answer to our dilemma here is obvious."

Again there was a flurry of comments and arguments, some even shouting for John that, for the good of the community, he had to go. He lowered his head, and finally it was Ernie who cried out for everyone to shut the hell up and listen to what John had to say in reply.

John finally looked back up, eyes fixed for a moment on his family. He separated out one sheet of paper from the others and held it up. "This is addressed to me personally. I'll not read it word for word; it's basically the same as the letters received by 113 others here. It states that rather than a request for my volunteering for national service to enter at the rank of major general in the ANR, I've been drafted for service."

"I thought it was a deal!" someone from the balcony shouted. "You volunteer and half our young people are exempt from call-up."

John shook his head. "I have now been drafted the same as so many of you and ordered to appear in the same manner as the rest of you, three days hence at 9:00 a.m. at the courthouse for induction. But yes, this notice I am holding still states that, though drafted, I will return to service with the rank of major general, and upon appearing to do so, half of those mobilized are exempt and need not report while the other half accompanies me to Bluemont. At least that is what I've been promised."

"Then do it, John!" someone outside in the parking lot cried. "And let my daughter stay with us!"

John stood silent, looking about the room as the shadows of evening began to lengthen. No one else picked up the cry.

He took a deep breath, held the letter up, and tore it in half. "I refuse to comply."

And now the room did erupt, some coming to their feet cheering, others cursing him, crying that he was a coward, others that he was damning their families to hardship, others shouting that he was a traitor, and yet others that he was a patriot standing up to a bureaucrat trying to turn the community against itself so that he could sneak in after John was gone and assert control.

Throughout it all, John stood silent, as if waiting for a firing squad to do the deed and end his misery. He kept his eyes fixed on his family, on Makala with tears of pride for him in her eyes, and on Elizabeth, as well, and Jen, who nodded approval, and poor little Ben wailing in fearful distress over the uproar of the adults around him.

Finally, it was Reverend Black stepping forward, holding his hands up and shouting for silence so John could explain his reasons for his decision.

"Thank you, Richard," John whispered, turning again to face the group. "You have the right to know my reasoning for my decision since it directly affects fifty-seven families in our community."

"You're damn straight we have a right to know!" someone shouted, but the rest of the gathering hushed the voice of protest.

John nodded his thanks and cleared his throat. "More than three decades ago, I gladly decided to serve my country and swore my oath to defend the Constitution of the United States. In that time, even when I disagreed with the decisions of my supreme commander, I nevertheless followed all orders, because they were moral orders, fitting within our Constitution and the military code of justice.

"I will admit here publicly for the first time that I hold our so-called federal director in Asheville, Dale Fredericks, in disdain, and from the first time we met, I felt uneasy about his ability to hold such an important position."

So it was out in public, at last. Makala actually smiled and gave him an encouraging thumbs-up.

"I welcomed the concept that our national government was coming back into power to reunify our nation after the most deadly blow inflicted upon any nation in modern times. When a battalion of our army came to this area a year ago, we greeted them with open arms and found in them so many of the traditions that had once bonded our country together. I had hoped for the same after they shipped out to Texas, and I went to meet the federal administrator who came to Asheville. I hoped his arrival was a clear indicator that our nation was finally coming back together, the first steps in what we all want—national recovery.

"Instead, I have come to disdain and loathe Fredericks. I saw far too many like him in the halls of power before the Day. Nevertheless, at the start, I felt I must accept his authority, which can be a tough decision for any man or woman at times, but the guiding principle was always the code I lived under as an officer and the same code I tried to teach some of you as students on this campus. It comes down to a profound question: Are the orders I receive lawful orders, and beyond even temporal law or the laws of Caesar, as some define that, are the orders given to me moral orders?

"Over the last week, I have reached the conclusion he lacks that moral authority, and sadly, by extension, I must include in that now those who appointed him to his post. They are not lawful orders, and most certainly they are not moral orders.

"The orders that this Mr. Fredericks attempted to impose on me and our community this morning are in violation of the traditions of military law—to turn over prisoners who had not just been captured in the field of action but had actually come to us for compassionate aid for noncombatants, placing themselves under our protection. That order I could not abide with and accept.

"If that were the only issue, I might still have accepted this juggling act of what should be apparent to all as an opening move of outright bribery to remove me as a troublesome thorn in the federal administrator's side— that if I enlisted, half of you would be exempt from federal service.

"Can you not see the hand moving behind this? Exemption for how long? I did ask that question the first time it was raised, and the answer was vague. A day? A week? A month or a year? Anyone capable of such sleight of hand I do not trust to hold to his word, and I suspect the rest of you would be drafted, anyhow, once I am gone. It is a game as ancient as recorded history. Promote a troublesome thorn up and out of the way if you cannot crush him, and then, once gone, impose whatever was planned in the first place. I refuse to play that game even though it was a decision that my action will result in twice as many of you being called to national service.

"I am not saying this as some sort of justification to cover my own personal decision. But how many of you now honestly believe that Fredericks will keep his word? What will prevent him, a week after I and the first contingent are gone, from sending out draft notices to those who stayed behind—or, for that matter, draft notices for two hundred more—and in so doing strip our community clean not just of our able-bodied defense force but even our ability to provide ourselves with a proper harvest this fall, thus forcing us onto the federal weal in meek submission to its authority?"

There were many nods of agreement now with that argument.

"But that is not my main reason for refusal," John quickly continued. "I assume most of you know of some means of accessing outside news. In the last few weeks, there have been reports via the BBC but noticeably lacking from Voice of America of a major offensive action to wipe out the gangs, similar to the Posse that controls Chicago. Several days back, the BBC reported that an entire battalion of the ANR was overrun, at least a hundred taken prisoner and later that day executed either by crucifixion or were hurled to their deaths from the top of the Sears Tower, which seems to be a favorite method of death for the madman Samuel who is running that place.

"In a tragic way, it should come as no shock, given what we faced at the Old Fort pass with the Posse who murdered thousands in a single day. But there is one key difference in our time of crisis. We had at least some time to train and prepare for their arrival and fought as a coordinated team as a citizen army. Those of you with prewar military service, or maybe some of you who studied military history, know that the total annihilation of a battalion of eight hundred or more of our troops on the field of battle has not happened in more than fifty years—and even then, it occurred when faced by well-trained and disciplined troops, such as the enemy faced in the Ia Drang Valley in 1965, the Chosin Reservoir in 1950, and the Bulge in 1944.

"I found that report profoundly disturbing. It tells me that this so-called ANR is being thrown into combat without proper training or leadership.

I refuse to participate in a system that treats the young survivors of the Day as if they are cannon fodder. If anything, after all we have lost, each and every life of our young men and women should be held in even higher value—and if sent in harm's way, it should only be done out of most dire necessity and when they are properly trained and equipped to do so."

He paused.

"I was suspicious from the start that an entity other than our branch of arms with centuries of tradition behind it was being formed. It reminds me too much of some other paramilitary organizations from the past, and the type of results witnessed here and reported by the BBC prove it.

"Second, it was also announced that the secretary of National Reorganization has received an executive order from the president releasing the use of nuclear weapons, so-called neutron bombs, for use on our own soil. The diplomatic threat is clear to our neighbors in Mexico and to the Chinese occupying our West Coast. Whether we buy their line that their presence is strictly humanitarian or not, the threat is clear—and with it the threat of an escalation to a second use of nuclear weapons in the wake of the bitter retaliations and counterretaliations after the first EMP attack.

"I cannot condone the use of nuclear weapons by our government on our own soil unless some other entity uses such weapons against us first. That convention on our part has existed for over half a century, the same way we have never used gas since the end of the First World War. With those factors in mind, I shall inform the administrator in Asheville that I will not accept my draft notice and refuse to report."

He forced a smile. "Since, in the eyes of this so-called federal government," he said, and there was a stirring in the room as to his choice of describing the government in Bluemont as so-called, "I am now, by their definition, an outlaw, the same as Forrest Burnett. Therefore, as of this moment, I am resigning as a member of the town council, resigning as military head of our self-defense force. I am retiring to private life and there shall await the results of my decision. It has been an honor to serve my community these last two years. I have tried my best for all of you."

He lowered his voice, struggling for control. "I ask forgiveness for any of the mistakes I made and for your prayers for guidance in the days to come. I thank you for all that you have done, the way you rallied together in the time of darkness, and I pray, as a hero of mine, Winston Churchill, once promised in the darkest days of his time, that 'broad sunlit uplands' are ahead for all of you. God bless you all."

He stepped away from the podium and walked off the stage to where his family waited in the front pew, the three most important women in his life up on their feet to embrace him, and together, with Elizabeth carrying a now sleeping Ben, they walked down the main aisle.

And together with his family, he walked out of the church. In silence, all got into the car for the short drive back to their home in the valley of Montreat.

He helped Elizabeth tuck Ben into bed while Makala helped Jen, the two of them whispering behind a closed door. John went out to his usual place to sit, pray, and meditate, picking up Rabs on the way out. He gazed down at Jennifer's grave. "I hope I did the right thing, pumpkin. I hope you approve."

CHAPTER THIRTEEN

This is BBC News. It is 3:00 a.m., Greenwich War Time.

It was announced today by the American federal government based in Blue-mont, Virginia, that a single neutron bomb was detonated over Chicago. The extent of physical damage to that already largely destroyed city is unknown, and there are no reports of casualties. The administration spokesperson stated that after the murder of several hundred prisoners taken from an ANR battalion sent there to suppress lawlessness and other depravations by the alleged leader of the city, who calls himself Samuel the Great, there was no choice left to the government other than to employ a tactical nuclear weapon.

There has been global condemnation. A spokesperson for the People's Republic of China forcefully declared that the Chinese presence on the West Coast of the United States is for humanitarian reasons only, and it sees the use of a neutron bomb against one's own people as a direct threat to China. The spokesperson in Beijing further declared that any use of such weapons in proximity to Chinese personnel within the continental United States will be construed as an attack upon all of China and result in a full retaliation. The Mexican government appealed to the Chinese government for support if such a weapon is used anywhere within, and I quote, "the former states of Texas, Arizona, and New Mexico," end quote.

A message now for our friends in Ottawa and Montreal: "By the waters of Babylon." I repeat, "By the waters of Babylon."

* * *

A general town meeting had been called for down in the park the day after the meeting at the chapel, a meeting that John had not attended. It was one aspect of his former duties of which he was definitely glad to be relieved. No more meetings!

He had come to dread them even as a junior officer, and though he truly loved his job as a professor, he dreaded just as much the interminably long faculty meetings and other committee meetings. An old mentor of his had wisely told him long ago that the more trivial the issue, the more it would be fought out in a meeting.

Makala, still part of the town council, had attended, along with Elizabeth, while John actually luxuriated in pulling down a copy of William Manchester's masterful biography of Winston Churchill, *The Wilderness Years*. The choice was a comforting one for guidance, and he had enjoyed the nearly four hours of solitude. For the first time since the beginning of spring planting, he had been able to relax. Jen had tiptoed out quietly several times, asking if he wanted some tea or a salad from the first greens of spring, though the salad was heavy with the pungent scent of ramps, and for the sake of politeness, he had accepted, picking at the salad while Jen settled into a chair to catch the early evening warmth and dozed off.

He looked at her lovingly. Makala was not her daughter; Mary, his first wife, had been her only child. In a way, Ben and Elizabeth were her only real blood kin in this world now, but even as Makala had come into the family, she had embraced the "intruder" with a warm, loving heart, the same way she had once embraced an uncouth New Jersey Yankee as her son-in-law.

John could sense that she did not have much longer with them.

She had always lived as a graceful, elegant Southern woman from something of a different age of genteel society. She was a bit of a paradox in that she had run the family business, the local Ford agency, with a hard-nosed, brilliant edge, and as for the culture she'd lived in long ago, she was proud to say that as a young woman, she and her husband had helped finance a bus from Asheville to participate in the famed March on Washington back in 1963. Their business had been boycotted, falling nearly to half of what it had been the year before, and when recounting it to John years later, she laughed that those who had boycotted her then were the loudest to proclaim they had supported her all along not long afterward.

So she was drifting away, dozing in the sunlight, radiating such a sense of calmness that John finally set the book down on the floor by his side and drifted off into dreamless sleep, as well.

"John?"

He half opened his eyes, saw Makala looking down at him, and smiled as she leaned over to kiss him on the forehead. He yawned and half sat up.

"The meeting." She chuckled. "Glad you weren't there."

"Why?"

"You were called everything from a traitor worse than Benedict Arnold to a hero."

"I don't care about that. What about the decision regarding the draftees?"

She smiled. "Six. Exactly six are reporting for duty."

"What?"

"Six, John."

"You sound happy about it," he gasped. "Do they realize what they are going up against?"

"Maury Hurt and Danny, both veterans, laid it out clear enough. Danny, as you know, was drafted for service back during Vietnam. He said that back then he hated the damn hippie draft dodgers, but after all he learned afterwards about the filthy politics behind that war, he wished he had dodged it, as well. Maury, who was in Desert Storm, spoke about the difference between a professional army in peace time—like we had even when fighting in Iraq and Afghanistan and on the day we were hit—and a draftee army. He closed saying he would refuse to be drafted into this ANR. They really helped to tip the scale."

"What about reaction to that BBC broadcast during the night?"

"That really threw things into turmoil," Makala replied. "Some said that if this Samuel character is anything like the Posse leader, then nuking him was too humane. Others see it as you do—a step back to the very brink. Most, though, were focused on the fate of that lost battalion of ANR troops."

John's feet were on the cold flagstone floor of the sunroom. Jen was still fast asleep. He could hear Elizabeth out in the kitchen, and she and Ben chattered away to each other in the language of mothers with their toddlers; the two understood every word exchanged, while the rest of the world just listened, smiled, and didn't understand a single word of the happy gibberish. He motioned for the door leading out to the garden, and Makala followed.

"Do they clearly understand what it means? In two days, failing to report, they will all be declared deserters and face execution." He sighed and sat down on the bench next to Jennifer's grave, lowering his head and covering his face with his hands.

"I never thought it would come to this. Fredericks will not sit back and let this go unchallenged. He's a climber, and he doesn't give a damn who gets in his way. I saw too many like him in the Pentagon and elsewhere, especially in the last couple of years of service. Friends of mine like Bob Scales were becoming a bit of a rare breed who would not hesitate to put their careers on the line if they felt the order was morally wrong.

"I suspect Fredericks will report my refusal back to Bluemont, and they'll seek to make an example of me. But as for all the others? How does he report that over a hundred have already told him to go to hell? That means failure, and in his game, especially if it is public and not hushed up, that means he loses his job and gets shunted off to one side. He'll force the issue before they find out, and from four hundred miles away, he can write the after-action report any way he wants, especially if there is no one to report differently."

"What do you mean?"

"He'll attack."

"Attack us with those black-uniformed goons? How many does he have at most? A hundred, maybe? They wouldn't last an hour against what we have."

"You know that means casualties on our side," John replied quickly, and she looked at him and then nodded.

"Yes," she whispered. "But I have to say the lesser of two evils. From all that you said about this ANR, if those kids go off, how many do you think will be back by Christmas as they promise? Or—let's get realistic—how many will still be alive five years from now?"

He lifted his face from his hands. "A suggestion, Makala."

"A suggestion? They voted for you to return as military commander during the current 'crisis,' as it was declared."

"I think it best I not accept. They vote me in, I accept it, the entire town is then culpable in the eyes of Fredericks."

"That's what Norm Schiach said—remember, he was a lawyer once with the army, so he is up with these kinds of issues. Nevertheless, he then voted for you to resume command of military operations if Dale makes an offensive move against us. But anyhow, what is your suggestion?"

"Clear the hospital, whether you think they can be moved or not. We always looked at the old Assembly Inn up here as a fallback position as a hospital if forced into a last stand and we lost control of Black Mountain. At least Montreat is highly defendable."

"Why?"

"Fredericks knows where the hospital is now. He has air assets. If they pull a raid on us as they did with the reivers, I want the downtown area evacuated beforehand. He lost face with not taking Burnett; I think that is where he'll try to take us first—a night raid to snatch Burnett. Catch us by surprise and make it a show of force. He'll argue he is not going directly against us but against a former enemy we are harboring. That divides public opinion in the town the following morning if he successfully drags Burnett and some others off. He then turns around and says the issue is settled, all is forgiven, so why fight any further. Yeah, there'll be some casualties on our side even with that, but then he blames it on me being such a recalcitrant bastard and suggests the rest come into line as long as I give myself up for leading everyone astray."

He paused, looking off.

"Crafty bastard," Makala said, sitting down by John's side. "But Maury, Ed, and others are on the same page with you regarding that. We're already evacuating the hospital."

He smiled. Of course they would see it clearly, acting already.

"The suggestion was made by some that you go into Asheville and make one more try."

"What do you think?" he asked.

"You'll be hanging from the courthouse steps ten minutes after you arrive."

He did not reply.

"Are you honestly thinking of turning yourself in?" she cried.

"It's crossed my mind. Strike a deal even now to reduce the draft. Once in Bluemont, see who is there—maybe some friends I knew before the war. I want to believe my old friend Bob Scales got out of D.C. alive and is out there somewhere. Even now, if I could serve with him in the regular army, I'd do so. If that was the case, I could make a difference."

"Like hell you will. He'll string you up in front of the courthouse as an object lesson and then break whatever agreement you made the next day. You even think of going into that city ever again while that pompous ass is in charge and I'll have Ed lock you up. In fact, it was made clear that if you try to go to Asheville, your friends will arrest you."

He could not reply. They were putting their lives on the line for him, and it made him decidedly uncomfortable. He sighed, shaking his head. "May I suggest, my dear, you get moving on getting the hospital cleared? It'll take a lot of work, and we don't have much time. I really should have suggested it earlier. I'm not officially accepting the offer to take command again, but maybe if Ed and a few others came by this evening, along with Kevin Malady and the other company commanders, we could share a few ideas."

The attack did come in precisely as John had predicted; the two Black Hawks swept in at just after three in the morning. The watch post John had suggested be pushed forward and concealed within spitting distance of the mall, which had been converted into Asheville's helipad, had warned of the liftoff ten minutes earlier.

The two helicopters touched down, seconds apart—one in the parking lot in front of the town hall, dropping its troops and then lifting off, and the second coming in thirty seconds later with a second squad. The second chopper remained on the ground, rotors turning at idle, while the other circled. Half of the first squad stormed into the town hall, weapons raised. A number of shots were fired, and at that same instant, the phone receiver John was holding, his link to the Swannanoa road barrier, went dead.

"They shot out our phone, damn it!" John snapped.

The second squad to land spread out in a skirmish line and raced toward the hospital . . . and found it and the town hall empty.

John, with Maury Hurt and a couple of the members of his first company mobilized down from the college, sat concealed in an abandoned apartment above the old hardware store, which looked straight out at the hospital and town hall. At least for the moment, they tried not to laugh, though the fact that some shots were fired as the assault team stormed into the town hall told him that their orders did carry deadly intent.

The assault unit that had charged into the hospital with weapons raised came out, and even in the dark, he could sense their confusion by the way they moved. He prayed that it ended this way, that confused and cursing, they'd get aboard their chopper, lift off, and the second one that was circling would pick up the rest, and they'd be gone. Maury had argued against John's plan, saying that if ever there was a time to capture one or maybe both of the Black Hawks, it was now. He did balk, however, at John's repeated query about whether he was ready to gun down the troops that had landed and whether he realized that even before they could snatch it and move it, chances were the Apaches would be on top of them in retaliation.

He wanted a message sent back to Fredericks, not the first shots of a full-scale war unless Fredericks ordered it first.

The troops headed back to their helicopter. No one in the town had night-vision goggles, but in the shadows cast by an early morning waning moon, he could see that the men were confused by the results, and several stopped alongside the small public bathroom in the town square to talk.

"Come on. Get back aboard and get the hell out," John whispered.

It was far tenser and more dangerous at this moment than the men who had come in realized. He had pulled everyone out of the town hall; it was too obvious that they might hit that first to try to take prisoners, but in the perimeter around the town hall and hospital across the street, he had over a hundred troops concealed, and they were trained killers. Survivors of the fight with the Posse and close to a score of small-scale skirmishes since—several of them with the reivers—they had stood many a cold, lonely night's watch at the hidden locations guarding the approaches into their valley. Their weapons varied from hunting rifles to what before the war were rather illegal automatics, a number of the weapons taken from the Posse dead. He had an RPG that had been captured from the Posse; a second RPG, a homemade affair, he entrusted to his best small unit, a group of Afghan and Iraqi vets.

Their orders were strict: no one was to fire unless directly fired upon or he popped off two green flares—green because they were the only two left in the entire supply of the town. But he knew from many bitter experiences and history itself that orders were one thing, but the tension of a moment like this another. A weapon accidentally discharged by either side . . . someone undisciplined or even drunk and pissed off . . . anything could happen when you put this many armed men and women with ever deepening antipathy in close range of each other.

The rotor of the copter on the ground began speeding up, the always distinct thumping echoing across the open plaza. The troops loaded in, and it lifted off. Even as it cleared the parking lot, the second chopper came back in from the west, flared, and settled down, troops loading in. As they left the town hall, there was more gunfire, and just as the last man loaded in, the door gunner unleashed a sustained volley into the building. Then the chopper lifted off into the darkness and was gone.

John breathed a sigh of relief and then sat back to wait. A standard ruse was for an enemy to come back into the same place fifteen minutes or so later. They undoubtedly had night vision, and he did not. He would not relax until his forward scout reported that all four aircraft were back on the ground, a report that did not come back for nearly a half hour. With the telephone switchboard in the town hall apparently shot out, it was a long wait until he heard a moped puttering into the town plaza, its driver circling several times, obviously a bit confused as to where to go, until John finally leaned out the window and shouted for the driver to come over. He then received the report from the courier that all four choppers were back at their base.

He shouted for an all clear. Kevin Malady stepped into the town square and repeatedly blew a whistle. Only a few appeared out of hiding; the rest remained concealed as ordered. A paranoia John had developed while waiting for this move was that maybe Asheville had more air assets than he knew about. More could be concealed on the far side of town or even called in from Johnson City or Greenville. Bureaucracies being as they were, he knew it would take a lot of wheeling and dealing to borrow more assets, but he was not going to bet anyone's life on that. He had passed the word that they had to assume that the sky above was now unfriendly and indeed watching.

He stepped out of the hardware store, looking up and feeling a bit naked. The first indicators of dawn were approaching as he walked up to Kevin, nodded, and shook his hand.

"Good job," he said, and then he headed for the town hall. It was Kevin who shouted for him to stop and to not open the door, and John inwardly cursed himself. They just might be capable of setting a claymore or IED on the way out, and Kevin shouted for a couple of his Afghan vets to come and check things out first. It was a long, tense fifteen minutes, the sky to the east shifting from blackness to a wash of indigo and deep gold before the two came out and said the building was cleared, but they were grim faced, angry.

John went in and stopped at the town's small telephone exchange.

"Son of a bitch." The switchboard had been blown apart, at least a couple of magazine loads poured into it. They had shut down most of the town's communications with this one wanton act of destruction, and John suddenly felt that the clock of their progress had been pushed backward.

His office had been ransacked, filing cabinets torn open, papers missing. Almost amusingly, they had taken the long-defunct computer, which had rested on a side table gathering dust.

On his shot-up desk was a manila envelope labeled "For John Matherson."

John went to pick it up, but one of his vets called for him to wait and then cautiously pushed the envelope with the muzzle of his M16 and flipped it over, finally opening it up himself before handing it to John.

What a pathetic world we are indeed slipping back into, John thought, *to again bring back these types of concerns.* It was too dark to read the note within, and not wanting to turn on a flashlight, he just held the envelope as he walked through the rest of the building.

Fortunately, they had taken the radio equipment set up by ham radio operators from equipment that had survived the Day and moved it to a secondary headquarters, which would now operate out of the basement of Gaither Hall until this crisis was resolved. Basing on the campus was inconvenient for many, but it had the tactical advantage of being in a narrow cove, with plenty of tree canopy for concealment.

John had left his far-too-easily identifiable Edsel in the garage of the house, and there it would stay henceforth, and he stood outside the hardware store waiting for a lift from one of Bartlett's recycled Volkswagen vans, which had become something of the community's bus service. Bartlett, being Bartlett, did feel it to be a bit weird that the vans were adorned with 1960s-style peace signs. It was all just too ironic at times.

John stepped back into the hardware store where he felt it was safe to turn on a flashlight and read the note sent from Fredericks.

John,

    The decision by you and by those who follow you to refuse the legal order to report for service with the ANR has now placed you—and all those who harbor you—firmly outside the law. I truly regret this. I thought we could work together for the common good of all. The fact that you are reading this note means that you and your followers have gone into hiding. There is no place to hide, and you know that. The deadline to report for mobilization has been moved up to noon today. If you are willing to comply as ordered, I am certain we can still work this out in a fair and equitable manner with all charges against you dropped. I know you are reading this within minutes of the departure of the troops. Since your phone service has been interrupted, raise a white flag at your boundary position at Exit 59 and remove all obstacles at that position at the same time, providing open access for the renewal of all traffic both ways will indicate your intent to end this crisis peacefully. This must be done immediately after dawn.

    Don't make any mistakes here. You are a military man who understands the chain of command and how each of us is a cog in the administrative system of state. It is time to do your part as expected.

                        Dale Fredericks
                        Director of Administrative District #11
                        District of the Carolinas
                        United States of America

He crumpled the note up and was about to toss it. There were a few things in his life that were hot buttons, and to be called a cog was one of them. It had been shouted at him repeatedly by an overly eager DI when going through boot camp, the sergeant taking delight in being able to harass ROTC trainees whom, months later, he'd have to salute for the rest of his life. It was a term constantly used by an officious XO of his division while stationed in Germany in the waning days of the Cold War. It was a term that was lifeless, stating they were all just simply part of some massive, Moloch-like machinery—the state, the company, the organization grinding relentlessly onward, and one either became a cog in that machine or was ground under it.

John stuffed the letter into his pocket and looked at Maury and Kevin. "Full mobilization. Our landline communications are down, but we've lived with that before and must again for now. We've never drilled properly for it before, but we have discussed what to do if facing an attack from the air. I'm expecting a full-out air-and-ground assault this morning."

He handed the note to his two friends to read.

"Son of a bitch, calling us cogs. I hate that," Maury replied.

"I want the entire downtown area evacuated immediately; get that siren going. Noncombatants are to be moved to designated shelters as planned and troops deployed in anticipation of an attack, as well."

In the months after the Posse attack, John had spent many a night developing contingency plans for a variety of scenarios, from the annoying border raids—which, at times, could turn deadly as several had with the reivers—up to taking shelter if a full-scale thermonuclear war was unleashed. They had given some thought to an aggressor who had managed to snatch a couple of aircraft or choppers. If the Posse had come at them armed with but one Apache, fully loaded, and done a proper air recon first of his deployment, it would have gone very badly for the town.

Never, though, had they thought along this line that they just might be facing not raiders or some gang but their own government, which he prayed was only one rogue administrator with a power complex.

The next eight hours would tell if this was a bluff or not.

Maury and Kevin both saluted and turned to run off, John instinctively returning the salute. Like it or not, formally accept it or not, he was again in command.

His retirement of little more than a day was over, and though in so many ways he hated it, there was, deep down, a certain thrill to it all, as well. He felt in control of his fate again. He absently rubbed his jaw. The tooth still hurt, but there was no time to worry about that now.

CHAPTER FOURTEEN

"Rook One to King Three, two Indians and two raptors are up and coming your way."

John clicked his mike twice to acknowledge receipt of the message and did not reply. Fredericks said they didn't have cockpit cameras, but they obviously did have night vision and undoubtedly radio-tracking gear, as well. Rook One was his new watch station based up along the parkway looking directly down on Asheville, a position the reivers had created over a year earlier, manned now by three watchers from those former enemies, concealed in a bunker that one could pass within five feet of and still miss.

"Sound the siren again!" John shouted, retreating back to his watch position above the hardware store across from the town square. Everyone in the council, now hunkered down in Gaither Hall, had argued he should be up there, but he felt compelled to witness what was about to happen, praying that Fredericks was just going to make a demonstration of force and nothing more. Surely he did not want a full-scale fight and that this was a bluff to overawe. If Fredericks put some troops on the ground from the Black Hawks and made no further moves other than have the Apaches circle for a while, then even at this late date, some kind of common sense would prevail.

"I think I hear them," Maury announced, leaning out the second-floor window above the hardware store.

"They can haul ass," John replied, looking off vacantly. "You've gone in aboard them, haven't you?"

"Yeah. Even though it scares the crap out of you, it's a rush every time."

"It's why kids are willing to get shot at; everything tied into getting shot at is such a rush, and they figure it won't be them that get it. I pray to God this is a bluff."

He could hear them now, as well, coming in fast, the thump of the approaching rotors echoing off the empty streets . . . louder and louder . . . and then a flash of light raced past the window.

"Jesus!" John barely had time to cry before the first salvo of rockets slammed into the town hall and fire station. There was a sound like tearing cloth, a rippling chaos of noise, another flash of light, and two more explosions tearing into the town hall complex, the concussion from the blasts shattering the windowpanes over John's head, showering the room with glass. The first Apache zoomed straight overhead so that John instinctively ducked as it roared over the town square, dodging into a hard bank to the right to avoid the billowing clouds of smoke. There was more gunfire and two more rocket impacts into what was left of the complex, the second helicopter peeling to the right, the two weaving, gaining altitude.

In response, there was a scatter of shots from the ground, nearly anything fired from the ground ineffective, even if it hit. The troops were breaking fire discipline, but it was understandable in their rage at such wanton aggression. These were not the vulnerable Hueys of Vietnam; the Apaches were ground-attack helicopters, the best that John's nation could produce before the war, designed to take nearly any small-arms fire from the ground and just keep on flying.

The Black Hawks? If they thought they were going to drop troops into the town square again after what the Apaches had done, it was going to be a very short and quick suicide mission, and something within John prayed that Fredericks would not be so stupid as to order his troops into such a mission. The entire perimeter was armed with troops far better trained than what Fredericks could throw at them.

"Better get back from the window, John," Maury said, pointing to the northeast where the two Apaches had leveled off and were now coming back in. And then, for a chilling instant, John's eyes were blinded by the distinctive red sparkle of a laser sight. He dived for the floor and scurried to the back of the room. If these choppers were equipped with the facial recognition technology rumored to be in development before the Day, they would have just painted him with that laser, and within seconds, the computer—if indeed such were on board and loaded with his profile and pictures—would have come back with a positive ID, and this building and all in it would be dead. There was no telling what high-tech equipment positioned in the Middle East on the Day had survived to now be used here.

Seconds later, every window in the hardware store shattered from the minigun bursts, and for a few terrifying seconds, John thought his worst fears were true. He crouched down low and was suddenly covered with green sludge from an exploding can of latex paint stored in the room, glass shards covering him. If they had put a rocket into the room, he now realized his folly for being here—he and his friend would be dead.

The two Apaches thundered past. He could hear the shifting of the rotors, the changing tempo as they arced up, breaking left and right and preparing for another strafing run.

"John, I suggest we abandon this place!" Maury shouted. "Once they're just past us, we break out the back door, head farther down Cherry Street, and hunker down there until this storm has passed."

John nodded agreement, peering up over the shattered windowsill to watch as the Apaches did another southwest-to-northeast strafing run. The hospital was going up in flames. Fortunately, all had been evacuated along with the precious supplies the evening before, and for the sake of their souls, he hoped the two pilots flying this mission knew that fact, because otherwise they deserved to be damned as three rockets slammed into the extensive array of buildings, and a fourth, going a bit high, took out the post office.

By the time they had passed, John and Maury, dragging the portable two-way radio, had retreated through the back door of a favorite old haunt, the used bookstore. The next strike strafed the length of State Street, incendiary rounds igniting several fires. The second helicopter followed, curving down along Cherry Street, such a beloved lane of their community, shattering windows, and then there was a distant explosion. John assumed they were hitting the empty Ingrams' market and the warehouse next to it where the L-3 had been stored. During the night, Billy had hurriedly taxied the precious plane along the interstate highway, concealing it within the cavernous remains of one of the buildings in the abandoned conference center at Ridgecrest.

The sound of the Apache rotors receded, and after several minutes, John ventured out onto Cherry Street, heart filled with a cold rage. Cherry Street. What threat did it ever represent? It was the heart of the old tourists' center, made up of antique shops, several restaurants, art shops, quaint and welcoming to him when he had first come here years earlier with Mary and two small girls. It was the street he had walked on bearing a dozen Beanie Babies for Jennifer's twelfth birthday on the Day—a remnant of all that his country had once been in a far distant, far more innocent age. Why tear this apart other than for the sake of willful destructiveness, piled on top of all the destructiveness of a nation collapsing, perhaps collapsing even before the Day?

Rather than tears, he felt nothing but cold rage and anger now.

"The Black Hawks!" Maury cried, pointing straight up.

They were indeed up, far up above any hope of ground fire, circling a thousand or more feet over the ever expanding flaming destruction of downtown Black Mountain.

"Observing, just observing for now," John said. Then he saw one of the two peeling off, heading north and then turning east for the valley of Montreat.

"No, not that." He sighed, but a moment later, he could hear the distant echo of gunfire and explosions.

"Try the back roads with the Jeep?" John asked his friend.

"I ruined the paint job last night, splashed it with a lot of camo. It's parked at my house."

"Let's go, then," John said bitterly, and the two set off at a jog up the three blocks up to Maury's house, which overlooked the park and Lake Tomahawk.

Minutes later, they faced a risky decision. For several hundred yards, there was only one road, devoid of overhead canopy, the final approach to the

Montreat stone gate from Black Mountain. Once past the gate, they could dodge up a side road and again be under cover.

There was definitely gunfire coming down from above, and he could hear staccato bursts of fire in return. Smoke was rising up, and his heart raced. Jen's old home in the once peaceful valley was just a short walk from the campus. Dale had knowledge of exactly where he lived. Had he gone so far as to target it? He had ordered Jen to go to the communal shelters, tucked into the basements of various campus buildings, and Elizabeth was to leave Ben with her and report to her unit. Makala was in the basement hospital in the Assembly Inn, and unless the helicopters were carrying Hellfire missiles, all should be safe there. But then again, if they had Apaches and standard air-to-ground missiles, might they have some of the deadly Hellfires, as well?

"Hang on to your ass!" Maury shouted, and he was half laughing as he shifted into low gear and peeled off the road, dodging through the kids' summer camp just below the gate, sprinting up torturous dirt roads, and splashing through a mountain rivulet. For the first time, John saw that there was indeed more than one road into Montreat, but one would have to be insane or desperate and in possession of a good four-wheel-drive Jeep or all-terrain vehicle to survive the passage. They dropped down at last onto a paved road, John shouting to just drive past his home. It was still intact, though an old cottage—as the locals called it—was in flames, and John wondered if the incendiaries poured into it had been misaimed and intended for his dwelling instead.

His heart sank as they came down Louisiana Street and saw plumes of smoke rising from the campus, and then they ducked low as a Black Hawk roared overhead, heading back down the valley.

The sound of its rotors receded, but off in the distance and high above, he could hear the other one still circling, indeed like a hawk waiting to pounce.

Strange how memory plays, he realized as the thought came of cartoons he had seen as a kid, where a hawk or other bird would suddenly transform into a World War II plane as it dived—if a bad guy, a Stuka, if a good guy, usually a twin-tailed P-38. Were the Black Hawks now indeed the bad guys? His heart rebelled at the thought. They were the tools of a bastard out of control.

As they turned onto the campus and raced past the small power station, which had been the source of so much hope and inspiration just a few weeks earlier, representing the best of what he believed his country would again be, he saw the roof of Gaither Chapel ablaze.

He cried out in rage as Maury raced them up the hill, swerving into the drive in front of the building. A score of his old students were up on the roof, armed with axes, and crowbars tearing back the shingling, buckets of water laboriously passed up along several ladders. Others stood guard, scanning the sky, weapons of every sort raised. Several observers with binoculars watched the horizon or focused in on the observation helicopter circling high overhead, and John just had an instinctive feeling that Fredericks was high up there, watching, and well out of range of ground fire.

Grace, carbine over her shoulder, ran up to him and saluted, face blackened from obviously having helped to fight the fire.

"Report. First off, any casualties?"

"Three dead, sir." She started to choke up.

He put his hand on her shoulder. "Focus, Lieutenant. Work with me. Who are they?"

She rattled off a few names, one of them an elderly professor who collapsed inside the chapel when it was hit and started to burn.

"Focus on now, Grace. That's your job, remember? Focus and go back to it."

"Sir, the command post down in the basement is still running. They asked for you to report in."

His admonishment to his young lieutenant of the college troops now reflected back on him. Again that nagging doubt. Was it the concussion of a couple of weeks back, or was he indeed losing his edge? Of course, after being out of touch for at least forty-five minutes, he should get a situation report and plot his next move. This first strike was a softening up; by this time, a ground assault could have rolled over his outpost on the interstate and be heading straight into town.

"Keep at it, Grace. You guys are doing great." He patted her on the

shoulder and then returned her salute before running down to the basement entry, the window shattered.

His communications team was inside, and they looked up at him with
relief as he came in. They had adroitly run their wires from a basement
window through the trees and anchored them to the roof of the adjoining
classroom building. Unless on the ground and staring straight up, no one
could spot them—though if they transmitted out for more than a few
seconds, an equipped unit could zero in on their location. Without Hellfire
missiles, fuel-air explosives, or a large, high explosive, digging them out
would be difficult, but it would certainly mean the ultimate destruction
of his beloved chapel. Once he had time enough, he would pull this command center out of here and move it to a less precious building, such as
the boys' dorm, a hardy structure of concrete and cinderblocks from the
1960s with zero sentimental attachment for nearly everyone, even those
who lived there.

"Any reports from our forward observers?" John asked.

One of his operators—it was Elayne from the post office—looked up
after removing one of the two decidedly old-fashioned headphones. "John,
forward outpost reports the two Apaches are back down and obviously re-
arming. No report of any kind of movement along the interstate, Highway
70, or anywhere else. We are getting an incessant signal in the last ten minutes from someone claiming to be Fredericks. He is on our primary frequency and is now at times overriding and jamming it."

John motioned for the headphones and slipped them on. They felt
strange, for after all, a few years earlier, he'd used earbuds, and these were
definitely retro from the 1960s or before.

There was static, and then a few seconds later, he heard the voice again,
and it was indeed Fredericks.

"Come on, John, that was just the first move. Talk to me before I send
them back in again."

Damn it. What to do? Transmit back for even more than a few seconds,
and chances were that Fredericks was indeed overhead, his helicopter
equipped with tracking gear, and they would get a rocket down their
throats, killing every kid on the roof of the chapel.

And yet he so wanted to reply to see if there was some way to call this madness off—and if not, to tell the bastard to go to hell.

He was being baited, played.

He looked at Elayne, removing the headphones and handing them back to her. "Code word scramble," he said. It was the signal for the teams on the net to switch to the first backup frequency, using old-fashioned ham radios and handheld units that the Franklin family had protected and stashed away before the Day and, in a surprise gesture, had offered to John just the day before. Elayne announced the one-word signal and then immediately shut down transmission and powered off, as did the others, and they would now be in the dark for the next thirty minutes before powering up again.

If the Apaches were back down to refuel and rearm, they could be back in as little as twenty minutes.

John could now guess what Fredericks was up to. There would be no ground attack for hours, perhaps not even for days. He would not risk his limited assets. He had tasted good blood with his deadly surprise raid on the reivers. He was now taking it up a notch. As long as fuel and ammunition held out, he would just keep sending the Apaches in, believing that it would wear John and those with him down.

If he needed to report back to Bluemont, there would be no casualties on his side, just a nice request for more fuel and ammunition, couched such that it would look like he was doing the most effective of jobs suppressing rebellions with minimum cost to his side—an efficient job that always looked good on paper.

Cursing under his breath, John dashed out of the communications room and onto the front lawn of the chapel. Each breath was painful and his jaw ached, but he needed to focus and ignore the pain.

The students had managed to contain the fires, but they were still tearing back shingles to get at the last of the smoldering blaze. The aged, dried chestnut within burned easily.

The sight of them up on the roof while others stood watchful guard reminded him of the heroic efforts of Londoners during the Blitz, the faded black-and-white images of crews struggling to save their beloved Saint Paul's Cathedral. Watching them at work, spotters ready to shout a warning to get off the roof, filled him with pride. He looked across the valley to the Assembly Inn, where the hospital was concealed in the basement. To his horror, he saw a couple of Bartlett's old VW buses racing up to the front of the building, the aging hippie now playing ambulance driver for the casualties in town. Surely the Black Hawk circling above was watching every move.

"Maury, we gotta move now!" John cried.

As he ran to the Jeep parked in front of the building, he looked up. The Black Hawk was still circling. He watched the chopper as he climbed aboard the Jeep, and Maury raced down the road around one of the dorms.

"Pull up to the old gym!" John shouted. "I'm getting out here. You take off the other way, find a place under good concealment to park, and make your way on foot to the Assembly Inn."

Maury grinned and nodded, and John jumped out of the vehicle. Maury continued on, and John stood for half a minute in plain view, looking straight up at the circling Black Hawk before going into the gym. If the chopper overhead did have advanced tracking capability, he now wanted to be seen going into the abandoned building. The cavernous basketball court was dark, empty, the air within dank and musty. It was a building the college wanted to replace even before the Day, and it had seen no use since. John loitered for five minutes or so and suddenly fought with the terrible urge for a smoke. He wished he had Ernie and his pocketful of cigars with him. He could sure use one now.

He finally slipped out one of the back doors and looked up. The helicopter had shifted a bit back toward Black Mountain. He took a deep, painful breath and ran behind the small dance hall barn. Rather than use the road bridge, he ducked down low and splashed through the tree-covered stream that fed into Lake Susan. He crouched for a minute between several abandoned cars parked on the far side and then sprinted the last few feet into a side entrance of the Assembly Inn.

If Fredericks had a means of tracking him, he had done his best to throw him off.

Once through the door, he was met by chaos. The basement had been converted into a temporary hospital. The Assembly Inn had once been a rather upscale hotel for conferences, and shortly before the Day, it had gone through an extensive remodeling. It had a long history, including housing enemy diplomats in the opening months of the Second World War. There had been little use for it since the Day. Of course, there were no more tourists and conferences, and with such a radical population decline in the year afterward, those who needed housing simply moved into abandoned homes while students remaining on the campus on the far side of Lake Susan had found that old familiar haunts were of the most comfort and stayed there. Those who married moved in together and lived not just with their spouse but beloved friends and even some of the staff who remained, as well. The college had become something of an old-style commune of sorts, led by the moral guidance of President King and Reverend Black while the beautiful Assembly Inn on the far side of the Lake Susan had slipped into disrepair. It had been designated a year earlier as the fallback position of a hospital and refugee center if ever Black Mountain were overrun or destroyed, but little had been done other than board up some windows damaged in an ice storm the previous winter.

But within the last twenty-four hours, it again had a use as Makala organized the transfer of the thirty-eight surviving wounded refugees and several dozen family members of the wounded who had trekked over the mountains in search of help. The town's precious reserve of gas had been nearly depleted as a result, but no one questioned that. She had even managed to get all their emergency medical supplies out of the hospital and fire station.

Several dozen wounded from the morning's first attack had been brought in, and again Makala had assumed her role as the "angel of choosing," marking each incoming case on the forehead with red lipstick, sending some into immediate surgery, the center rigged up in a former classroom illuminated by the morning light streaming in through east-facing windows. Those marked as ones were sent to wait in the rear of the foyer, and the tragic threes were sent into another back office with the minimal comfort of mattresses and slightly moldy sheets dragged down from long-vacant rooms on the upper floor. No Red Cross flag had been set up out front or atop the building. That would only draw Fredericks's attention.

As John walked down the packed corridor, Makala looked up from her work with a young woman in her late teens, obviously very pregnant but with no sign of injury.

"Sweetheart, you've gone into labor," Makala announced, smiling at her, clutching the frightened woman's hand. "You're most likely hours out, and once things settle down, we'll get you a comfy bed, and I know a granny who was a midwife who will help you. Okay?"

The girl tried to smile, her face soaked with sweat. An elderly couple, perhaps her grandparents, braced her on either side while a young nurse, dressed in camo but wearing a medic's armband, said she'd lead them to a safe place.

Makala looked up at John, smiled, and then dashed the few feet between them to embrace him tightly. "I've been worried sick about you all night." She sighed. "Thank God you're safe."

"How are things here?" John asked.

"Not bad, but not good." She drew closer. "Actually, when compared to the before times, it's practically medieval," she whispered. There was pain in her voice. "The ones I mark as threes? Nearly all could have been saved before this, and John, everyone in this town knows what a three means. They look up at me wide eyed, saying, 'I'm not a three, am I?' I lie to nearly all of them. Damn all this."

She held him tightly, and then he tensed, looking toward the open window. The helicopters were coming back to Montreat.

"Everyone!" John shouted, breaking the hushed whispering—which, even now, everyone felt was the way one should talk in a hospital—his loud, booming voice even startling Makala. "It might get a bit rough in the next few minutes. I need all of you to work with me as a team. Any wounded in the rooms facing Lake Susan, we have to get them out now and into the back rooms away from any windows. Those of you with vehicles, get them the hell out of here. You only got a minute or so to do it. Now move!"

John looked passed Makala and saw the elderly couple helping the young pregnant woman, who was bent double from a contraction and crying out. John ran up, shouldered her family aside, and picked her up. Ignoring the sharp pain in his chest and dashing for the back room, he set her down none too gently.

Makala had taken charge, as well, shouting for people to move as she ran into the surgery center that needed as much lighting as possible and thus had been set up in an east-facing room. John looked out the window and saw one of the Apaches swinging up over Lookout Gap, lining up for a strafing run across the valley, the second one turning behind it.

Surely the son of a bitch had not ordered this!

"Move them now!" Makala shouted. "Move them now!"

Three surgeons were working on wounded set side by side, one of them Doc Wagner, a young assistant by his side handing him instruments as Wagner bent over to pull something out of a boy's chest, which he had split wide open.

"Doc, go now!" John screamed.

"Not now, I can't!" Wagner shouted back, still intent on the forceps buried in the boy's chest.

John looked from him to Makala, who had shoved aside two nurses struggling to stop the bleeding from an old man's shattered arm and was trying to maneuver his makeshift gurney out of the room. John looked back out the window. The Apaches were skimming down the slope of Lookout Gap, guns blazing, shots ripping across the campus and now slashing the waters of Lake Susan, coming straight toward them.

He tackled Makala, knocking her to the floor and rolling with her up against the outer wall, the window a foot over their heads shattering into a thousand shards. A split second later, Wagner was dead, nearly torn in half from a bursting twenty-millimeter shell that also killed his assistant and the boy they were both trying to save. For a second, the room was a cacophony of exploding twenty-millimeter shells, shattering glass, blood splatters, screams, and hysteria. John's memory flashed to the videos posted on the Internet showing the work of gunships killing terrorists in the years after 9/11, the comments on the web pages nearly orgasmic with delight, laughter, and jokes. Yeah, they had been enemies who deserved to die, but had all those commentators ever seen people up close as twenty-millimeter shells exploded in their bodies?

Makala was screaming not with fear but horror at the sight, and John buried her head against his chest, holding her tightly, forcing her up against the wall and shielding her with his body. Where were Elizabeth and Ben in all this madness? Elizabeth's post was on campus. He had caught a glimpse of her as he'd left the communications center, but he had not had time to speak to her. Ben, thank God, was in a shelter in the basement of the girls' dorm.

He spared a quick glance up over the edge of the windowsill and then instantly ducked back down. The second helicopter was nearly on the tail of the first, which had roared overhead in a sharp banking turn to avoid slamming into the mountains that bordered the northwest slope of the valley. Another volley of fire ripped into the room, but there was nothing left to kill or destroy; all three surgical stations were a shambles. The chopper roared overhead, and John stood up, pulling Malaka to her feet.

"Run!" he screamed. "Get into the back rooms. If they had put a rocket in here, we'd all be dead. Now run, and keep down until they're gone!"

She looked about wide eyed, and for the first time since they had met long ago, he could see that she had become completely overwhelmed with the horror of it all.

John pushed her into the hallway, which was a sea of chaos. He heard the helicopters coming back, and a few seconds later came that surreal sound almost like yards of cloth being torn, but it was not hitting the Assembly Inn this time. He cracked open an emergency exit to look out and saw the old gym getting torn apart, and this time, two rockets were unleashed into it, blowing off part of the roof, igniting fires within.

He smiled grimly.

So you did see me go in there, he thought with bitterness. He wondered if their supply of rockets was running low, perhaps the last two reserved for a personal strike against him. If so, it had spared those in this building.

The helicopters continued on down the valley after the two strikes, and he slipped out the door, crouching low. A minute later, he heard distant explosions. They were back to ripping Black Mountain apart.

He went back down the corridor and spotted Makala in one of the storage rooms, struggling with a set of forceps to dig into an elderly woman's arm to close off an artery and clamp it shut. Though the woman was obviously in agony, she was talking calmly to Makala, reassuring Makala that she was doing a wonderful job. Makala clamped the forceps shut, telling the woman to hold on to them with her good hand and that someone would be along shortly to tie the artery off.

In a gesture John thought nothing less than surreal, the elderly woman first reached out with her good hand and gently stroked Makala's cheek, telling her that she was a beautiful woman whom she would pray for. Makala actually leaned against her for a moment, beginning to sob again. The woman saw John, and he recognized her as an old friend who had worked in the bank and then disappeared into retirement some years earlier.

"John, I hope you are well," the woman said in a soothing voice. "I think your wife needs a good hug before you go running off again."

Her tone so startled John that it actually did take him aback. He smiled, thanked her, and put his hands on Makala's shoulders, turning her around.

"Sweetheart, I have to go now. And you have to do your job. I love you."

She hugged him tightly, then exhaled deeply, drew in another breath, and stepped back.

It was mostly just acting now, but for the moment, she had regained some control. The shock, the nightmares, the waking up screaming in the middle of the night, that would come afterward, as it did for so many veterans, but for the moment, she could still do what she was trained to do.

"I love you," he whispered. "Be safe."

"And you too, John."

As he turned to go back out into the madness, the old woman looked at him and smiled. "God will watch over the two of you," she said. "I'll keep an eye on her, John."

That nearly broke him as he came back to kiss her on the forehead and then went back out into the fight.

He found Maury with his Jeep, tucked into a side road a couple of blocks to the south of the Assembly Inn. As he climbed into the Jeep, he heard more gunfire and looked back to see one of the Black Hawks circling high, undoubtedly to avoid small-arms fire, pouring a long stream of tracers and incendiaries into the campus, igniting numerous small fires.

"All right, let's try to divert that son of a bitch," John announced, Maury grinning at him as he reversed the Jeep out of the driveway of a private home.

"Where to?"

"Right down Montreat Road, but get ready to break up a side road."

"Sure thing."

They turned out onto the main road in and out of the cove, most of it well covered with trees. Once the gate was in sight, John told Maury to slow down while John stood half up and kept a very close watch overhead. It sounded like the Apaches had finished up their third run over Black Mountain and were most likely heading back to Asheville to rearm. But one of the armed Black Hawks was still up there, and though John wanted to be seen, he definitely did not want to get the last surprise of his life by a Black Hawk suddenly rearing up from behind some trees and unleashing on him and his friend.

The observation Black Hawk remained, slowly circling above Montreat for another half minute while Maury guided the Jeep through the stone gate and continued on the main road into town. The circling helicopter swerved slightly and turned south.

"Okay, get us the hell under some cover!" John shouted, and Maury pulled into the camp just south of the Montreat gate, the forest-canopied hiking paths and bridle trails the perfect place to hide from eyes looking down from above. John prayed they didn't have infrared, as well, because if so, the hot block of Maury's engine and exhaust could be their death signature.

A Black Hawk suddenly came swooping in from the east and banked up sharply. It was a tense moment, as if they were probing, trying to flush game, John feeling like a terrified rabbit that knew it must remain absolutely still even though the hunter was but a few feet away. The helicopter then leveled out, continued on a few hundred yards, and hovered for a moment, shooting up an abandoned convenience store farther down the road before continuing on with its search.

Continuing along back lanes, the two pressed back into town. Parking in an alleyway on the north side of State Street, John and Maury slipped across the road and back into John's first observation post above the hardware store. A fair part of the downtown had been shot apart, a dozen or more buildings aflame. The Posse had never gotten this far, the damage of that battle confined to the east end of the town. It was heartbreaking to see the devastation wrought by two helicopter air strikes. Though shops had been long closed, their owners who were still alive were desperately trying to contain the flames to salvage what little they had left.

His firefighting teams were under the strictest orders not to mobilize out except for fires that threatened shelters and hospitals. Several residents of Cherry Street, seeing John slipping along a back lane and into the rear of the hardware store, called out to him for help. He paused.

"God forgive me, we can't help you!" he cried. "Any crowd right now will draw fire from those bastards up there!" No one argued further or cursed him as the bringer of this doom, a curse he half felt he really did deserve.

Once back in this reserve position, he took in the sight of the wreckage, the smell of wet, charred wood, and the stoic gaze of the two old radio hams who were monitoring traffic.

"News?"

"Three choppers are back on the ground, according to our observer up on the parkway. They also report it looks like their fuel bladders are running low."

John nodded at that. They certainly had been profligate these last two days, burning more fuel than he would ever dream of allocating for months of productive labors. With a regular army unit of Apaches going into action from a forward deployment, there would be enough fuel, ammo, and rockets on hand to support several dozen sorties before calling up the chain of command for additional support. In Desert Storm, an entire brigade of airborne—the largest air assault since the Second World War—had gone in with scores of helicopters and set up a forward base inside Iraq with dozens of the new fuel bladders and had torn the hell out of the rear lines of the Republican Guard. It was the first full demonstration of air/ground warfare that had been refined in the long years after Vietnam.

Fredericks was most likely operating on a short leash, and he had to gamble on that one now. A strike against the reivers, with four aircraft or sorties. Upward of a dozen more sorties now against him since early this morning. Surely he was beginning to come up short on fuel and ammunition. Hopefully the air attacks were finished, at least for now.

"Report coming in that a fourth helicopter is coming in to land," one of the hams announced.

John nodded. "You still have the frequency they are operating on?"

The ham nodded.

"Switch to transmit."

"John, they'll track us the same way they tracked that forward recon unit."

"He's on the ground or just about down. Now's the time to send him a message, and then we move this unit down south of the railroad tracks."

The ham smiled, nodded, and handed John the mike. "Fredericks, do you read me?"

There was a moment of static and then the click of another radio coming online. "Who is this?"

"You know damn well who it is."

A pause.

"You drag out your response to more than thirty seconds, and I shut down," John replied sharply.

"You called me," Fredericks replied.

"Just to tell you this, Fredericks: I'll not be satisfied now until I see you dead, and I hope your people are listening to me. Your alleged leader has violated the most fundamental laws of humanity, of warfare, and of what our country and Constitution stood for. Refuse to obey his orders, and you'll be spared. Comply further, and you are as guilty as he is, and in the eyes of the world, you are no longer any part of what America was and will continue to be."

He clicked the transmission off before Dale could even reply.

"Let them stew on that," John said coldly. "Wait twenty minutes, then get on the horn and send out the coded message for our unit leaders to meet in the Ingrams' building at six tonight. It is time for some payback. I'm heading back to the hospital."

Though there was no indication that another strike was up, Maury maneuvered cautiously until they finally pulled up a block behind the Assembly Inn, and he walked the rest of the way.

He thought he had learned to get used to it; an essential part of his job had become visiting the wounded and dying on a near daily basis after the battle with the Posse and the numerous other skirmishes afterward. He had dealt with bullet wounds to the gut, students facing death with all painkillers depleted, asking him to hold them and pray. He had dealt with

far too much, but this was different. The hospital had been deliberately attacked, nearly a hundred within, most of them already wounded and torn
apart by the strafing attacks.

Drying blood was splattered against the walls in the corridor. Out
behind the Assembly Inn was now an open-air morgue. More than seventy dead from the attack lay side by side, covered with blankets and blood-
stained sheets. Families and loved ones were sitting beside bodies, lost in
shock, and he recognized many of them, horrified to see a former student
holding the lifeless hand of a girl he had married but a month earlier.

All of it filled him with cold, intent calculations as he sat down beside
Forrest's cot, his room a storage closet that was windowless and stifling hot
in the late-afternoon heat, the scent of unwashed bodies, blood, and filth
hanging strong in the room. John coughed to conceal his gag.

Forrest chuckled weakly. "Guess I stink like shit," he whispered.

"Well, you ain't no bouquet of roses, Forrest."

"How bad is it out there?"

"Bad." John sighed. "More than a hundred dead here and a couple of
hundred wounded downtown. It is devastating."

"I feel responsible for this," Forrest said. "You doing what you did for us."

"What the hell was I supposed to do? Turn away a bunch of kids?"

"You could have taken the kids and dumped me by the side of the road
or turned me over to Fredericks, and all this could have been avoided."
He pointed out to the hallway that was a charnel house.

John shook his head. "We both went through the same training a long
time ago, Forrest. Our wars were different, we took prisoners and treated
the wounded."

Forrest chuckled. "Well, at least when CNN was around." He paused.
"But yeah, unless we were dealing with a sniper or some bastard who had
killed a lot of innocent people, we still took them in."

"Handing you over to Fredericks is not what this community is about.
And besides, I owed you one. That guy with you, George, tried to take me
out, and you were the one who put him down. So what the hell was I supposed to do? But honestly, I didn't expect this level of retaliation."

"And now you wish you had done different?"

"Hell no! If that bastard is willing to do this, he would have wound up doing it anyhow at some point, to others if not to us, Things are spinning out of control. I pray it's not all the way up to Bluemont, but this is not the way to pull this country back together."

"So why are you here?" Forrest whispered.

"I think you and your people are the experts we need now."

"Go on."

John ran his idea past Forrest, who nodded with approval. "You have to act now, tonight," Forrest replied, "otherwise, tomorrow will be even worse. You have to assume he has at least a few people infiltrated in here who are reporting on everything, and more targets will be pinpointed." He paused and smiled weakly. "Hate to admit it, John, but in those first minutes when my encampment was hit, I thought it might have been some of your people who called it in. Sorry."

"No need to apologize. Remember an old song—Crosby, Stills & Nash—the line 'Paranoia strikes deep, into your soul it will creep.'"

"Never heard of them."

John forced a smile. "Different generation, I guess."

"Anyhow. Get some of my people in here, John; we'll go over the plan. They know the way in and will be your point men."

CHAPTER FIFTEEN

As each member of the lead assault team went into the drainage pipe that ran under Interstate 240, John offered them a pat on the back, a soft word of encouragement. Seventy were going in, divided into five assault teams, each one guided by one of the reivers. It was a route they had used for over a year to infiltrate in and out of the area of Tunnel Road to scavenge for supplies from the abandoned stores that had once lined the road—and also for raids for food. They had even been so bold as to pull a raid and holdup on Mission Memorial and disappear back through this concealed approach, which emptied out onto a trail that took them back over the parkway and then over the mountains to their home base.

This whole thing was one desperate gamble, but the report that had come in even as he was leaving Forrest's bedside had sealed the decision for John. A transport plane had touched down at the Asheville airport, apparently loaded with supplies for the choppers. If they didn't do this now, come morning, the nightmare over Black Mountain would resume. It was obvious that Fredericks would just keep pounding from the air until either they submitted or the entire town was destroyed.

John looked down at the illuminated dial of his old-style wristwatch. *Five minutes to go.* He leaned back against the embankment, breathing hard. It had been a day and a half since he had slept, and he cursed the fact that he was getting older. He felt utterly exhausted, his chest, head, and mouth aching, but in the next few minutes, he had to be sharp and ready to go.

Everyone had made clear to him that his forays to the front were finished, and he reluctantly agreed. The concussion was clearing up, but all the running, ducking for cover, and slamming Makala up against the protection of the wall in the surgery ward had cracked his barely healed rib open again. Each breath was a stabbing pain, a sneeze or cough absolute agony.

To ensure he stayed back from the front line, Kevin Malady gladly conspired with the town council, assigning Grace and a half dozen of their best as his security and communications team, along with his neighbor and friend Lee Robinson, who was given the order that if need be, he was to knock John down and sit on him, something Lee could easily do.

He kept staring at the watch. It was still three more minutes before everyone was to be in place, especially the one crucial player for this entire attack plan who needed the most time to infiltrate into position.

Suddenly, a shot rang out, and then another, and then a long staccato burst of automatic fire, followed by a white flare going up, the magnesium light burst flooding the area around the mall with startling brilliance, revealing many of his troops out in the open, not yet across Tunnel Road.

"The shit just hit the fan!" Lee whispered. John looked back at his reserve team, mostly students but veterans, as well, whom he would have to commit if the lead assault failed—which, at this moment, he feared just might be happening.

Deployed out on the east side of I-240 were several hundred, nearly every person in Black Mountain and the reivers who could carry a gun and were not part of the lead assault teams. They had force-marched seven miles after sunset once dropped off near the Exit 59 barricade.

The only vehicles he had dared to send beyond that point were those that were relatively quiet, which would serve as ambulances. Nearly everyone else had come up on foot. Leading the advance were carefully picked teams of "hunters," mostly reivers. They had to run on the assumption that the enemy had night-vision gear and would have advance patrols out. If his assault columns were spotted, the entire plan would disintegrate, and chances were that nearly his entire force would be annihilated, caught out in the open if the Apaches got up.

There had indeed been a couple of patrols out, and John now had a night-vision set, old military issue from fifteen years earlier, to observe the action. The other night goggles were issued out to Iraq and Afghan vets in the lead assault teams who knew how to use them.

The bursting of the flare blinded him for a moment. Snapping off the headset, he could see by the light of the flare several of his people, caught out in the open as they attempted to sprint across Tunnel Road and the approach to the helicopter base, being cut down by a sustained burst of machine gun fire.

"Go, damn it, go!" John hissed as more and yet more weapons opened up. And then he heard it—one of the Apaches was starting to wind up. If it got airborne, the entire operation was finished.

Fredericks had committed one serious tactical blunder: basing the helicopters at the abandoned mall on the far side of Beaucatcher Mountain rather than in the middle of downtown. It was a logical position in some ways; it had several acres of open tarmac, the old Sears building—which had not been gutted out and was a good location for barracks, storage, and workshops—and the covered parking lot behind Sears as a place to move the choppers in bad weather and for maintenance. The tactical mistake was that it was indeed on the outskirts of town, closer to Black Mountain. If he had positioned them on the west side of town, across the French Broad River, this plan would have been next to impossible.

The rotor of the first helicopter was picking up speed, even as his assault teams continued to charge in. No one needed to be told that if even one of the copters lifted off, all was lost. John grimaced at the sight of half a dozen of his troops crumpling up and collapsing, those surviving continuing to press in toward the defensive perimeter of concertina wire and piled-up highway barriers.

The helicopter began to lift, and in spite of the random shots streaking over his head, John stood up, binoculars focused on the Apache. In a few more seconds, it would be clear, and he prepared to give the signal for retreat.

From the roof of the mall, there was a flash of light. *An RPG!*

Handled by an old marine with the reivers who had been handed the launcher and two warheads taken the year before from the Posse, it was the one heavy shot the entire community had other than homemade shoulder-mounted weapons that might be good from fifty feet away but not much beyond that and were as much risk to the shooter as the target.

The marine had grinned with delight when handed the weapon, promising to get the job done or die trying. The missile streaked in, striking just behind the tail rotor assembly, knocking out horizontal control. It was a very good shot, shrapnel tearing into the gearbox housing and the spinning rotors. The Apache lurched sideways from the blow, the pilot struggling to throttle the engine back.

The Apache careened in nearly a full circle before crashing into the parking lot, pieces of rotor flying off in every direction, igniting into a fireball as its fuel tanks ruptured, the blast engulfing the second Apache. The pilot of the second Apache popped the canopy, he and the gunner attempting to roll clear.

Regardless of his feelings for the Apache crews and what they had done, John felt a wave of sick remorse. They had been on his side at one time, and he could see the two men writhing in agony as they struggled clear of the spreading fire and then collapsed.

John held up his flare pistol and fired off a round—green, the signal for the reserves to come in. Turning to his own unit, he shouted to get up and move forward.

The advance assault teams were into the concertina wire that had been strung around the makeshift base, throwing heavy planking over it to form pathways in. An old pickup truck, which had been hand-pushed the last mile to its preattack position down at the bottom of the long, sloping road approaching the mall, had roared to life and careened up the hill, a plow mounted to its front. It crashed through the gate and then burst into flames as the security team riddled the vehicle.

They were taking heavy casualties, and John was furious. The driver was ordered to wait until it was clear that fire from within the compound had been suppressed, but he had charged in regardless and was now undoubtedly dead, as were many who were trying to weave through and over the wire. A couple of explosions ignited—claymores—cutting down more of John's personnel.

The attack, which he had prayed would infiltrate, gain positions, and take out the Apaches with two RPG rounds, had unraveled. His advance teams were pushing in regardless of loss, now seemingly an attack of desperation.

He could not stay out of it any longer. "We're going in!" John shouted, and before anyone around him could object, he sprinted up the last few feet from concealment and started across the highway, his security team racing to catch up and then push ahead, Grace in the lead, Lee Robinson by his side, cursing at him to hang back.

His communications team, a man with a portable ham radio strapped to his back followed by two gunmen and Maury—who just still might be the most valuable person in this attack other than the marine who had knocked out the Apaches—was by John's side.

"John, we're too old for this crap!" his friend gasped. "And both of us wounded already."

John did not reply, trying to ignore the pain in his chest with each breath he took. Maury no longer had his arm in a sling, and he could see his friend wincing with each step, as well.

More explosions echoed around the mall—claymores and grenades—and they were taking a devastating toll.

The rotors of one of the Black Hawks started turning, and an instant later, sparks from half a dozen semiautomatic and full automatic weapons slapped against its side. Smoke began to pour out of the engine housing, the pilot and copilot bailing out. The fourth chopper had not started up yet and John hoped that the plan just might work.

And then a roar of gunfire erupted from inside the abandoned Sears building at the north end of the mall. The gunfire rose to fever pitch, rounds, perhaps fired from his own side, zipped over John's head, causing him to duck down below the edge of the road bordering the mall.

And then, just as suddenly as it started, the firing slacked off, cries going up to cease fire, Grace on the one megaphone owned by the town ordering the opposition to lay down their arms and surrender and that prisoners would be taken.

The firing had all but ceased, and John finally stuck his head above the berm and cautiously stood up. He could see his people inside the perimeter, weapons held to shoulders, shouting for the security force to get down on their knees, hands over their heads. Several were up alongside the fourth chopper, weapons aimed at the cockpit, the pilot and copilot coming out with hands raised over their heads.

A burst of explosions erupted, and all ducked, ammunition aboard the first Apache cooking off, and all stayed low for a minute. Finally, they were back up, and John trotted across the road and through a gap in the wire that someone had cut open. The cry was up for medics, wounded being carried out to the side of the road.

John turned to his radio operator, motioning for the mike. "Position secured. Bring up the ambulances. I want our wounded out of here now!"

He handed the clumsy mike back to the ham operator. Malady was shouting orders, calling for all prisoners to be herded to the north side of the compound, wounded from both sides to be carried out to the road for the ambulances, which were mostly pickup trucks, now coming out from the reserve position they had taken back on Highway 70.

A scuffle broke out with the prisoners. John turned and saw two of them being dragged out of the lineup, one of his men—a former student— kicking a prisoner in the groin and then straddling his writhing body and pulling out a pistol.

"You there!" John cried. "Stop!"

The former student ignored him, shouting curses at the prostrate man at his feet, holding his pistol up and then lowering it to aim at the man's stomach.

"Stop him!" John shouted, and several now rushed in, pulling the young shooter's arm up. The gun went off once, and the prisoner on the ground began screaming. The more than fifty who had been taken prisoner recoiled back, several of them trying to break free but quickly stopped at gunpoint or clubbed down.

John strode up to the shooter, whom Kevin had personally disarmed. John slapped the young man hard across the face. "What in the hell are you doing?"

"He's the pilot of one of those damn Apaches. They killed my wife, and damn him to hell, he is going to pay now!"

"I was following orders!" the prisoner gasped, curled up in a ball, his scorched face contorted in agony. "I was following orders."

John looked down at him with contempt, half tempted to kick him, as well, so sudden was the rage he felt at what this man had done and the words he chose to defend his actions.

John turned away before he lost control.

"All prisoners to be checked for weapons, hands secured behind their backs." He paused for a brief instant as if to indicate that he was debating a decision, knowing that cruelty should be beyond him. "My people will escort you down the road to the pickup point for transport back to safety. As long as you cooperate, no one will be harmed. Do all of you hear that?"

There were cries of relief, several actually going down on their knees, sobbing with relief, so intense had been their terror. As he gazed at them, he could sense that these troops were barely above the rank of amateurs.

"Are you ANR?" he asked, focusing on a girl who looked to be in her midtwenties with bright twin bars on her shoulders. He motioned for her to come over and pointed at her shoulder bars. "Incredibly stupid to be wearing something like that, especially at night."

"Me?"

"Yes, you. I'm not talking to the lamppost behind you."

"Yes, sir, Army of National Recovery."

"How long have you been in?"

"Six months."

"Merciful God," John whispered, turning his back on her for a moment. Her words had at least deflated a bit of the battle rage with his troops of a few minutes earlier.

He turned to look back at her. The young woman's dark features were drenched with sweat, and she was actually trembling with fear, almond-colored eyes wide, gazing at him with obvious fear. He stepped forward and put a reassuring hand on her shoulder and could feel her shaking. "The fighting is over, Captain. No one is going to hurt you. Are you hearing me clearly?"

She stifled a sob and nodded.

"I want you to help me with your people to make sure there are no mistakes now. Will you work with me on that?"

"Yes, sir," she answered, her voice trembling.

"Where are you from?"

"Plainsboro, New Jersey," she replied, her Jersey accent obvious.

"I grew up near there," he replied as an offer of reassurance. "Now tell me why are you here?"

"I was drafted, along with most of the others here. I got to be captain because I had a college degree."

"In what?"

"Business leadership."

"Oh, just great." John sighed. "All right, Captain, what's your name?"

"Deirdre Johnson."

"Listen to me, Deirdre Johnson. We don't abuse or execute prisoners here, and I want you to work with me to keep your people in check as we get them the hell out of here. Can you do that?"

She took his words in wide eyed, and her shoulders began to shake again.

"Why are you crying?"

"We were told that you rednecks—" She paused. "Sorry, sir. We were told you people execute prisoners." She paused. "That African Americans would be lynched and women raped, so I'm down on two counts."

He stepped closer, shaking his head. "How they turn us against each other," he said sadly. "Look at me. Do I look like a racist and rapist to you? How many women do you see in my ranks? How many of African descent? Tell me!" His voice rose in anger so that she recoiled and then lowered her head.

"You really promise none of us will be hurt or killed?"

"I was a colonel in the United States Army, and on my word of honor, I promise you that as long as you listen to my people and do not try to escape, you will be taken back to Black Mountain and there held until I figure out what to do with you—most likely paroled after this is over." He looked past her to the others. "Did you all hear me clearly?"

There were nods of thanks and several replies of "Yes, sir," more than a few openly crying.

"Are you the superior officer here?"

She looked around at the group and then shook her head and nodded to the pilot still writhing on the ground. "Major Cullman there. He was in overall command here for the airbase. The helicopters crews and maintenance teams were National Guard units, the rest of us ANR."

John stepped away from her and knelt down by Cullman's side, roughly grabbed him by the hair, and pulled his head up. The man's face was scorched, the scent of burned hair and flesh wafting around him.

"You hear me, Major?"

There was a barely audible reply.

"Are you army? I sure as hell can't see you flying the way you did with six months' training."

"Yes. Six years."

John leaned forward, his voice barely a whisper. "Personally, I would like to shoot you myself for what you did to us and the reivers. You broke the code, Major, and I detest you for it. But I won't shoot you, nor will you face trial, because—let me guess—you were only following orders."

Cullman gazed up at him, eyes wide with terror, unable to reply.

John looked over at Grace. "Make this bastard walk, no matter how badly he hurts. Lock him up in some basement along with his gunner and the other pilots and ground crews if you can find them still alive. Regular army we hold for negotiated exchange after all this is over. Now get him out of here before I change my mind."

The sad procession started to shuffle toward the gate that the truck had burst open, while out in the street, the first of the pickups converted into ambulances had pulled up to haul away the wounded.

Maury came up to his side, grinning. "The first Black Hawk is badly shot up, looks like the engine is fried, but the other one is checking out okay, no leaks sprung. I'm going to make a go of it."

John smiled and nodded. "Let's see if you can remember anything." He followed Maury over to the Black Hawk, which several members of his team were guarding. The first of the reserve attack wave was across Tunnel Road and fanning out, scrambling over the supply trucks that apparently had come up from the Asheville airport just after dark.

Another of his strike groups should have been hitting the airport ten miles to the south at this same moment. If the transport plane was still there, it was to be captured or burned. All supplies found were to be taken, and then, in a most crucial move, work crews were to tear up the runway and taxiway at five-hundred-foot intervals, marking both ends with broad *X*s, the international sign that a runway was shut down. There would be no more transports from Bluemont, Charleston, or anywhere else until this issue was clearly resolved.

Maury, favoring his wounded arm, climbed awkwardly into the pilot's seat of the Black Hawk and strapped himself in.

Billy Tyndall, who had never even had five minutes in a chopper, took the copilot's seat, looking over at Maury wide eyed as he flicked on a flashlight, pulled out the preflight checklist, and scanned it. He then looked back at John. "Like I told you, John, it's been more than twenty years since I flew one of these, and that was in an old Huey with the National Guard."

"I heard it's like riding a bicycle," John offered, trying to sound humorous, but given the moment, his comment fell flat.

Maury shook his head and looked over at Billy. "Do you have any idea where the starter button is?"

If not for the seriousness of the situation, John would have started to laugh, but all were interrupted by a shout from out in the compound.

"Incoming!"

A couple of seconds later, a shell impacted a couple of hundred yards to the south.

"Mortar!" a cry went up.

"Maury, stop screwing around! Find the damn starter, rev her up, and get the hell out of here!"

Maury fumbled with various switches, cursing under his breath, and then he finally found his goal, the rotor overhead beginning to turn slowly, turbine engine whining to life. It sounded rough, rumbling, Maury working what he thought was the primer, adjusting the fuel mixture, grasping a lever, the pitch of the rotors changing, cutting deeper, louder.

"I'm not sure if I got it yet!" Maury cried. "Get the hell off, John, unless you want a quick ride to Black Mountain or one helluva crash!"

John stepped back out of the chopper, ducking low and looking to the side of the road where medics were working on the wounded.

"Worse cases that won't make it back to the hospital, load them up!" John shouted.

Six of the wounded, two of them their foes, were carried over. One of the wounded was the old marine, a close friend of Forrest's who had nailed the Apache with the RPG. He was suffering from multiple gunshot wounds across his stomach. John doubted he had more than a few minutes left, but those carrying him did so with tenderness and respect.

John grasped his hand and squeezed it. "You won this one for us, gunny, knocking out that Apache," John said, voice even, the man's eyes drifting out of focus. "Semper fi."

"Didn't get time to fire the second one. Did it get away?"

John held his hand tightly. "You got both with that one shot, Sergeant."

"Incoming!"

John crouched down, the gunny's stretcher-bearers dropping him down and covering him with their own bodies.

The shell detonated fifty yards to the north. They were definitely bracketed, most likely a firing position staring down their throats atop Beaucatcher Mountain.

"Get it up, Maury! Get it up!" John shouted.

The speed of the rotors picked up, Maury working the collective to get the feel of it, sound changing to the distinctive helicopter *thwump, thwump, thwump.* For a brief instant, it flashed John back to Desert Storm, the fleet of helicopters passing overhead in the opening moments of the attack into Iraq.

John ducked back down, and the next mortar round blew just twenty yards away, over near where the wounded were waiting to be loaded onto trucks. More screams echoed even above the roar of the Black Hawk as it lifted half a dozen feet, dropped back down, and began to lift yet again. Then its tail swung violently, nearly crashing into John so that he dived for the pavement. As the chopper swung back the other way and started rising straight up, another mortar round exploding in the wreckage of the burning Apache.

"Come on! Get out! Get out!" John cried, and he could see that most of his personnel were ignoring the incoming, looking up at the captured Black Hawk as if willing it to get up and away. It banked slightly, nearly drifting into the roof of the mall, rotating drunkenly, nose edging over, and then it just sped off into the darkness toward Black Mountain, disappearing into the night.

Another mortar round clipped the procession of prisoners, dropping several along with one of his guards. Grace shouted for them to run down the street to where the flatbed truck waited, John crying for the ambulances to back up, as well.

A thought seized him, and he shouted for one of his troops standing nearby to run down to the prisoners and bring back their captain, and then he ordered everyone to take cover inside the mall.

There was no need for urging. John shoved Kevin Malady through a shattered doorway, his ham radio operator behind him. Lee Robinson brought up the rear, cursing out John for being in the middle of it all.

Within was a dark and haunting sight. He remembered the weekly trip here with Elizabeth and Jennifer years earlier and the ritual of having to drag Jennifer past where the Disney Store had been, negotiating with her as to whether she wanted a Beanie Baby that week or one of the Disney stuffed animals—they cost more and were equal to two Beanies—Economics 101 for a four-year-old. Though painful in a way to recall, he did smile for an instant as he gazed down the darkened corridor, as if half expecting to see his little girl alive again.

Beside her would be Elizabeth, reaching the age where she would slow at the sight of the gaudy jewelry offered at a corridor kiosk, and then they would head to the food court for a snack before going across the street for a movie, where minutes earlier he had ducked low along the roadside to avoid getting shot.

All of it was abandoned ruins, completely looted out in the first week after the Day, though there was hardly a store in the vast complex that contained a single item necessary for survival. Much of it had then been burned by looters gone wild and left to sink into moldy ruin. Once one of the iconic images of affluent American society, a shopping mall, it was now a ghost building filled with ghost memories. He turned away from the memories to examine the building they were in.

The huge Sears building had been turned into a barrack and storage area for the chopper crews and their security team. There was even an electrical generator still running, some fluorescent lights casting an eerie glow on the ruins of fire-gutted wreckage—shattered display cases, a mannequin with a broken face sporting what would have been the summer fashion of two years earlier, debris of a squatter's camp, most likely driven out by the arrival of Fredericks's troops. A disquieting stench of moldy, decaying clothing and waste hung over it all. The wreckage had been pushed back to make way for nearly a hundred bunks, a chow line, and storage area in what had once been the first-floor section devoted to tools and automotive supplies, which of course had been one of the first areas looted.

Several mortar shells crumped onto the ceiling high overhead, but nothing collapsed down from the upper floor.

"Malady, post security. Once the annoyance stops outside, get people into their supply trucks and move them into hiding; get others to check out what we have here."

John took a moment to get on the radio and announce in the clear. "We have one chopper—a Black Hawk—coming back. It is definitely ours."

If Fredericks was monitoring that, it would certainly set him off, and he could imagine the cheers erupting back in Black Mountain.

"Prepare the hospital for at least fifty more wounded coming in."

He clicked off and looked around as his troops, many armed with flashlights, began to search about, and as they rifled the personnel bunkers, there were cries of excitement as MREs, snacks, comfortable sleeping bags, and personal items were snatched up.

"All right, people, listen up!" John shouted, his voice echoing in the cavernous room. "Personal looting stops now. Second squad to secure a perimeter around this building. They won't take their defeat lying down and might try coming back before dawn. Set up firing positions as you were trained to do, keep back from the doors, and stay low. I want the chow area secured by first squad and what rations we can find, one only to then be distributed to each of you. Third squad to that storage area over there; I bet we'll find one helluva stash of weapons and ammunition. Fourth squad to the vehicles outside once the shelling stops, and get them moved. Keep your ears open and ready to run if the shelling resumes. If any of the fuel bladders have not been hit, find a way to move the damn things. They'll weigh several tons each and that is gold for us."

He turned back to his radioman and clicked back on again. "Reserves, move to objective two, then hold in place."

Within the half hour, he wanted them holding the southeast-facing pass of Interstate 240 cutting through Beaucatcher and the old tunnel of Tunnel Road.

John came up to Kevin and put a hand on his shoulder. "Pick out half a dozen of your best, and find the surviving reivers with us; they should be good at this. Give them fifteen minutes to rest and get something to eat, and then I want them to get up atop Beaucatcher Mountain, hunt down that mortar team and any observers, and take them out."

Kevin nodded.

"And, Kevin, what was the butcher bill?"

Kevin sighed and shook his head. "Didn't have much time to tally it yet." He reached into his pocket and pulled out a cluster of dog tags that had been manufactured for every serving soldier in the town's battalion, stamped with name, blood type, and next of kin. "I've collected eighteen of these so far."

He offered them to John, but John did not take the burden. There would be time later after the fight was truly finished.

"Let's see what we've captured," John said softly, a reassuring hand on Kevin's shoulder, "and what can be used immediately." He looked at his wristwatch. It was ten past four local time. All of this in little more than an hour. Sunrise in another hour and a half, and then to the next step, which he prayed would end without another fight. "Where's the captain we took prisoner?"

Malady gestured to where one of his troops was escorting the girl. Someone had tied her hands behind her back.

"Wake me at six, but I want to talk with her first."

John went over to the prisoner, and as he approached, he drew out his pocketknife and snapped it open. At his approach with knife drawn, the prisoner looked terrified, and that reaction filled him with pity. The kid thought he was going to kill her.

"Deirdre, turn around, please."

She just stood their gazing at him.

"Oh for heaven's sake, Deirdre, I'm just going to cut your handcuffs off. Now turn around."

She complied, still nervous, as he carefully sawed through the twist of rope that bound her wrists while telling the prisoner's guard to get something to eat and relax.

Once freed, Deirdre turned back to face him, rubbing her wrists. "Thank you, sir."

"I have your word you won't try to bolt?"

"Yes, sir."

"Fine, then. Now let's go over to your food supply, find something to eat, sit down, and talk."

He let her lead the way to where a small crowd was rummaging through shipping boxes stamped with the old FEMA logo containing old commercially packaged cans. He pulled out one stamped Bacon and Eggs and a plastic-wrapped packet of utensils. He motioned for her to lead the way, and she walked over to a small temporary cubicle.

"This was my bunk," she announced as she sat down on the collapsible camp bed. He looked around. Pinned to the canvas wall that had offered her a modicum of privacy were half a dozen photos.

"Your family?" he asked, his gaze lingering on what was obviously her college graduation day.

She nodded.

"Mind if I look?"

"No, sir."

He unclipped the photo and held it close, examining it with his flashlight. Deirdre was in the middle, beaming with pride, holding her diploma, a tall young man by her side, elderly couples to either side of them, several children in their early teens on both sides and standing in front of her. He forced a smile, yet another frozen memory of the time that was lost, and he respectfully handed the photograph to her. "Who is in the picture?"

She did not reply.

"If you don't want to talk, Deirdre, I understand. I have a photo of my daughter in my wallet. She died from diabetes. It's still hard for me to talk about."

Deirdre looked at the photo, hands shaking slightly.

"That's my parents to my right. My fiancé, Jim." She paused. "He was going on to med school at Rutgers. Those are his parents. The kids are his younger brothers and sisters."

He did not reply. Either she would end it with that or, in a moment, blurt out the rest.

"My parents owned a nursery for roses. I was helping them to run the business side of it." She sighed and then chuckled. "What with the way developments had swept through the area, land value was through the roof. I kept telling them to sell the place; they were sitting on millions, but they loved their rose business. When everything hit the fan, it was only a matter of days before we got looted. As if a dozen acres of a rose farm actually had anything of value to keep you alive. That's when Daddy got killed."

She continued on, falling into a monotone, a recounting of the horrors that to John had become all so familiar, the story of survivors, repeated over and over in a flat, emotionless tone, the story of a nation going into collapse.

She and her mother managed to scratch by until the first winter, thanks to a small garden. Fending off other groups of looters, killing a rapist, not being so successful with killing the second one until after he fell into a drunken sleep, waiting for her fiancé to show up but never hearing from him again, her mother dying of pneumonia the first winter . . . it was a somber, ten-minute recounting of horrors spoken of without emotion.

"When I heard of the ANR, they had set up a recruiting station in Princeton. I joined. I actually believed their line that they were helping to rebuild America, and besides, it was a couple of real meals a day, and frankly, it was safety, as well. They were taking anyone who walked through the door voluntarily. An hour later, they said I'd make officer. I went into a training camp at the university campus, and it darn near felt like heaven at first. A warm building, real food . . . I actually put ten pounds back on within a month, and then they shipped us out.

"My first tour of duty was guarding the approach out of New York City. My unit was down in Hoboken with orders to shoot anyone trying to get across the river."

"What?"

She gazed at him and shook her head. "Didn't you hear, sir? Plague, ebola—you name it—was rampant on the other side of the river. Rumor was there was still a hundred thousand or so living in the wreckage. It was medieval, the way the city was still burning. Hard to believe anything could still be found to burn. Those trying to get out we were ordered to shoot on sight."

"And did you?"

She sighed. "At first, I couldn't. Tried warning shots. They'd be in rafts, small boats, even some trying to swim across. But after a while, it was them or us." She lowered her head.

"Yeah, I helped shoot them. We were told if any of us even touched one of them, we would be shot, as well." She looked up at him. "What would you have done, sir?"

He had no reply for her question. "Go on, tell me the rest."

"After that my unit was pulled with orders to report to Bluemont for special training."

He sat up a bit at the mention of Bluemont. At last, someone who had actually been there other than Fredericks.

"What did you see? Did you meet the new president? Is the government really up and functioning?" The eagerness in his voice was obvious.

She sighed and shook her head. "I didn't see anyone other than our trainers. Our unit was there for a month of advanced infantry training in urban combat. Sorry, sir, but that's all I saw."

He sat there silent, frustrated.

"We thought it weird. I mean, I had some interest in history, even thought of majoring in it in college. Old films of presidents and generals talking with troops. Morale boosting and all of that. We just went into an encampment in a town nearby that any surviving civilians had been cleared out of and practiced taking buildings. Rumors were that we were going to be sent to the Midwest. No one wants to go to Chicago, Cleveland, Pittsburgh, and that had us worried."

"Why?"

"Haven't you heard the news?"

"We tune into BBC, that's about it."

She shook her head. "Other ANR units were coming in, same as us. Forming up into battalion-level strength. We bunked in with a unit recruited out of Ohio. They said most of that part of the country is level five. Gangs forming into their own armies, some of them nut job religious cults, others just, well, just barbarians."

He thought of their own fight with the Posse but said nothing, just letting her go on as she talked about the rumors, the execution of a trooper who tried to desert, the fact that there appeared to be an abundance of food and supplies—at least in the Bluemont area—that lulled them all into compliance, and then finally the wave of fear when their company was pulled out of the assignment to Chicago with orders to accompany a new administrator to North Carolina.

"Why fear?"

She hesitated.

"Go on. There's nothing to be afraid of now, Deirdre. Once all this gets straightened out, I'm giving prisoners with the ANR the option of staying on with us or trying to make their way back to their homes."

"Really, sir?"

He actually reached out and took her hand. She was only a couple of years older than the students who formed his own "army," and though battle hardened, he still at many times saw them as his kids.

"We were told that you people didn't take prisoners. And like I said earlier, me being black, we were told . . ." Her voice trailed off.

"Those sons of bitches," he whispered.

She just looked at him.

If her words were the truth, it was a stunning revelation of just who was in charge in Bluemont and reinforcement that his decision not to comply, to fight back, was the right one.

"Remember, I'm from Jersey too," he finally replied.

"Which exit?" she asked with a touch of a smile, offering the old standard joke.

"Near Exit 150 off the GSP."

"Around Newark?"

"Yeah."

"You don't sound it now, sir."

"Live here for a while; it changes things."

He smiled and then turned serious, feeling that they had broken down barriers a bit. "I first came south over thirty years ago to go to Duke. Yeah, all the old stereotypes had me going too. Friends up north used to joke that I'd wind up like that guy in the movie *Deliverance*."

"They actually showed us that movie one night. Said things had reverted back to that way down here."

"Those bastards." John sighed. It was the standard routine of dividing one off against the other with fear. No wonder the prisoners were petrified. Some of the reivers were definitely tough looking, but to play on that sick stereotype? "So you got shipped down here and thought we were all toothless rednecks and moonshiners?"

"Yeah, something like that. The entire unit is recruits from Jersey. I did start to wonder about that, why were they shipping us here and taking recruits from down here and shipping them up north."

"Standard routine, Deirdre. Never set one's own people against their neighbors and kin. Tell them the other side is different and hates you. They were going to take a hundred or so from my community and offered me the job of major general."

"You a major general?" she asked, obviously surprised.

"Something like that."

"And you turned it down?"

"Again, something like that. It's kind of what this entire fight is all about."

She was silent for a moment. "I'm sorry, sir. We didn't know. We were kept separate from the day we got here. Told any of the civilians we encountered could be terrorists and all of you were in open rebellion against the new government."

"If you guys had been allowed just a few days' leave to mingle about a bit, you'd have seen different. We're still Americans here."

"What about Chicago, Cleveland, places like that?"

"I know just about as much as you do, Deirdre. Yeah, we faced gangs, and chances are they're still out there. But most of us who survived the Day? I think we want nothing more than to come together again as a country and rebuild. Instead, it seems like some are turning us against each other."

"Bluemont?"

"If Fredericks is representative of what they are, I'll have to say yes."

She took that in and sighed. Absently, she popped the lid on the can of dried scrambled eggs and bacon, scooping up a handful to munch on and offering the can to John, who refused.

The sight of it was tempting; he could not even recall the last time he had actually tasted real bacon. He recalled reports of how, prior to the Day, the government had brought up literally billions of dollars of such rations on top of the huge stockpile of MREs the military always kept on hand. Except for the day a battalion of regular army troops had come through Black Mountain more than a year earlier, he and his neighbors and friends had never seen such emergency rations. It filled him with a deep bitterness.

"We both need to get a little rest. But first, a few questions. You don't have to answer them if you don't want to."

"Name, rank, and number—type things?" she asked.

"Yeah, you could call it that."

She did not reply.

"How many troops came with Fredericks?"

She hesitated.

"Deirdre, you're going to have to make a choice. If you don't answer, I'll leave it go at that. No torture or any of the other crap they filled you with about how we fight down here. Regardless of what you decide, there is going to be one helluva fight for Asheville in a couple of hours. Maybe what you tell me can help save lives, both of my people and those with your unit."

She took another handful of the dried eggs and bacon, started to chew, and then began to shake, stifling back a sob. "Seventy-five here as security for the helicopter pad, a hundred or so downtown, billeted in the county jail," the other half garrisoned in the county jail downtown," she began softly. "Nearly all of us came in within the last week by transport to the airport south of town. We thought it strange the way we were moved in at night and forbidden any contact with the locals. Also a tech and support unit from what was supposedly the old army for the four choppers. And finally, a personal security squad for Fredericks. Those bastards, we don't know where they came from, but none of us liked them, and they were kept separate."

He patted her on the shoulder as she truly let go.

"Guess this makes me a traitor."

"A traitor to traitors, Deirdre?"

She looked over at him.

"You did the right thing. Now try to get a little rest. I want you with me when we go in; maybe you can help convince the others not to fight and save lives."

He stood up, and she curled up on her cot, clutching the open can of dried eggs and bacon.

He walked back over to Kevin, who had been conveniently standing close by.

"You hear all of that?" he whispered.

"Everything."

"Let's hope it doesn't turn into a fight; we've lost too many already."

Kevin was silent.

"I need a few minutes' sleep. Is that okay with you, Kevin?"

"Wide awake here, sir."

John smiled and patted him on the shoulder. He hated to admit it, but he was pulling rank. Twice Kevin's age, he was definitely feeling it now. He found a quiet corner, lay down on the bare floor, and slipped into dreamless, exhausted slumber.

CHAPTER SIXTEEN

"Sir, it's time."

Startled, John looked about in surprise. Daylight streamed through the blown-out doors and windows of the store, and he sat up, shocked by—of all things—the smell of coffee.

One of his troopers was kneeling down by his side, smiling broadly, holding out a cup.

"I remember how you used to come into class every morning with a steaming cup—black."

John nodded a thanks. "Where in the hell did you get this?"

"Sir, they must have a couple of thousand MREs back there and cases of that survival food. Check this out." He offered John a plastic container filled with something dark red and in slices. "Freeze-dried strawberries. We each got a handful. Just stick them in your mouth; it's a real treat."

John tried one and nodded again. It did indeed taste heavenly, and so did the real coffee. *When was the last time?* And then it hit him: Forrest had given him a cup every morning while he was a prisoner. But other than that, coffee had run out within the first month after the Day.

The rush of caffeine startled him, and he was glad when another one of his troops, a sergeant in his late thirties, came over to share a plate of beans and a hunk of cheese. All around him were wolfing down their meals, and then—the temptation of temptations—he smelled cigarettes. Several of the reivers had found a stash in someone's personal locker. It was such a dreadful siren call, but he resisted it.

His radio operator was sitting up, working the dial on the set that he had taken off from his backpack, the two dials glowing dimly.

"Anything?" John asked.

"Chopper is safely down, wounded are in the hospital, and our observers up along the parkway report a lot of activity around the courthouse— they say they actually have a Bradley Fighting Vehicle parked out front of it. They've ringed the place in tight."

"I've monitored a number of urgent broadcasts saying they are about to be overrun by 'terrorists and rebels.'" The old man sighed. "Us, *we* are the ones branded as the terrorists and rebels even after what they did. They're sending out an urgent appeal for immediate help from Greenville, South Carolina, and Johnson City, Tennessee."

"The reply?"

The old man laughed. "Basically, it was 'You are up the creek without a paddle, and screw you.' Typical, John. Everyone covers their own turf, and to hell with anyone else. Johnson City claims a fuel shortage but might be able to send a convoy later in the day if Asheville can promise that the Interstate 26 pass over the mountains is secured from the reivers."

John chuckled.

"Hope you don't mind, but I took the liberty of cutting in when they weren't chattering and said we own the pass."

"And Greenville?"

"No response. Not a word back."

He took that in. They could have switched to another frequency. Greenville had good access to the coast; they could move a lot up quickly if motivated to strike back.

"And then there was the BBC again. Caught their 5:00 a.m. broadcast before the signal went weak." The old man sighed.

"Well?"

"China repeated the threat that if any neutron bomb is used anywhere near them in the continental United States or anywhere on a demarcation line that I guess runs down the Continental Divide, they will construe that as an attack upon their homeland and retaliate with a full nuclear strike on Bluemont and a number of other cities, including Charleston. John, it is getting damn ugly out there. There were other reports of global condemnation of the neutron bomb strike on Chicago. BBC is reporting chaos over here, and then I lost the signal."

Suddenly, the coffee in John's stomach felt sour, nauseating. No matter how horrid the gangs, mobs, or just plain insane characters that had risen up in the wreckage of those once bustling cities, there was something about hitting them with neutron bombs, slaughtering nearly all that still struggled to survive within the cities who were hiding out from the gangs, that was beyond his grasp of understanding. Hunt down the criminals, yes, and execute those who had turned to the lowest barbarism, such as the Posse, but to indiscriminately kill all in what was left of the cities, claiming that all were now in rebellion against some central authority?

He stood up, shaking off the gloom that this news had cast as Kevin approached, grinning broadly.

"My God, sir, have we got a haul!" Kevin announced loudly. "Thousands of rounds of twenty-millimeter shells, .50 caliber, case after case of .223, grenades, rockets for the Apaches, over a hundred shoulder weapons of military grade, and—as you can tell by the scent—rations to feed this entire army for several days. A case of handheld two-way radios of variable frequencies, a dozen night-vision goggles, cases of various batteries, electrical generators . . . the list goes on. Six trucks they had stashed down below the old Lowe's building have yet to be inventoried, along with two fuel bladders—one with jet fuel for the choppers, the other with gas—pure, clean gas! Five hundred gallons' worth, not counting the topped-off tanks in the trucks."

"All that for what?" John sighed. "What does it mean?"

"To kick our asses back into the Stone Age."

"Yup."

What a fool Fredericks truly is, John thought as he took in this latest information. All that equipment and helicopters, but positioned out here rather than somewhere deep within the city. Was it that he mistrusted the civilians still trying to survive in Asheville? Regardless, it was a stupid position to take, perhaps motivated in some strange way by a memory of things past—the American shopping mall as a place of comfort, indulgence, and security—even though John had always detested them and went there simply to please his kids. It was Dale's stupidity and now definitely his gain for the final move.

He stepped outside for a moment to relieve himself while still nursing the soothing cup of coffee. Up along Tunnel Road, some reserve troops were breaking their temporary camp and shouldering up their backpacks, now loaded with extra ammunition and rations. Like any father, he could spot his own child in a crowd of thousands, and he saw that Elizabeth was with the column.

Elizabeth? With the stress of preparing for the attack, he had tried not to think about her. She had insisted that she fall in with the reserve battalion. John could not veto her demand and had simply nodded agreement, unable to speak.

As he watched them head out, spreading out into combat column spaced far apart on either side of the road, he remembered the legendary story of General Robert E. Lee at Antietam: at the climax of the battle, the Union troops about to break through his center, he had personally ordered in a reserve battery of artillery only to then see his beloved youngest son, not yet eighteen, going into that most deadly of fights. But he did not stop, did not call out to the battery commander with orders to send his child to the rear. He had turned and rode away to other sectors of the line. Only at day's end, having barely hung on to fight another day, did Lee return to that stricken position, breaking down in tears when he saw that his boy had survived unscathed.

If Elizabeth demanded to serve with the reserves that would now be the main assault force, if an attack was needed to finish this fight, he could not stop her. He recalled as well a much-beloved film, a favorite of his students when he showed it in class, about a Quaker family during the Civil War, the father portrayed by Gary Cooper, who, when confronted by his son's decision to fight, had replied, "I am only his father, not his conscience."

He went back into the Sears building where his troops where strapping on gear, gulping down the last of their cups of coffee, and forming up to move out. They truly did look like combat veterans, youth with old eyes, a sense of perpetual weariness at age twenty. But regardless of their weariness, they were ready to go into the next fight.

"The mortar position and their outposts?" John asked Kevin, forcing his thoughts away from his daughter.

"Took them out nearly an hour ago, though not sure we have all the outposts. But we did capture the mortar intact with fifty rounds."

"Our losses?"

"Two dead, one wounded," Kevin replied.

"Prisoners?"

He shook his head, and John did not ask. The fight was getting ugly, and after the outrages committed against the reivers and his own town, unless he was present to enforce discipline as he knew it, the passion of the moment was bound to take hold. He had come dangerously close to it himself with the Apache pilot.

He stood up, stretched, and nodded to the door. "Time?" he asked, gulping down the last of his coffee.

"Five minutes to go."

John nodded. "Saddle up."

Out the door of the Sears building, he started the long walk up Tunnel Road, passing the collapsed sign of the Old Mountaineer Motel, a favorite diner of his from before all of this started across the street. It was a walk he wouldn't have thought of doing three years earlier when one had a car to go from parking lot to parking lot. But now? Though far more fit, he was feeling his age, and his cracked rib hurt like hell. Within a few hundred yards, he felt a bit winded as his far younger troopers, support units, and personal security squad kept sprinting ahead while his fractured rib throbbed with every step. The radio crackled with a report from an observer that she could see black-clad troops running down from the tunnel entrance and into the twin courthouses and the county jail alongside it, with positions manned behind heavy concertina wire. Dale had played it as he had hoped—pulling all his assets back into that complex of buildings, most likely assuming his Alamo could hold out until help from the outside finally arrived.

Not a shot had been fired so far as he paused for a moment to catch his breath at the entry to the tunnel that passed under Beaucatcher Mountain and emerged on the far side with the courthouse complex straight ahead. Several squads were running through it, their footsteps sounding hollow while the main assault force pressed through the gap of I-240, flanking wide before infiltrating into the center of town above the courthouse center.

He followed the lead elements, flanked by Lee Robinson, still ready to haul him out of harm's way, his radio operator, security team, and message runners squinting from the morning sunlight as they emerged on the far side and gazed down at last on Asheville. It was once a vibrant, bustling city of a hundred thousand. At last estimate, there were fewer than five thousand still alive in its abandoned buildings and streets, most huddled along the French Broad River on the west side of town—and hopefully well clear of a fight if one was about to happen.

The skyline was still essentially the same, though shortly after the Day, the old Battery Park Apartments had burned to the ground. The BB&T building was somewhat intact, though a number of windows had been knocked out, a perfect place for a heavy-weapons squad to set up on an upper floor—a position that Kevin Malady, leading a unit burdened down with captured armaments along with a dozen reivers toting deer rifles and high-powered scopes, was racing to secure. He heard a distant humming that grew louder, and then he saw the L-3 passing overhead, Billy Tyndall at the controls, undoubtedly far more comfortable in his old plane after the experience of flying in a helicopter with Maury. The radio with John crackled to life.

"Bravo Xray online and overhead. I'll call it as I see it."

Unlike Don Barber, who had come in far too low during the fight with the Posse, John had ordered Billy to stay at least fifteen hundred feet above the fray and to get the hell out if any fire came up his way. He had not even considered the prospect of putting Maury and whatever helicopter they were lucky enough to capture into this one. He'd either crash out of sheer amateurish piloting or get shot down within five minutes. That asset was to be cherished for some future use.

He looked at his watch. It was a quarter to eight. Fifteen minutes more to let his far more fleet-footed young troops sprint to the far side of the court-house, enveloping it from the north and south and cutting off retreat, while some of the captured heavy weapons were moved up for the assault from the east.

The minutes clicked off. There was an occasional explosion of small-arms fire, either a sniper taken out or trigger-happy troops on his side reacting to a shadow in the window.

Two minutes before eight.

John turned to his radioman. He had feared that the batteries for the old-fashioned unit would not have held out this long, but they had captured a supply in the cache at Sears. D batteries were a thing of the past, but with a little twisting of wires, his man had rigged it up to work for several hours more using captured double As.

"All positions reporting in," was the report, and John nodded. He felt obligated to try one time, and he took the mike, clicking it several times first.

"Fredericks, I know you are monitoring this channel. The game is up. We've captured your helicopter base, along with a Black Hawk. You can hear one of my planes overhead; we own the air now. The courthouse is surrounded. There is no alternative but surrender. Tell your people to drop their weapons and come out with their hands up. All who surrender will be treated by the rules of war and will be exchanged or paroled. That is my one and only offer, Fredericks. I have someone else here who wants to speak to those under your command."

He held the mike open, and nodded for Deirdre to speak.

She identified herself, repeated John's offer, and added that what they had been told about the treatment of prisoners was a lie. All had been fed and treated with respect, and the wounded were already back in a hospital. "What they told us is a lie!" she cried. "I know many of you. Please surrender. This is a senseless fight. Please listen to me."

John took the mike back. "Any of you serving under the lying despot, this so-called administrator Fredericks, put your weapons down now, come out with hands up, and you will receive parole and exchange and returned to your families. You have one minute to act. Otherwise, may God have mercy on your souls."

"Sir, can't you just wait?" It was Deirdre. "Sit it out for a day or so, and I know most will crack. Let me keep talking to those with the ANR. They don't want this fight any more than you do and will surrender if given a chance."

He wanted to agree with her. He knew taking on troops dug into the courthouse, county office, and county jail would be costly. But time most likely would be on Fredericks's side. If Greenville responded with air assets, they could be here in little more than thirty minutes, and everything would unravel. A couple of Apache helicopters circling overhead would switch the odds back to Fredericks's side. If there was any chance of taking him out, it had to be now.

He shook his head, hoping her appeal for surrender worked.

There was a flurry of shots from within the courthouse, half a dozen running out. One dropped to the pavement, shot in the back from within the courthouse.

John clicked the mike back. "All units, hold fire! Hold fire! Let them surrender!"

The half dozen did not make it far, a burst of automatic fire from an upper floor of the federal building slaughtering them. There was more fire from the county jail, flashes of gunfire from within. A door burst open, and two more ran out. They were dropped, as well.

"Those were friends of mine!" Deirdre cried. "His security team is killing them!"

"Damn you, Fredericks!" John shouted. "For God's sake, show some mercy!"

Several more tried for a run from the county office. All died within seconds.

"It's on your soul, Fredericks!" John cried. "And those who stand with you!" He had one flare left. He raised the pistol over his head and fired it off.

A fusillade of fire erupted seconds later from the three-hundred-plus troops deployed around the courthouse. He now wanted to keep his losses at a minimum; it was simply a question of overawing or—if need be— waiting them out unless he received word that Greenville was sending choppers up. He prayed that resistance would collapse before then, that there would be no need for a frontal assault or charge and resulting slaughter out of some Civil War battle or amphibious beachfront attack.

Overawe in the first minutes. Break the will of the jittery ANR troops inside.

With the captured armaments from the helicopter base, there was a surfeit of ammunition for once. A .50-caliber machine gun moved up by a team of Afghan vets to a position on the roof of the BB&T building poured an arcing stream of heavy fire down on the three main buildings of the courthouse complex, incendiary rounds igniting fires in the upper floors of the courthouse. He held back the two dozen air-to-ground rockets designed for the Apaches, because no one was sure of how to properly mount and shoot them, but half a dozen of the town's homemade RPGs were fired, several going off wildly but two striking the county offices, igniting yet another fire in an upper floor. In an amazingly lucky strike, one hit the Bradley, the crew within abandoning the vehicle and running for the security of the courthouse, though there did not appear to be any real damage to the vehicle.

After the initial rain of fire in an attempt to overawe, the situation settled down to near silence and carefully aimed shots by trained snipers on John's side. If Deirdre's ridiculous stereotype of mountain rednecks had one true point, it was that John had in his ranks dozens of highly skilled hunters armed with deer rifles and high-powered scopes, and it was doubtful that his opponent had the same.

The morning dragged on, heat increasing, John looking at his watch ever more anxious, his radioman catching several quick appeals from someone other than Fredericks to Greenville calling for air support.

John could feel the pressure building. Greenville to Asheville was indeed within air-support range for Apaches. From liftoff to attack, they could be on him in little more than twenty minutes. Billy had returned twice to Black Mountain to refuel, and John sent an order for him to climb up to at least eight thousand feet, move south to over Hendersonville, and report in if any kind of air support or ground movement up from South Carolina was approaching.

They were four hours into the siege. In his mind, he felt he could, if need be, let it drag out for days since Greenville had not yet taken any action, but if they did, the tide could turn in a matter of minutes, and this chance to end the madness would be lost.

The top two floors of the county office were completely ablaze, black smoke billowing straight up in the hot, still noonday air. In the county office building adjoining the courthouse, numerous smaller fires were burning on nearly every floor. The sight of it sickened John in a way. Everyone who lived in the region knew the legend of how, during the Second World War, the local hero, Bob Morgan, pilot of the *Memphis Belle*, one of the first B-17 bombers to complete twenty-five missions against the Germans, had flown his plane between the two buildings in an ultimate buzz job. His grave was at the veterans' cemetery in Black Mountain, where those who died fighting the Posse rested. Before his death, Morgan was a regular guest visitor to John's class. John connected those memories to this tragic moment, where the buildings now housed an enemy and those dragooned into serving him and what he allegedly represented.

"White flag!" one of his team cried.

John raised his binoculars, focused on the county building, and there was indeed a white sheet or towel hanging out of a window, a floor above where the fires raged. Someone was standing in the window, waving, making the gesture of throwing his weapon out to clatter on the pavement below. Smoke began to billow out of the room he was in so that he climbed out onto the window ledge.

The sight sickened John. It was, of course, a gut-wrenching reminder burned into the heart of every American, the memory of the morning of 9/11.

The man tried to crawl along the ledge, and John felt a swelling of pride in his troops in that no one fired at the man, and several around John were whispering encouragement.

And then he lost his balance, tottered, and fell, plunging twelve stories to his death, and John heard groans of anguish erupting around him.

He turned back to his radioman and took the mike. "For God's sake, Fredericks! Your people are burning alive on the upper floors! Get them the hell out! We will not shoot!"

He paused a few seconds, clicking the mike five times to signal it was a message to all units. "All units, all units. Cease fire unless directly fired upon. Let them surrender. Let them surrender."

Apparently, there was more than one radio link between the three build-

ings under siege monitoring his own broadcasts. Within seconds, a dozen
more white flags were out from upper floors. Someone in the prison building had managed to find enough bedding; after shattering a window,
someone tossed a rope ladder of sheets out the window and started rap-
pelling down the side, reaching the pavement six floors down and holding
the rope ladder taut as a woman in black uniform came out next. But before
she had dropped a floor, shots rang out from the county courthouse, and
she plunged to her death. The man on the ground ducked low and ran hard,
dropping as puffs of shattered concrete erupted around him, but then he
was up again, reaching a low stone wall and tumbling over it.

"Send someone down there and try to find that man and bring him to
me!" John shouted, and one of his security team got up, crouched low, and
sprinted off.

Apparently, at least one sniper in the upper floor of the federal building was still alert and nearly hit his runner, triggering another explosion of
return fire that plastered the side of the building for several minutes.

"Deirdre, you got the guts to get closer?" John asked.

She looked over at him and nodded. "Yes, sir."

He motioned to his radioman. "Ready for a little running?"

"John, I'd prefer not, but I'm game if you are."

"Damn it, John," Lee snapped. "You can control things just fine from
here."

John looked at his old friend and smiled. "Okay, everyone, take a deep
breath." He hesitated. The order was indeed so hackneyed in so many bad
movies. "Follow me."

He got up, crouched low, and started to sprint down the Tunnel Road,
zigzagging every few seconds, startled a bit when he heard a bullet slap by
close to his face. It was a long two-hundred-yard run down to the base of
the hill, every gasp for air an absolute agony, until he finally dodged into
cover behind a building at the northwest corner of the traffic circle below
the courthouse complex.

He looked back. One of his team was down, clutching his leg below the
knee, a medic dragging him to cover, shots kicking up around them. He
did not need to call for suppressive fire. Several hundred rounds slammed

into the three buildings, any window that still had a pane of glass shatter-ing. Whoever had fired on him and wounded one of his team was either dead or cowering.

"Deirdre, you can talk your people out better than I can. You've seen how we've behaved since taking you prisoner. Do you trust me?"

She looked at him and nodded.

"Try to talk them out and end this before any more people get hurt. I promise you, I will move anyone with the ANR who surrenders to arrange their repatriation back to their homes as quickly as possible."

At this point, as to the fate of Fredericks and others, he was making no promises after more than four hours of this day's madness and the weeks leading up to it.

Deirdre took the megaphone and began to appeal to those within the courthouse complex to surrender and end the killing. Her appeal was heartfelt at times that she was in tears, begging those within to just give up and come out with hands up. Then she made a gesture John had not antic-ipated, and it happened so quickly he did not have time to react. Deirdre suddenly stepped out into the middle of the traffic circle, megaphone still raised.

"Please, all of you. Surrender. I promise you, you'll be treated fairly. It was those who brought us here who lied."

A single shot clipped her shoulder, spinning her around and dropping her in the middle of the traffic circle.

John, horrified, sprinted to where she lay writhing in pain and scooped an arm around her, pulling her up as he started to drag her back. One of his security team leaped out, weapon raised to cover the two, and he top-pled over backward, shot in the forehead.

Lee reached out, grabbing the two, dragging them the last few feet back into cover, the brick from the corner of the building peppering them with fragments.

Lee grabbed the radio mike. "Leader okay. Now tear the bastards apart!" he cried.

John cradled Deirdre as a medic came up to their side, crouching low. The medic, carrying a standard pack looted from the stockpile in Sears, cut Deirdre's shirt open. She had been punctured just below the left collarbone, and contrary to all movies, a shoulder wound was not merely a nick with the bundle of blood vessels, nerves, and bones just above the rib cage and heart. The medic slapped on a sterile compress, pumped a morphine vial looted from medical supplies found in the Sears building into the young woman's upper arm, stuck the empty syringe to her collar to indicate the dose she had received, and called for stretcher-bearers to take her to the rear.

"Sorry, sir," Deirdre said, looking up at John. "Thought if they saw me they'd lay down their arms."

"It's okay, Captain," he gasped, a wave of pain hitting him from his fractured rib. "You are one helluva brave woman, even if you are foolish."

He looked back out to the street where the young soldier of his security detail was dead, blood pooling on to the pavement. Yet another kid from one of his classes. It wasn't Deirdre's fault; it was war with all its stupidity and random violence that had killed the young man.

Stretcher-bearers came up and lifted Deirdre to carry her off.

"When all this is over," John said, "I hope you stay on with us. We need soldiers like you."

She forced a weak smile of thanks. "Nothing to go home to now, anyhow. Thank you."

The next ten minutes were an explosion of unrelenting fire poured into the courthouses, and he sat silently, staring at the young man lying dead in the middle of the traffic circle. A decent lad caught up in madness who had died trying to do the right thing. And chances were that so many down in the courthouse complex believed they were fighting for the right thing, as well. But they had to be defeated now if his community had any hope of survival.

Finally, after the long, sustained barrage, white flags began to appear in windows in all three buildings, but he let the fusillade continue on. It was time to break them entirely.

"Tell all units to cease fire," John finally announced.

His radio operator looked over at him. "Billy reports he thinks he sees at least three helicopters coming up from Greenville."

"Scan the frequencies. See if you can find the one they're operating on— most likely one of the aviation ones, perhaps the standard 122.9 of uncontrolled air space."

As the gunfire slacked off, with only an occasional return shot from the county building where it looked like part of the roof had collapsed in, John edged to the corner of his concealment and held the megaphone up, clicking it on. "This is John Matherson of Black Mountain and commander of the forces engaged against you. I am giving all of you five minutes to surrender and come out with hands up. This is my final offer. If you do not comply immediately, we will storm the buildings, and no prisoners will be taken. You have five minutes to surrender unconditionally but with the promise that you will be treated by the Geneva Accords. Otherwise, you damn well better be ready to die for that scum leader of yours."

In less than a minute, a side door of the county prison burst open, the first few stepping out looking about nervously and then breaking into a run down the street, staying close to the north wall of the building. From the office building next to the courthouse, it was the same, several score pouring out from a south-facing door, out of view of the county building. From the county building, the fugitives dashed out the side door facing Tunnel Road. Several ran from the main entry, and again, a flurry of shots from inside the building dropped some, but the majority were now making it to safety. Return fire tore into the front entry even as those pouring out of the other buildings raced across the potentially fatal open ground. The first of them reached John's position, having no idea who he was. They were wide eyed and terrified, begging for mercy. He would rather spare them than kill them, but after all that had happened, he gazed at them with disgust and shouted for someone to take charge of the prisoners and get them to the rear.

After ten minutes, no one else emerged. His radio operator announced that someone inside the building was desperately calling for air support from Greenville, the choppers going into a holding position just south of Hendersonville, which was only a few minutes away by air.

It was a moment where Maury, back in Asheville, knew what to do, starting up with spoof radio traffic on the same frequency, announcing he and his assets were up and waiting to take out any approaching aircraft, the frequency jammed up with signals that John prayed was buying them time.

It was a risk John could not tolerate. Fredericks would spin out his account of the disaster in the manner all such stories were spun going back thousands of years, and though John doubted the government Fredericks represented would be willing to drop a neutron bomb on them, two or three fuel-air explosives could nevertheless destroy his beloved valley and all whom he held dear. It had to end now.

"All units. At my signal, once those surrendering are clear, suppressive fire for two minutes, assault units to go in and secure the buildings."

He half stepped out from the safety of where he had set up his command post. A dozen or so black uniforms were running for their lives, a few shots coming only from the county office.

"On my mark. Now!"

There was another explosion of fire, all of it focused in on the county office, and there was a fury to it now, a release of rage by his troops, fed up with all that had transpired and knowing that the cause of it was at last pinned down to this one final corner of trapped bastards.

The assault teams started to dash in, crouching low under the suppressive fire, those racing for the federal office and county jail not showing too much concern as they burst into the buildings, but the county office was a different story. A heavy weapon, concealed and silent throughout the fight, now opened up from the third floor, dropping half a dozen of the team heading for the front entry. The way one of them was running, John—like any father—could recognize it was his daughter. A girl running next to her crumpled over, but his daughter pressed on. He watched, heart racing as she disappeared from his sight, his view of her blocked by the building. John could not contain himself. He stood up and started for the side entrance, his security team cursing him soundly, shouting for him to stay back as they sprinted ahead with younger legs and stronger hearts.

None of them were hit, but out at the front of the courthouse where his daughter was looked bad. The assault team dived for cover and scattered, even as John's team reached the side entryway where, across the years, those waiting for their cases—from traffic tickets to divorces to civil suits and criminal charges—had stood wreathed in cigarette smoke, waiting for the courthouse to open. It was a tawdry place in John's mind, having stood out there himself when he had decided years earlier to fight an unfair traffic stop from an overeager trooper on Route 70 who claimed he was two miles per hour over the speed limit. His angry comment to the judge that the trooper was just looking to make her quota for the month had lost him his case, but it was worth it for being able to at least say exactly how he felt about things.

And now he was running for that door as if his life depended on it, which it most certainly did. The glass door was shattered, his team leader diving through it and coming up with weapon raised, sending a burst of fire down the corridor to cover the others storming in.

John lagged far behind, cursing the day he had taken up his first cigarette. The long-abandoned and defunct metal detector that guarded the entryway was still there, his team pushing past it, heading for the stairs that led up to the main floor. The foyer had been built in a grand old style, soaring up three stories, ringed with balconies along the four walls leading to offices on upper floors, and the foyer was thus a death trap. There were several explosions; someone was dropping grenades from above. One of his team dropped and was being dragged back to cover.

Damn it. When will they ever give up? John thought, boiling with rage.

His people were pouring in enough suppressive fire to disrupt the defense against the main entryway facing downtown Asheville, several dozen charging in, creeping up stairs one at a time, firing toward the balconies, and dropping several of the defenders. And then suddenly, the firing slackened, several weapons being thrown over railings to clatter onto the floor of the foyer, black-clad troops, crying that they were surrendering, holding up their hands and nervously coming down from the upper floors. Nearly all with him held fire, though one of his troopers, filled with rage, nearly reignited the fight when she shot one of the surrendering foes in the head as she turned the final bend of the staircase. She was jumped on and dragged back as she screamed at those surrendering that they were all murderers.

John did not react but knew he'd have to deal with it later.

Shots erupted from the corner office suite that John knew was the nerve center and where Fredericks, he hoped, was most likely dug in. Sandbags had been piled around the entryway, the gunner guarding the approach collapsed and dead.

"Fredericks, it's over with. Your people have surrendered!" John shouted. "You got thirty seconds to come out, or we blow the rest of this apart and leave you to burn to death, because this building is coming down in flames once we pull back."

A broken door ever so slowly cracked open, and to John's utter disbelief, the man was looking out at him, wearing his ubiquitous jacket and tie as if ready to head off for a noonday power lunch meeting.

"Matherson, you could have written your own ticket, and I was ready to write it for you."

"Just come out slowly, you bastard. Hands up."

"For what? A trial by you and then a hanging?"

John would not admit here that was precisely his intent after the crimes that Fredericks had committed, the hundreds who were dead because of him.

"John, I was only following orders, and I suspect you do hate those five words, 'I was only following orders.'"

"You're damn right, I do!" John shouted in reply.

"Were you only following orders in Iraq? Were your minions only following orders when you executed the leaders and followers of the Posse?"

He did not reply.

"Greenville's air-assault team will be here any minute, and if you kill me, John, the word will come down from Bluemont to neutron or fuel-air your precious hick village."

It was precisely what John feared, and Fredericks had hit a nerve.

"Ah, I sense hesitation," Fredericks taunted back. "So what's it going to be, John? We talk this out like two reasonable men, or your community ceases to exist. You'd better call it now; the clock is ticking down."

Damn, he is good, John thought. As good as so many he had witnessed long ago, stalking the halls of power, amoral sociopaths drawn to power who, behind the smiles and handshakes and backslapping, held men and women of moral convictions and a soul-stirring love of a concept of the Republic in contempt. He knew far too many like Fredericks who, while mouthing platitudes, actually held everyone in secret disdain, because they as "leaders" knew what was best "for the people."

John took several steps forward. "It's over, Fredericks. And no, I will not trade you back. You will stand trial in front of the people you ordered murdered where a jury of twelve of your peers shall decide your fate."

"You mean you don't have the guts to just order me hung now, as you did that Posse leader?"

"I hold you in contempt lower than that sick bastard I hung," John replied. "He was driven by hunger and a twisted belief in his Satan that he worshipped. You, you son of a bitch, were driven by something far deeper and darker. You are beneath contempt."

John stepped closer, pistol in his hand half-raised. "Hands up, Fredericks, and step out slowly."

Fredericks lowered his head, and his voice began to choke up. "Okay, John, I quit, but know if you kill me, you've lost your best bet to negotiate your way out of things with Bluemont. I'm worth a helluva lot more to you alive than dead."

John sighed and nodded. The bastard was right. "Someone arrest him and get him out of here. And clear the wounded before his damned place collapses on all of us."

He turned his back and began to walk away, disgusted with the entire end of this affair. His rage of minutes before had cooled. Fredericks would live, and chances were, trial or not, he'd be a bargaining chip with Bluemont in the end to spare further retaliation, and then another Fredericks would eventually arrive, for vermin like him certainly did breed like lice and had been a plague since the first day that someone had figured out that while some labored, others would "administer."

"Down, John!"

He barely had time to turn back when a flurry of shots echoed, stitching Fredericks across his chest. He staggered backward and collapsed into his sacred office.

"What the hell?" John cried.

"Bastard was drawing a gun on you," someone said even as the sound of gunfire echoed in the foyer.

John saw his old antagonist Ernie Franklin stepping out of the gathering that had come into the foyer to witness this final confrontation.

"What?"

"He drew a pimp gun and was about to blow your brains out, you damn fool. You're a damn fool, Matherson, turning your back like that, so I covered your ass."

John looked about in confusion. No one spoke. There were faint grins from several as Ernie walked across the foyer, stepped over the sandbag emplacement, and leaned over Fredericks's body. Ernie's hands were out of view for a few seconds as he appeared to pat down Fredericks and then stood back up holding a small pistol.

"Pimp gun. Bastard like this couldn't even carry a real gun." He then turned his weapon on Fredericks and put one more round into his head. Without further comment, he turned and walked out of the foyer, pausing to toss the "pimp gun" on the floor by John's feet. "Historian, know your history. 'Sic semper tyrannis.'"

CHAPTER SEVENTEEN

John had called for the meeting in the Fellowship Hall of Gaither Chapel at 10:00 p.m. for a reason. His trusted team was now augmented by Forrest and also by Ernie, who had simply just bulled his way onto the town council, like it or not. It was something John did not really object to given that he had essentially done the same thing immediately after the Day. Kevin Malady was with them, as was Lee, his arm in a sling from a bullet taken in the final assault. There were also representatives from Swannanoa, a couple of police officers invited from Asheville who, word was, represented a good grasp of public opinion in the survivors of that town, one of the two the cops John had befriended long before in the first days after the war had started. There was even a doctor from Mission Hospital—which, once the fight was over and it was no longer under Fredericks's thumb—had thrown its support into caring for the injured and wounded.

Only a little over five thousand civilians were still alive in Asheville proper, and John had won most of them over with a most simple gesture. The ANR troops had over one hundred thousand rations stockpiled, and John decided they would be divided evenly between his community and Asheville. The following day, after the storming of the courthouse complex, a delegation had come to Black Mountain seeking John out with the request that, during the current crisis and until things were "straightened out," he and the citizens of Black Mountain would consider a "consolidation."

It was a decision he could not just make on his own. Ever since the Day, there had been a deep sense of division between Asheville and Black Mountain, fueled by the leadership there in the beginning, brought together somewhat when the army was in direct control, and then driven wide open again by Fredericks. As to the old pre-army leadership—which had stayed on but faded into the back while the army occupied the town, only to reemerge after the military left and then fallen in with Fredericks—the last of it was gone. Several had died in the battle for the courthouse, and the others—so typically—had excused themselves before the fighting even broke out and tried to flee to Greenville. There were rumors that a reiver group that at times had control of the two main roads leading out of the southern mountains down to the piedmont of South Carolina had captured the group. No one was discussing the treatment quickly meted out to them.

Both the town council and a vote by paper ballot of the community had been overwhelming to end the standoff, the more pragmatic and savvy politically noting that if they did not try to merge now and offer enough rations to stuff everyone for a couple of weeks in the immediate wake of the shocking battle fought downtown, some new bloc would try to rise up. The strain of it was that the spring planting and acres of fields now under the plow, along with the birthing of pigs and cattle and the hatching of chickens, promised that come fall, for the first time since the start of it all, there would actually be not only enough food properly stored away to see all through the winter but even a surplus. The edge of starvation up until this current crisis seemed finally to be pushed back, but the overnight doubling of mouths to feed would again mean living on the edge.

The alternative, though, could be infinitely worse, and the situation out in the rest of the world had helped seal the deal up, as well.

The argument to work toward a new union carried additional weight after the conversation that occurred with—of all people—a reporter with the BBC. The radio on the captured Black Hawk could be spun through a number of frequencies, and earlier in the day, Maury had been conversing with the chopper pilots down in Greenville, trying to talk them down from any follow-up action when, of all things, someone else had chimed in, identifying himself as a BBC reporter based in Canada who had been monitoring their conversation.

Maury had fetched John, and it had turned into a regular interview with John presenting his side of what had occurred. The signal was sketchy, wavering in and out, but John had at least been able to get a few questions answered.

"Bluemont declares itself to be the legitimate government of the United States," the reporter had replied. "But as for my country seeing it thus, I can't speak to that. England is still hanging on, just barely. We were not hit by the EMP directly; that was focused more on central and eastern Europe. The power vacuum afterward has triggered fighting between Russia on one side; Poland, Germany, we're trying to stand clear. Neither side has stepped to nukes; my government pledged its arsenal to Germany if Russia should go nuclear, and it is tense, damn tense, and your government's decision to pop that neutron bomb over Chicago has the Chinese ready to push the button.

"I don't know who you really are, John Matherson," the reporter concluded, "though there have been rumors of folks like you trying to reestablish order in spite of what is claimed to be the central government. But I can tell you this: either you take Bluemont out, or they will take you out—and in the process perhaps retrigger a nuclear war that will burn off the rest of this insane world."

After that, they had lost the signal, and his words had rested heavily on John's heart. If true, this was no longer about the survival of his town and the reivers from the other side of the mountain and the frightened survivors in Asheville. It was far broader, and he dreaded the sense of responsibility it now carried.

It was just about ten, and John nodded to his radioman to switch on his best radio, a small generator outside the room powering up to supply juice. The dial was already set, but it took a slight fiddling to bring the broadcast in clearly with the always soul-stirring ringing of Big Ben and then the always well-modulated voice of the announcer.

This is BBC News. It is 3:00 a.m., Greenwich War Time, and here is the news first from overseas.

Today, the federal administration of the United States in Bluemont announced a deepening crisis, declaring that twelve more administrative districts have descended into what it defined as "class-five status." Here is a listing of those districts in alphabetical order:

Asheville in the Carolinas, Administrative District Eleven, where it was announced that the director of that district and his entire team of ANR troops were murdered by terrorists, many of the prisoners being summarily executed.

Bismarck in the Dakotas . . .

The broadcast was drowned out by the cries of protest erupting in the room. John stood silent, gazing out the window. Ernie had brought him the report of the broadcast two hours earlier; apparently, the radio set in his enclave just below Ridgecrest had picked up the first of the early evening broadcasts.

It really came as no surprise, though he had hoped that his conversation earlier in the day with the BBC reporter had somehow been relayed back to England. It undoubtedly had been, but at this stage, they would most certainly not claim it as fact.

All of the radio gear Fredericks and his troops had been using in the courthouse had been lost in the fire minutes after the fighting was finished; the fire of the upper floors had so weakened the roof that the entire building started to cave in. It had cut John off from any means of reaching Bluemont to try to negotiate or at least report in as to what had really happened with the tin-pot dictator whose body had been left behind to be consumed in the flames.

John motioned for order, and the crowd settled down in the room. He had taught many a class in this same room when a larger area was needed for special events that drew larger crowds. The acoustics were terrible, and without a mike and speakers, it could be tough to be heard at times.

The radio was still on.

And Syracuse, New York, Administrative District Three, where there are reports of a rebellion and the murders by terrorists of over eighty troops of the ANR.

The administration repeated its announcement again today that the draft for the million-troop mobilization for the ANR is moving forward smoothly in most areas, cooperation with the draft being a factor in defining a district as not in rebellion, but it cautioned that those not in compliance will face the full authority of the law and appealed for those districts not yet reporting in to do so immediately. There has been no response of just how many administrative districts are in compliance so far.

In a surprise move, the administration also announced that it is rescinding for the moment the authorization to theater commanders of the ANR to use neutron bomb weapons within the continental United States, except when receiving a direct order and release by the administration.

The repeated queries by our embassy in Bluemont to respond to the rumor that the acting president was either forced to resign yesterday or has been removed from office have not been answered.

Again there was an eruption of comments. That news had exploded around the world early in the day. It was one of the reasons everyone listened to the shortwave edition of the BBC; few now trusted the Voice of America for anything other than a highly censored version of the news. The implications were profound. Had the administration that sent people like Fredericks out into the field collapsed? Was there a coup d'état taking place in Bluemont? If true, were they sliding into civil war, or could one hope that more reasonable heads were prevailing and the announcement of the pullback on the use of neutron bombs was a signal of serious change?

John kept his ear to the radio speaker, but there was no more news on that front, though there was an announcement of a discussion to ensue with various "experts" as to what might be transpiring in America.

The crowd settled down so that the radio could be heard again.

And for our friends in Hong Kong, "The sun is rising in the west." I repeat, "The sun is rising in the west." And now to our discussion about events transpiring in America today . . .

John nodded for the radio to be turned off.

"I wanted everyone here," John announced, "representing the town council of Black Mountain, Montreat, and Swannanoa—along with our friends from Asheville and representatives from the group some called the Mount Mitchell Reivers—to gather together in one place, garner what news we can from the outside, and decide if we will henceforth move forward in mutual accord. This could go on for some time, perhaps most of the night. I guess I'm stuck with moderating, and I will ask that those representing different perspectives try to limit themselves to five minutes. Let's work toward points of mutual agreement rather than tear each other apart. We have a rare chance here to settle issues that have divided us for far too long. Let's bury them here and now."

He looked around the room. "There is one issue I have to present to you first before we move on to other business, and I am afraid I'll have to hold the floor for this one."

All knew what he was about to raise and fell silent.

"It is impossible at the moment to raise Bluemont. The communications gear to do so was destroyed in the fight at the courthouse. It was undoubtedly on a secured scrambler, so we are in the dark there. I have tried to reach out to Greenville by radio, so far without success other than conversations between Maury and the chopper pilots. At least from that, those pilots know our situation, and Maury feels they just might disobey orders if directed to attack us. They have made no aggressive moves toward us yet. I pray it stays that way. If we cannot raise them within the next few days, I'm asking our friends who lived north of Mount Mitchell to head down toward Highlands, talk with the folks there, and see if they'll honor letting a convoy with a team to visit Greenville to pass safely. Also, that will open up a conversation with folks in the southern mountains to consider joining in with us."

There were nods of approval to that.

"What do you think Greenville will do?" someone in the back of the room asked.

"I can't say for sure. We do know that when the fight was on in Asheville, they did send several attack choppers up, but they stopped while over Hendersonville and the Asheville airport, one of the pilots repeatedly asking for a decision as to whether to go in or not. They turned back about when their signal to the courthouse was lost. We do have the radio in the captured

Black Hawk. Maury Hurt has raised one of their pilots several times, told him what happened here and why, and made it clear we had no desire to see any more Apaches up here and will react accordingly. I listened in and felt that the pilot Maury was talking to was of the same accord and less than happy with the prospect of turning his weapons, as he said, 'on our own people.' So I want to believe there are second thoughts down there, perhaps even at least an 'administrator' we can deal with in a friendly fashion."

"Why not just fly someone down there in the Black Hawk or L-3 to negotiate a truce with them?" someone asked.

"I'll not risk such precious assets outside our own territory for now," John replied, and there were again nods of agreement.

"Once we get the road secured, I've asked Ernie Franklin to be the one to head the team going down."

That did draw some comments, not all of them happy, but more than a few were laughing.

John smiled and held his hand up for silence. "We want straightforward, no-nonsense talk; Ernie is the man to deliver it straight from the shoulder. Do any of you disagree?"

Many turned to look at Ernie, who smiled and then finally replied, "You're just trying to get me the hell away from these meetings."

"Maybe so," John replied, and there was a round of laughter and then applause. "So that is the situation with Greenville and Bluemont. Are we in general accord to try to reach out to Greenville and ensure no aggressive action will be taken against us?"

His question was greeted with approval.

"But until we have a clear answer, at least from Greenville, the military is to stay on full alert, dispersal of population and assets against air attack to stay in place. You all know the mobilization alarms; if you hear them, act immediately." He sighed. "And let's pray the war is over. So with that said, I open the floor for comments."

For a man who hated meetings, this one, illuminated by candlelight, had something of a different feel. The illumination, the rather sacred nature of the room actually called Fellowship Hall, triggered the historian in him. Perhaps it was a touch of the romantic in looking at it in such a way, but he could not help it as person after person stood to speak, appealing for a joining together, to set aside past differences and even expressing the optimism of expanding their reach to all the mountain communities of western North Carolina.

By midnight, there was a near consensus to have a charter drawn up for the various representatives to sign, and for the moment, John would be tasked as an emergency commander, but any actions regarding life or limb of a citizen or relations with communities outside their own would be referred to a council made up of representatives from each of the communities.

The establishment of an actual elected government was then brought up, and it was decided that, this time, they would indeed take a census of all those over eighteen, identifications would be issued, and in one month's time, elections would be held for all posts.

Some were so exhausted at this point that there was a call to close the meeting, but for once, John refused such a request, feeling there were still some details to be hammered out and that now was the moment to do it, when a wave of near idealism filled the room. He suggested that those who needed a break could go into the chapel and stretch out in one of the pews.

John, taking a break himself, went into that special place and looked up at the starlight, the sight of the scorched beams and part of the roof missing reminding him of photos of churches and cathedrals in war-ravaged Europe of many years earlier. Makala came out to join him, taking his hand, again recalling the first time they had met here. The room was silent; there was no one at the piano at this hour of the morning—and besides, the piano was gone, crushed under a collapsing beam, a heartbreaking sight for both of them, though someone had pulled a scorched flag out of the rubble and pinned it to the far wall.

"They're already talking about this fall election with enthusiasm and hope."

He looked at her and smiled. "Maybe there'll be a painting some day, like the one of the signing of the Declaration of Independence."

"You are sounding more like a historian every day, Makala."

"Kind of rubs off after a while. Besides, it is what I want for our child."

"Elizabeth and little Ben, I do pray that they see it. I was scared to death when I caught a glimpse of her in that final assault wave. I'm so damn proud of her, but now that this moment is over with, I just wish she would go back to being a mother for a while."

"I do too, especially when Ben has a brother or sister to play with, though technically, I guess it'll be his aunt or uncle."

It took a moment for that to sink in, and then he turned to her in surprise.

"Yup, we're pregnant." It was all she could get out before he pulled her in tightly, hugging her fiercely.

"If she's a girl," Makala whispered, and she started to cry, "can I have your permission to name her Jennifer?"

And now both of them cried together.

EPILOGUE

"Well, here it goes!" The expectant crowd fell silent. Paul and Becka Hawkins stood in the open doorway of the rough-hewn power plant, Becka with a hand on the main switch, snapping it down.

An instant explosion of light enveloped the crowd of nearly half a thousand who stood around the building and had spilled over on to Montreat Road and the parking lot of Anderson Hall. A long line of festive Christmas lights, strung from the power station to a telephone pole and down to Anderson, sparkled to life. And then there were shouts from farther up the hill, lights in the chapel humming back to life after more than two years of darkness.

A phone in the power plant rang. Becka picked it up, chatted for a moment, and then looked to John, smiling. "It's for you, sir."

Though badly shot up in the fighting, parts of the switchboard had been salvaged, and with that as a template, several old phone company technicians had actually begun to assemble an entire new board based in the new town hall in an abandoned day care center a block away. Only a dozen connections were back in place, but it was a highly symbolic start in John's eyes. They were not scavenging items from the past, retro equipment of a hundred years ago, but were beginning to build things from scratch. Psychologically, John saw it as a major step forward for the entire community.

He took the phone from Becka, putting a hand over one ear.

"John, we've got electricity up here! How long will it stay on?"

John looked at Becka and repeated the question to her, having to shout to be heard. Becka looked at the old-style analog gauges, measuring the energy output coming from the full-size turbine that was humming away beneath their feet, the generator in the next room whining at a high pitch. The air was redolent with the scent of ozone, and the way it was all rigged up, it did have a bit of a "Frankenstein's laboratory" feel to it.

"I think it's holding together okay. We're shutting things down at midnight to go over all the equipment. After that, if it is holding together, we'll throw the power back on for an hour, three times a day, then on full-time come evening to midnight."

There were so many factors at play, John realized. Though running smoothly at the moment, this was their first truly operational generator, though work had already begun on a second, and work crews were already busy rebuilding the original power dam for Montreat a couple of miles higher up along Flat Creek. For the moment, this was their one and only power source with no reserve yet in place, and it was not to be stressed. Turning it on at hour-long intervals and then off for four throughout the day would allow the hospital to chill down the freezers and refrigerators, his communications teams to recharge batteries, and—luxury of luxury—to run a hot-water heater at the college and hospital and then washing machines. Hand scrubbing had just become a thing of the past, though the decidedly old-fashioned ritual of hanging out clothing on clotheslines would continue for a long time to come before they had become so profligate with electricity to actually run dryers.

The power supply for right now was wired to just the campus and Assembly Inn, the town council for the time being forbidding anyone to try to tap into the power line for home use. With the second station going in above the first, plans were already afoot to put in a third unit in a cove above Black Mountain—actually over in Ridgecrest where there had been a power station over a hundred years earlier—again a dam that had to be rebuilt. Once in place, that would provide electricity straight into the town. Paul calculated it would provide enough energy to be wired into one of the town's old water pumps. Homes below 2,400 feet in altitude were still receiving a trickle of water from the gravity-fed pond, but it had to be boiled, and two years of no maintenance on the lines meant that nearly all the precious water was now hemorrhaging out. With a town water pump back online, twenty thousand gallons a day could be pumped up to the old water tank that overlooked the village and then gravity fed back down and run through the small filtration plant. That, in turn, meant that they were going to have to find or make new filters and some way of getting chlorine or some other purifier. But what a blessing. That most simple of luxuries would again become commonplace and with it hopefully eliminating *E. coli* and other illnesses that still plagued the town at times, caused by the lack of public sanitation.

So the complexity of it all would then start to multiply. Water going out meant bringing sewerage filtration back online, setting up some kind of public hot showers and laundry facilities, and then . . .

"John? You still with me?" It was Makala on the other end of the phone.

"Oh yeah. Ah, Becka said they'll run to midnight. Can you come down for a few minutes? Something of a celebration kicking up."

"Be right down, and I'm bringing someone with me." She hung up.

It was indeed turning into something of a celebration. The students had rigged up a small stage with a CD player and speakers. One of the kids, who again for this moment appeared to be "just" a college kid, was up on the stage, shouting for requests. Then held up his hands in acknowledgment and rifled through a stack of old CDs, but he first turned on the player and ran the volume up, and the crowd fell silent for a moment. It was "God Bless America," and within seconds, all had joined in, more than a few with tears streaming down their faces.

He saw Makala approaching him through the crowd with Doc Weiderman by her side, carrying his medical bag. He tried not to blanch at the sight of the dentist.

"Yeah, John, let's get it done. It'll only take a minute."

John gulped and then nodded in submission to fate. It was time to get the tooth out. "Give me a minute. Okay?"

"Yeah, but no escaping this time."

He smiled, nodding to where Lee Robinson, arm in a sling, was standing behind him, ready to snag John if he tried to slip away. Then he felt a reassuring hand slip into his. It was Makala, and she was in tears, standing silent, looking up at the lights and listening to the chorus singing.

"We got to get you fixed up proper, John," she whispered, drawing in close to his side.

They stood in silence, listening as the chorus sang the last refrain of the song, and then the party started, dancing beneath the brilliant array of lights, the cares of what tomorrow would bring—or what John had to face in a few minutes—forgotten.

"We're still America. We'll always be America," Makala whispered, drawing in closer by his side.